MIDLOTHIAN LIBRARY SERVICE

Please return/renew this item by the last date shown. To
renew please give your borrower number. Renewal may
be made in person, online, or by post, e-mail or phone.
www.midlothian.gov.uk/library

Also by Andy Mulligan

RIBBLESTROP
RETURN TO RIBBLESTROP
TRASH

RIBBLESTROP FOREVER!

LIFE IS DANGEROUS

Andy Mulligan

SIMON AND SCHUSTER

First published in Great Britain in 2012 by Simon
and Schuster UK Ltd, a CBS company.

Text copyright © 2012 Andy Mulligan
Cover and title page artwork © 2012 Serge Seidlitz

www.andymulliganbooks.com

Simon & Schuster UK Ltd
1st Floor, 222 Gray's Inn Road
London WC1X 8HB

www.simonandschuster.co.uk

Simon & Schuster Australia, Sydney

Simon & Schuster India, New Delhi

A CIP catalogue copy for this book is available
from the British Library.

ISBN: 978-1-47112-155-5
Ebook ISBN: 978-0-85707-801-8

1 3 5 7 9 10 8 6 4 2

Typeset by Hewer Text UK Ltd, Edinburgh
Printed and bound in Great Britain
by CPI Group (UK) Ltd, Croydon, CR0 4YY

For Michael and Anita

Map of

High School — Museum

RIBBLESTROP Town

RIBBLESTROP EDGE

our lake

our school
(Ribblestrop Towers)

Treehouse camp

First Glade Path

RIBBLEMOOR

the river

Absolutely NOT to scale!

N
W   E

TIVERTON

still the
river

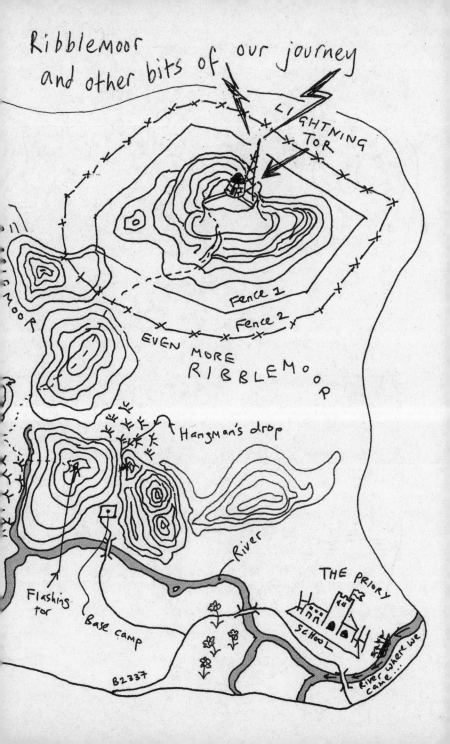

Chapter One

It was the end of the Easter holidays.

Millie, Miles and Sanchez had flown first class from Bogotá, home to Sanchez's father. They hadn't intended to visit him but, in the end, the thought of South American fiestas and fireworks had proved too seductive and they'd rushed out for a few days of excitement. They'd returned to Heathrow airport, however, to find their onward travel plans to Ribblestrop – all arranged on brand new cellphones – in tatters. They had been hoping to share a taxi with their friends, Sam Tack, Ruskin and Oli. Mr Tack had booked it, to drive them right to the school gates, but he'd got the dates mixed up, and after a whole series of confusions he'd been forced to drive the children himself. There was room for just four in his tiny hatchback, so Sanchez, Millie and Miles were in a fix.

They were desperate to be at school for six o'clock as the orphans had promised a trapeze display that very evening, in the dining hall. The orphans had arrived that morning as well, after a sell-out run of Circus Ribblestrop in New York. Captain Routon had hired a coach and driven up specially to collect them. Sanchez phoned his father, explained the muddle, and a light aircraft was chartered within the hour.

The three children found themselves in a limousine on their way to a private aerodrome near Reading, and soon they were shaking the firm hand of veteran pilot, Timmy Fox.

'Welcome!' said Timmy. 'This is what we call "scrambling a flight", eh? In a hurry, are we?'

'We don't want to hang around,' said Millie.

They walked towards a pretty little aeroplane, alone on the tarmac.

'It's no distance at all,' said the pilot. He raised his eyebrows and grinned. 'Flown in one of these before, have you? She's sweet as a songbird – *Maisie*, I call her.'

'Never,' said Miles.

'Single engine, but still packs a punch. We won't go over fifteen hundred feet, so you'll see the landscape. I bought her six months ago and she handles like a baby. Quick and bright with a mind of her own. We can actually land at your school, can we? I've not filed the old flight plan yet, but I think this Mr Sanchez character cut a bit of red tape for me, eh? We can improvise a bit, I imagine?'

'There's a long driveway,' said Millie. 'And a big lawn.'

'We'll be fine. She can land on a sixpence, this one.' Timmy led them to the steps. 'Once we're airborne,' he said, 'I'll radio Bristol and tell 'em what we're doing. They're pretty flexible with the Foxter.' He lit a cigar and climbed aboard. 'Timmy's been around a bit. Now, anyone get sea-sick?'

'No,' said Miles.

The pilot pushed back his cap. 'Not like flying in a jet, you know! You're going to feel every bump. I used to do stunt work in the movies. Bit of action over Iraq too – came in low to Afghanistan a couple of times . . . but we don't talk about that. No looping-the-loop today, eh? Not unless you twist my arm. Now, buckle yourselves in, boys – I want to catch this westerly breeze.'

A moment later they were taxiing and, the next second it seemed, rising in a great vibrating, roaring rush. The world was suddenly nothing but sunshine and blue sky, with a patchwork of fields revolving below. Timmy Fox wore a headset, and he turned and winked at his passengers.

'I went up without clearance,' he shouted, putting up his thumb. 'I'll get a bit of a talking to, but they know the Fox. They know Foxy bends the rules! Smooth as a bird, eh? Whoops!'

A patch of turbulence caused a sudden roll, but the pilot laughed as he righted his craft.

'She's a bag of tricks is *Maisie*!' he cried. 'Oh my, this is flying!'

It was at this point that Miles unbuckled his seatbelt, and stood up. There wasn't much room in the narrow cabin, but he leant over Millie and peered through her porthole. The plane banked to the left, and the city of Reading appeared and slipped by.

'You know, I'd stay in your seat if I were you!' shouted Timmy.

'Why?' said Miles.

He hauled himself into the cockpit and crouched beside the pilot. Cigar smoke filled the little cabin, which was a mass of dials and switches.

'Is it difficult?' said Miles. 'It looks easy to me.'

Timmy grinned and coughed. 'They don't fly themselves, chummy, that's for sure. You take a jumbo – that's pretty much flown by computers, these days. Your air-jet pilots spend most of the time doing crosswords. It's these little chaps that take control and ... well, I'll say it myself, sonny: skill – nerve!' He puffed at his cigar. 'Maybe judgement's a better word. You have to feel the wind, hear the way she's handling. It's not child's play, that's for sure.'

3

Miles was nodding. 'What's that knob there?' he shouted.

'I can see you're interested. I like that in a boy! Now, that's my air-speed indicator, okay? That stops us stalling.'

Miles pointed to a dial. 'What's that one telling you?'

'Ah, don't look at that. That's the fuel in the primary tank. It's as good as empty, but the reserve's full, and I reckon a forty-five minute journey's okay on reserve. We won't need more than . . . oooh, thirty litres? We should have filled up beforehand, really, but the wind was perfect. I didn't want to miss it! Who are your friends, by the way? The dark boy seems pretty important – some kind of prince, is he?'

Miles smiled. 'No. He's a mafia gangster's son. Drug-running mainly, so he has to be careful of kidnap.'

'Right. I thought as much.'

'The girl's called Millie. She's been expelled from four schools, which is one less than me. We've been on holiday together.'

'Ah.'

'You've probably heard of Ribblestrop.'

'Have I?'

'It's the place where the chaplain got eaten by a crocodile, and before that the deputy head was killed by a train. The headmaster's great, but he doesn't really have much of a grip. Oh, and the local policeman hates us too – but that's all right now because he got sacked for attempted murder. I think most of our problems are solved. Do you want one of these?'

'One of what? What are you offering the Fox?'

'Colombian gobstoppers. They're mixed with coca-leaves – they give you quite a buzz.'

Timmy Fox stubbed his cigar out and looked at the bag in Miles's hand. It was an innocent-looking brown colour, crumpled from its time in the boy's blazer pocket. Miles held it under pilot's nose.

4

'Looks pretty tasty, I must say,' he said. 'That's one thing about old Foxy – he's got a sweet tooth and tries anything once.'

'These are beautiful. They last for two hours each.'

The pilot grinned and eased his craft into a gentle climb. He had felt the vibrations of turbulence again and he flicked some switches in the roof. 'I shouldn't really, sonny. My dentist says I'm a little bit too partial to – whoops!'

The plane juddered into an air pocket and Miles was butted forward.

'You see?' said Timmy. 'It's a roller-coaster, sometimes – she's as game as a bird, is this little girl. I'll just take the one, thank you. What's your name?'

'Miles.'

'Thanks, Miles. Here's to you.'

He took the offered sweet between forefinger and thumb and rolled it. It was smaller than a ping-pong ball and up close it had a peppering of purple spots. Putting it into his mouth, he tested it with his teeth.

'Oooh! Hard!' he mumbled, trying to get his tongue round it.

'You can't crunch them,' said Miles. 'Don't even try. I've got a suitcaseful, for the orphans.'

It was at this point that Millie came forward. She put her hand on Miles's shoulder, and then leant on his neck. The plane soared upwards, so she had to grab his shirt collar.

'Are you flying the plane, Miles?' she cried. 'If you are, I want to know where the parachutes are kept.'

Timmy Fox laughed long and hard. 'No parachutes today!' he shouted. The sweet bounced against his tonsils and he tried to get his tongue behind it.

Miles squeezed to his right in an attempt to make room for Millie. The plane came out of the air pocket into a gust of hot air. Timmy hadn't felt it coming, so the plane rose again, more violently, as if caught on a wave. Then the wave was gone and the nose came down, hard and fast. Millie and Miles were jerked backwards, while Timmy Fox – who was safely belted into his seat – received a violent jolt. The gobstopper spun against his uvula, where the digastric muscle strained at once to eject it. The plane bobbed yet again and the pilot panicked. He tried to swallow and disaster struck. The gobstopper was sucked straight into his windpipe where it lodged like a cork in a bottle.

Timmy Fox's eyes bulged. He did his best to cry out, but his airway was blocked – all that emerged was a choking groan.

Behind him, Miles was laughing. He'd fallen against Millie and caught her with his elbow, so she was clutching a bleeding nose. Sanchez looked mildly concerned, but had been reading a magazine – so wasn't sure what had happened. Their expressions changed, however, when the plane suddenly keeled over to the left and the engine started to scream. An alarm sounded at once and then pulsed urgently.

'Miles!' shouted Millie.

They saw, with horror, that their pilot was clawing the air, completely helpless. He was spluttering too and changing colour before their eyes. He managed to get one hand back to the controls and they were level again – but only for a few seconds. Timmy Fox grabbed his own throat, gagging, and a moment later, there was a sickening lurch to the right. His headset fell onto his knees.

Sanchez was up now, but it was Millie who reacted fastest. The cockpit was tilting heavily, but she managed to dive forward and get her hands onto the joystick, her nosebleed forgotten. Miles was beside her in a moment, grabbing at the gasping pilot. He was bright red and the red was turning to purple.

'Heart attack!' shouted Millie. 'Do something!'

Miles guessed what had happened and tried to slap the man hard on the back. The blow bent him forward and he managed to disengage his seatbelt so he fell heavily onto the controls. Sanchez was now right behind them, while Millie leant through the confusion of arms and knees to steady the all-important joystick. Miles tried to thump the pilot again, but the control area was too congested. Timmy Fox levered himself up somehow and fell backward into Sanchez's arms. With Miles's help, he was lowered to the narrow strip of carpet behind, where he lay gasping. Millie jumped straight into his empty seat and gazed through the cockpit window as fragments of cloud hurtled towards her. Seconds later, Miles was back with the headset clamped to his ear.

'Do something!' Millie was shrieking. 'Get the pilot!'

'Fly the plane, Millie!'

'Oh my God! How can I? I don't know how to fly a plane!'

She eased the joystick back and they rose slightly. The alarm stopped, but a red light kept flashing and a buzzer was buzzing. An oxygen mask had fallen from above and bounced uselessly, knocking at their heads.

'Hello?' shouted Miles, into the mouthpiece of the headset. 'Is anyone there, please? Hello?'

'I don't know what I'm doing, Miles!' cried Millie. 'Get help!'

'Just do what you're doing. Keep us up. Hello? Is anyone there? Mayday, mayday – come in, please. Ground control, this is . . . oh God . . . this is a very small plane up in the sky. We've lost our pilot and we don't know what to do.' He turned to Millie in despair. 'How do you work these things?'

'I don't know. I don't know anything. Ask Sanchez!'

Her eyes were dancing from dial to dial, from switch to switch. Some of the needles were moving up and she spotted two that were moving down. She pushed the joystick forward and felt the plane respond and sink – but whether that was good or bad, she couldn't say. There were pedals under her feet, but she didn't dare press them. At least they were going straight and, though everything was vibrating, it seemed like they weren't about to fall out of the sky.

Miles, meanwhile, was experimenting with a small black knob on the headset. When he turned it, a green light came on.

'Hello?' he said, again. 'Is anyone there, please? This is a real emergency – I'm not playing games here. Help!'

A man's voice answered, utterly calm. 'Come in, *Maisie 202*. State your position, over.'

'What?' said Miles.

The voice remained relaxed. 'Come in, *Maisie 202*,' it repeated, slowly. 'This is Bristol control. State your position, over.'

Miles swore under his breath. 'I think our pilot's dead,' he said. 'That's the position.'

'OK, *Maisie*, can I ask you to identify yourself and repeat that, please? Over.'

'Yes. My name is Miles Seyton-Shandy. I'm going to school, but I'm on a plane without a pilot because the pilot's choking to death, and my friend is trying to fly the plane. I have no idea where we are except up in the sky. Over.'

Miles's eyes were full of tears. He had just realised the danger. They were racing along at more than a hundred miles per hour.

The voice on the radio seemed to become even calmer. 'Okay, good … That's good, Miles. I'm reading you – sounds like you've got a situation up there, so I'm requesting priority airspace. Can you re-confirm, please? Your pilot is down? Over.'

'He's unconscious,' said Miles, taking a quick look behind him. Sanchez had the man laid out in the recovery position. He had his knee in the pilot's back and was jerking his shoulders. 'I don't know if he's breathing or not. He swallowed something and it got stuck.'

'That's good, that's fine. You're going to have to stay very calm, Miles, and relaxed. You're going to have to answer all my questions, clear as you can. When you finish what you say, try to remember to say "over", because that makes communication simple. First question: who is at the controls of the plane? Over.'

'Millie Roads. But she doesn't know what she's doing. Over.'

'You're doing fine at the moment. We're getting a fix on you, and we're going to pull all air traffic in the area well back. You've got a completely clear corridor, okay, so there's no emergency if you hold her steady. I want you to look at the controls and tell me when you have located a black dial with two white needles. They're like the hands on a clock. Over.'

Miles scanned the forest of dials. 'Black with white needles,' he said to Millie. 'Can you see anything like that?'

Millie pointed and put her hand straight back on the joystick. She was rigid with concentration.

'I've got it,' said Miles. 'Over.'

'Good boy. What's it reading at the moment? It's going to tell us your altitude. Over.'

'The big hand's on six. The little one's on two!'

'Excellent. Ask Millie to ease the joystick back, very gently. Can you do that? Over.'

'Millie,' said Miles, 'pull the lever back a bit. Slowly.' He held the mouthpiece. 'We're doing it. We want to come down, okay? We want to be on the ground!'

'The numbers should be falling now —'

9

'Over!'

'What? No, listen: when the big hand's at zero, that's the altitude to hold. So we're bringing you just a little lower, where you've got a good, safe space and visibility's best. Is that okay, Miles? Over.'

'It's okay. Yes, we're going down a bit. Can you send us a new pilot or something?'

'I'm handing you over to a colleague now, Miles. She's senior to me and she's going to keep you safe and get you on the ground. Is that okay?'

'Don't go!' said Miles. 'Don't leave us!'

'I'm right here, but Sandra's taking over communication now. She's more familiar with your craft than I am.'

'I'm right here, Miles,' said a woman's voice. It was deep and wonderfully sensible. 'I'm with you, okay? I'm with you all the way. We're going to get through this together. We're clearing an emergency landing site for you in Bristol; the only problem at this stage is the airfields you're passing are all short runways. Now, in normal circumstances, a short runway would be fine for your craft, but—'

'You think we can land this?' said Miles.

'We'll talk you through it. We're with you every step of the way.'

'We're going too fast!'

'No, no. We're going to find a nice, long airstrip for you. We're going to practise your approach, give you a couple of dry runs. It's much easier than you think. '

'What about petrol? The pilot said we were flying on reserve.'

'Flying on reserve. Are you saying your first tank's dry?'

'I don't know.'

'How do you know you're on reserve?'

'The pilot told me. He didn't fill up. He said he normally would, but he didn't want to miss some wind or other.'

'And he said you're flying on reserve?'

'That's what he said. What can we do?'

There was a pause.

'Miles,' said the voice. It was just a little firmer. 'We're going to try something a little bit different in the light of what you've just told me. Can you take a look at the reserve gauge? That's three dials to the right of your altimeter. It's a needle over a white strip about three centimetres long – have you got that?'

'The needle's at half,' said Miles. 'Is that good?'

'The needle's at half of the white area. So you're how far from red?'

'About one point five centimetres.'

'Okay.'

'It's bad, isn't it?'

'No, it's—'

'We're running out of fuel! Oh God!'

'No, no, no. There's enough fuel, just not enough to give us too much leeway. We're going to have to make some more emergency arrangements. I'm going to leave you for a moment. I'm going to brief my colleagues and scramble a helicopter.'

'Don't go!' cried Miles again.

There was no answer. He glanced at Millie and saw that her face, like his own, was a mask of terror.

'Are we going to die?' she said.

'I think so,' said Miles. 'We'd better tell Sanchez.'

Chapter Two

Sam saw the little plane through the window of his father's car.

He didn't mention it to Ruskin, who was sitting next to him, because he seemed to be dozing. Oli was in front, deep in an instruction manual and definitely not to be disturbed, and his father had his nose close to the windscreen. He pulled the new phone out of his pocket and polished the display panel with his tie. His parents had told him that he was to hand it straight in to the headmaster when he got to school, and he was wondering if he was going to obey them. He had promised he would – it had been a condition of his keeping it. But what was the point of having such a thing if you couldn't actually use it? Anyway, he was still getting used to the device, which seemed to have so many different functions. It was quite a large phone, and a sticker on the box had said, *Special offer, line discontinued.* He needed two hands to operate it, because it was as heavy as a brick. It had a stopwatch and a countdown facility. It had a calculator too, but that was quite tricky to operate and seemed to get even the simplest sums wrong. It had an alarm clock, and you could also check which year you were in.

As he held it, it vibrated and emitted a piercing bleep.

'Oh!' he said. 'I've had a text.'

Ruskin opened his eyes. 'Another one? That's number seven.'

'How do you get at it?' said Sam. 'Do you have the instruction book?'

'You just press the . . . you press that little digit there, under the screen.'

Sam pressed it and the words *Address book* appeared.

'You've pressed the wrong one,' said Ruskin. 'Give it to me.'

'I think that plane's in some kind of trouble,' said Sam, glancing out of the window again. 'Unless it's just practising stunts or something. It was low and now it's high.'

Ruskin pressed another button and found *Games*. 'Did you know you had games on this thing?' he said.

'The man in the shop said there were games, but he showed me so quickly that I could never find them.'

'Texts. I've got it. Inbox.'

'So who was it from?'

'I'm in your inbox. This is such a crafty gadget: it actually stores all the texts you receive, so you can go through them. Oh, it's from Millie again.'

'She's probably at school by now. What does it say?'

Ruskin blinked and held the phone higher. 'I can't see. There's a reflection. Looks like, *Why R U so crap?*'

'That was the last one,' said Sam.

'Oh. Right. Scrolling down . . . hang on a moment. Here we are.' He tilted the screen again. *Goodbye all. We R going . . .*'

'Going where?'

'It doesn't say. What a strange message. Maybe she was interrupted.'

'Go down a bit, Jake. If you press the down arrow, you can see the rest of the words.'

Ruskin pressed the arrow and the sentence continued.

'Ah!' he said. 'There is more. *Goodbye all. We R going to crash. We R all going to die. Millie.*'

'Crash where? How can you be about to crash and have the time to text someone?'

'Maybe she's joking. I'm not sure it's something to joke about, though, Sam – you remember that crash we were in last term?'

'Shall I phone her?'

'It's quite expensive, isn't it? Making calls?'

'Can I have it back a second? I've got five pounds credit, so I might as well use it.'

'Don't waste it, Sam. What if there's an emergency?'

'I'll give her a very quick call – just check she's okay. Oli? Look, sorry to disturb you, but you're better at this than me. Can you give us a hand calling Millie?'

Millie, Miles and Sanchez were now all pressed together in the cockpit and Miles was still relaying information from the headset. Timmy Fox was alive, but hardly breathing. The three terrified children watched as the fields rolled beneath them and the electricity pylons spread their cables inches under their wheels. Millie had pulled the craft upwards several times, but for some reason it kept wanting to descend. She had worked out that the pedals on the floor stabilised them somehow and had got used to pressing them carefully.

They all knew the fuel supply was getting lower; the needle was even closer to the red. Millie slipped her phone back into her pocket and concentrated on the controls again. 'There's some kind of river ahead,' she said. 'What if I aim for that? What if we go straight into the water?'

'No,' said Sanchez. 'We're going way too fast.'

'You're doing okay,' said the voice in Miles's ear. 'We're finding you an airfield. Now, if you –'

'We keep going down, Sandra,' said Miles. 'Over.'

'I think you may have a headwind. It's decreasing your speed and your trimmer needs adjusting.'

'What's a trimmer?'

'It's the adjustable flap at the back of the plane tail. It keeps you level, so the pilot has to compensate —'

'I don't know where the controls are! Can't we just land? Please?'

'Look for a wheel about the size of your hand. It's between the two seats and it's got a bumpy edge to it.'

Miles repeated her words and Sanchez located it. He leant behind Millie, so she was free to move the joystick.

'Got it.'

'Roll the front downwards. Nice and slow.'

Sanchez did so and the plane's nose lifted. They felt a buffet of air and the plane tilted to the right and set off in a dramatic curve. They rose steadily, Millie doing her very best not to scream. She played the joystick back and depressed one of the pedals. The curve grew dangerously tight. In the next minute they completed three-hundred and sixty degrees and were heading for the water again. Millie pulled the nose back up and everyone sighed with relief.

'Are we back on course?' said Sanchez.

'What is the course?' said Millie. 'Where are trying to get to? Are you sure we shouldn't just ditch? We can all swim.'

'Listen carefully,' said the voice in Miles's ear. 'I'm going to teach you how to decrease your speed. You have to do it very gently, and you keep your eyes on the air speed indicator. That will tell you if there's any danger of a stall. '

'Right,' said Miles.

'You've got nothing to worry about if —'

There was a silence.

'Hello?' said Miles. He could hear a strange pulsing noise.

' — in the first instance, can you do that?'

15

'What?'

There was silence again.

'Tell me what to do, Miles!' said Millie.

'I'm not hearing you,' said Miles. 'Can you repeat what you just said? Over, please.'

The pulsing turned into a crackling and, when it returned, the voice was furred over in static.

' – indicator to the top of the control . . . intensify all exifi-cation . . . can you . . . hello?'

'What?'

'Are you there, Miles? Come in, Miles – are you there? Over.'

'I'm here. You're breaking up!'

'Is somebody using a cellphone? If someone –'

Sure enough, he could hear the ringtone of Millie's mobile, getting louder and louder. The voice of the control-ler disappeared in static and some of the needles seemed to be flicking abruptly backward and forward.

Millie snatched out her phone and clicked it open. 'Sam?' she said. 'Where are you?'

'It's Oli, actually. We're in a car on the motorway. Where are you?'

'Oh God, Oli, we're in a bad situation. We're in a plane. We've lost the pilot. We're about to run out of fuel and we don't know what to do.'

'Millie!' said Miles. 'The phone's screwing up the controls!'

'What kind of plane?' said Oli.

Millie pressed the phone to her ear. 'What?' she cried. 'What do you mean, "What kind of plane?"? A little plane, with wings, and a tail, with us inside it –'

'Are you red and white, by any chance? One propeller, just going over a river?'

'Yes! Shut up, Miles! Oli, I don't know –'

16

'You're just to our right. We can see you. I'll tell Sam to wave.'

Millie looked down, trying frantically to remember her right from her left. The river ran next to a dual carriageway and, though the vehicles on it were small, they were getting larger every second. Again, Millie realised that, through no fault of her own, the plane was descending. She eased the joystick back and this time nothing seemed to be happening. There were more pylons ahead and a great spider's web of cable. A power station was looming with red, winking lights.

'We're going down,' she said.

'Turn the wretched phone off!' shouted Miles. 'Turn the bloody phone off!'

'No!'

A little red car was speeding along in the outside lane, and Millie fixed her eyes onto it, easing the plane closer. It was hard to be sure, but something black appeared to be flapping out of the rear window and a tiny face was gazing up at her. There was a new sound now in the cockpit – and it chilled everyone to the very bone. A bell was ringing, one urgent chime at a time, as if sounding the ominous arrival of midnight. It didn't stop at twelve, though; in fact, it showed no sign of stopping at all.

'Fuel!' shouted Miles. 'Oh my God, look at the fuel gauge! Help us, Sandra! Where are you?'

He put his finger over the needle and the three children saw that it was well into the red It twitched as they stared, and dropped further to the left.

'We're going to have to land,' whispered Sanchez. 'Swing her to the road, Millie.'

'What do you mean, "Swing her to the road"? You think I can—'

'You're at the controls?' said Oli's voice, right in her ear. 'Are you flying that thing, Millie?'

17

'Yes! Of course I am!'

'Okay, it's easy – I had a radio-controlled version. You've got to take the rudder to the right, that means right foot down, nice and gentle. That's the yaw control. Then you're probably going to need some upward thrust if you're losing speed.'

'I don't understand.'

'Right foot down a little. Yes! You're coming in! Beautiful.'

'We're going to land on the road,' said Miles to the mouthpiece. All he heard was static and the chiming bell. More pylons came under them and all three closed their eyes, waiting for their undercarriage to be chopped away. It didn't happen, but they were far lower than ever before. The engine was beginning to splutter. They came over the road and tried to follow it – but the plane had a mind of its own now, and a breeze seemed to lift and push it over the top of the red car, and they were heading straight for a concrete cooling tower.

'Go right!' shouted Oli.

Sanchez said, 'Look. There's an emergency fuel switch. Shall I press it?'

Millie and Miles had their eyes closed, however, and for the first time in his life, Miles was saying a prayer.

Chapter Three

The orphans were watching the plane too and most now had their hands over their mouths.

They were in their school uniforms again, for the black-and-yellow tracksuits were in a laundry basket. Circus Ribblestrop was all in the past and Professor Worthington – who had rounded them up at the airport terminal – had insisted that everyone travel looking smart and ready for an exciting new term. It had been an emotional reunion, of course; Doonan had come up on the bus with Tomaz and Imagio. Caspar Vyner had not been allowed, unfortunately, for Lady Vyner's hatred of the school had been rising as Monday morning came closer, and he was locked in his room. Henry was making his own way down, but they were still a large party.

'I want you to stay together,' Professor Worthington had called. 'I want blazers buttoned and ties straight.'

She'd led the gaggle of excited children through the crowds and out to the car park. Captain Routon had been waiting for them with drinks and sandwiches, so there were more hugs and handshakes. As they pulled onto the road, his ears were ringing from the third rendition of the school song. He inched forward carefully, for the bus was towing a long trailer carrying the boys' luggage and equipment.

As they came towards Bristol, he became aware that the traffic was slowing on both sides of the carriageway. He saw at once what the cause was: a light aircraft was in difficulty. In fact, it was on collision course, and he touched the brake instinctively, almost in sympathy. Sanjay and Anjoli both cried out and pointed, and within a moment everyone was crammed against the windows, following the course of the troubled little plane. The singing had died and there were five seconds of agonising silence.

'Go up, man!' whispered Sanjay.

The plane was heading straight for a wall of concrete. Then, at the very last second, it seemed whoever was flying it woke up and pulled the craft upwards. It seemed to clip the top and then it rose like a rocket. It couldn't stop rising, in fact. It hit vertical and then doubled back on itself in a remarkable loop-the-loop, clearing the top of the power station and banking steeply round as if it wanted to do the whole thing again. It swept behind the bus and the orphans rushed to the back seats to follow its course.

Kenji, one of the youngest orphans, was crushed against the window and was astonished to see a little red car accelerating towards them. There was a boy leaning out of the window waving a black-and-gold blazer in the jet stream.

That boy was Sam.

'We've got more fuel!' shouted Sanchez. 'Well done, Millie.'

'It was you,' gasped Millie. Her face was white. 'Sanchez, you saved us! It must be some kind of injection system. Oh God, Oli . . . Miles has been sick.'

Miles was wet with sweat, clutching the arm of Millie's seat. He had dropped the headset and was blinking in amazement.

'Millie, you're still there?' said Oli.

'Yes!'

'Okay. The best thing you can do is come round again and land on the road. Sam's dad is going to slow down a bit and try to hold the traffic back. Do you want to try an approach?'

'I don't know if I can.'

'Oli,' said Ruskin, staring upwards, 'I might be wrong, but . . . I don't think they've got both wheels anymore.'

'What do you mean? Who hasn't?'

'The plane. Look at it!'

Ruskin was kneeling on the back seat, peering through the window. He rubbed his glasses and grew more positive. One of the plane's wheels had dropped off completely and the other was at a strange angle. The aircraft tilted right and the wheel he was watching sheered off and dropped like a bomb. It was suddenly bouncing along the road so fast that it overtook the car.

'Can they land without wheels?' he said. 'They've lost both.'

'Millie,' said Oli, 'you've lost your undercarriage.'

'What does that mean?' said Millie. 'Was that the bump we felt? I thought we'd hit something!'

'Come in, Miles!' said a small voice from the headset. 'Please come in! Over!'

Millie gripped the phone tighter. 'What can we do, Oli?'

'If you try to land, you'll just dig into the road and . . . you'll either burst into flames or you'll start cartwheeling over the tarmac. Either way, you won't survive. I was looking at the map earlier and I know we go over the River . . .'

'Oli, please!'

'Hold on, Millie. Jake!' he hissed. 'Who's in that bus? Why are they staring at us?'

Sam had noticed too. The rear window of the vehicle ahead was filled with grinning faces and waving hands.

One of them – Podma – had found a piece of paper and had written the words *Hello Sam!* in thick black crayon.

'This is a stroke of luck,' said Oli. 'This could be just what we need. Excuse me, Mr Tack, can we pull alongside that bus, please?'

'What bus?' said Sam's father. 'I'm really not up to all this, you know.'

'You're doing fine, Dad – just put your foot down a bit.'

'I don't want silly games. Not on the road.'

'I know, Dad—'

'That bus with the trailer,' said Oli. 'Can you get round it?'

'I don't like overtaking, boys. We really should have stuck to the B-roads.'

'It's all clear,' said Ruskin. 'Just pull alongside and keep with it. This is so lucky.'

'Oli,' said Millie, again, 'I don't know how much longer we've got up here. What's your plan?'

'We've got an idea,' said Oli.

'Well, it better be a good one, all right? Only the best will do.'

'Hmm,' said Oli. 'I'm going to hang up for a moment, okay? I'll call again in a second, so keep the line open. You see the bus next to us? Purple and blue?'

'No. Yes!'

'Great big trailer? We're pretty sure Captain Routon's at the wheel. So I'm going to give him a call now and see if he can help. Overtake us, Millie – that's the safest thing. Turn right and do a great big circle so you're approaching again from behind. You're going to have to land on the roof of the bus.'

'Are you joking, Oli? Is that your idea of comedy?'

'It's a question of matching velocities. If you can dock the plane on the roof of the bus, the bus can decelerate at an appropriate speed. It'll take a bit of nerve, I imagine, but I can't see any other way of getting you down safely.'

There was no reply. He heard a stifled sob and then the plane he was gazing at came over the car, lower than ever. It hovered and then swung gently away, gaining height.

Millie was doing just what she'd been told.

Captain Routon didn't like to take a call when he was driving, but the ringing seemed so insistent. He put the phone to his ear and heard the excited voice of Sam Tack.

'Sam,' he said. 'Where are you, my boy? Everything okay?'

'Just coming alongside you, actually, sir. Can you see me? Look right.'

Captain Routon looked down to his right and was delighted to see three smiling faces. The orphans were clogging the right-hand seats again, waving and calling. He took one hand from the steering wheel and waggled his fingers. The traffic had picked up speed and he was aware of hooting behind.

'Sir,' said Sam. 'Did you see that little plane? The one that nearly crashed?'

'I did, Sam. Yes. I'm not sure I should be on the phone when I'm driving, son. Is there a problem?'

'Well, there is really, sir. You probably won't believe me, but Millie's at the controls – of the plane, I mean. They had some kind of emergency and their pilot's unconscious. How would you feel . . . this is Oli's idea. How would you feel if they landed on top of you? It's a matter of life and death, apparently.'

Chapter Four

The orphans had always worked well together.

They had lived as a family for two terms in Ribblestrop's east tower and, though they fought and argued with ferocity, when it came to a crisis they observed strict lines of command. Their experience in the Ribblestrop Circus had made those lines firmer than ever, and the three teachers could only sit back in awe.

Captain Routon handed his phone to Asilah, the oldest of the boys, and a moment later the five skylight windows were not just open, they had been removed completely. An advance party was swarming through them, barefoot, onto the roof. Meanwhile, Eric ran to the emergency exit at the back and swung with Sanjay and Imagio onto the bars over the vehicle's rear bumper. They were doing a steady sixty miles per hour – the road a blur beneath them – but it wasn't difficult to make the leap onto the long, flat trailer behind. They soon had the tarpaulin off and, since Eric was chief packer, they knew exactly where to locate the gear they needed. They clambered over the trunks and cases, clinging with toes and fingers as the trailer bounced under them. Soon, they had their trapeze pulleys and cable, and had thrown a rope up to Podma, who was firmly anchored on the bus roof by human chain. Other vehicles were nosing up to them now, then falling back in wonder. There was more hooting, and then flashing lights, including blue ones. There was a helicopter, too, directly above.

The boys tried to ignore it, for this was the tricky bit. Podma pulled on the rope and hauled the heavy cables out of the trailer onto the roof. A forest of hands received them and started to uncoil the thickest. Anjoli started to stretch it, splayed out like a lizard on the juddering roof. Podma had taken the precaution of roping everyone together, and Professor Worthington, her head and shoulders rearing up through the front skylight, gripped the end of the line for dear life. The boys held onto each other, communicating with signs rather than words, and it wasn't long before Anjoli's cable was as tight as a tennis net, raised up a good half-metre by carefully wedged crowbars. The plane was a speck, some distance behind them, but there was clearly no time to be lost. It was making its final approach.

'What's your speed, Millie?' said Oli, as Mr Tack dropped behind the bus. He let a queue of furious vehicles past, his knuckles white on the wheel.

'Ninety,' whispered Miles.

'We're doing ninety,' said Millie.

'Can you slow down? We can't go that fast!'

'I don't know how.'

'Try. You can see us okay? Can you see the bus?'

'Not yet, no. I've got the road and the river. The road's right under us, but . . .'

'You're coming in nicely, but you've got to get lower and slower. You've got to come in as low as you can, all right? You need to come up behind us and Captain Routon's going to try to match your speed and carry you. We're going to lash you on as well, so you don't fall off. Everything's ready.'

25

'This isn't going to work, Oli!'

'Yes, it is. The maths is perfect. How much fuel have you got?'

'There's no way of telling. The alarm's getting louder all the time and we're juddering about. Oli, there are helicopters too! I can see fire engines!'

Miles was pressed against the cockpit glass and had managed to turn to his right. The helicopter had come from nowhere and was keeping pace with them. He could see the pilot yelling orders and instructions, but his own headset was still on the floor, a shrill voice gabbling through static. He looked down and the road was even closer – the blue lights had multiplied and he could see a column of ambulances off to the left. The traffic was being held back – a great, open swathe of tarmac appeared, though a police Land Rover was streaking ahead into it. Miles could hear its siren wailing and he wondered, for the hundredth time, why the police used sirens, when all they did was paralyse everyone with terror. He looked at Sanchez, who was holding the phone to Millie's ear, his jaw rigid with tension.

'I can see you, Oli,' said Millie. 'I've got the bus!'

'Slow down!' cried Oli.

'I'm trying. I just don't know how.'

She pulled the joystick back a fraction and felt the plane swerve to the right. She pressed the left pedal and they were back on course, the road skimming beneath them and the bus and its trailer coming ever closer. If they had wheels, she thought, a landing might be possible. Then again, she had no idea where the brakes were – should she simply run into the bus and use it as a buffer? She didn't dare, because she remembered Oli's words about fireballs.

'You can do this,' said Sanchez, quietly. 'I know you can.'

'No I can't,' she said.

26

'Just a bit lower,' said Miles. 'They've got a flag, look. They're showing the height with a flag!'

Sure enough, Kenji and Israel had leapt back onto the trailer and were sitting at its far end with one of the black-and-gold circus flags. They unfurled it in the gale and anchored it between two packing cases, hoping it might give Millie a clearer target. There were two police Land Rovers now, both keeping pace with the plane, just behind it, lights flashing madly. The rest of the children and their teachers were clustered on the back seat of the bus, watching anxiously.

'You can do it,' said Sanchez again.

'If I can't,' said Millie, 'you won't blame me, will you?'

'I love you,' said Miles. 'I want you to know that. Both of you. If we don't make it, I want you to know—'

'Shut up!' shouted Millie. 'Tell me what to do! Higher or lower? My hands are shaking!'

'You're dead on,' said Sanchez.

'Maybe down just a tiny bit,' said Miles.

'Down,' said Oli in Millie's ear. 'Just a tiny bit down and . . . okay, okay!'

Oli gestured at Sam, and Sam waved at Captain Routon, who sat rigid at the wheel of the bus.

'Faster, Dad!' shouted Sam, and Mr Tack increased his speed as Captain Routon did the same. They could hear nothing any more, except for the screaming engine of the aeroplane, which even obliterated the police sirens. It was so low its undercarriage touched the tarmac and there was a burst of sparks. If Millie felt the bump, she remained in control and lifted her craft just a fraction. At eighty miles an hour, decreasing due to wind resistance down to seventy-six, she came over the little car and then the trailer.

The orphans lowered the flag and threw themselves down amongst the luggage. Captain Routon held the wheel grimly. He pressed the throttle, pushing his speed up to seventy, seventy-two. The road ahead was clear, thank goodness – the police must have closed all junctions – in fact, he could see a road-block in the distance. He checked his mirrors and saw that the aeroplane's propeller was sweeping up behind him. It was on a collision course, and he braced himself, fighting his instincts to brake or swerve. There were blue flashing lights everywhere it seemed, but only the sound of howling engines and he clamped his jaws so tight his fillings were hurting.

He felt the crunch of contact like a blow.

For a moment he lost control, the back wheels simply sliding off to the right, and he heard the rending of metal as if the bus roof were being ripped apart. He steered into the skid and felt the wheels come true again. Then his bus was accelerating, as if some awful force were driving him forward – as if he was about to take off. The plane was down, the remains of its undercarriage snagged on the cable: the combined speed was terrifying. He touched the brake again and felt his tyres bursting. Left and right, he saw them in his mirrors – great chunks of rubber sheered off and flew into the distance. He could see luggage bouncing away as the trailer fish-tailed amongst fountains of sparks. Any moment, he thought, the bus would somersault over its nose.

He saw that the orphans were streaming out onto the roof again, grabbing at the plane. For one precious second he allowed himself to close his eyes. When he opened them, he saw fire engines ahead – a whole line of them up on a road-bridge. Despite his ruined wheels, the bus showed no sign of slowing, and there were emergency vehicles to the left and right, reversing quickly out of his path. The bus sped through them and Captain Routon tried the brakes again, knowing that if he pressed too hard he'd spin everyone into oblivion. There was a stink of burning, and he glimpsed in his mirror the shape of Doonan, on his knees in the middle of the aisle, praying hard.

Touchdown, from Millie's point of view, was yet another miracle in a life crammed with so many.

Miles and Sanchez were cowering beside her and, as the bus beneath them accelerated to match their speed, there was a curious slow-motion about it all. They could see the cable stretched across the roof. They could see Professor Worthington, Asilah and Anjoli gesturing with their hands, hair flapping wildly over their faces. Millie let the plane drift in and came lower still. She felt the cable catch the undercarriage and felt the nose dip suddenly. She eased the joystick back, compensating, and the craft sunk with a crunch that made the bus skid and sway beneath her.

She had no idea how to turn things off, but it was Sanchez who did the obvious. He closed the emergency fuel line and, after an agonising ten seconds, they saw the propellers slowing down. That was when a boy in a black-and-gold blazer appeared on the end of a rope, clambering onto the right-hand wing.

It was Israel, fighting the jet stream, and he had a bundle in his arms. There was activity on both sides, and Millie recognised the long hair of Anjoli. It looked as if another cable was being slung right over the top of them, as half a dozen orphans battled with the wind. It was Miles who had the sense to go back to the door and in a moment he'd hauled it open and the cabin was blasted with air.

Nobody could speak. The bus was skidding and slipping, and the noise was unbearable. Podma was first into the plane, Israel behind him. It was the rope ladder they carried, and it was soon unfurled and drawn tight. Miles was out, and there were hands everywhere, steadying him as he descended. Millie was next, and then Sanchez was heaving at the half-conscious pilot. The bus swerved again and took out a road sign. The orphans grabbed wrists, hair, collars and knees, and somehow, everyone was inside the bus.

There was wild cheering and a scrum of embraces. This might have continued had not Doonan's voice soared out over the din.

'Look out! Oh no! Sweet Jesus, no! Brace, children! For God's sake, brace! Bridge! Bridge!'

It happened so fast.

Captain Routon was simply trying to keep the bus on the road, because it was shimmying wildly. They were almost at the bridge, and the blue lights were blinding. There was snow in the air, too, thick on the windscreen and flying all around them. It was foam from the fire engines, and even as Doonan shouted they felt themselves spinning into a vast cloud of bubbly whiteness.

The bridge was just low enough to catch the upturned nose of the plane, and flipped it backwards. The cable round the plane didn't snap, it simply tore the whole roof of the bus right off and sent it spinning onto the road. One of the police vehicles that was following skidded and hit the wreckage broadside. The other managed to brake, but was then whisked away on a lake of gobstoppers – Miles's suitcase had fallen onto the road and burst, spraying them in all directions. The car pirouetted into the central reservation and slammed into a Portakabin. The children emerged from the foam clinging to their bus seats. The bus then shouldered its way through a crash barrier and down a steep embankment – just where the elbow of the River Ribble was at its widest. A handful of fishermen jumped for their lives, and could only gape as the mangled vehicle slipped hissing and steaming into the deep, dark water.

Mr Tack pulled up neatly on the hard shoulder and put on his hazard lights. Ruskin, Sam and Oli raced to the river-bank in time to see the bus, with everyone onboard, sinking fast. A strange, awestruck silence descended, then the three boys rushed forward to save their friends from drowning.

Chapter Five

Ribblestrop's headmaster was in his study when the call came through.

He had ignored the phone all day, thinking it was one of the school parrots. There were two, and they'd been learning more and more sound effects ever since they'd arrived. Now they'd gone to roost up in the rafters above his desk, and it seemed their chief occupation was to torment him. Telephones, door-knocks, children's voices; Doctor Norcross-Webb felt he was being haunted. He was quietly seething, because on the last day without children he'd hoped to get some concentrated work done on the school song. There was still only one verse, and he was determined to write the second before the big assembly at six o'clock. He'd brought his accordion down from the attic, but the birds had even started to imitate that. He closed his eyes, put his fingers in his ears, and sang the opening lines of his latest effort:

'*Ribblestrop, Ribblestrop, jewel within my breast.*
I will hap'ly die for thee; I will stand the test.'

He paused.

Was the allusion to death wise? He knew that 'jewel' was an awkward word to sing, and he wasn't at all sure why a child should have one buried in its breast. Would anyone understand that 'hap'ly' was 'happily'?

He looked at an earlier draft.

'Ribblestrop, Ribblestrop, let me hug thy stones . . .'

It was worse, and he knew it.

He gazed out of the window again. The breeze was warm and it ruffled the heads of the spring flowers. They were the product of Captain Routon's gardening club last term and overflowed from the pots on the terrace. Pinks, whites and blues – it was a perfect scene. In the distance one of the school donkeys cropped the grass beside the camel, and the sun gave the lake a silvery glimmer. He gazed, and tried not to let his eyes drift to the furious letter in his in-tray. It was the second of the day, from Lady Vyner, and had been hand-delivered.

To the so-called headmaster of Ribblestrop,

So-called 'school' for dysfunctional reprobates and vandals.

That was just the opening.

You are ordered, by law, to vacate these premises. You are instructed to pack your bags, as I've got a court order now, so I'm changing the locks and hiring a security firm . . .'

The rest of the letter degenerated into obscenities, so he pushed it to one side, wincing. Beneath it was an altogether more charming communication from the new sports teacher at Ribblestrop High. Since the sacking of Gary Cuthbertson – brother to the infamous ex-police inspector, Percy Cuthbertson – a closer tie with local schools seemed possible. The new coach there was a Mr Johnny Jay, and he seemed positively friendly. He was reminding the headmaster about a match they'd confirmed, saying how much he was looking forward to it. The headmaster wrote the date in his diary and wondered where the football had been stored.

The phone rang again and he ignored it.

He turned back to his song lyrics and was seized by inspiration.

'Ribblestrop, Ribblestrop, what a lovely day!
This is where we come to work, and where we come to play.'

It was promising. He could imagine the orphans in particular singing it with gusto. He had missed them so much, for a school without children was a forlorn place. The least he could do was have everything ready for their return, so he stood up with his notes and prepared to try the words out loud. At that moment, the phone rang again, and he swung round, hunting for a missile to throw at the parrots. This time, however, he noticed that the receiver was visibly vibrating in its cradle. He snatched it up and put on his most responsible voice.

'Ribblestrop Towers,' he said. 'Headmaster speaking.'

'Oh, Giles. Thank goodness.'

It was Professor Worthington, and the relief in her voice was palpable. She sounded close to tears.

'Hello, Clarissa. Where are you?'

There was a silence.

'Giles,' said the Professor, at last. 'Where have you been? I've been trying to reach you for the last two hours.'

'I'm so sorry. I didn't think it was a real call. How are you getting on? By the way, I had a thought about supper. Why don't we just order a huge load of fish and chips—'

'Giles?'

'And I had a call from Sanchez's father. Mrs Tack as well, and it all seems fine. They're on the road at the moment.'

'Giles, I've got something to tell you. Can you listen to me, please?'

'Yes, of course. You've met up with the orphans, I assume?'

'Are you sitting down?'

'What's wrong?'

34

'We've lost our school.'

The headmaster was silent for a moment. 'Who has?' he said.

'We have. Doonan, Routon and I. We had everyone together, but various accidents have occurred, and—'

'Are you still at Heathrow?'

'No! No, we left Heathrow ages ago. We had them all in the bus. And we . . . met up with Sam and Oli and Ruskin. And then we ran into problems.'

'Where are you, Clarissa?'

'I'm in a police station, Giles. We've all been arrested, pending a full-scale investigation of traffic violations – and that includes air traffic. But the children aren't with us. They're gone.'

'What? How?'

'We've been arrested for endangering the lives of . . . well, just about everyone, I think. And we've caused about a billion pounds' worth of damage. The thing is, Giles, the children slipped away and nobody's looking for them. They just disappeared into the river and the helicopter wouldn't go after them, so . . . we've lost our school!'

There was a silence.

'Where?' said the headmaster, at last.

'On the edge of Ribblemoor. In a river. How soon can you get here?'

The roofless bus had slipped into the river and sunk like a stone. Water filled the vehicle in about five seconds and the bus was soon sucked out into the deepest channel. Doonan had managed to shout, 'Swim for it! Everybody – ahh!' before the deluge had swept him under the seats, filling his lungs in an instant. Captain Routon was a strong swimmer and grabbed the young man by his belt. He was soon up and out, kicking against the vortex that was swirling around them. They broke the surface together and a fisherman on the shore threw them a lifebelt. Other heads were popping up one after another, and in an instant Routon and the Professor were diving to look for those who might be trapped. There was zero visibility, however, and the only way they could do it was by touch. Routon went back in the bus, swimming among the seats, mindful that he only had enough air to search a fraction of the area. When he surfaced for the second time, he saw Professor Worthington crawling up the bank with the dazed pilot under her arm. A human chain was forming, but now Sam and Oli were nowhere to be seen. He also saw that the long trailer he'd been pulling had broken free of the bus, and was afloat some way out to midstream. A lot of the children were clinging to it and, as he watched, he saw one child diving back into the river, presumably to search for the missing.

He took a great lungful of air and plunged again.

Ruskin was in difficulties. He had rushed gallantly into the water, determined to save his friends, and only when he was completely out of his depth and sinking fast did he remember that he couldn't swim. He hadn't even taken his blazer off and it was waterlogged at once. His school shoes were soon deep in mud and, as he flailed blindly, it was a stroke of luck that he caught Imagio's elbow as he swam by. Imagio grabbed his wrists and towed him to the trailer. Then he too jumped back in for another search.

The two smallest orphans, Kenji and Ron, did a head-count. Amazingly, once Anjoli, Miles and Millie had been called in from a splashing fight, everyone was accounted for. The trailer they were on, however, was drifting fast. It was caught in a strong current and was already more than a hundred metres from the bank. They could see policemen in the distance, struggling through the undergrowth in pursuit – but they were disappearing behind a line of trees. The policemen were shouting and whistles were blowing but they had little chance of keeping up, because the craft was so buoyant and the river so fast. The adults watched in disbelief as the children floated behind an island, out of sight. The boys and Millie sat clutching each other, gazing back – they were helpless to steer or paddle, and in another half-minute the blue flashing lights, the bridge and all the spectators had simply been erased from the landscape.

A strange silence fell.

'We're on our own,' said Sam, quietly.

'Totally,' said Ruskin.

'I didn't say goodbye to my dad. He drove us all this way and I didn't even say thank you.'

'What about Captain Routon?' said Oli. 'We didn't get a chance to thank him.'

'What if we swim for it?' said Miles. 'We could probably make it.'

'No way,' said Sanjay.

'I could swim that,' said Anjoli. 'I could swim back there.'

'You want a race?' said Vijay, pulling his shirt off. 'First one back to the road and you've got to touch —'

'No!' shouted Asilah, grabbing hold of him. 'No way. You just sit down – all of you – and you stay sat down. All right?'

'We're lucky to be alive,' said Sanchez. 'That was the most amazing bit of flying I've ever seen, Millie. That was a miracle.'

'It was Oli's plan,' said Millie. 'He's the genius.'

'How did it happen?' said Imagio. 'We're just on our way back to school and . . . it was like a disaster movie. And what do we do now?'

'What can we do?' said Tomaz. 'We just have to wait, I guess. They'll follow us, won't they? They'll send that helicopter.'

'Stay together, that's for sure,' said Sanchez. 'I suppose everyone's phones are ruined?'

Miles, Millie and Oli pulled them out of their pockets and water streamed from the cases.

'I might be able to clean Sam's,' said Oli. 'The circuitry's pretty basic, but it won't be a quick job.'

'Do your best,' said Sanchez. 'We need to get back to civilisation – Captain Routon's going to be worried sick about us.' He turned to Asilah. 'Why is it that getting to school always involves these ... diversions? Whenever we split up, that's when the trouble happens. If we stay together, we'll be safe.'

'I say we just go with the flow,' said Eric. 'They'll find us soon enough.'

'They'll be round the next bend,' said Miles. He laughed. 'This is our last few minutes of freedom, guys, we might as well enjoy it. I've been here before, by the way. I'm sure of it.'

'What do you mean?' said Millie. 'When?'

'I don't know. It's just familiar.'

'We can't be that far from school,' said Asilah. 'We'd driven for hours and I saw a sign to Ribblemoor.'

'Did you see the faces of those policemen?' said Vijay, grinning.

Eric laughed. 'The ones by the river? They were not happy getting their shoes wet.'

'There's going to be a lot of angry people back there,' said Millie, and there were murmurs of agreement. 'We'll be on the news again. I think we're best off getting as far away as possible – hiding out, even. I mean, how much does a plane cost? We smashed it to bits.'

'And a bus. And two police cars. You think we killed anyone?'

'I don't think so,' said Sanchez.

'Fine,' said Imagio. 'Let's just keep going and see where we end up. If we see a house or a bridge or something, we can stop and make a phonecall.'

'It's a very pretty river,' said Sam. 'I just saw a kingfisher.'

Chapter Six

After another half-hour, the river divided for the third time.

'How far do you think we've come?' said Sanchez.

'A long way,' said Tomaz. 'It's a maze, isn't it? They're never going to find us – and there's still no one about.'

'Hold on, that's not a field,' said Ruskin. 'Look to the right – look how flat the grass is.'

'That's a cricket pitch,' said Asilah.

'There's one on the left, as well.'

Miles was staring, screwing up his eyes. 'I have been here before!' he said. 'I thought I recognised it, way back. I know this place, I'm sure of it.'

'You are such an attention-seeker,' said Millie. 'When have you been floating on a river?'

'It's The Priory,' said Miles. 'On the edge of the moor – The Priory School. These are the playing fields.' He stood up and went to the prow.

Sanjay said, 'There's a sign coming up.'

'*Private property*,' read Israel. 'How can you make a river private?'

'There's something written under it.'

They came closer and peered at a line of smaller letters.

'Miles is right,' said Vijay. 'It's just what he says: *Property of The Priory*. I guess they mean the land's private and they don't want trespassers. Oh, and look at that.' He read carefully. '*These premises are patrolled by Stillwater Security Sytems. SSS.*'

'You think they're guarding the fish?' said Anjoli.

'You think they're watching us?' said Sam.

Miles was still gazing around him. 'It's my old school,' he said, quietly.

'Which one?' said Millie.

Miles ignored her. 'You can see the pavilion. And the chapel, on the other side of those trees – can you see the spire? This is the worst school in the world.'

'It looks quite grand,' said Ruskin. 'Do you think they'd help us?'

Sure enough, some formidably grey school buildings were emerging, the windows blank and black. The river bent to the right and took the children closer, under a line of willows. There wasn't a pupil or teacher in sight, and still nothing but birdsong.

'You really went here?' said Israel. 'You must be loaded.'

'When was it?' said Tomaz.

'Two years ago. I was eleven.'

'Is it as posh as it looks?' said Sam.

'Oh yes,' said Miles. 'The poshest, snobbiest place I've ever been. I got kicked out and went up to some dump in Scotland. Then I went to Canada.'

'It certainly has character,' said Ruskin. 'The facilities look excellent. Oh, and there's another sign –'

'It was a prison camp,' said Miles. 'Look! You can see some of the kids in the distance.'

Everyone strained their eyes and, sure enough, a line of blue-clad figures jogged out of the trees. They kept in strict formation, trotted round the pavilion, and disappeared again.

41

'I could tell you some stories,' Miles whispered. 'And I'll tell you something else: we don't want to get caught here. I want to get back to Ribblestrop.'

'We're being filmed,' said Vijay. 'Everyone smile.'

They were floating slowly under a spread of tree branches, and the next sign was right overhead, bigger than ever. *Stillwater Security Systems*, it read. *We are watching you!* A small black camera sat at the centre of the sign and Miles made an obscene gesture at it.

'How do we get home?' said Asilah. 'That's the question, isn't it? Does the river lead anywhere?'

'I can't remember,' said Miles. 'There was a whole maze of rivers, all round the grounds – and we weren't allowed to go near them. If you were caught playing by the river, you got a Sunday detention. Or worse. I think we just need to keep going.'

'Why did they kick you out?' said Eric.

Miles shook his head. 'You won't believe me if I tell you. Let's go left here – it might take us away from the place. All we did was work and do cross-country running and tests the whole time . . . I hated it. Go left – please!'

The children on the right side of the trailer paddled as best they could, for the river was dividing again. Vijay leapt onto the bank and found a couple of long branches. He re-joined the craft and he and Asilah punted them in the direction Miles had suggested. The river narrowed at once and took them past yet another cricket field and a row of huts. After some time, the land turned to fields again, but their way was suddenly blocked. There was an iron bar stretched right across the water, wrapped in barbed wire.

Strictly private, said a sign. *The Priory School – Rector's House. No admittance to pupils or public.*

The initials *SSS* were stamped on a little plaque and there was another camera rearing up from behind on a metal arm.

Millie whistled softly. 'They think they own everything,' she said.

'They do,' said Miles. 'The founder was some saint. We had to bow to his statue the whole time. We had to wear cassocks on a Sunday.'

'Should we go back?' asked Ruskin. 'If Miles doesn't like it, maybe we should just turn around.'

'I'm telling you, we don't want to get caught here,' said Miles. 'They might remember me.'

Sanjay was peering through the trees. 'There's someone in that field,' he said. 'We could just ask for directions – they can't stop us doing that. Maybe we can find a bus or a railway station.'

'That's the first person we've seen,' said Asilah, 'apart from those kids. Let's stop and ask.'

'Maybe just one or two us should go,' said Sam.

'Yes,' said Miles. 'The rest of us should stay in the boat.'

'No,' said Sanchez, firmly. 'No. We stick together now. We are not splitting up.'

'What are you so worried about, Miles?' said Imagio. 'You must have had friends here. Maybe you can find one, and—'

'They all hated me,' said Miles.

'What a surprise,' said Millie.

Miles turned on her, angrily. Asilah held him back.

'Don't let her get to you,' he said. 'We won't stay here long, okay? We'll just walk over to that person in the field, get directions and go.'

'He's just standing there,' said Sanjay. 'He hasn't moved in the last five minutes.'

The children pulled on their blazers and stamped back into their shoes.

The trailer had come to rest against the metal barrier, so it was easy to use the two branches to push it to the bank. In less than a minute, everyone had disembarked, and Imagio was leading them up a narrow path. 'I don't know where I'm going, all right?' he said.

They came to the top of the rise, the trees giving way to brambles and nettles.

'If we've been seen on camera,' said Ruskin, 'then they might be sending someone to help us.'

'We just say we're lost,' said Sam. 'It's the truth, isn't it?'

Sanjay said, 'I can see more of the kids.'

'Where?'

He pointed and another column of running figures came into view. They were dressed in blue overalls.

'They do look like prisoners,' said Vijay. 'You think they're being punished for something?'

'No,' said Miles. 'They run all the time.'

The column came closer and it was obvious that the runners were in some distress. They looked tired and strained and they were concentrating hard. There was no cheerful banter and nobody stopped to dawdle. They ran almost in formation – left, right, left, right – and the one straggler, who was a plump girl with glasses, seemed desperate to keep up. Her face was wet with sweat and her mouth was set in a thin, determined line. The Ribblestrop children crept back out of sight and watched them pass. Half a minute later they had disappeared over a hilltop and the birdsong resumed.

'Let's go,' said Tomaz. 'I agree with Miles. I want to get to Ribblestrop.'

Miles was nodding and his face was pale. 'I'd rather get back in the boat and go back the way we came. If we get caught here, they'll lock us up.'

'It's getting late,' said Asilah, reasonably. 'We can't just stay on the river, Miles – we can't spend the night in the open. I really think we've got to find civilisation. We'll stay together, like Sanchez says. We'll ask the guy we saw in the field and get moving.'

With that, he led everyone out of the brush and over the rise. The figure was still there, with his back to them, just as before. He wore a bright red waterproof, and was standing by a low hillock. As they moved towards him they saw that there were several of these hillocks, rising like pimples on the plain.

'It's a woman,' said Sanjay, after five minutes of walking.

'What's she doing?'

'No idea. Looks like a . . . survey, maybe. She's got some kind of tripod.'

'She's looking at the burial chambers,' said Miles, softly. 'We were never allowed near them, but we did some project—'

'Who's buried there?' asked Sam.

'No idea. I hated rubbish like that. I know tourists used to come and look at them, because we had to tell a teacher if we saw any. They have rich kids here, so they're terrified of kidnappers.'

Millie grinned. 'Just like Sanchez, huh? Feeling nervous?' she called.

'No,' said Sanchez. He looked grimly around him. 'But I want to find the road, so let's ask her if she knows the way, and get out of here.'

The figure still had her back to them as they approached. A stiff breeze was blowing her hair about and flapped the hood of her anorak. She was so immersed in her work that she didn't look round, even as Asilah coughed. Her eye was in the viewfinder of a large camera and she seemed determined to get close-ups from above and below. They could see now that she was focusing on a pale white stone that was embedded in the hill, about the size of a small tombstone. The children stopped, not quite sure how to start a conversation with someone so intent.

'Hello?' said Sanchez. 'We're sorry to bother you . . .'

The woman didn't hear him. She moved her tripod again, a metre to her left. She lowered the legs and crouched, and they heard her camera click. The white stone had lumps and carvings on it and she was zooming in on the fine detail.

'Hello!' called Sanchez more loudly. This time she swung round and started with surprise. The tripod fell onto its side.

'Good afternoon,' she said, frostily.

The children came closer and saw that her face was pink and weathered. 'Sorry to bother you,' said Sanchez, 'but —'

'I know what you're going to say,' she interrupted. 'I was told the same thing yesterday. By a little crowd of joggers and your wretched teacher.'

'Oh.'

'You may as well save your breath.'

'Yes,' said Sanchez.

'Why it's any of your business,' she cried, 'I just don't know. I'm on a historic bridleway and I have every right to be here.'

Sanchez swallowed. 'I see. We were just wondering—'

'Apart from that, I'm doing absolutely no harm – so why you children can't live and let live is quite beyond me. I do not recognise your school's jurisdiction over trade routes that have existed for five thousand years, so I suggest you clear off.'

The children stared from the woman back to Sanchez and waited for him to reply.

'Oh,' he said. 'Thank you very much.'

'We're actually looking for a telephone box,' said Ruskin. 'So we can phone someone.'

'Do you know the significance of this stone?' said the woman. 'I bet you're not even interested.'

Miles spoke up. 'We didn't want to bother you, honestly. It's just that we're a bit lost and getting quite hungry.'

'Then I suggest you go back to school!'

'Er . . . that's what we're trying to do. But not this one.'

The woman put her hands on her hips, and looked harder at the children. 'You're not from The Priory?' she said, slowly.

'No,' said Millie.

'Oh. I thought you were another bunch of those snotty-faced little snobs. Sorry, I rather jumped to that conclusion because . . . well, there's so many of you, and I . . . No, your uniform is totally different – I'm so sorry.'

'We're from Ribblestrop Towers,' said Ruskin, showing a damp blazer badge. 'Though we're not from there, as such. We're trying to go there.'

'We've just come down the river,' said Anjoli. 'We had some accidents.'

'Ribblestrop?' said the woman. 'Ribblestrop town, formerly the settlement known as Volara? Gateway to the silver and tin mines of Ribblemoor? Market town, granted its first charter in 1302, but a thriving Iron Age trading post on account of the minerals? I was there last week, at the museum.' She swallowed. 'I got the wrong end of the stick, my dears. That seems to be something I do rather a lot, so people say. I'm Ellie Mold, by the way – Doctor Ellie is what people call me. You want the nearest road, right? That will mean following the bridleway I mentioned back to the school's main entrance. Or you can take the shortcut I took and hop over the gate. Rather depends where you want to get to.'

'We're trying to find some shops, and a phone box, and—'

'We're starving,' said Israel. 'We got lost and we haven't eaten for about a day.'

'Anjoli!' said Asilah, sharply. 'Don't touch it!'

Everyone swung round in time to see Anjoli step back abruptly from the fallen tripod. For the first time, the woman smiled.

'Oh, don't worry,' she said. 'You won't damage it. I've knocked seven bells out of it over the years and it's pretty much indestructible. Rather like me. You can have a look through it, if you want. I was about to pack up now the light's going. It's part of a project I'm working on – decoding the stones. Ribblestrop Towers, though ...' She thought hard. 'Doesn't that belong to the Vyner family? You say it's a school?'

'It's a kind of school,' said Miles. 'It's a pretty strange place.'

'So you're a kind of schoolboy, are you? You do look a bit unusual, you know. The Priory children dress rather more smartly.'

Miles grinned. His shirt was more torn than usual and the tails came almost to his knees. 'They have to,' he said.

'So why are you taking so many pictures?' said Oli. 'Are you an archaeologist?'

'Yes,' said Doctor Ellie. 'I don't want to bore you, especially if you haven't eaten, but that's exactly what I am. I'm an amateur archaeologist – full marks for guessing. And these stones are a mystery I'm determined to solve. They're part of a very elaborate system of markers, but what they mark exactly ... well, that's the mystery. They've been found all over the moor, though I expect you know that if you live at Ribblestrop – you study local history, I assume?'

'No,' said Sam.

'Look, why don't I get you to the road, and I can ... well, I can drive you to the nearest supermarket, I suppose. I can at least get you fed.'

48

'All of us?' said Millie. 'Have you got a bus parked somewhere?'

'I've got a fairly big van, so it depends how small you can make yourselves. It's in a lay-by over there – other side of that hedge. If The Priory lot haven't towed it away, that is. They think they own the whole earth and sky. Follow me, why don't you? We can slip out quietly. Oh ... too late. Dammit.'

'Why?' said Eric.

The children turned to look where Doctor Ellie was looking, and a voice floated over the field towards them.

'You there! Stay where you are!'

'Oh Lord,' said the woman. 'Here comes the tyrant.'

'Who's he?' said Sanchez. 'Is that the teacher?'

A large man was hurrying over the grass with another figure behind him. He had an arm raised, and his anger was obvious even at sixty or seventy metres.

'It's the same one as yesterday and one of the guards. He's an absolute rogue – no manners at all.'

'We could run,' said Israel. 'They don't look too fast.'

'Why should we?' said Doctor Ellie. 'We are not trespassing and I will not be chased off like a peasant. You have to stand up to these fellows.'

The two men broke into a jog and the children saw that there was yet another cluster of blue-suited children behind them. The taller of the men blew a whistle and waved. His voice floated across the plain again. 'Stay exactly where you are, please! You're under arrest.'

'He's a history teacher,' said Doctor Ellie. 'Can you believe that? He teaches history and knows nothing about it. They call him "Mr Ian".'

'Mr Ian?' said Miles. 'History teacher?'

She shuddered. 'He's completely ignorant. We'll ignore him, I think. Follow me.'

49

She started walking purposefully towards the hedge and there was another long blast on the whistle.

'I order you to stop!' shouted Mr Ian. 'I order you to stand still!'

Chapter Seven

Doctor Ellie held the children to a dignified walk and it was soon clear that the two men would cut them off before they reached the hedge.

There was a gate through to the road but it was padlocked. Everyone converged and Mr Ian thrust his way to the front, blocking all chance of escape. He was puffing and wheezing, and his security-guard companion was red-faced too. This man was dressed from head to toe in black and the letters *SSS* were inscribed on both breast pocket and cap.

'Mr Ian,' said Doctor Ellie, politely. 'How nice to see you again. I expect you're going to give me a good telling off, aren't you? But do you really think you have the power of arrest?'

Mr Ian fought for breath. He wore a tracksuit with a shapeless tweed jacket over the top, both elbows patched. His eyes were bulging slightly and he was chewing his lips through a shaggy, sandy beard.

'I thought I told you,' he said, at last. 'I told you to . . . to stay off our land!'

'I thought I told you,' said Doctor Ellie, 'that it's not your land to control.'

'It most certainly is.'

'No, it's not.'

'You had your warning. I am now—'

'This is a path,' said Doctor Ellie, 'that has existed for thousands of years, and if you think your tin-pot college can privatise and close it, you're demented. Now, does this gargoyle have a key to the gate, or do we have to remove you and climb over?'

The children could see that there was a lay-by on the other side of the gate with a large blue van parked at the end of it.

'I do have a key,' said the guard, 'but Mr Ian's quite right. The fact you've ignored the sign means that you are in breach of by-laws, and—'

'The by-laws are illegal.'

'Oh no they're not!'

'I also happen to know that your security company – this SSS nonsense – is unlicensed and unregulated.'

'We are not!'

'Yes, you are, and—'

'This is school property, woman!' exploded Mr Ian. 'You can't just clamber over our gates and go where you like!'

'I can and I do. This land was made public by Oliver Cromwell, and the right to freedom of passage—'

'You're trespassing!' shouted the teacher.

Doctor Ellie nodded. 'Well, I can see that there's no point standing here contradicting a fool,' she said quietly. 'You're not a man who listens, and I should save my breath. But I can tell you now what I told you yesterday: no court in the land would uphold your fraudulent claim and, if you molest and bully me, then I'll be bringing a civil action against you. The land is free and part of our heritage. I've been showing these lovely children living history, and I defy you, sir. You should be looking after your own pupils, not harassing mine.'

Mr Ian had turned crimson and his lips twitched. He turned to see that the cluster of blue joggers had come close. They had overheard every word – and one or two were smiling happily. They were gazing at the Ribblestrop pupils with fascination.

'Get back to the house!' barked Mr Ian. His voice was a curiously high squeak. 'Get into your togs – greys only – and get to prep.'

'It's Monday, sir,' said a boy. 'Shouldn't we wear our –'

'Get back to the house!' roared Mr Ian, and the children fled without another word.

Doctor Ellie broke the short silence that followed with a cool line of contempt. 'You know, I have always despised grown men who shout at small children,' she said. 'Herodotus, writing in 429 BC, tells of a tutor in third century Athens. The man was stoned out the city for that offence, because it was seen as an affront to civilised values. It also suggests mental infirmity.' She turned to the security guard. 'Unlock the gate, please.'

The guard did as he was told and wrenched off the chain.

Mr Ian stood aside. 'You are all on camera, you know,' he said. 'We shall be circulating your images.'

'Completely illegal,' said Doctor Ellie as stepped into the lay-by. 'Any film you've shot is protected material and cannot be circulated by civilians.'

'Now you listen to me!' said Mr Ian, pushing through the gate after her. 'We have a duty of care here to all our pupils. Who are these ... ruffians, anyway? Look at the state of them!'

His eye had been caught by Anjoli, who had one arm round Sam and the other round Israel. He was bare-chested, his blazer tied round his waist. He stuck his tongue out rudely.

'I will have your names, every one of you,' hissed Mr Ian.

His hands were clenched into fists and he snatched a pen from his jacket pocket. 'I will be making a formal complaint to your so-called school.'

'Shall I call the police, sir?' asked the security guard.

Mr Ian swung round and glared at him. 'Yes!' he cried. 'I thought they were on their way!'

The man muttered into his radio and the children pushed through the gate towards the van. Doctor Ellie strode ahead to its rear doors and pulled them open. The first orphan struggled up onto the step.

'All aboard!' she cried.

'Do not attempt to leave!' shouted Mr Ian. 'I need names and addresses!'

'It's all right, sir,' said a voice. 'I've got her.'

Everyone looked down to see who had spoken. There was a second security guard who had been hidden by the side of the vehicle. He was kneeling close to the back wheel and was smiling grimly.

'Two-hundred and fifty pounds,' he said. 'That's just the release fee.'

'They've clamped us,' said Doctor Ellie, quietly. 'How typical.'

'College property, madam,' said the man. 'Signs up for all to see.' His radio squawked like a bird and he spoke into the microphone. 'Unit Foxtrot reporting. Blue van immobilised, driver and passengers apprehended. Can you send recovery asap – need a ten-tonne flat-bed, couple of crew. Police alerted – she's about to get nasty, by the look of it.'

'Do you have a tool kit?' said Sanjay, quietly.

'What for?' said Doctor Ellie.

'Get Cuthbertson,' said the first guard. 'Might need a bit of muscle.'

'Miss,' said Asilah, 'we don't really want to meet up

with the police right now. It would be best to get out of here.'

'I don't either, but I'm not sure we've got much choice.'

Even as she spoke, Israel was emerging from the driver's door with a long metal box in his arms. The wheel-clamper stepped back as the boys pressed in to look at his work. The tyre was encased in yellow bars and familiar letters were stenciled over their centrepiece: *SSS*.

'Stay away from that!' said the guard. 'Don't even think about interfering – that's another offence.'

Seconds later, however, Podma had a crowbar slotted behind the clamp. One quick jerk twisted the main hinge clear of the hubcap.

The guard was outraged. 'That is vandalism!' he cried. 'Come and look at this, Brian! They're forcing the metal!'

The children took no notice for, once again, they were working together. Podma bent the second part of the mechanism, while Miles added his weight. Vijay moved in under them with a large spanner and eased it in over one of the wheelnuts. A number of other boys had dragged suitable stones from under the hedge, and Sam and Israel had crawled beneath the chassis on their bellies with a jack. In half a minute, a large rock had been rolled into position and slid through the mud. The jack was under the axle, and the corner of the van was rising into the air.

'Do not remove that wheel!' said the guard. 'That is forbidden, totally, and there's a fine of six hundred pounds—'

'Excuse me,' said Vijay, adding his weight to the spanner.

Mr Ian could stand it no longer. 'Give that to me, you little beggar!' he cried. 'Give that thing to me!'

He was a big man and he strode into the scrum of children, knocking two to one side. He slammed Vijay against the side of the vehicle and went for Anjoli, who was working on the second nut. Anjoli ducked, but the man was too quick. He grabbed the boy by the hair and drew him backwards. The next instant, however, his legs had buckled under him, and he was on his back. Asilah crouched over him, trembling with rage, a finger close to the man's nose. Sanchez tried to hold him back, but Asilah was bristling.

'Don't ever, *ever* do that,' he hissed.

'Assault,' said one of the security guards, backing onto the road in terror. He had a small camera in his hand. 'Did you all see that? That was a martial arts move, that was! Did you see what he did?'

Mr Ian lay still, winded and shocked. He had received a sharp kick to the back of his left knee, and it had completely disabled him.

'You touch one of us again,' said Asilah, 'and you'll get badly hurt.' He looked up at Vijay. 'Finish the job. Help him, Miles.'

'I say, leave this to Cuthbertson,' said the guard. He was filming everything. 'This is one of those London schools, isn't it? Thugs and druggies, that's what you lot are.'

Mr Ian managed to sit up, but he still hadn't caught his breath. There was blood on his beard from where he'd bitten his lip, and he was shaking his head as if to clear it.

'Miles,' he said, quietly. 'You said Miles, didn't you?'

Anjoli said something in his own language and started to slide the wheel off. Mr Ian was staring round the group, his eyes wild. 'I thought I . . . Where is he?'

'Take no notice,' said Sanchez. 'Get the job done and let's get out of here.'

Miles had moved to the other side of the vehicle, but he couldn't resist a sideways glance at Mr Ian. He found a pair of astonished eyes gazing back into his and the man's mouth dropped open.

'Seyton-Shandy,' he whispered. 'Miles Seyton-Shandy!'

'What about it?' said Miles, nervously.

'Of all the kids I've ever taught . . .' He was losing his breath again. 'Of all the children . . . you were the devil.'

Chapter Eight

The children worked even faster.

They pushed the clamped wheel into the van and the spare was swiftly fitted. In another moment, the jack was down and the stone that had supported it was hauled back to make a step up to the rear doors.

'In you get, boys,' said Doctor Ellie, cheerfully. 'That's enough bother for one day. Could you go in the front, please, dear?' Millie did as she was told, dragging Miles with her. Everyone else started to clamber in through the back doors. 'That's it,' Ellie cried. 'Pile in any old how – I want to get out of here as soon as possible. Let's get you back to your nasty London school.'

She was just about to close the door, when her eyes fell on the step they'd been using and her heart lurched. She stopped and leant against the frame. Her mouth opened and she couldn't close it again.

'What's the matter, miss?' said Sam. He noticed the woman's face changing colour and jumped out to help her.

'I'm not quite sure. This can't be happening.'

'Are you sick?'

'No. Wait. This is remarkable.'

'We ought to go,' called Millie, anxiously. Podma had started the engine and was revving it. 'What's the problem back there?'

Doctor Ellie was staring downwards. 'This is impossible,' she whispered.

'What is, miss? Come on!' cried Sam.

The children at the back were craning their necks, confused by the old lady's sudden stillness. One of the security guards came closer and followed her gaze.

'Can you help me for a moment?' she said to the boys that were nearest. She was holding Sam's arm, using him for support. 'You've made the most . . . This is not possible! Help us here!' she cried. 'Please . . . Boys?'

She went down on one knee and several boys leapt out and clustered around her. She now had both hands on the stone.

'I've been looking for this for years. It's part of the keystone.'

'What is?' said Israel. 'What are you looking at?'

Podma blasted the horn twice, but Doctor Ellie was oblivious. She was brushing muddy footprints from the milk-white stone with a paintbrush plucked from a pocket. She pulled the block towards her, swinging it round in the mud, and found an eye-glass. It took her seconds to check, and she was aware that she had to make a quick decision. The problem was that she couldn't stop her hands shaking, and as she lay her fingers gently over the indentations she could feel heat rising. There were stars and half-moons. There were crosses, lines and dimples and they ran in long swirls, over every visible face. Her eyes filled with tears as she traced them blindly, sensing the tools and the hands that had cut them.

'Put this inside, please . . .'

'What's the matter, miss?'

'D'you need some water, miss? Do you want to lie down?'

'No. No – just . . . Put this in the van, would you?' She started to lift and there were suddenly five pairs of hands helping. 'We may, um . . . need it again, boys, if we have to . . . You know, if we have to change a wheel or something. Just pop it in the back – mind your fingers.'

The guard's radio squawked again. 'Back-up on its way,' said the man. 'Is that you, Mr Cuthbertson, sir? We've been assaulted and vandalised. There's a situation here and our assailant's absconding. How close are you, over? . . . Well, can you hurry, sir?'

'Quickly,' said Doctor Ellie. 'Quick as you can! And make a note of where we are. Oh Lord – I need my maps!'

'Cuthbertson,' said Millie. 'He said Cuthbertson, didn't he?'

Doctor Ellie was still talking. 'It's heavy, isn't it? Of course it is. This is a most extraordinary find. Hurry!' She closed the doors from inside, and pushed through the van. 'I've been looking for that for . . . It's the second piece! It has to be, I saw the crack. The crack!'

She hauled herself over the driver's seat, behind the wheel. Her chest was heaving and she let in the clutch way too hard. The van catapulted backward and Mr Ian – who was still on the ground – scrambled to his feet just in time to avoid being squashed. He banged on the vehicle's side and made a grab through the window.

Doctor Ellie flapped his hands away and a charge of euphoria hit her. 'You're a fool, you know,' she cried, braking sharply. 'You're totally unaware of what's under your nose! But I am a step closer to solving the mystery!'

'Give me the keys!' cried the teacher, holding tight to the steering wheel. 'That boy! Miles! We have unfinished business . . .'

'Your pupils are terrified of you, aren't they?' said Doctor Ellie, calmly. 'And I imagine . . .' She shunted forward into the lane, dragging Mr Ian alongside her and squeezing him into the hedge. '. . . I imagine you lead a life without love, so you compensate by being a monster. You are to be pitied, sir. Now, for the last time . . .' She lurched forward and then braked, spinning Mr Ian into a nettle patch. 'Goodbye forever.'

The two security guards were both blocking the lane, their hands upraised. They leapt to one side as she accelerated towards them. She found second gear and pushed the vehicle so hard up the hill, the children were pressed back on top of one another. They were clapping, though, and cheering. She could see them in her mirror, waving their fingers, and she felt dangerously light-headed. Her mind was whirling and she was starting to laugh.

The children had started singing and she could hear the words, 'Ribblestrop! Ribblestrop!' They were chanted in the style of a football song. Some boys were whistling too, for another security vehicle had been forced to skid sideways off the road as she thundered past. The driver gawped in horror. Doctor Ellie shouted with joy as she swung round it and shot to the left down a tiny, random lane. What if they chased her? What if they discovered the stone and took it away again? They wouldn't know what it was, but the very thought that they might claim it made her accelerate faster and faster. In a moment, they were between deep, high hedges, racing away. For five full minutes they hurtled through the lanes. Only when they'd turned and twisted for a good few miles did she slow down and relax. She knew they were safe.

'What a remarkable group of children you are,' she cried, gulping fresh air. She had tears in her eyes. 'I can't believe what's just happened! This is destiny!'

'You were great, miss,' said Miles. 'That took guts, that did. You told him!'

'Thank you, my dear. Oh, what a team we are – that was teamwork, pure and simple.'

'I bet he's never been spoken to like that,' said Podma.

'I bet he's never been immobilised like that,' said Doctor Ellie. She shook her head and laughed. 'I can see you're not to be trifled with, any of you. We've made enemies, though, and they have got my number of course. They'll get straight onto the library services. Never mind! Who cares? If they behave like that, they have to expect retaliation. Now, let's get back to civilisation and if I have to ditch the van . . . then so be it. Where do you want to get to, children?'

'Ribblestrop!' shouted someone. 'Drive us home, miss! Come home with us!'

She indicated left and inched the vehicle onto a wider road. She picked up speed and they were soon joining a busy dual-carriageway. The school song was blaring yet again.

'What are you doing here?' shouted Millie, over the noise. 'Is it your job, taking photos of stones?'

'Oh no!' laughed Doctor Ellie. 'I'm unemployed and on the run. In fact – to be honest – I'm a criminal.' She smiled grimly. '*Qui scelera evitant mox inter se coalescent!* Do you know your Virgil? It means, "Those fleeing evil will soon join together". Now, there is, I believe, a supermarket off the next roundabout and it has one of those family rest-areas. It was built on a sixteenth century monastic site – two monks were burnt in a barrel, courtesy of Henry the Eighth.' She smiled again. 'So I think the first thing is to hide this vehicle, and the second thing is to get some food in our stomachs. Then, we plan the glorious future.'

She laughed and blasted her horn long and loud.

'I want to look at my stone!' she cried. 'You don't know what you've found, do you?'

'Picnic area!' cried Sam, seeing a sign. 'Can we stop there?'

Doctor Ellie was already indicating and the bright lights of a superstore were getting closer and closer.

They nosed into the car park and made for the remotest corner, sliding the van into the shadow of some trees.

Chapter Nine

Meanwhile, the Ribblestrop teachers were taking tea. The mood was understandably sombre. Doonan had been the last out of the cells, for the station sergeant found his soft Irish accent suspicious, and his interview had seemed never-ending. When he emerged, and had claimed back his belt and shoes, he found Captain Routon, Professor Worthington and the headmaster waiting for him in the car. They drove out of town and stopped when they saw signs to a supermarket – none of them had eaten for hours. They sat in the refreshment area, and tried to make sense of their experience.

'I just don't understand why the police didn't follow them,' said the headmaster. He looked more haggard than ever. 'How could they simply watch helpless, vulnerable children drift down the river?'

'They were more interested in arresting us, sir,' said Captain Routon.

'But they had a helicopter. Why didn't they use it?'

Professor Worthington laughed bitterly. 'The pilot needed a rest, Giles,' she said. 'He'd done a two-hour shift and was entitled to a coffee break. We begged them to go up but they said it was against health and safety rules. Clock-watchers, all of them.'

'That's why they sent for the dinghy,' said Captain Routon. 'I don't know what happened to that.'

Doonan sighed. 'I do,' he said. 'That sergeant told me.'

'What happened?'

'It ran aground after about ten minutes and they had to wait for a salvage crew to get them back in the water. They want us to pay for all that, as well.'

'Meanwhile two dozen children are left to their own devices and could be anywhere. They could be at the bottom of the river, or victims of some nutcase on the road —'

'No chance, sir,' interrupted Captain Routon. 'Don't start panicking. They pull together in a crisis, we all know that. They've probably found a railway station by now – they're probably waiting for a train to Ribblestrop.'

'Is that where we should go?'

'I think we should get back to the school,' agreed Professor Worthington. 'That's where they're heading, after all. They won't want any more adventures. Try Sam's phone again.'

'You do it, Routon – I can hardly see the numbers.' He passed his mobile across the table and sat back. 'I had such high hopes for this term, you know. I wanted it to be nice and quiet, with the focus on botany. A bit of football and a nice exam or two at the end. I thought we might even have one of those award ceremonies.'

'Like a normal school,' said Doonan.

'Exactly.'

Doonan smiled. 'I thought we might start a cricket team instead of football. My brother said he'd send my bat over.'

'Well, at the moment the only player's going to be Caspar. And Henry, if he comes back.'

Captain Routon peered at the phone and tapped in a message. 'I imagine Sam's will have been soaked, same as mine . . . No, sir, I still can't get anything.'

'We should sue the police,' said Professor Worthington. 'It's gross negligence.'

'That's what they said about us,' said Doonan. 'They said we were the most irresponsible so-called teachers they'd ever come across.'

'They were extremely unpleasant,' said Captain Routon. 'We can expect a full prosecution, they said.'

'Don't tell me!' said the headmaster. 'I've had eviction notices from Lady Vyner again and threats from her solicitors. She wants to start a nursing home, she says, so she's hell-bent on getting rid of us.'

'Why a nursing home?'

'Money. Someone's told her there's a fortune to be made from old people with nowhere to go. We'll be lucky if she hasn't changed all the locks and thrown our stuff into the street.'

Professor Worthington took the headmaster's hand and pressed it. 'Don't despair, Giles,' she said. 'We've come through worst crises than this.'

Captain Routon sat back and threw the phone onto the table. Then, just as it bounced, they all heard the soft buzz of an incoming text. He snatched it back up and clicked to the message inbox.

'What is it?' said Doonan.

'I don't believe it, sir.'

'What?'

'They've made contact. They've picked up our signal and they've made contact!'

The headmaster jumped to his feet. 'What does it say, Routon? How long's a text take to come through?'

'I don't know,' said Professor Worthington. 'I thought they were pretty much instant. What's it say? Open it!'

Captain Routon dropped the phone in his haste and it was batted between hands. 'I can't get at it ... I'm all thumbs.'

Doonan grabbed it.

The adults strained their eyes to see, shielding the little screen from the overhead striplights.

'Hello,' read Doonan, slowly. '*I hope u r well. Is that a teacher??? We r fine dont worry cannot take calls at the moment we are shopping.*'

'They're fine!' hissed the headmaster. 'They say they're fine!'

'Shhh, sir! What else?'

'*If that is you, sir, did my dad get home ok?*'

The headmaster stood, motionless. 'That's Sam!' he said quietly. 'That's Sam, isn't it? Oh, dear me, they really are safe! Safe enough to text, anyway. Shopping, for goodness' sake! Why don't they say where they are?'

'Text them back!' shouted Captain Routon. 'Ask them!'

The phone bleeped again, unprompted, and there was a follow-up text.

'*We r having a bbq. ShoppaLot Superstore nr A30 ring-road home soon. Sam xxxx.*'

It was Doonan who looked up first and saw the large banner stretched above their heads. His eyes instantly filled with tears and he crossed himself; he could not believe that a prayer could be so promptly and favourably answered. Not only were the children safe, but they were close – for the banner read, *Welcome to ShoppaLot. You'll be Amazed At What You Find* . . .

It seemed pre-ordained then, that Anjoli should drift past the window at that very moment, sitting high on a shopping trolley. There was a slow-motion quality to the scene, because it was laden with food. Sanchez and Millie were pushing and, one by one, the whole line of boys passed with bulging bags. Black-and-gold blazers, muddy knees and shoes . . . Doonan watched as Sanjay tried to trip Ruskin's heels, prompting Asilah to give him a sharp slap. He saw

Oli drop a lettuce and Miles take a large box from a friendly-looking old lady, who pinched his cheek. Last in line were Tomaz and Imagio, hauling yet another trolley, this one packed with what looked like sacks of charcoal.

'They're there,' whispered Doonan. *'Though I walk through the valley of death, I will fear no evil, for Thou art with me . . .'*

Now all the teachers were staring, unable to move, paralysed with wonder. The children disappeared into the crowds of shoppers and crossed the car park.

Somehow, the teachers came to their senses.

They crashed through the doors, fearing that, if they delayed a second their pupils might be snatched away again. For an awful moment, that's just what happened, for they emerged totally disorientated at the rear exit and had to race round the front of the complex to get their bearings. Had the children been a mirage and would they ever be reunited for the start of term?

Routon spotted Kenji and Nikko, who had dropped some eggs. He broke into a run, calling their names at the top of his voice. Cars screeched to a halt to avoid the racing figures and at last the children saw them.

There was an immediate scrum of welcome. An attendant tried to intervene, for the traffic was at a standstill and a crowd had gathered to watch. He had no success, for there were too many hugs and handshakes to be enjoyed and repeated. Only when cars started hooting long and loud, did Professor Worthington manage to get everyone moving.

There was too much to say, of course. The teachers lost track of who had and hadn't been properly welcomed, so the only solution was to start all over again, embracing and asking the same questions. By the time the children had finished pouring out their stories, they were back at the picnic spot and the sun was setting. They perched on the picnic tables and opened bags of sweets, some weeping with laughter. Captain Routon was listening to Miles and Millie re-enacting the collapse of their pilot – Anjoli playing the pilot. The headmaster was trying to follow the exact course of the bus, car and plane as Oli laid out little models made of tin foil and Sam did the noises. Doonan was going through his interrogation for the fifth time to an enthralled audience of orphans, who had their hands over their mouths in horror.

It was Tomaz – wearing a brand-new apron – who called for order.

'Excuse me, everyone,' he said. 'I don't want to break up the party, but we've started the cooking and . . . well, it's almost ready.'

Everyone turned and was amazed to find that whilst they'd been talking, he and Imagio had been working. The charcoal was blazing and two shopping trolleys were on their sides, acting as the perfect grills. A pall of sweet-smelling smoke floated by, for sausages, burgers and steaks were sizzling. On a table nearby there were loaves of bread sliced and buttered, there were salads in bowls and two huge tubs of ice-cream. The box that Miles had received from that sweet old lady was also open. She had taken it through the till for him and pretended she was buying it. Miles had convinced her it was vital medicine for his sick mother.

It contained six bottles of rum and a stack of paper cups was ready beside it.

Chapter Ten

'Hey,' said Sanchez, as he finished his third burger. 'Where's Doctor Ellie?'

'Who?' said Doonan.

Asilah looked around guiltily. 'We forgot all about her!'

'How did we do that?' said Eric. 'Without her we wouldn't be here!'

'Oh man,' said Vijay. 'She probably thought we didn't want her, because . . . well . . .'

'She's fine,' said Sam. 'We just took her some food. 'She's got half the school with her.'

'What do you mean?' asked Doonan.

'Captain Routon's there. So's Professor Worthington. They're looking at that stone she found. The white one.'

'You should see the van, sir,' said Sanjay, who had come back for another sausage.

The headmaster swallowed. 'Whose van? I'm really not following this . . .'

'She lives in a van,' said Ruskin. 'It's like a little house-boat only with wheels.'

'This is the lady who brought you here?'

'She's amazing,' said Sanchez. 'She knows everything.'

The headmaster wiped his chin with a napkin. Like

most of the children, he was on his third helping of food – it had seemed in never-ending supply. Where the money had come from he didn't dare ask, but the children had bought enough for an army twice their size. The cooks had been round again and again, pressing more onto everyone. He looked at all the empty tables, immediately guilty that he had – yet again – let half the school drift off without really noticing. He also realised that his first priority should have been to meet and thank the children's saviour.

'I must be introduced,' he said. 'It sounds as if we owe this lady a very great deal. It also sounds as if she's rather special.'

His first impression was that he was looking into a gypsy caravan.

The back doors stood wide open and the interior of the van was bathed in cosy light from two pink lampshades. It was crammed with teachers and children, who had found places to perch on what appeared to be shelves, alcoves and ledges. He could make out a low bed with a silk coverlet, and under people's feet he could see Indian rugs. The old lady herself – Doctor Ellie – was sitting on a stool, with a glass of rum in her hand. The other hand rested on a slab of white rock and from time to time she stroked it, as if it were a favourite pet.

'. . . so, you see,' she was saying, 'the Romans took advantage of civilisations that were already highly developed. The idea that they came along and taught everyone how to live is absolute poppycock.'

'Were there Romans actually on Ribblemoor?' said Anjoli.

'Oh yes. There's a hill fort quite close to your school. I'm surprised you haven't seen it.'

'Were there battles and things? Wars?'

71

'There certainly were. There's a grave site quite close to Lightning Tor. You've heard about Lightning Tor, I would imagine?'

'We don't really know the moor at all,' said Millie.

'Ah, well – you have a treat in store. Lightning Tor's at the centre of things, I'm pretty certain about that. The scandal is that nowadays, nobody's allowed near it. A clan was wiped out just beyond the boundary fence, probably on Hadrian's orders. If you can just . . . can you pass me the book behind you, Vijay? The one with the axe-head on the cover. There are some very good photographs.'

'Why were they wiped out?' Miles asked. He was sitting next to Podma, who was gazing at a book of fossils.

'Impossible to say,' said Doctor Ellie. 'Who knows what quarrels took place as the Romans pushed west? It was a Roman atrocity, though, because the wrists of the victims were tied and the skulls had been smashed with hammers – which was a Roman way of execution. They kept their swords for combat, you see; they were far too precious to be used on slaves, or those who were considered slaves. A Roman sword – this will interest you – would have cost a soldier more than a year's salary. It's the equivalent now of buying a top-of-the-range Mercedes or BMW – something to be looked after very carefully and not used for a bit of casual butchery. And, of course, a good sword was believed to hold magical properties. If you could forge metal in those days, well . . . you would have been considered a god.'

Doctor Ellie glanced up and noticed the headmaster. Oh,' she said. 'I'm so sorry . . .'

'What for?' said the headmaster.

'Don't stop,' said Sanjay.

'I'm just sitting here rabbiting,' said Doctor Ellie, struggling to her feet, 'when I haven't had the pleasure of introducing myself. You are the headmaster, I presume?'

The headmaster was pressed against the doors now, leaning in.

'Come in, sir!' said someone.

'Is there any room?' he said. 'That was the most fascinating story.'

'We can make room,' cried Eric. 'Shift up! Sanchez, sit here!'

Bodies heaved and shifted, and somehow room was made. Doctor Ellie, meanwhile, was peeling off a pair of latex gloves. The headmaster was at last inside and extended his hand. Doctor Ellie clasped it.

'What a school you have, sir,' she said. 'What remarkable children! I've been getting to know them, and I have never met a group more fearless, more hungry for knowledge – and more instinctive. I expect people say it all the time, but you are a magician and you should be proud of yourself.'

There was a burst of applause and the headmaster found himself blushing to the roots of his hair.

'No,' he said. 'Honestly . . .'

'They saved my bacon today and they made the most extraordinary find. A find of genuine historical interest that means I am even closer to my goal.'

'Which is what?' interjected Millie. 'What is this goal of yours? You never actually tell us.'

The headmaster found that he was sitting down and that there was a glass of rum in his hand. There were books everywhere and many of the children were sharing them. The axe-head book was now open on Sanjay's lap and heads were poring over photographs of skulls and skeletons.

'Have I not told you what I'm doing?' said Doctor Ellie.

'No!' cried the children.

'I keep getting side-tracked! I try to explain and you keep interrupting with questions!'

'You take your time, miss,' said Captain Routon. 'Are we in a hurry? Of course we're not.'

'Is everyone here?' said Asilah. 'Are we missing anyone?'

'Just tell us,' said Millie. 'We met you in a field, taking photos of a stone. You live in a van . . . or do you? Do you actually live in this? Or are you on holiday?'

Doctor Ellie smiled and sipped her drink. 'I think I told you a few things as we fled from that awful Mr Ian,' she said. 'I'll be totally honest and admit that I am, in fact, a criminal-fugitive. On the run and desperate. And, to answer your question, yes, I do live in this vehicle. I had a flat in London, but couldn't afford to keep it, so I ran away and went on the road. I'm surprised you haven't guessed, my dears! I'm an out-of-work librarian. This is a library, and I stole it.'

There was a stunned silence.

'What you're sitting in,' she continued, 'is the mobile unit for North London District Council – but they decided they no longer needed it. It was my job to drive it round that bit of London, you see. I went to schools, community centres, old people's homes. I used to go to a maternity hospital, a couple of day-centres . . . and anyone who wanted a book could come onboard and choose one.'

'Did they have to pay you?' asked Imagio.

'Good Lord, no,' Doctor Ellie said. 'It was a free service, because the people of London had paid quite enough already in taxes, rates, insurances – oh, don't get me started on that. No; it was a free service. But, of course, when times got hard and money was scarce, somebody somewhere decided that what I did was far too costly and needed to be stopped.'

'That's happening everywhere,' said Captain Routon.

'I arrived at work one morning and was told my job would only last another six weeks. They also told me that the van would be scrapped and the books recycled as pulp for chipboard furniture. Could I be taken on by another library? I asked. No, they said, because the libraries were all shrinking. They might be able to get me a few hours a week in a school-dinner factory, putting lids on those little trays of chemicals ... but that was about it. Sorry, I'm losing my thread again. The point was that everything was coming to an end, and I was about as useful to the world as a chocolate teapot. So I found myself driving back from this particular old people's home, on the last day of the sixth week ... and I'd been chatting with a man, who was one of my regulars, about the flare paths of Ribblemoor. He'd been a very keen walker and had mapped one of them. And I had all that churning about in my head, and I have to admit I'd been quite emotional saying goodbye to him. And I was on the road, coming towards the garage where we kept the van – and I just drove past it. I ... I just drove on until I found the M25. I made a phonecall, and a friend brought me some clothes and a few suitcases of books ... and I thought: dammit. This is not the end of something, Ellie. This is the beginning.'

'Wow,' said Miles. 'That's brave.'

'There's always a good reason when you break the law,' said Doonan. 'I tried to explain that to the police sergeant.'

'Why did your mobile library van have a bed in it?' said Oli.

'Good question,' said Doctor Ellie. She turned to the headmaster again. 'This is what I mean about your students being so intelligent. The reason there's a bed in the van, Oliver, is that I had one built. I spent the weekend with a friend who used to build boats and he helped me kit it out the way you see it now. There is actually a little stove, just behind where Tomaz is standing. I've got running water, a place to cook. I've got a small dynamo. And the wonderful thing is, because I have *Mobile Library* on the side of the van,

75

people tend to leave me alone. They assume I'm on library business, so the only time I'm disturbed is by people who want to borrow books.'

'Do you let them?' said Ruskin.

'Yes. Of course.'

'How do you get them back, though? Do you have to hang around and wait?'

'I don't bother. If someone wants a book out of this library now, I simply give it away. Whatever book they choose, even if it's one of mine, I let them have it and they can keep it forever.' She laughed. 'One day I might be driving around with just one book left, looking for the person who needs it.'

'That's crazy,' said Millie. 'You should sell them. You could make a lot of money.'

Sanchez looked at her. 'How is it you always miss the point, Millie? Whenever anything serious is being talked about, you just don't get it.'

Millie turned on him, but they were interrupted by Vijay. 'Look!' he shouted. 'I found your name, miss! Look, guys, look at this!'

Vijay was standing and the book he'd been leafing through was cradled upside down in his arms. There was a large black-and-white photograph of a line of white stones that disappeared over a hill.

He held it under the headmaster's nose. 'Read the bit at the bottom, sir!'

The headmaster took the book, aware that half a dozen heads were pressing against his. The print was small, but he was just able to read it when he took his spectacles off.

'*View of the Hatchington Flare Path, Ribblemoor – the only documented Caillitrian flare path in the British Isles. Photo by Ellie Mold, Doctor.* Well, well, well! You wrote this, did you?'

'You wrote a book?' said Kenji, in an awestruck voice. 'You actually wrote that?'

Doctor Ellie was turning pink. 'No,' she said. 'I submitted a few photographs and sent in my dissertation on that particular site.'

'But what are they?' said Professor Worthington. 'You keep mentioning the phrase "flare path", but I don't think any of us know what you mean.'

'Flare paths are runways, aren't they?' said Captain Routon.

Doctor Ellie nodded. 'Yes, they are – you're right. But in the context of Ribblemoor, they're rather different. I don't want to be a bore, though – if you get me started –'

'Tell us!' cried various children.

The rum bottle was being passed again and someone leant in to give Doctor Ellie another generous measure.

'I don't know how much you know about the area your school's in.'

'Nothing,' said Imagio. 'I'm stupid.'

'Shhh!'

'I'd better start from the beginning, then.'

Chapter Eleven

Doctor Ellie sipped her rum.

The children sipped theirs. Tomaz arrived with Eric, who'd been toasting chocolate brownies. The van was soon heavy with their scent, and the old lady continued.

'Ribblemoor's been the centre of all kinds of activity for many thousands of years,' she said. 'There are tunnels underground, ancient quarries – tin and silver mines. The flare paths were early roads and they were laid out long before the Romans. We call them "flare paths" because they were illuminated by moonlight. The moon rose and the white markers would shine in the light – then these special paths would have been passable, even in darkness. It's my belief that the ancient tribes needed to pass over the moor at night, perhaps for religious reasons. Perhaps because they were trading in precious goods and wanted the cover of darkness. I don't yet know. What I do know . . .' Her hand rested on the stone at her feet again. 'What I do know is that the stones we find are always inscribed with a pattern of hieroglyphs that is totally unreadable. It's a language that remains secret, and I've spent many years trying to decipher it. I fell in love with Ribblemoor and . . . this is going to sound odd . . . but I fell in love with the people who carved the flare paths. They were called the Caillitri, which means "those who pass" – I fell in love with their customs and their lifestyle. They did not bury their dead, for example, nor did they cremate them. I'm getting bogged down again, but it was one of the details that caught my imagination all those years ago. When a member of the tribe died, the body was cleaned and dried, and it was folded somehow – shrunk, of course. I'll show you pictures, or you can visit Ribblestrop Museum. They put the bodies into earthenware jars which were then sealed, and they carried them around, strapped to their backs. So, if you lost a child, for example, you had it with you still, under your bed, or even under your arm when you went for a walk.'

The van was silent.

'I believe the Caillitri – the tribe whose carvings are so impenetrable – came from the Far East. They may have been trading in gold. They may have brought spices all the way from the Indus valley . . . which is where I think some of you come from?'

She was looking into Anjoli's soft eyes, and he held her gaze.

'I don't know,' he said.

Asilah said, 'We're from the mountains.'

'Ah, but your ancestors,' said Doctor Ellie. 'They would have fished in the Indus Valley, before climbing into the snowline. They would have met Alexander the Great and built cities with him. They would have walked the Silk Road all the way across Persia and west into Greece. They would have sailed past Crete and Sicily, and waved to the Carthaginians – can you imagine that? Finally, they would have come all the way west to Ribblemoor – that's my belief. And there they stayed, for quite some time.'

'We've been here before, then,' said Sanjay.

Doctor Ellie smiled at him. 'I rather think you have. And what you found today is a keystone,' she said, stroking the white rock again. 'This is no simple marker of the flare path; this is part of the coding stone, which I have been hoping to find for years. I think it's in three or four parts, and now we have two. And I think it's going to help us decipher the language we've lost.'

The headmaster found that he had moved closer to Doctor Ellie and that his hand was on her arm. How it got there, he didn't know – because he rarely took the liberty of touching anyone. He found, as well, that everyone in the van was looking at him, waiting for him to speak.

'You are coming to Ribblestrop, aren't you?' he said. 'You wouldn't think of deserting us?'

There was a silence.

'Oh,' said Doctor Ellie. 'That's very kind, but . . .'

'We mean it, miss,' said Sanchez.

'You said the police were looking for you,' said Oli. 'You said you were on the run, so . . .'

Anjoli spoke. 'So live with us. Teach us. Be our history teacher.'

'Oh no,' said Doctor Ellie. 'No, no, no!'

'Why not?' cried Sanjay.

Doctor Ellie shook her head. 'No. I am the most boring woman on the planet,' she said. She tried to laugh, but the laugh died under the children's gaze. 'I'm dry as a stick, honestly – children can't stand me. All I talk about is the past and . . . people find me very, very dull. I will kill you with boredom – you don't realise what you're getting into.'

Podma said, 'I want to know about the Caillitri tribe. We all do.'

'They're our ancestors,' said Vijay. 'That's what you said, wasn't it?'

'I want to see that Lightning Tor place,' said Eric.

'Anyway, miss,' said Sam, 'we can help you, can't we?'

'Yes!' cried Kenji. 'We can help you discover things. We can carry your camera and write things down for you. You can show us the flare paths – we can go on walks together. Can't we?'

The headmaster interrupted. 'I don't think we're going to take no for an answer, Doctor Ellie. The school needs you, and you need a place to be safe. I think a lot has happened today that may have been . . . Well, forgive me, because I am actually a rationalist, the same as Clarissa over there, so I do not believe in mysterious happenings. But a lot has happened today, and –'

'It's pre-ordained,' said Professor Worthington. 'That's what the headmaster's saying, and I completely agree. I hate all that destiny twaddle and I certainly don't believe in the mumbo-jumbo of miracles. But what's going on here is right – and if you try to get away, Doctor Ellie, I think we'll have to kidnap you.'

Israel laughed, but was shushed by Eric.

'Do we have a deal?' said Miles.

Doctor Ellie looked from face to face, and sipped her rum. She wiped her eyes, blew her nose, and went to speak twice. The children simply waited.

'Very well,' she said at last. 'We have a deal. I would be proud to come to Ribblestrop, of course I would. But I do so on the very strict condition that when you realise how boring I am, you ask me to leave.'

'That's not going to happen,' said the headmaster, shaking her hand. 'At Ribblestrop, we're family!'

It took three hours to drive across the moor, because they wanted to use the back roads – just in case there were police patrols looking for a stolen library van or a party of wheel-clamp thieves. They stopped once for coffee and drank it under the soft gaze of a yellow moon. Some children slept and others read as the van rocked comfortably along. The headmaster drove behind.

When they turned into the gates of Ribblestrop, it was already light and there was a bubbling of birdsong. When they came down the drive and caught the first glimpse of the school building, there was a hush of expectation. Those who had dozed woke up and pressed their noses to the windows. Doctor Ellie slowed down, so they could enjoy the wonder of a dawn arrival. The sun was just up and had painted the Neptune statue pink, so he lay like a great baby in glittering water. Rays of light hit the windows, which flashed, and the walls turned solid gold. Suddenly it was as if the school was illuminated from within like a great lantern.

The children moved up the steps to the front door and there was a huge banner pinned across them, the words scrawled in a childish hand. *You made it! Welcome home!*

Under it lay two sleeping forms – a little one, wrapped in the folds of a huge blazer, that belonged to the larger one. It was Caspar, who had somehow escaped confinement and had wanted to be there for his friends' return. The bigger boy was Henry, and he had also succumbed to sleep on the doorstep, his enormous bicep pillowing Caspar's head.

The school was complete, with every child safe and well. The new term had started – one day late, but in a blaze of morning glory. There was no need to stand and sing the school song, because everyone was singing it already in his or her heart. They walked through the corridors in a dream, and failed to notice the posters taped to the stairs. *Do not enter!* they read. *Strictly Private!*

The letters screamed in reds and blacks. There was even tape across some of the corridors and staircases, but the Ribblestrop children moved wearily past them all and staggered to their dormitories. They were asleep before their heads touched their pillows.

Chapter Twelve

Millie had heard the word 'Cuthbertson' – one of the security guards has used it, several times. She had shuddered, but put it from her mind. After all, there were many Cuthbertsons in the world, and it had seemed highly unlikely that the Cuthbertson mentioned could be ex-police Inspector Percy Cuthbertson, the monster that had tried twice to murder her.

It was, however, the very same person, and he'd recognised Millie as she swept by in the library van. What was he doing by The Priory School in a Stillwater Security patrol car? What monstrous coincidence could this be? The answer was simple. Having been sacked from the police force, he'd found work with the SSS. It was a company run by his son-in-law, and he'd bullied his way into a job out of sheer desperation. He was plain old Mr Cuthbertson now, working with men he despised for a pittance of a salary and very few perks. But as he was virtually penniless, he had few choices. His savings had all gone to pay the bribes that had kept him from prosecution. His wife had left him. He was a sad and bitter man.

Naturally, he blamed Ribblestrop Towers for his misfortune, and his hatred of the children had grown like a tapeworm, deep in his gut. All he could think about was revenge, destruction, kidnap and murder. He drove around the lanes and planned increasingly elaborate schemes to bring the school he loathed to its knees. His files on the children and their teachers grew thicker, for he knew that he had to make his move soon.

To see the black-and-gold blazers again – so close and so unexpectedly – had almost made his heart stop. He jumped out of his van and his suspicions were instantly confirmed: it had been the whole Ribblestrop gang. Mr Ian described the mayhem and there were images that confirmed everything on the digital camera. He thought fast and in a moment he was frog-marching the teacher into a quiet corner. The two men had known each other for several years; it was a relationship born of shame and blackmail, and within half an hour they were sitting in a nearby pub.

'Look,' said Mr Ian, anxiously. 'I'm supposed to be doing a roll call. If I get seen having a drink with you, I'll be in serious trouble.'

'You're in serious trouble already, my lad.'

'No, Cuthbertson –'

'You've been in trouble for years. It was me that got you out of it.'

'I don't mean that. I'm not referring to the past.'

'I am. I can dig up that paperwork any time I choose.'

'It happened ages ago!'

'Drink your drink and listen to me.'

Mr Ian went to speak, then thought better of it. For a man so used to being in charge, he seemed curiously smaller in Cuthbertson's presence. He was also curiously obedient. He took a sip of his orange juice and waited, his eyes on the table.

'The payment is tomorrow,' he said at last. 'I can't pay you today.'

'Sounds like you won't be paying at all – if you've had your wallet stolen.'

'Look. I'll find the money.'

'Just been to the bank, had you?'

'Yes.'

'How certain are you he nicked your wallet?'

'Positive.'

'You don't want to check back at the school?'

Mr Ian shook his head. 'I had it when I came out onto the playing fields. I remember feeling it.'

'Five hundred pounds, Ian. What a misfortune.'

Mr Ian nodded. 'I have never let you down, have I, Cuthbertson? It was all ready, I swear it.'

'I believe you.'

'I had credit cards, too.'

'And you think it was the same lad?'

'Yes. Miles Seyton-Shandy.'

'Such a coincidence.'

'What's he doing back here, Cuthbertson? He went up to Scotland – I thought I'd never see him again!'

'Your nemesis.'

'Why would he roll up, out of the blue?'

'Because they always do. Because they always appear where they can do the most damage. Did he recognise you?'

'Of course he did.'

'You thrashed him half to death, didn't you?'

'You know what happened. He nearly cost me my career!'

Cuthbertson laughed. 'Pity you didn't finish him off. Then again, maybe you'll get another chance. I've got plans for the lot of them, and they're all coming together. The South American boy, did you notice him? And the girl – she's the one I want.'

'I didn't notice a girl. I was too busy fighting off the little foreign thugs who attacked me. What plans have you got? What are you talking about?'

'They're going to be homeless tomorrow.'

'Who are? What do you mean?'

'They don't know it yet, but I struck a nice little deal with the Ribblestrop owner, Lady Vyner. She's brought Stillwater in to evict them. I've been helping her with the paperwork. She's got a good lawyer and there are men down there today, changing all the locks. She's even cut off the water supply.'

'So . . .'

'They'll be out on their ear, Ian.'

'And what's this got to do with me?'

Cuthbertson laughed. 'I think we can work together again.'

'No.'

'No? You haven't heard what I've got to say, yet.'

'I don't want any part in anything. I keep my nose clean. I haven't struck a child for . . . I keep my temper in check.'

'I need your help, Ian.'

'No. I don't want any involvement.'

'You're involved, my friend. Always have been – always will be. I'm working out a nice little kidnap venture, and you're perfectly placed. You're in this up to your neck – and you still owe me money.'

Mr Ian's lip was trembling. 'I will have the money next month, Cuthbertson!'

'It's due tomorrow.'

'One missed payment! In over eighteen months!'

'You think I should be merciful, do you? That's not a word I understand. I saved your skin – I told lies for you and buried paperwork that would have put you in jail. That makes us partners.'

'Look!' hissed Mr Ian. 'Even if I wanted to help, what could I possibly do? I'm a small teacher at a well-known boarding school—'

'Befriend them, Ian. Offer them help, just when they need it – schools share facilities sometimes, don't they?'

'What do you mean?'

'They visit each other – cricket matches and what have you.'

'We would never visit a school like Ribblestrop.'

'You might just have to.'

'To what end, though?' He lowered his voice. 'To kidnap a child? Are you serious?'

'What if they visited you?'

'No. It's out of the question. Anyway, this is our outward-bound season – we're going to be out on Ribblemoor for some of the time. It's the Pioneers' Award.'

'Get them involved.'

'No!'

Cuthbertson reached across the table and took the lapel of Mr Ian's jacket between his fingers. The two men stared at each other.

'I'll make a little promise to you, Ian, my friend.' Cuthbertson was smiling. 'If you do the necessary – if we work together on this – I'll call it quits forever. I'll even split the ransom and I'll make sure you get the chance to finish the job on Miles Seyton-Shandy. You can break every bone in his body.'

'Look. I hear what you're saying—'

'Don't decide anything now. We'll meet again.'

There was the sudden revving of engines and both men swung round in alarm. A television set had burst into life behind them and a news bulletin was in progress. The pub was filled with the sound of a helicopter, which was hovering over a long stretch of motorway. Strewn along it were parts of a small aeroplane and, as the camera inched towards the elbow of a river, the wreckage of a bus was visible too, being dragged out of the water.

'Good Lord,' said Mr Ian, standing.

'That's the M5,' said Cuthbertson. 'Looks like an air crash. Look at that mess . . .'

Both men moved towards the screen, which was now filled by a grave-faced police officer. He summarised the full horror and the mugshots of three bemused adults were flashed up, one after another. Cuthbertson found that his mouth was open and he felt light-headed again.

'It's them,' he whispered. 'Again!'

'Ribblestrop? Are they the teachers?'

'Yes. No control whatsoever. How can one bunch of kids cause such chaos?' He turned back to Mr Ian. 'I'll tell you another thing; that was Eddie Shackleton talking – the deputy chief.'

'I've lost you, Cuthbertson.'

'That copper talking to the camera. Eddie Shackleton. Deputy Chief Constable now. My God, the favours we've done each other . . .'

Cuthbertson downed half his beer and wiped his mouth.

'I need to see him, don't I? This could be an opportunity for me. If he hates them even half as much as I do . . . If he wants them closed down, I might be just the man he's looking for. Dammit, who's that?'

His phone was ringing. The ringtone was the siren of a police car and the volume was rising dramatically. He checked the number and winced.

'Lady Vyner,' he whispered. 'I said I'd call her at lunch.'

A furious voice buzzed from the speaker and Cuthbertson closed his eyes.

'Good afternoon, ma'am,' he said, at last. 'I've been so busy —'

The buzzing intensified.

'I'll get there as soon as I can,' said Cuthbertson, loudly. 'Of course, ma'am. We can't seal the place until the notice has been served, that's the law of the land.'

The voice grew shrill, as furious as a half-swatted hornet.

'Look,' he said. 'I will come as soon as I can. I have to be disguised, though, don't I? I need the ice-cream van. My men will do their best and I will call the squad leader. Right now, yes. I'll do it now. Yes! Did the dogs arrive? Good.'

He switched the phone off and sat back down.

'She's another one who needs murdering,' he said. 'Every day she thinks of something more insulting to say. I'd better do what she asks and get down there. I have to wear a wig. Sunglasses. That's what it's come to, Ian. And it can't go on much longer.'

Mr Ian stared at him.

'We'll get them all, lad. We'll have them yet! Those kids don't know what they're in for.'

Chapter Thirteen

The grand eviction took place the very next morning.

In the relief of getting home safely, the children hadn't noticed a thing. Once they were up and about, however, they discovered dramatic changes.

'What's going on?' said Ruskin. 'There's no electricity.'

Israel said, 'There's no water, either. And half our stuff's missing.'

Everyone gathered outside the dining hall. There was an enormous *Keep Out* sign screwed right across the doors and a coil of barbed wire under that.

The headmaster arrived, looking agitated. 'Stay calm, everybody,' he said. 'I think there's been a slight misunderstanding. Lady Vyner's gone on the offensive, by the looks of things, and taken advantage of our absence yesterday.'

'I think you're right, sir,' said Captain Routon. 'There are guards everywhere. Doesn't look pleasant.'

'I've been trying to find her, but she won't see me.'

'They're boarding up the windows,' said Oli.

'We can soon un-board them,' said Eric. 'If they think we're leaving, they're going to get the shock of their lives!'

'We can get this open,' said Sanjay, nodding at the dining-hall doors. 'Just a couple of grinders. There are bolt-cutters in the stable.'

'I daresay there are,' said the headmaster. 'I don't really want a pitched battle here in the corridors, though. Someone's going to get hurt and ... the last thing we want is more policemen chasing after us. Clarissa, are you all right?'

'No, Giles, I'm not.'

Professor Worthington had appeared round the corner and was trying to control her fury.

'There are hooligans in my laboratory.'

'Who are they?'

'These ... I don't know who they are. This security firm – they're everywhere.'

'SSS?' said Sam.

As he spoke, two men in black overalls walked past carrying what looked like a tank-trap, festooned in chains. They wore peaked caps and the initials flashed yellow.

'They're working for my gran,' said Caspar, in a small voice. 'I heard her on the phone.'

'What did you hear?' said Sanchez.

'She wants you out. You know that, but –'

'She's wanted us out ever since we arrived,' said Millie.

'She said this time we're finished,' said Caspar. 'Because of the nursing home. Read that notice – I saw her writing it.'

A large paper banner had been pasted onto a wooden barricade, some distance down the corridor. Everyone moved towards it. There were similar barriers going up behind them, hemming them in. The paper was still wet with glue and the heading had been scrawled by a savage hand. *Get out now!* it said. *And stay out forever!*

Vijay was a good reader and he started at the top.

'By order of Lacson and Lacson, solicitors to Lady G Vyner – undisputed owner of Ribblestrop Towers, henceforth to be known

as "the premises". Lady G Vyner, henceforth to be known as "Chief Prosecutor" wants it to be known to all adults and children in the so-called school known as Ribblestrop Towers but henceforth to be known as "the illegal and unwanted occupying colony of filthy squatters" that . . .' Vijay gave up. 'Sorry, I'm lost,' he said. 'I don't understand any of it.'

Doonan took over, and read more slowly.

'The prosecutor wants the squatters – that's us – to know that they have absolutely no rights any more. They would not have come back last night, if I'd had my way. Their worldly goods – which is mainly junk anyway and belongs on a bonfire – have been confiscated. They are now in a big pile and will be released only when the squatters gather up the last few crumbs of their tatty, stinking garbage and vacate the premises, which they need to do now if they know what's good for them or I'll be setting dogs on them. This, by the way, includes my so-called grandson.'

The children glanced round to see that Caspar was turning pink.

'He was always a bitter disappointment and running away the other day was the final straw. Well, he's made his bed so he can lie in it and dream about all the things he won't be inheriting when his loving grandmother succumbs to her broken heart. The Vyner name will live on in some other way and he can take to the road and die in the gutter.'

'Good day to you all,' said a voice.

The children swung round.

'I wrote that last bit this morning, Caspar. Especially for you.'

It was Lady Vyner in person. She was more ghastly then ever, for she was smiling. Her mouth looked like a purple gash in a face that had been squeezed in a vice. It was tilted sideways above the sepia yellow of her nightdress. She was rubbing inky hands in glee and a high-pitched laugh – not

93

unlike the whine of a bandsaw – echoed down the corridor. A small man stood behind her.

'Your school's finished!' she cried. 'I've even taken the pencils! What's left, I wonder? Just a bunch of shabby teachers, cluttering up my home with their luckless pupils. You didn't expect a full-on takeover, did you, headmaster? Oh, this will be money well spent! Come on, Lacson. Read the eviction order!'

'Lady Vyner,' said the headmaster. 'I must protest –'

'You can protest outside!' snarled the old lady. 'You can hire yourself a lawyer and do all the protesting you want. But I'll tell you something for free: you don't stand a chance. Do you know how much this man costs an hour?'

She had reached behind her to clutch the tie of her companion. She dragged him forward and pushed him sharply in the back.

'This is Donald Lacson himself, straight from the law court. He may look like a constipated clerk, but believe me he'll scalp you and skin you, won't you, Mr Lacson?'

Mr Lacson gaped. He found himself standing between the Ribblestrop party and the demonic form of Lady Vyner, whose smile now hovered over his shoulder, her drool dripping onto his jacket.

'Read it,' she spluttered. 'I want to hear it again. I want to watch their dreams ending, Mr Lacson, I want to hear the weeping of orphans.'

'By the powers invested in me . . .' mumbled Mr Lacson.

'Louder, man!'

' . . . under sub-section thirty-two of the fourth statute . . .'

'Oh, you're half asleep! Cut to the last bit!' She jabbed a finger at his paper, then snatched it from him. '*Leeches,*' she cried, '*you are to leave forthwith. You are to exit the building, which shall be closed against you.*' It was as if she was in church, ejecting devils. *'Out, vile ones! Re-entering the said building will render you liable to immediate arrest and prosecution!* Which is why we've got cameras!' she laughed. 'Listen to this bit, this is the best. *All expenses for this eviction shall be paid by you. The fees of Lacson and Lacson shall be paid by you. The services of specialist security guards and their expenses, shall be paid by you.* By you! Ha! Are you understanding this, headmaster? Or do you need to sit down and have the children explain it to you? The school's at an end; finished and dead, and I'm starting the Ribblestrop Nursing Home. First customer arriving this evening.'

There was an awful silence.

'I just wonder if that's actually legal,' said Ruskin. 'I think we ought to have a good look at those papers.'

A large envelope came whistling through the air and split at the headmaster's feet. Documents splayed out of it.

'Mr Lacson,' said Doonan. 'I think we need a bit of give and take here and—'

He was silenced by a volley of ferocious barking. An enormous dog burst from a side passage, a security guard straining to hold onto its chain as it dragged him behind it. When the dog saw the children, it went into a frenzy of howls and foam flew from its jowls.

Sanjay, who'd been in charge of the big cats in the circus, stepped forward, but Asilah held him back. The dog barked at him savagely.

Lady Vyner laughed again. 'I've got three of these monsters,' she cried. 'I press this button and the dog squad's here in seconds.' She held up an electronic device, which was flashing red between her fingers. Another dog appeared, this one silent but mad. It saw Sanjay and a yellow, rabid look came into its eyes. It started to snarl.

'Are they ready to leave, m'lady?' said the first handler, hauling the beast backwards. 'I'm not sure I can hold 'er! They 'aven't eaten for days!'

'I think so,' said the old woman. 'You don't want your throats torn out, do you?'

Mr Lacson stepped forward with a piece of paper raised high above his head. The dogs came either side of him, baring teeth and gums. Lady Vyner stood back with her fists clenched, her face a rictus of ecstasy. One guard hauled the main doors open and the children looked at one another, bewildered. The dogs barked yet more furiously.

'Come on,' said the headmaster.

'We can't give in!' said Millie. 'I am not leaving!'

'Yes we can!' he shouted, taking her arm. 'We will not win this particular battle.'

'But this isn't fair!' said Sam. 'We've only just arrived.'

'I can deal with the dogs,' said Sanjay. 'They're pussycats, all of them – give me five minutes.'

'No!' said the headmaster. 'No. A pitched battle won't help us and I will not take unnecessary risks. As I said before, the last thing we want is another police visit.'

'Where do we go, sir?' said Sanchez.

'I don't know,' said the headmaster. 'But—'

'I do,' said Captain Routon, grimly. 'And I think you're absolutely right, sir. Follow me!' he cried. He raised an arm and signalled. The dogs set up another hysterical volley, their claws skittering on the flagstone floor. Lady Vyner was yelling abuse, but she was inaudible, and Captain Routon led the children past her without a glance.

'Keep together!' he shouted. 'Onto the lawn, please! Follow me!'

In a moment the entire school had left the building and was blinking, homeless and stunned, in the bright sunshine of the courtyard. Two of the youngest orphans were crying and Ruskin had his arm round Oli who was white-faced. The doors slammed behind them and they heard the clanking of chains.

'Thank goodness for that,' said Captain Routon, after a moment.

'What do you mean?' said Sam. His voice was shaking. 'Where do we go? We haven't got a school any more.'

'Round the back!' shouted Anjoli. 'Get in the back door!'

'No,' said Captain Routon. 'We stay here. We stay together.' He smiled suddenly and rubbed his hands together. 'It's the summer term, isn't it? Who needs classrooms in weather like this? I think we need to find Doctor Ellie . . .'

Chapter Fourteen

The teachers conferred.

'Where do you think Doctor Ellie is?' whispered Ruskin.

'I don't know,' said Millie. 'Are you thinking we can live in the library van?'

'No. I'm just thinking how shocked she's going to be.'

Captain Routon stepped up onto the fountain to address them. He was still smiling – in fact, there was an unusual smugness about his smile, as if something had excited him.

'We'd been looking for a project this term,' he said, 'and I rather think we've found one. We'll live off the land.'

'How?' said Asilah.

'Why not go underground?' said Kenji. 'There's space in all the tunnels and—'

'My cave home's available,' said Tomaz. 'We could have classes there.'

'There's the chapel,' said Doonan.

Captain Routon was shaking his head. 'We can do better,' he said. 'Follow me, my dears – and never say die.'

Captain Routon turned away from the school buildings and crossed the courtyard. He was soon walking fast over the lawn and the children duly followed.

'He must have a plan,' said Imagio. 'Do you think he knows of a barn, or a —'

'Don't bank on anything,' said Millie, bitterly. 'I remember the first time Captain Routon led these guys on a nature ramble. They ended up under a train.'

'He knows what he's doing!' said Sanchez.

'We're going to be in an army tent,' said Miles. 'Could be fun.'

'You can't have a school without classrooms,' said Sam. 'He knows that . . .'

Millie sighed. 'It's so typical, though, isn't it? We only just get here and now suddenly we're worse off than when we started. We should have stayed in the building.'

'And the police would have come,' said Israel.

'I guess we didn't pay the rent again,' said Asilah.

'Why not?'

'I think it all went on the circus.'

'And Flavio,' said Sanjay, remembering the owner.

'You know he's starting an animal retirement centre? I think the headmaster gave him money for that.'

Eric laughed. 'We need Kenji to make us a million again.'

'Hey, Caspar!' said Millie, irritably. 'Why didn't you stop all this? She's your gran and you knew what she was planning!'

'I was a prisoner,' said Caspar. 'I was locked up, right through the holidays!'

'Look, maybe we ought to wait and see where we're going,' said Sanchez. 'There's no point getting angry and judgemental.'

'My God, it's the head boy speaking,' said Millie.

'I want to stay positive!' said Sanchez.

Millie laughed. 'We haven't even had breakfast! I'm sick of it and, I tell you, if there isn't a good alternative waiting for us, then I'm going back to London.'

They were moving into the woods.

Captain Routon consulted a piece of paper and found a footpath that went steeply downhill. Soon, they came to a stream and then rose up again, climbing into thick undergrowth. Five minutes later, they were in a part of the school grounds they'd never seen before. The trees were tangled in creeper and bramble, and soared upwards, blotting out the sunlight. Captain Routon checked his paper again and led them to a small waterfall. Everyone paddled happily up the stream for ten minutes, before branching off into an unexpected clearing. A bad-tempered braying noise greeted them, and the children were astonished to find the school donkeys tethered to a stake in the ground. Further off, behind some low bushes, they could see the camel.

'What's going on?' said Miles. 'Is someone expecting us?'

'That's not possible,' said Tomaz.

'Where are we, then?'

'Quite a secret bit of the wood, this,' said Captain Routon. 'She's chosen well.'

'Who has?' said Millie.

The headmaster was red-faced from the exertion and had been at the back of the group. Kenji and Nikko had been helping him. 'Is this the spot, Routon?' he said. 'It's certainly private enough.'

'So we're camping?' said Eric.

'The circus tent!' said Israel, with a tremor of excitement. 'We could make space for that, pitch it by those trees.'

'This, I imagine, is where the tribe lived,' said Captain Routon. 'This is one of the oldest bits of the forest.'

'What tribe?' said Vijay. 'I don't understand.'

'The lost tribe of Ribblemoor. Doctor Ellie was telling you all about them – weren't you listening?'

'Come on, Routon!' said Professor Worthington. She was smiling, broadly. 'They don't want guessing games, they just want to know where they're sleeping tonight. Now spill the beans properly.'

Captain Routon was smiling too. He was about to reply, when there was a shout from the trees.

'*Féarrad, kengets! Fearrad na fáilte!*'

The children turned, but the speaker was invisible. After a moment, though, they saw a head poking up from a hole in the soil. A pair of elderly blue eyes flashed with excitement and a hand rose up in salute.

It was Doctor Ellie and she was beaming.

'That means "Welcome to the brave",' she cried. 'I was trying out my proto-Celtic. I'm not sure I should be using it really, as they probably spoke one of the Indus languages. It's all guesswork, history!'

She pulled herself up out of the hole and dusted herself down. She was wearing a long dress made of sacking, belted in the middle. There was a canvas cloak over her shoulders. 'You found me, then! What do you think of the camp?'

'It's a good spot, Doctor,' said Captain Routon.

'I did an archeological dig here some years ago – found all kinds of things. The water table's higher here and there's access into some of the tin deposits. It's never been properly excavated – we only had a weekend to potter about. There was something in the air, though, and it's stronger than ever now. I would bet the tribe passed through this very clearing, settled for some time, possibly. Who can say? Anything they built would have been wood, and wood disappears.'

'What was that hole you were in?' said Israel.

'Oh, that's just a little clay pit. It might be useful for the bread oven. If we're going to cook here, then we'll need two more fire-pits at least. Do you want to make a start on them, or think about shelter?'

'Are we eating here?' said Ruskin.

'Are you suggesting we *stay* here?' said Millie.

'Well, yes. I thought you'd had it explained,' said Doctor Ellie. 'Are they not up to speed?'

Captain Routon was still smiling. 'Why don't you tell them?' he said.

'Certainly,' said Doctor Ellie. 'It's only a thought, but it seemed a pretty good one last night, because you were all so interested. Routon and I stayed on in the van, you see, and we were looking at a few pictures and maps ... and we thought a good outdoor history project would be just right for the summer.'

'We've been wanting to do a bit of outward-bound for some time,' said Captain Routon.

'So I said, why not link the two?' Doctor Ellie grinned happily. 'Why not reconstruct the tribal village and live in it? We'd end up re-discovering some of the skills they must have had and we can document things as we go. We've got fresh water over there, so we'll be re-constructing on an authentic prehistoric site. What do you think?'

'That's brilliant,' whispered Miles.

'Actually stay here?' said Asilah. 'Like the tribe did? Is that what you're saying?'

'Build stuff?' said Israel. 'What, mud huts and things?'

'Oh, they didn't live in mud huts,' said Doctor Ellie. 'They were much more sophisticated than that.'

The headmaster was nodding. 'You see, children?' he said. 'A disaster suddenly turns into the most unique opportunity. We rise to the challenge.'

'How, though?' said Imagio. 'How did they live?'

'Well, they were farmers, of course,' said Doctor Ellie. 'They had to be. They would have had a stockade for the animals, so that's why I grabbed the donkeys. They would have had some kind of meeting hall, probably here where we're sitting – a big fire for the cold nights and a cooking fire as well. Workshops, of course, a kitchen, a butchery ... They were undoubtedly experts in metalwork, we can tell that from the jewellery in the museum – which we must take you to, as soon as possible, you must meet Vicky. There would have been a forge and –'

'Where did they sleep?' said Anjoli. 'I mean, where will we sleep?'

'Here,' said Kenji. 'In huts!'

Every child was now staring at Doctor Ellie. Their eyes had been flicking between her and the headmaster, but now, in the growing excitement, they gazed at the old lady with a new fascination.

'Where would you want to sleep?' she said, slowly. 'Think carefully.'

'Together,' said Podma.

'Together, of course. That goes without saying. But this tribe faced the unknown. They faced predators, of course, and . . . well, my understanding of the stones they left is still incomplete, but judging from the symbols, I'm not sure they favoured huts and earth. I'm not sure they felt safe on the ground.'

'In caves then!' cried Ruskin. 'You said there were tin mines, so maybe they –'

'You're not safe in a cave,' said Asilah. 'Not unless it's one like Tomaz's, where you hide the entrance.'

'Dark as well,' said Sanjay. 'Gloomy.'

'Trees,' said Vijay, suddenly. 'Maybe they just climbed trees, and made little . . . you know, hammocks – like in our village.'

'Come here,' said Doctor Ellie.

'Pardon, miss?'

Doctor Ellie was standing. She beckoned to Vijay, smiling – and when he was close, she turned him gently so he was looking back at his friends. 'You know, you're a very bright boy,' she said. 'You have intuition. You're sensitive to the ways of a people who passed through here more than two thousand years ago. So look around you and tell me which trees you'd choose to live in.'

Vijay was embarrassed, but excited. His eyes scanned the edges of the clearing and rose up the trunks of several ancient oaks. It was dark under the leaves, and he was aware of how huge they were and how their limbs knotted and stretched. He said, 'I'd choose the biggest. I'd choose where the branches were flat, like that one there. But I . . .'

'What?'

'I wouldn't just put a hammock up. I mean, that's just when you want a snooze.'

'So what would you do?'

'I'd build a tree house.'

There was a gasp and the phrase was immediately echoed in hushed whispers.

Doctor Ellie said, 'Tree houses, eh? They were people who certainly loved the air. They understood water and most of all they loved moonlight and sunlight. Why would you take the risk of being surrounded on the ground? There were wildcats and wolves. I believe you're right, Vijay. I believe they had the most intricate system of tree dwellings, interlinked by bridges and swings. We'd have to design carefully, of course – and getting the structural timbers won't be easy. Are you up to a job like that? Is it too ambitious for you?'

The children stared at her, in a silence so profound it seemed unbreakable. Nobody wanted to speak, in case such an extraordinary fantasy were snatched away. For what if they were all dreaming together and they suddenly woke up in their dreary dormitories, incarcerated in the grey walls of an old school building? Ribblestrop Towers suddenly seemed like a prison . . .

The headmaster spoke softly and carefully. 'What we will do,' he said, 'is spend tonight in the circus tent. We can start construction tomorrow.' He looked at Captain Routon. 'First of all, though, I propose a vote of thanks to both Captain Routon and Doctor Ellie. They have saved the day again. I vote that this term is given over to what I believe is called, "Living History". We will throw away these modern clothes and go back in time. We will learn a new way of life. Do I have your agreement, children? Raise your hands if I do.'

Every hand went up.

'Very well. Asilah, could you organise the tent, please? Tomaz and Imagio, can you pick some helpers, and we'll get fire and food on the go – another barbecue, I'm afraid. Sanchez, Miles and Millie, look into sanitation and drinking water, please.'

He paused, smiling.

'Off we go, children.'

'You know, Routon,' said the headmaster, a little later, 'I can't help feeling rather glad we've been evicted.'

'Every cloud, sir, a silver lining.'

'I wouldn't have said that a few hours ago. But I'm pondering this business of fate. Maybe the gods are with us at the moment.'

'It's going to be a good term, sir. Perhaps the best yet.'

The headmaster nodded. 'Let's just hope the police leave us alone.'

'They won't interfere. They won't stop us. I was in Eastern Turkey years ago . . . little skirmish on one of those islands, dispute over the border, usual thing. We found ourselves cut off from the main force, just the five of us. We were outnumbered, outgunned. They had the air power, of course, so we were like rats in a trap.'

'You were being bombarded, were you?'

'Oh yes. They were dropping everything they had. We thought our number was up.'

'But somehow . . .?'

'We worked together, sir. We stayed in control.'

'Reinforcements were sent, I suppose?'

'Oh no. No. We were abandoned. We . . . we had a good commander, though. He knew when to give orders and he knew when to listen. He let us function as a team and, because of him, we found a way. We waited until nightfall and we scaled the cliff everyone knew was unscalable. We swam a sea everyone knew was unswimable. One rope between us, no moon in the sky, one man with a broken leg. But we took our time and we made it. He was a bit like you, sir.'

'Who?'

'Our commander.'

'Routon . . . It's kind of you, but I never know what to do in a crisis.'

'Oh, you're our guiding light, sir. Always have been.'

Chapter Fifteen

The children worked as they had never worked before.

The roofing project of term one, and even the circus training of term two, would seem inefficient and unambitious in comparison to the creation of the tribal village. Asilah and Imagio harnessed the camel and dragged the circus tent in on an old boat trailer. Willing hands unpacked it as others dug the fire pits. The orphans had pitched this tent so many times that they could do it in darkness – and this was lucky, for it was soon twilight.

The great canvas rose and they drove in the pegs and tightened the guys. Soon they were sitting wearily, ready for supper. This time their burgers were squeezed between hunks of home-baked bread, for Doctor Ellie's bread oven was impressively efficient. It was her hope, she said, that the children would soon be grinding their own corn and doing all their own baking. Later, they would learn the arts of the smithy.

Candles were soon lit and the layout of the village was hotly debated. An exercise book was produced and soon diagrams covered the floor.

As the younger children dozed, Asilah said, 'Can I ask you something, miss? Are we going to do everything the way they did it? Every single thing?'

'I'm hoping so, yes.'

'Isn't that going to be a bit difficult?' said Miles.

'It will be a challenge, of course.'

'I think it's going to be hard cutting wood,' continued Asilah. 'If we don't have tools, it could take quite a while. And I'm thinking we ought to have boots and gloves – just because if we don't, we'll probably get splinters. We don't want to waste time in hospital.'

'Yes,' said Doctor Ellie. 'They would have used natural medicines, from plants and so forth. But if we don't have the immunity they had . . .'

'Can't we cheat a little bit?' said Sam. 'You know, just have a few things that are modern?'

'I think we should have toilet paper,' said Ruskin.

'And soap,' said Israel.

'I think we need chainsaws,' said Captain Routon. 'I don't think much can be done without them. And a block and tackle for lifting. Nails, of course.'

'Rope,' said Vijay.

'Hammers,' said Kenji. 'Brace-and-bit.'

The list went on and Doctor Ellie thought hard. 'I do understand,' she said. 'We mustn't let the project founder because of some slavish desire to imitate every detail. I think we have a few modern things so as to get going and then we become more authentic later. The tribe would have bargained for things, after all, in the outside world.'

She pulled a blanket around her shoulders. 'Now I'm going to suggest we have an early night and resume this in the morning. We need to be up with the sun, you know. We'll be adjusting to totally new rhythms.'

The children slept well and rose before the birds.

They were lucky; one of the old chainsaws was found in Flavio's storage shed and, once it had been cleaned and greased, it was ready for action. Breakfast was eaten quickly – coffee, wild goose eggs and toast – and the clearing was soon ringing to the sound of a throbbing motor.

They selected six trees for felling and worked as a single organism. The first came down fast and was cut up into trestles and a wood-working bench. The other five were lowered gently onto logs, so they could be rolled and split. Captain Routon showed them how to crack the trunks with wedges and the children found that they came apart easily if you worked with the grain. Oli and Israel lashed the chainsaw to the edge of a plank, the blade rearing upwards at forty-five degrees. Henry was in charge of feeding the lumber into it, though everyone had to help at first. Henry held the wood steady as it bucked in his hands and, by the time the sun was above the trees, there was a large pile of useable wood. It was soon rising into the treetops on pulleys and the foundations of houses were soon secure.

The younger orphans gathered brushwood and stripped branches. They soon learnt how to bend and weave and, before long, roofs were taking shape. They had selected three massive oaks, but nobody had realised just how much movement there was in a tree when you were twenty-five metres off the ground. The lashing of the platforms was a tricky business and, though they used creeper whenever they could, thick rope was essential for the main mooring points – especially around the stairways.

Just before lunch, Doonan returned from his shopping expedition.

He asked for six willing helpers and he led his volunteers to a flat-bed truck that had braved the mud and reversed as close as it could to the construction site. There were a dozen more bails of rope, plus a stack of boots. There were torches, tools and a variety of sealed boxes that had been ordered by Professor Worthington for her metallurgy classes. By the time it was all safely stowed in the camp, everyone was even more ravenous than last time.

'You're doing well,' said Doonan. 'So I'm going to suggest something controversial.'

'What?' said Sanchez.

'Look what I found in town. I bought it in a charity shop.'

Doonan revealed an old, battered cricket ball. He tossed it from one hand to the other, smiling happily.

'Cricket,' said Miles.

'I thought we might have a game this afternoon,' said Doonan. 'All work and no play, after all!'

The children stared at him. 'It's the most boring game in the world,' said Miles. 'I played it at The Priory and it stinks.'

'We're a football school,' said Millie. 'Or we were.'

'And talking of which,' said the headmaster, 'we should be training for the High School match, Routon. I've got a feeling that's next week.'

'No time, sir,' said Asilah. 'We've got other priorities at the moment.'

'Oh, come now,' said Doonan. 'We must make time for a bit of leisure. We could have a nice little wicket set up here, just by the . . .' He looked around the clearing. 'Where's the tent gone?'

'We took it down,' said Israel. 'We're going to cut it up for costumes.'

'Oh. Well, that gives us even more space. I don't mind whittling the stumps and we've enough for two teams—'

'We're busy,' said Israel. 'We don't have time.'

Professor Worthington stood up. 'Doonan, I don't mind playing, if you're desperate. But I don't think we should get in the children's way. They've got quite a schedule.'

'I agree,' said Captain Routon. 'I think we should go back to the drive and find a bit of flat land there. I'd better call the High School and cancel that football match.'

So it was that the teachers spent the afternoon batting and bowling, while the children worked. The headmaster returned once to the site, for an ice-cream van passed along the drive in the mid-afternoon and he couldn't resist the choc ices. The driver – a slightly curious-looking fellow with frizzy hair and sunglasses – offered them at a very reasonable price and even found a box of them to sell. The headmaster met Podma in the trees.

'Didn't you hear the chimes?' he said. 'We thought you'd all come running.'

Podma was gleaming with sweat. He was stripped to his shorts, and a black-and-gold tie held his hair back.

'Sorry, sir. Would you mind not coming into camp until later?' he said.

'Why not?'

'We want it to be a surprise, sir. So they sent me to help you out.'

'Oh. Of course. When do you want us?'

'Late as possible, really, sir. Just before sundown?'

'Eight or nine o'clock. Certainly. It's all going well, is it?'

Podma nodded.

'You will have time for the ices, won't you? You must take a break at some point.'

'I'm sure we will, sir. Thank you.'

Podma took the box and trotted away up the path. The headmaster turned, and headed back to the slap of bat and ball. The ice-cream van, he noticed, was now parked under Lady Vyner's tower.

Oli, meanwhile, was labouring over the plans. It had become his job to approve and modify, and make sense of the enthusiastic sketches of the previous evening. Nikko – one of the youngest orphans – worked as his assistant and they were now on their fifth exercise book. Each one was smothered in red pen. The pages were carefully cross-referenced, so it wasn't hard to find the section dealing with rope-bridge communication and exit strategy, which was the current phase of construction and had meant yet another meeting.

'We have to link them,' said Asilah. 'We don't want anyone isolated.'

'It's fine,' said Kenji, 'but we have to use intervening trees, and that means losing more branches.

'We don't want them visible from the ground,' said Miles.

'They won't be.'

'I think that if they lived in the trees,' said Vijay, 'then they would have been able to travel right through the forest, up in the branches. We can't make bridges for the whole forest!'

'We could,' said Sam. 'Like in one of those adventure centres.'

'Sam,' said Ruskin, 'this is real. This isn't an adventure centre. If we— '

'We'll use swings for some parts,' said Oli. 'Look at this – 18B. But there are some stretches – I would say here and here – where we definitely need tightropes.'

'More wood, then? For anchor-points?'

'Definitely. And more rope.'

'We're going to get attacked at some point,' said Millie. 'We have to assume that. Lady Vyner's going to want us right out of the grounds, so we want to be able to protect ourselves.'

'That means man-traps,' said Miles. 'Serious ones.'

'What about weapons?' said Israel. 'I think we should split into two teams—'

There was a buzz of anger and excitement.

'No!'

'We said we wouldn't!'

'Tomorrow,' said Sanchez. 'We do weapons and man-traps tomorrow. We've got to be sensible and finish the houses.'

'Bows and arrows,' said Caspar. 'They're easy. I could make them now.'

'Come on, they're toys,' said Anjoli, scornfully. 'If we're protecting ourselves, we're going to need proper stuff. We'll need to go hunting, too.'

'We're not going hunting,' said Asilah. 'What are we going to hunt?'

'We are! Doctor Ellie said!'

Asilah grabbed Anjoli's arm. 'You are not going hunting until the houses are finished. I saw you, Anjoli, mucking about with . . . what is that supposed to be? War paint?'

Anjoli blushed. There were stripes of charcoal round his eyes, and he'd found a reddish clay for his chest. Caspar was similarly decorated and had a grass frill round each wrist.

'You look like a silly kid,' said Asilah.

'It's just an experiment,' said Anjoli, quietly. 'I've done as much as anyone else – I don't see why we can't experiment a bit.'

Asilah said something in his own language and Anjoli blushed deeper.

'Are we going to get on?' said Millie, in the silence that followed. 'I want to sleep off the ground tonight and we've got loads to do.'

Sanchez stood up. 'Let's do it,' he said. 'Boots on, every-one. And gloves.'

Chapter Sixteen

The sky had turned pink when the teachers returned.

Doctor Ellie was with them. She'd had to drive into town in the afternoon, as she wanted to leave the precious white stone at the museum. Anjoli and Millie met them outside the camp, with four strips of tent-canvas in their hands.

'We're going to blindfold you,' said Millie. 'You can't come in without blindfolds.'

'Oh,' said the headmaster. 'Is that going to be entirely safe?'

'Don't you trust us?'

'Of course, Millie. But if we're climbing ladders . . .'

'You're not a prisoner or anything,' said Anjoli. 'And you'll each have a guide.'

Doctor Ellie nodded grimly. 'It's entirely sensible. I'm sure the tribe would have been cautious about those who strayed in from outside. The instincts are kicking in, you see.'

'We're going quite high,' said Millie. 'So don't make any sudden moves.'

'Lead on, my dear,' said Captain Routon. 'We'll be careful.'

Minutes later, the adults moved cautiously into the camp, aware that there was a hush all around them. Not a foot stirred. An occasional bird chirped, but there wasn't a hammer or saw to be heard, and nobody was talking. They could smell the resin of wood and smoke from bonfires. Seconds later, the headmaster found his hands on the uprights of a crudely made ladder.

'You all right, sir?' said a voice in his ear.

'Yes, thank you, Israel. Perfectly.'

'Okay, miss?'

'Right as rain. Is that Nikko?'

'Yes. Just feel with your feet. And don't be scared.'

'It's sixty-eight steps,' said someone. 'Are you sure you're okay?'

'We're all fine,' said Professor Worthington. 'I just hope these knots have been checked. If I do have an accident, I'm going to be looking for the culprit. Assuming I survive, that is. How high are we going?'

Vijay climbed first, and soon the ladder up to Tree House One was thick with children, gently guiding the adults. The ladders twisted and turned and bent back on themselves in complicated elbows. A breeze was soon rustling the leaves and swaying the branches. Gentle hands steered, and when the orphans spoke, it was softly, in their own language.

At last they felt a solid floor under their feet and they were aware that it was moving.

'All right, Doctor Ellie?'

'Splendid, thank you. Are we there, at last?'

'Yes,' said Sanjay. 'First platform.'

The blindfolds were removed, but the adults kept their eyes tight shut. The headmaster had his hands over his face.

'Can we look?' he said. 'I've got a feeling this is going to be wonderful.'

'Oh my goodness,' whispered Doctor Ellie.

'What?'

She had opened her eyes.

She stepped back into the guiding arms of Asilah and Imagio. The headmaster blinked and he too nearly fell forward – there were hands to steady him. Captain Routon uttered a groan and Professor Worthington gasped. The headmaster was immediately dizzy and grabbed at a supporting beam, sure that he was falling. They were way too high – it was like being up in a balloon at the top of the world. There were walls to the tree house, but they were woven like a bird's nest and had wide windows. Through the windows he could see the tops of the trees, undulating on all sides in golden sunlight. Above the trees he could see a sky that was turning to rich purple, with the first peppering of stars.

There was a staircase up to an even higher platform. It had handrails and the children led the teachers up again. It was like a veranda, floating on two massive branches, rearing high over the forest. In the distance they could see the school, a blush of pink beside the lake.

The tree houses were huge. Other platforms floated in the trees nearby and there were bridges so carefully made they looked like extensions of the trees themselves.

Everything was shifting slightly and whispering, as timbers rubbed against timbers. There was an allowance for movement – nothing was straining, for the wood moved with the trees.

'We thought the lower room could be the main teaching area,' said Imagio. He was perched on a branch, the other side of the handrail. 'If you wanted to . . . you know, do a lesson or something.'

'This is a boys' dormitory too,' said Sam. 'Millie's got her own platform a bit lower.'

'We started on the next one, but we didn't get far.'

'We ran out of time.'

'What do you think, sir?'

'Do you like it, miss?'

'Miss? What are you thinking?'

The questions persisted, but the adults were speechless. They had to be sat down and given time, for the house they were in was simply too magnificent for words. Professor Worthington put her hand on the headmaster's shoulder and patted it. Anjoli gave her a rather dirty handkerchief and everyone watched as she blew her nose and dabbed her eyes.

Doctor Ellie said quietly, 'Could it have been as good as this? For the lost tribe of Ribblemoor – was Eleudin held here, to gaze over trees like these?'

'Who's Eleudin?' said Tomaz.

'Oh, you'll be meeting him soon. He's a sad little chap. Could they have had as much fun as this, though, when it was their forest?'

She went to the rail and leant on it, gazing out.

'There are ladders on the stone, you know,' she said. 'I've been at the museum most of the day. Ladders, fish, trees . . . lightning bolts. This . . . this isn't a fantasy.'

'What's the matter, miss?'

'I can see them. I can see them, in the trees. Can't you?'

'Who?' said Miles.

'It's the light. It's my eyes, maybe, but . . . Can't you see them? I didn't tell you, did I? People swear they do see them sometimes and hear them laughing. Out on the flare paths, when you come across them. I thought I heard someone then – listen . . .'

She heard a clink of glass and turned to find Sanjay with the inevitable tray of rum. She took one and turned back, straining her eyes and ears. The new homes had to be blessed, of course, for the sun was giving way to the moon.

If the Caillitri were laughing, then their laughter was swallowed up in the final cries of birds and the whispering of the children.

'We are going to find them,' she said, smiling. 'I can feel it. They're closer than ever – and I think they want to be found.'

That night she produced a flute and played soft melodies in the treetops. The children slept and dreamt of ancient music.

Chapter Seventeen

A few days later, a hot-air balloon was seen in the sky.

Sanjay spotted it first and alerted the others. Everyone had worked so hard at disguising the homes from below that it seemed an outrage that anyone could be watching from above.

'They won't see much,' said Millie. 'Just trees.'

Israel disagreed. 'They might see our smoke,' he said. 'We ought to train more green over the platforms. It would make them cooler too.'

'We should put the forge on the other side of the spring,' said Tomaz. 'I told Professor Worthington, but she wouldn't listen.'

'Who do you think's coming to get you?' said Sanchez.

Millie looked at him. 'Oh, nobody,' she said. 'We have no enemies. We're a peace-loving people.'

'You think the police are up there?'

'Maybe.'

'You're paranoid.'

'I've always preferred paranoia to stupidity. And remember something, Sanchez. I've been right twice. You've been wrong twice. Now don't those statistics tell you anything?'

Miles said, 'I believe in predators, so I suggest we upgrade all weapons. We need long-range spears. The stuff we're making at the moment is for kids.'

'Doctor Ellie said no weapons building,' said Sanchez. 'So did Professor Worthington. So I don't think we ought to be . . . going behind their backs.'

Sanchez found that everyone was looking at him.

'Okay then,' said Vijay. 'Let's call it "tools building".'

Millie laughed and punched Sanchez on the shoulder. 'Got you!' she cried. 'A weapon's a tool – get out of that one.'

Sanchez kept his patience. 'They were a non-violent people,' he said. 'That's what Doctor Ellie told us, again and again.'

'That's why they got wiped out,' said Miles. 'If they sat around eating nuts and playing flutes, they were pretty much asking for it. We're just learning from their experience.'

'I'm going to sit at the forge and make a big, sharp battle axe,' said Millie, slapping Sanchez again. 'And I'm going cut another of your toes off, Head Boy . . .'

In the basket of the balloon stood an ex-pilot: Timmy Fox.

He gazed down through binoculars and licked his lips. A week had passed since the trauma of meeting Miles, Millie and Sanchez – and he could still feel the bruise of the gobstopper, deep in his windpipe. He was still prone to hot flushes and fits of trembling.

He was bankrupt and he'd been stripped of all licenses.

'There's a clearing,' he said, quietly. 'No signs of life, though.'

'They're down there somewhere,' said his passenger. 'I sold them twenty choc ices a few days ago. They're in the woods, playing games.'

'Do you want me to go lower?'

'No, Foxy. I don't.'

'What do you want to do? What exactly are we here for?'

'Monitoring, lad. Hovering and thinking. I'm enjoying the breeze and you're getting over a nasty experience.'

Ex-Inspector Cuthbertson had not found it difficult to trace the unfortunate airman. He had visited Deputy Chief Constable Eddy Shackleton, and doors had been opened. Old friends tapped into police computers and he heard the whole story of the ill-fated flight. He went straight to the hospital.

'Lost everything, have you?' he said. 'I saw the newspapers.'

Timmy Fox barely registered his presence. '*Maisie*,' he said, at last.

'Maisie who?'

'I'd had her less than six months, you know. Half a million pounds, spread all over the motorway.'

'And the insurance, Timmy?'

'No.'

He raised damp, sightless eyes and blinked. He shook his head and the ex-policeman drew his chair a little nearer.

'No insurance, Timmy? How's that then?'

'No flight plan,' whispered the Fox. 'I didn't file a flight plan, so I don't get a penny. I've got creditors chasing me. My wife . . .' He laughed a thin, unnatural laugh. '"Final straw," is what the wife says. She visited yesterday, you see. Took away my door key. That's her ring, look. Next to my tablets.'

He blinked again, as if trying to focus. Tears rolled down his cheeks.

'What am I going to do? Just a few, reckless minutes and the Fox loses everything. They're going to prosecute, there's no two ways about that. Had the accident investigators in all morning. I'll never fly again.'

Cuthbertson touched his arm. 'I think you will, son. If you want to, that is.'

The airman shook his head and laughed. 'I broke too many rules. It's over . . . and all because of a South American gobstopper.'

The ex-policeman pulled out a small hip flask and poured whisky into a nearby beaker. He passed it to the Fox and poured another for himself.

'What if I made you a little proposition?' he said, inching even closer. 'What if we threw our fortunes together, so to speak? I might pull a few strings for you.'

'How?' said Timmy Fox. 'Why?'

'I'm looking for someone I can trust. I need a fearless pilot, who doesn't ask questions and takes a few risks. A man like you, Timmy, who breaks the rules now and then, and isn't scared of danger. I know people in high places, son – are you listening? Friends, Foxy, who just might make a certain prosecution disappear if you could see your way to helping me out.'

He let the words sink in and watched the colour return to the man's face.

'Go on,' said the Fox.

'Not yet. It's complicated, Timmy. I need air cover – and that's why I thought of you.'

That evening, Timmy Fox discharged himself and drove with his new friend to the Somerset and Devon Balloon Club. They filled out some forms and by the end of the week they were floating high over Ribblemoor.

Timmy Fox was nervous. 'This is their school, isn't it?' he said. 'Ribblestrop Towers.'

'That's where they come from, son. And this is reconnaissance. All we do at the moment is monitor.'

'There's a car coming down the drive. Is that what we're looking for?'

'That's a friend of mine working on phase two. Let's just go up a bit, eh, Foxy? I don't want to be recognised . . .'

Lady Vyner saw the balloon, too.

She was standing in the window of the east tower, which was the former orphans' dormitory. She gazed out over her grounds and she saw the little burst of flame which made the thing go higher. She even saw a glint of sunlight on the binoculars and then she turned her eyes back to the drive. There was a car, zooming closer, and her first thought was that it might be another customer for the nursing home. She turned to the door, noticing the orphans' hammocks that still hadn't been cleared. Scribbled timetables were tacked to the wall and a soft toy lay abandoned on its side.

She smiled. The school had withdrawn – retreated – and she was in charge of the building again. She wasn't sure it was total victory, yet, because she didn't trust the headmaster or the pupils – and she'd heard the sound of chainsaws. It had all been much too easy. Nonetheless, it felt good to wander at will from room to room and take possession of each tower. She had been going through the children's things, wondering if there was anything that old people might like. When she had money, she mused, she would have a lounge for them with a huge television. Drugged, they could watch it all day – all night if they wanted to. For now, they would have to share her flat. The two that arrived seemed comfortable enough, though their chatter got on her nerves.

'Junk,' she said, turning over a discarded sock. 'All of it.'

'That's kids for you, isn't it?' said the guard who'd been helping her.

'What do you mean?'

'I mean, it's all kids' stuff.'

'Obviously, it's kids' stuff. It was kids who were living here – what do you expect it to be?'

The guard decided to be silent. Lady Vyner came closer.

'How does a grown man like you force himself into a uniform like that?' she said. 'You look like one of Hitler's bully-boys. Don't you have any kind of conscience about what you do?'

The guard looked baffled. 'Just doing a job, ma'am.'

'That's what the gas chamber repairman probably said in Belsen. What I want to know is where they've all gone? They've not disappeared, you know!'

'Who?'

Lady Vyner swore under her breath. 'The children, you dolt.'

'We evicted them.'

'I know you evicted them. That's what I'm paying you to do – not that I'm paying a penny until the job's done properly. They didn't vanish into thin air, that's what I'm saying. And what was that noise coming from the woods? Have you investigated that yet?'

'I don't know nothing about no noise.'

'I spoke to you about it. Three days ago.'

'This is my first shift.'

'Is it? Well, you look all the same to me. You ought to have your names on your foreheads, then I'd stand a chance. You do have a name, do you?'

'Terence Perkins, ma'am. Lads call me Terry.'

'Well, Perkins. I want you to have a word with these so-called "lads", and find out who investigated my complaint about chainsaws in the woods. You can do that, can you?'

'Yes.'

'Yes, *ma'am*. It's Cuthbertson I need to see again. He can lead a manhunt – we've got the dogs for it, haven't we? Get

124

him on the phone for me. You won't get a farthing, you know, until the whole site's been checked and cleared. I'm going to need to talk to that Lacson fellow too – is he around still? Why isn't he suing them properly?'

In the distance, a doorbell rang.

'Ah!' cried Lady Vyner. Her eyes gleamed. 'That will be another inmate, I presume. Do me a favour, Jenkins. Trot down to the main door, quick as you can. We don't want anyone escaping. I'll be right behind you . . .'

The guard set off, relieved to get away. Lady Vyner followed more slowly, clinging to the banister. By the time she reached the bottom step, she was dizzy again, and her head was full of the barking of dogs. She leant against the wall and felt for her vodka flask. It was all the way upstairs, in her own flat – she remembered Crippen, her butler, refilling it. Now someone was shouting and she felt a wave of irritation rise up like a sickness. She tottered towards the confusion, cursing under her breath. She could hear someone yelling and the barking was constant.

'Silence!' she yelled.

The dogs backed off at once.

Mr Ian lay between them, curled into a ball. One trouser leg had been ripped off and he was hyperventilating.

'He just barged through the door!' said a guard. 'Tried to stroke Buster – there was nothing I could do!'

'Who on earth is he?' hissed Lady Vyner. 'Has he brought someone?'

'Said he was from a school, but—'

'Get him on his feet!'

Mr Ian was helped into a standing position and he gazed around him, white-faced. There was blood in his beard again. Some bristles had been torn away.

'I'm . . . I'm . . .' He could barely speak.

'You're what?' said Lady Vyner. 'You're who? What's your business?'

'I've come . . .'

'You have old people for me? Where are they?'

'No. I—'

'This is a nursing home.'

'I thought it was a school.'

Lady Vyner cursed. 'Put him in his car,' she said to a guard. 'Turn him round and get him out of here.'

'No, wait!' cried Mr Ian. He gulped a deep breath and wiped his eyes. 'Norcross-Webb is who I'm looking for. Ribblestrop Towers, headmaster. I've been phoning and writing and—'

'You know him, do you?'

'I don't know him—'

'He's here somewhere, though – isn't he? What's your business with him?'

'I have a proposal. I'm from The Priory, and I'm hoping we can work together. I've even brought a couple of pupils! I was hoping to introduce them.'

Lady Vyner looked him up and down. 'They're out in the woods. Somewhere. You can help me find the wretch if you want to. If you can walk, that is.' She turned to a guard. 'Get the door open! Idiot.'

Chapter Eighteen

The camp, of course, had been substantially developed.

In addition to weapons-construction, the children had enjoyed a whole range of fascinating craft classes. They had developed several more buildings, including a thatched roundhouse – perfect for meetings and feasts. It had a chimney, so cooking could be done inside, and Tomaz led a team of cooks, experimenting with forest produce. Breakfasts and snacks tended to be eaten in the treetops, and there were now three lifts up to the highest platforms, running on counter-weighted ropes. Substantial loads could be hoisted, and many evenings had been spent nibbling rum-and-wild-berry quiche, out on the sun decks. The lifts were enormous fun, for a child could sit in the basket and be shot up at alarming speed. Vaulting and swinging had developed too and there were now trails in several directions. The challenge was to cover long distances without ever touching the ground. Anjoli said he held the record for the fastest aerial journey from one side of the wood to the other, but this was hotly disputed. Young Nikko had been the star acrobat in the Ribblestrop Circus and when he got going, his thin body was a blur, hurtling from creeper to creeper. He hardly disturbed the leaves as he dived and dipped, and he hadn't been formally timed because the time-keepers always lost track of him.

Metalwork had been a huge success. Professor Worthington had run two classes on metallurgy and shown them how to build a furnace. The highest temperature reached so far had been seven hundred and fifty degrees, which was enough to make steel. They made nails, ladles, buckles and bridles. They'd been toying with the idea of chariots, so they made an axle and then rimmed two large wheels, bolting spikes in the centres. When Professor Worthington was called away, they made arrowheads and daggers. Imagio had been brought up in a Colombian favela and knew all about sharpening blades. He showed them what kind of stone to use and how to hold it. Everyone was amazed, and even frightened, by how cruel a properly honed edge could be and how easily it could cut.

The question of the tribe's peace-loving ways continued to cause controversy. Miles, in particular, was keen to discuss the question.

'How do you know they didn't fight, miss?' he asked Doctor Ellie.

'Because no evidence has ever been found of war.'

'But all that means is it hasn't been found,' said Tomaz.

'You're right, of course. But there have been Celtic finds and endless Roman finds. The stone, too, makes no obvious mention of combat.'

'They must have been able to protect themselves,' said Israel. 'Everyone has to.'

'I daresay they did. That doesn't mean they made a fetish of it.'

'What's a fetish?'

'I mean, they didn't elevate war to some high art, like so many cultures have done. They didn't become obsessed with it, the way you are.'

'Maybe they should have done,' said Miles. 'They might have survived.'

Doctor Ellie nodded. 'I know. You think being peaceful is a weakness rather than a strength. You wait till we go to the museum and meet Eleudin – that might challenge your way of thinking.'

'When are we going?' said Sam.

'When will the chariot be ready? You want to travel in style, I presume?'

'Soon,' said Asilah. 'We're giving the donkeys every chance, but . . . we're going to have to get rough soon. They just don't want to work.'

Miles stood up. 'Gotta go, miss,' he said. He pulled on a feather headdress. 'I'm in the hunting party.'

'That's another thing I'm dubious about,' said Doctor Ellie. 'They were farmers rather than hunters and a vegetarian diet would have been quite sufficient.'

'Not for us, though.'

'I think you like killing things, Miles. You're making me nervous.'

'We'll protect you, miss. The hunters are guards, as well, and we're always vigilant.'

So it was that Mr Ian and his two small Priory children were spotted that very afternoon, as they fought their way through the forest.

Mr Ian was in the lead, followed by his blue-blazered pupils. Lady Vyner was lagging behind, dehydrated and giddy. She had fallen twice and the absence of alcohol was causing severe distress.

'I have no idea where you're taking me,' she wheezed.

The two children looked at her with undisguised fear. They were Mr Ian's special ambassadors, selected because of their neat haircuts and polished faces. Unfortunately, the heat was getting to them too and they were now dripping in sweat. The little boy's cap was damp and his knees were filthy. The little girl's jacket was wet and muddy down one sleeve and she had lost a shoe.

They had both been trained, however, never to cry in public.

'Are we even going in the right direction?' said Mr Ian, trying to keep his temper. 'You said you saw smoke?'

'God knows. It looked like smoke, but then again everything's pretty blurred. You haven't got any water, or . . .?'

'Nothing.'

'This isn't really a footpath, is it?' said the boy.

'Shut up, Scott. How is that a helpful remark?'

'Sorry, sir.'

Mr Ian brushed at his tie, which was dotted in the old lady's spittle. He had dressed extra smartly for this meeting and his clothes were now in ruins. He was supposed to be back at school that night for boarding-house duty and there would be many questions if he and the pupils were late. He felt a pang of hatred for ex-Inspector Cuthbertson and wondered if he should simply abandon the mission. If he did, he would face curses, followed by sarcasm, followed by threats. And he'd most likely be forced to make the journey again. The kidnap plot was thickening around him and he was powerless.

He would have to press on.

'Have you been eating sweets?' he said to Scott.

'No, Mr Ian.'

'Well your mouth's disgusting. Wipe it.'

He took the child's ear and drew him closer.

'I'm very nervous at the moment,' Mr Ian whispered. 'I won't deny it. And when I get nervous, boys like you suffer. Do you understand me? There's a lot at stake here today, so I need best, best behaviour and a positive attitude. I don't know where this mad woman's taking us, but we're going to smile and be nice and get what we came for.' He pinched hard. 'Got it?'

'Ow! Yes, sir.'

Mr Ian turned to Lady Vyner, and called out brightly. 'Shall we press on? It can't be *much* further.'

'What?'

'Their hideout. Whatever it is.'

Lady Vyner swore obscenely and spat onto a rock. 'I've had enough,' she said. 'I should have brought the dogs. Dogs and policemen, that's what we need. Which way's back?'

'Well, I'm not entirely sure.'

'Downhill, I know that much. Wretched, evil nonsense of a school . . .'

She swore more brutally and turned back the way she'd come. A moment later, she had disappeared into thick brushwood and her cursing faded from earshot. A bird cried out, there was a flapping of wings, and then silence. Mr Ian stood with his two miserable pupils and wondered what to do.

Chapter Nineteen

Vijay saw them first.

He was in the stream below. Miles and Nikko were close by, comparing arrowheads. He shushed them with the cry of the raven and they turned to him, frozen. They had got tired of hunting some time ago, for there were no birds or animals to be seen. Instead, they had worked on another man-trap, binding timbers and fitting weights for an hour. Mr Ian's voice carried through the trees loud and clear, and there was a great deal of twig-crunching.

'No,' shouted the teacher. 'We're going on! If you didn't bring water, that's your problem.'

A plaintive voice said something inaudible.

'I don't need this, Jacqueline! I have no time for weakness! Not today!'

There was another crack of brushwood and they heard a squeal.

The three boys grabbed their spears and shouldered their bows. They moved noiselessly into the undergrowth and Nikko led them up the nearest trunk, into the treetops. They crossed carefully from branch to branch, following a creeper trail. They were soon directly over the intruders, looking down.

'I don't believe it,' said Miles, peering through the leaves.

'What?' said Vijay.

'Mr Ian. The Priory.'

Nikko took his arm. 'What? That guy from the crazy school?'

'He must have come for his wallet. Damn, this could be bad. How did he find us?'

'Who are the little dudes?' whispered Vijay. 'They look scared as hell.'

'What do we do?' said Miles. 'Can we lure them to Anjoli's pit? Where is it?'

'They're walking in the woods, Miles! You can't drop them in a pit for taking a walk. Anyway, they've stopped.'

'You think they're lost?'

'Maybe. They may have come in peace – we need to find out. Nikko, swing down and see what they're saying.'

Nikko did so at once. The orphans had set vines in many of the key trees, so it was easy to wrap one that was close to hand several times round his middle. Pushing off from his branch, he let himself down silently, until he was a couple of metres above Mr Ian's head.

A minute later, he'd wound himself up again.

'He's rude as hell,' he said. 'He's in a bad, bad mood – gave the boy a slap, right in the face.'

'What's he saying?'

'He said they're going to go on looking, through the night if necessary. He keeps telling the kids they're useless. Boy and girl, about ten years old. They're pretty done-in, by the look of it. They're nice kids, though ... they're brave, anyway.'

'He's a barbarian,' said Miles. 'I wonder if we can separate him from his pupils. We could lead him back to the stream and drop a rock on his head.'

Vijay laughed again. 'He's a human being, Miles! You can't murder him – you'll go to prison.'

'You don't know how bad he is. If I told you what he did to me, you'd have a different attitude.'

'What did he do?'

'Whipped me till I bled.'

'Everyone gets whipped,' said Nikko. 'Maybe we should just—'

'Shhh!' hissed Vijay.

They listened carefully and through the trees came a long, sweet trill, rising to a piercing warble.

'I don't believe it!' hissed Vijay. 'What's Doctor Ellie doing? This is bad . . .'

'What?' said Miles. 'What is that?'

'She's playing that damn flute again. Listen! It's getting louder.'

The flute became penetrating, for the notes were climbing higher and higher, like the call of some magical bird. The three boys looked down and saw Mr Ian turn and sniff the air. He said something to the little girl, and the boy put his cap back on. Mr Ian led decisively, turning right through some bushes and then left towards an enormous beech. He soon found a track and started to climb. Nikko and Vijay followed in the trees above, keeping pace. It was twenty minutes later that they caught their first whiff of woodsmoke and Mr Ian's voice rang out confidently.

'I think we're warm, you know. You let me do all the talking, all right? I want nothing from you but smiles. If the teachers speak to you, you agree with whatever I've said.'

When they came into the village, the first thing they saw was half a pig roasting. Tomaz was under it, basting carefully. When he stood up, the three visitors could only stare, open-mouthed.

'Sir,' said Tomaz, 'we've got company.'

'What's that, Tom?' said the headmaster. 'The trotters won't cut . . .'

'Later, please, sir. It's easier when the meat's cooked. I said we've got company. I think it's that teacher. From that school.'

'What school? Where do you mean?'

The headmaster had been crouched down in one of the fire holes and, when he stood up, Mr Ian's mouth opened still wider. He was wearing a tunic made of old circus tent, with a handwoven cloak attached round his shoulders by a black-and-gold tie. The loom classes had started on day four and most of the children were now dressed in appropriately tribal gear made of multi-coloured wools and feathers. Doctor Norcross-Webb had wild flowers in his hair and an amulet made of twisted straw and pheasant bones.

Mr Ian came forward. His ripped trouser leg flapped damply.

'I'm sorry to bother you,' he said, 'but I'm looking for the headmaster of Ribblestrop Towers.'

'Are you?' said the headmaster. 'I'm happy to say you've found him.'

'Oh. Where?'

The headmaster clambered out of the fire hole and dusted himself down. 'I am he,' he said, 'and you're our very first visitors from outside, so you're particularly welcome.'

'You're . . .'

'Who are these youngsters? What a lovely surprise.'

His eye had fallen on the two children, who were hanging back, bewildered and nervous. A crowd of Ribblestrop tribesmen had gathered and, as some were now experimenting more confidently with war paint, the effect was alarming. The flute music was strangely disorientating too. It had attracted birds that wheeled screaming overhead and there was also the sound of hammers on metal. Into the mix came the occasional bray of a donkey.

'Is this . . .? I'm looking for a school,' said Mr Ian, trying to bring his voice under control. 'I'm looking for a Doctor Norcross-Webb.'

'Yes. That's me.'

'I've been trying to telephone, but—'

'Ah, was that you calling? I am so sorry – to me, a cell-phone is more of a curse than a blessing. I find it so hard to see the numbers and reception . . . well, I'm never sure if it's me or all these trees. Where are you from?'

'I'm Ian Keith. From . . . The Priory School. We've come to . . .'

Words failed him again.

The children he was looking at were staring at him with cold dislike. He could see that one of them was the girl and she had her hands on her hips. Over her shoulder she wore a longbow and a quiver full of lethal-looking arrows. He looked around for the boy that had kicked him to the ground, but couldn't find him . . . nor could he see Miles, which was an encounter he'd been dreading. At once, Cuthbertson's instructions came back, like an inner voice, and he managed to force his lips into a smile. He was, after all, making progress, and he was in no danger. Against all odds, contact had been made.

'You must be doing a project,' he said. He tried a chuckle, and the laughter emerged like a series of sharp coughs. 'How absolutely wonderful. How absolutely . . . Ha! Ingenious! Can you see what's going on, Scott? Jacqueline? We've walked slap bang into a history lesson.'

The headmaster nodded. 'I can see I'm talking to a fellow teacher. Some people would look at us and think we'd all

136

gone mad, but this is a very scientific exploration of Ribblemoor's history and an ancient tribe. Can I offer you a drink or a snack?'

'Oh!' said Mr Ian, remembering to smile again, for the smell of cooking fat was making him feel queasy. 'How thoughtful. We are a little parched, aren't we, children? We've been wandering for some time, you see.'

'Come into the roundhouse. We can have a proper parley in there. Unless, of course, your pupils . . . would they like to see round, maybe?' The headmaster went down onto his haunches and addressed them kindly. 'You must be very hot, Jacqueline. Scott. Why don't you loosen up a bit? Give us your coats. Israel, could you get some water? What's that noise? Oh dear! Sounds like trouble.'

The donkey they'd heard earlier was now braying almost continuously and the headmaster had to raise his voice. 'See if those biscuits have cooled, would you, Kenji? Come on into the shade – oh my word, look out!'

A part of the fence behind him gave way with a crunch of timber and there was another almighty bray. It was the donkey, of course, making a desperate bid for freedom – but it was attached to a huge chariot, the wheels of which gouged ruts into the earth. It was held back by the mighty arms of Henry, but the beast was enraged and desperate. It tried to charge and everyone leapt for their lives. Asilah was on the animal's back, surfer-style. He dropped astride her and yanked at her ears. Sanchez was being dragged along under her muzzle, holding the reins in both fists, and at last they got the animal still.

It reared its head back and kicked viciously. The front of the chariot was split wide open. Asilah twisted the creature's ears again and the poor animal bared her teeth in rage and brayed what had to be a string of pure donkey obscenities. Mr Ian realised he was sitting in the mud. He had jumped back and lost his footing. Scott and Jacqueline were nowhere to be seen.

'Dear oh dear,' said the headmaster when order was restored. 'I'm so sorry about that! These creatures are proving impossible and we thought . . . Are you all right, sir? Do you want a hand?'

Mr Ian was holding his mouth.

'We're desperate to be mobile, you see. We want to do some serious racing – this chariot is one of two.'

Ruskin and Sam eased Mr Ian to his feet. He had bitten his lip again and there was that tell-tale smudge of blood in his beard.

'Do you have donkeys at The Priory?' said Ruskin, politely.

Mr Ian couldn't speak.

The young boy, Scott, emerged from under a small sapling. 'No,' he said. 'We don't.'

Jacqueline, who had got halfway up a tree, said, 'We do have ponies, but they're for riding. We don't . . . We don't really do what you're doing.'

'Well, we're way off schedule, to tell you the truth,' said the headmaster. 'The plan is to take a ride into town on Tuesday and there's no way we'll be ready. We've booked the Ribblestrop Museum, you see – for the whole day. We thought it would be rather a hoot if we arrived by chariot, but the best laid plans, eh? What do you think, Asilah? Would you trust old Mildred?'

'She's learning, sir,' panted Asilah. He was still astride her, holding the reins firmly in both hands. 'She knows we mean business, now, so I think we can try again tomorrow.'

'Never give up, eh?' said the headmaster.

'Never, sir,' said Asilah.

A lot of the children were staring at Mr Ian still, with undisguised hostility. He could feel their eyes boring into

138

him. As far as he could tell, there was still no sign of Miles, and that comforted him a little. He remembered his mission and tried to think of something to say.

'Quite a project,' he managed to whisper.

'Oh, we don't mess around here,' said Asilah. 'Maybe we didn't make that as clear as we should have done.'

'What are you here for, Mr Ian?' said Millie.

Somehow, Mr Ian flailed his face into a smile. He was sticky with sweat and his head was aching. He had a feeling that his trousers had split when he sat down, but he was determined not to draw attention to the fact. He tried to think himself into more comfortable surroundings, and thought of the cricket pitch at The Priory. He imagined himself talking to parents with tea from the marquee . . . and the thought calmed him a little. He would get back to civilisation. The nightmare would end.

'Lord,' he said, hoarsely, 'what a wonderful day we're having. We didn't expect this, did we, Scott? The fun they have at Ribblestrop, eh? Ha!'

Israel appeared with three clay cups of water on a tray made of bark. Mr Ian took one and drank deep. He tried out his laugh again and heard it emerge with a retching sound.

'Can we take our blazers off yet, Mr Ian?' said Jacqueline.

The headmaster clapped her on the shoulder. 'Of course you can, my dear! I'll find you a costume if you want. That's Anjoli, there – under all that face paint. He'll show you round, let you try out the bridges. They're too high for me, but I'm something of a coward. What about you, Scott? Do you want to unbutton your jacket?'

Scott's eyes dilated with fear. 'Oh no,' he said.

'Ha!' said Mr Ian, quickly. 'There's nothing we'd like more than a good old . . . you know . . . tour. To get stuck in. Wouldn't we, Scott? But the fact is, we've got quite a drive if we're to get back for prep. It's nearly five as it is and I—'

139

'We don't use watches,' said Millie. 'We go by the sun.'

'Do you have prep every day?' said Ruskin. 'Prep is homework, isn't it?'

'We have it all the time,' whispered Scott. 'If we don't finish the work, we just have to stay in hall till we do. And it affects the food we get – you know, the portions. If we get things wrong, the portions get smaller.'

'Oh,' said Mr Ian, laughing again. 'That's, er . . . what we call an "urban myth", Scott. I don't think that's ever actually happened, has it?'

'It happened to my brother,' said Jacqueline. 'Last Monday. The prefects see to it.'

'Oh, only in fun. We believe in pupil leadership, you see, so the prefects –'

'They gave him one scoop of mash and a bean. He got fifty-six per cent in a vocab test and, as a scholarship boy, that's not allowed –'

'Vocab?' said Imagio. 'What's vocab?'

Mr Ian laughed again and clapped his hands. 'This is what I call a real getting-to-know-you session. It's like two tribes meeting, isn't it? Discussing customs, and . . .' He hunted for the word. '. . . rituals. If we had more time I'd like for nothing more –'

'Why doesn't he loosen his tie?' said Caspar, who was the one boy still in the chariot. 'He's going to faint in a minute. Look how red he is.'

The hunted look came back into Scott's eyes and his hand leapt to his throat. 'I'm fine,' he said.

'You get crosses if you're out of uniform,' said Jacqueline. 'Three crosses and you go to The Darkroom.'

Mr Ian was caught off-guard again. 'Oh, Jacqueline,' he said, gently. 'You're going to give the wrong impression if you carry on like this. The Darkroom, I should say, is what we call . . . well, it's a kind of small room –'

'I remember it,' said Miles.

Mr Ian swung round and saw two unblinking blue eyes gazing at him. The boy's arms were folded and he held a long knife.

'I remember it well.'

'It's really not that dark,' said Mr Ian. 'Just a tradition, really—'

'I don't want to go there,' said Scott, suddenly. 'I haven't taken my blazer off, sir. I'm wearing it!'

'You're not going there!'

'I don't want to!'

'Look,' said the headmaster in a decisive voice. 'I can see that this gentleman's come to see us for a reason, and it's very rude of me not to find out what that is. So, here's a plan. We're going to have a private chat, and I want you children to give Jacqueline and Scott a tour of the camp. I'm putting you in charge, Sam – you're the most sensible. Back here in half an hour. Asilah, can you get the donkey into its paddock? And Mr Ian . . . let's go in here, the children will be fine, I promise you. No need to worry. We're having a pig-roast later and you are welcome to join us if you're able to change your plans.' He took his guest by the arm and led him forward. 'Ah, Captain Routon, in the nick of time, that's lucky . . . This is Mr Ian of The Priory School. I have a feeling he's got something up his sleeve and I'm dying to hear what it is.'

Captain Routon was bare-chested, wearing a canvas cloak and army trousers. 'How do you do, sir?' he said, extending his hand.

'Well,' said Mr Ian, weakly. 'Thank you. I wonder if—'

'Step this way,' said the headmaster. 'Your pupils will be fine. We aren't cannibals.'

Mr Ian was staring after Jacqueline and Scott, who were surrounded by tribesmen. Even as he watched, they were moving away from him and their blazers were being peeled from their shoulders. He felt a hand on his arm again and he was ushered by two adults into a tall, thatched construction, the floor of which was strewn with reeds.

Chapter Twenty

'So,' said the headmaster. 'How can we help?'

Mr Ian could feel the phone in his pocket buzzing and he knew at once that it was Cuthbertson. He felt a pang of helpless fury – the man would be asking for a report, already. He knew the visit was today. He sat in the shadows, cursing his luck and wondering, for the hundredth time, if there was any way out.

There wasn't.

'Well,' he said, at last. 'You're right, I have come with a . . . proposal.' He drank more water and remembered his manners. 'A request, actually. I'm here to ask a favour and . . . well, if you gentlemen can help me out, I'd be in your debt forever. The whole school would be, actually.'

'I'm intrigued,' said the headmaster.

Mr Ian looked him squarely in the eye and asked the question that Cuthbertson had told him to ask. They had rehearsed it together. 'How seriously do you take outward bound?'

'Very seriously.'

'Oh good. So do we. It's pretty much at the heart of The Priory's curriculum.'

'I wish we could say the same,' said Captain Routon.

The headmaster nodded. 'We've often said that with the moors on our doorstep and all this land we should do a lot more outward bound than we actually do. Especially in the summer term.'

Mr Ian felt encouraged. He was over the first hurdle. 'Do you by any chance do the International Pioneers' Award?'

'No,' said Captain Routon. 'Never heard of it.'

'It's quite a high-level programme,' lied Mr Ian. 'It replaced the, er, Queen's Orienteering Medal about three years ago. The Royal Marines designed it, so it's quite . . . arduous.'

'I'm interested already,' said the headmaster. 'What's it involve?'

'Map reading. Survival. A bit of climbing. It's a bit like the Tor Trail. Did you ever do that?'

'I did,' said Captain Routon. 'Quite a few years ago. I was a marshall for that in Scotland with the paras. That's when you have to climb at least three peaks and pick up coded information. One of the lads took a bullet in the shoulder – that's how competitive it got.'

'Yes,' said Mr Ian. 'That's . . . probably a bit more serious than the schools' version, of course.'

'Our kids don't get enough competition.'

'Don't they?'

Routon shook his head. 'Soft as butter, half of them.'

'Oh.'

'We go for a co-operative approach,' said the headmaster. 'As Routon says, it means some of our boys can be a bit a little retiring.'

Mr Ian nodded. 'Well, the Pioneers' Award is a pretty tough programme and it does mean spending a few days out on the moor. Living . . . without the supervision of adults, in wild isolation.'

'And I take it you do this at The Priory?' said the headmaster.

'We most certainly do.'

'Is it popular?'

Mr Ian nodded again, more fiercely. He was going to go through with it. Cuthbertson's plan was about to be unveiled. A boy had appeared in the shadows with a cup of something and he took it gratefully. The Ribblestrop teachers were staring at him, keen to hear more. 'It's gone down an absolute storm,' he said. 'These outward-bound activities, they really help separate the weak from the strong – and it looks so good on a child's resumé. It helps us too, because we can find out who the cry-babies are and crack the whip a bit.' He paused. 'In a protective and supportive way, of course.'

'So what has this to do with us?' said Captain Routon, clapping his hands. 'What's brought you all the way to Ribblestrop?'

Mr Ian smiled. 'Ah,' he said. 'Now we're at the crunch.' He sighed and sipped his drink – it had a taste like ammonia and his gums instantly smarted. 'I'd better lay my cards on the table and be completely honest. We need a partner school for our next outing. We hoped it would be you.'

'Excellent!' said the headmaster.

'Yes. We had a bit of a set back last term with an outbreak of mumps, which put us behind schedule. We have to go out again, in the next couple of weeks—'

'My word,' said the headmaster. 'As soon as that?'

'Yes. We want to take advantage of the good weather.'

'I can see that makes sense,' said Routon.

'We also have exams looming,' said Mr Ian. 'So we haven't much time to sit around.'

The headmaster sat forward. 'Exams, eh?' he said. 'That's something else I'm trying to get started. What kind of exams do you do?'

'What kind?'

'We want difficult ones. Soon as possible.'

'We do the scholarship tests, of course. Profile A and B. Most boys take the Common Standard and Extension papers and everyone has Creativity Checks. We do the Cambridge Numeracy Programme in early June and our top set does the Oxford High-Flyers. Later in June it's Mods and Consolidation Tests. And we finish with Career Profiling, so every child knows what it's aiming for.'

Mr Ian sipped his drink again. The phone buzzed in his jacket and he ignored it. Captain Routon was looking at the headmaster, who was nodding thoughtfully.

'I'm keen,' he said. 'I love the sound of this award and I think our lot would jump at the chance to get out on the moor. I don't want to tread on Doctor Ellie's toes, that's the only drawback. This history project's been inspired by her and she's the one steering it.'

Mr Ian stared. 'Doctor Ellie, the . . . Not the elderly lady who photographs stones?'

'You've heard of her?'

'Yes.'

'She's a marvel, isn't she? She gave the most splendid lecture last night on natural poisons. There's a very potent lichen that grows near here. You wet it in urine apparently, add boiling water, and it becomes quite deadly.'

'That's . . . extraordinary.'

'One mouthful's enough.'

'Can we combine the two projects, sir?' said Captain Routon.

'Ah,' said the headmaster. 'Lateral thinking. I find Routon often sees a way forward when lesser men see obstacles. What are you thinking?'

Captain Routon put his fingertips together. 'If the Pioneers' Award is Royal Marines,' he said, 'it's going to be top-dollar. Tough but fair. No better training for the would-be warrior. So why don't we combine it with the flare paths and go off on a proper adventure? This is a gift horse, sir. We should not be looking in its mouth.'

The headmaster was nodding. 'I think it's a yes,' he said. 'We'll run the idea past Doctor Ellie and, if she's as happy as we are, we can get things moving at once.'

The three men walked back out into the sunlight to find the camp almost deserted. A few boys were tending to the pig-roast and Doonan was peeling potatoes. Miles was tending one of the fires. He got to his feet when he saw Mr Ian and smiled his friendliest smile.

'Hello again, Mr Ian. Are you all right?'

'Yes, I'm . . . The sun seems rather bright. I might need to sit down.'

'How was your coffee? We're experimenting with some herbal infusions.'

Mr Ian tried to smile, but his facial muscles were paralysed. His cup was half empty and the ground was spinning.

'I wonder what's happened to your two?' said Captain Routon. 'We said half an hour, so we can't really expect them back just yet. Do you know where they went, Miles?'

'Tree House Two, I think, sir.'

'That doesn't surprise me,' said the headmaster. 'It's the prettiest. How's your head for heights, Ian? You're looking pale.'

'I'm fine! Lead on, please . . .'

He managed to get his legs moving. Before he knew it, he was climbing, rung after rung, and he recalled a nightmare he'd had once in the middle of a terrible fever. He'd been trying to climb out of hell as demons and devils poked at him and laughed. When he got onto the tree house platform he couldn't bear to look around him, for the wind had risen

147

and his stomach was heaving more wildly than ever. He could still taste the strange brew but now there was a stink of coconut in his nostrils because – unbelievably – a boy was crouched over a small fire cooking some kind of sweet sludge. Other children were eating it with their fingers. There were savages down on their haunches, playing a game, and when he was drawn forward he saw, with another awful rise of nausea, that gambling was in progress. They were betting on the progress of slugs and caterpillars, and the cheering was cacophonous. Worst of all, he could see the blurred figures of his own pupils, Jacqueline and Scott – the boy's shirt was torn and the tail was filthy from where he'd been sitting on it. They were tie-less and dishevelled and had long feathers behind their ears . . . He could stand it no more and only just managed to get to the tree house window before he vomited copiously into the leaves. He sank to his knees.

Yet again, the phone in his pocket was ringing. He wanted to hurl it over the treetops, but he didn't dare. Cuthbertson had to be obeyed and he had to get down and out and back to The Priory. The first part of the mission was a success, surely. He comforted himself with that thought as he wiped his eyes and mouth. He might, possibly, have got what he wanted. They might have swallowed the bait. If he could hang on to that positive fact, he might just get back to order and sanity.

'Would you like to spend the night here?' said someone behind him.

He swung round and saw Millie staring at him. Asilah was close by.

'Your kids are human,' she said. 'Even if you're not.'

'No,' he whispered.

'They don't want to leave. It's the first time they've ever had fun.'

148

'We're leaving now,' said Mr Ian, quietly.

'But we'll see you again,' said Anjoli.

Mr Ian glared. 'When we get back to school,' he said, 'we'll disinfect ourselves, head to foot. You stink of corruption, the lot of you!'

'Can we guide you to your car?' said Millie. 'We want to hear more about The Darkroom and what you did to Miles.'

'Sounds like you had a jolly time,' said Asilah. 'What did you hit him with, Mr Ian?'

'He got nothing he didn't deserve. He got what *you* deserve – all of you. A good old-fashioned, uninterrupted thrashing.'

Millie stared. 'You believe in pain, don't you?' she said. 'I wonder how much you can take?'

Chapter Twenty-One

The donkeys didn't improve.

The orphans tried carrots and sticks. Then they tried sharp sticks. They heated the sticks in the fire and put chilli pepper on the tips. But the animals just bared their teeth and endured. They would not pull the chariots.

Luckily, Israel had a reasonable relationship with the camel and she was reversed into the harness. The arguments raged about historical authenticity with some children saying that camels were a relatively recent invention. Eric and Podma had done their research, however. They had spent two hours in the library van and argued that, as the lost tribe of Ribblemoor had come by the silk route, they would have undoubtedly brought such a beast. When the camel herself proved willing and strong, her critics fell silent. Everyone piled on and there was a certain grace to her hip-swaying, Egyptian roll. They trundled out of camp, singing lustily. Oli and Sam had translated the school song into Latin and, though the tune was more awkward now, the words sounded heroic:

'*Ribblestrop, Ribblestrop, nobis super omnia*
– amaaaa-ta!
Deliciae somni puerisque academia – (ooh la!) cara!'

They waved their spears and stamped to the beat, and they came, after some time and some grass nibbling, along the old Ribblestrop High Street.

They had high hopes of the great museum, for Doctor Ellie had often spoken of it. Ruskin had described his trip to a museum in London, years ago, and had mesmerised his audience with tales of wonder. He explained that he'd seen only a fraction of the exhibits, for the halls were too vast to see everything in one day. There had been a space rocket that really flew and a full-size battleship. There were two raptors fighting a whale and a room full of mummies in bandages that sat up and spoke. He recalled the last dodo, flapping in a cage, and a real volcano that erupted over your toes.

It was inevitable that the Ribblestrop Museum would be a disappointment in comparison. When they pulled up outside the address they'd been given, the grey façade was an instant let-down. It stood next to Spare Ribb – a kebab shop that had closed soon after opening, due to its undisguised foreignness.

'It's a house,' said Anjoli. 'Just a normal little house.'

'That's not quite true,' said Doonan, who was wearing a dressing gown and pith helmet. 'It's a *converted* house. A very old one, apparently.'

'It's so tiny,' said Podma.

'It's closed, as well,' said Sanjay, looking at a scrap of paper taped to the window. 'It doesn't open till nine.'

The children had been up with the dawn as usual, so they were very, very early. This had been lucky from a traffic point of view, as the handful of cars they'd passed were distinctly unnerved by the slow-motion chariot – there had been two near-collisions. Doonan suggested they stayed put and waited – so Miles went off with Henry to get refreshments. Dave's Diner was nearby, open for bargain breakfasts, so he used the last of Mr Ian's cash to buy bacon butties. By the time they were finished – and Doonan had collected all the rubbish – they could see Doctor Ellie.

She was walking briskly along the pavement with an extremely pretty young woman, and they were in such deep conversation that they didn't notice the chariot and camel until they came alongside it.

'You made it!' gasped the librarian. 'You got the thing working and you're all in one piece! Look at the costumes, Vicky! Aren't they wonderful?'

There were a few shy thank yous, because for the first time in a while, the Ribblestrop pupils were rather lost for words. Some were even blushing under the intense gaze of Doctor Ellie's companion, whose jaw had dropped wide open.

'I've told you all about this young lady,' said Doctor Ellie, nudging her forward. 'It gives me great pleasure to introduce her in person. Our curator, our inspirational leader – and very personal friend – carrying a torch in the darkness! I present, Vicky Stockinger.'

Vicky blinked and smiled. Several orphans blushed more deeply and wished they were wearing shirts. Vicky's smile was the prettiest thing some of the boys had ever seen.

'I'm hardly any of those things!' she said. 'But I'm so pleased to meet you – I've heard all about you and I'm so glad you're here. You're so punctual, too!' She was searching the pockets of her dungarees. Her long hair was tied back into two bunches and she wore a striped sweater that blazed with every colour of the rainbow. Her mouth settled naturally into a grin and her eyes were the luminous blue of bright skies. She produced a key with a cry of triumph.

'Here we are! I thought I'd left it at home. Now, I hope you're not expecting very much . . .'

'They're expecting everything,' said Doctor Ellie.

'It's a very small collection and it's so dusty. The ceiling collapsed last week and we're still in chaos. Now, if you've got questions, I can't promise to answer them, but I will try.' She laughed. 'I'm not an expert on anything, whatever Ellie says. You're very welcome, that's the main thing – and I have to say I've been looking forward to meeting you for since I saw your circus.' She smiled at Anjoli. 'I recognise you!' she said.

'Me?' said Anjoli.

'Oh yes. You were so fearless! '

The children leapt down from the chariot and filed in through the doorway. Vicky was chattering all the time and, if she was surprised by how close some of the boys were pressing, she didn't say anything. 'Now I know you're doing this project on the Caillitri,' she cried, 'so I have mugged up on them. Oh, and I've been hearing all about the tree houses! So . . . let me just get the lights on. Ah, now this is one of my favourite items! Can you see? Stand back a little . . . Oh, the light's gone out. Can you jiggle that switch, one of you?'

The door had opened straight into a room the size of a small classroom. It was wallpapered in ugly brown and cream, as if an old-fashioned family had recently lived there. The musty smell suggested that they might have slept there too, or even died and been buried under the floorboards. Whoever cleared up their mess had left a tatty rug and an old gas fire. Dark cabinets were ranged along the walls, some high, some low. There were pictures and postcards with inscriptions in faded ink on the wall. Several fluorescent tubes flickered and Vicky pushed at a wire so another popped on in a dazzling burst.

'What do you think it is?' she said, excitedly.

The children weren't quite sure what they were being asked to look at, but they did their best to work it out.

Vicky's voice was musical and they wanted to enjoy themselves. The problem was, all they could see was a handful of tarnished coins and what might have been mouse droppings. Next to them was a chunk of old food, possibly discarded banana, turning from yellow to brown.

'We've got three of them,' said Vicky. 'Can you guess what they are?'

Nobody could.

'Is it someone's thumb?' said Ruskin.

'No.'

'A sweet?' said Imagio.

'You're not even warm. They're from a children's game, we think. I can't get it out, but it's a bit like a chess piece. We've also got . . . over here . . . what we think might be the first ever playing cards. Can you see these?'

They shuffled to the next case and saw six metal disks the size of small plates. There were designs etched on them, but it was hard to make them out. 'Playing cards were first found in China,' said Vicky. 'So this tribe – the one we're studying – brought them to England. We think they were the first people in the whole of the British Isles to play games and make music! They had the time and the imagination to create little sets of cards and . . . they're very lovely. Now, come and have a look at this. There!'

She turned to the far wall and there was a rather childish painting of some semi-naked people grouped on the brow of a hill. The colours were lurid and it reminded Millie of something she might have drawn when she was five.

'Is that the tribe?' she said. 'The lost tribe of Ribblemoor?'

'Well, it's just an impression,' said Vicky, apologetically. 'It's based on a grave site that was found.'

'Did you paint that?' said Israel.

'Yes. I used to be an art student. Can you see what they're wearing?'

'Is it jewels?' said Nikko. He had managed to get close and his nose was up against it.

'Yes! We're sure they wore jewellery. It was the obvious way of carrying wealth, of course, as well as being decorative and fun to make. I'll show you downstairs. We've got quite a little collection . . . And there's our prize exhibit, of course. You've heard about Eleudin?'

Vicky led them down to a cellar where there were yet more cases. The children moved among them, trying to conceal their disappointment. It was tempting to call it junk, for everything was so mottled and decayed, and the light wasn't good. Gradually, though, as Vicky explained, they started to realise that what they were looking at was a kind of treasure. They began to understand that when you dug treasure up, this was what it looked like, and a little thrill of reality went through the group. Vicky fluttered around them, pointing out hairpins and anklets. Then she turned on a projector and an enormous bracelet was thrown up onto a blank wall. Some of the younger children gasped.

'It's a reconstruction,' she said, for it was gleaming brightly. 'We tried to imagine what it would have looked like . . . Ellie and I went to the British Museum and talked to one of their experts. You see, we're confident that the Caillitri were metalworkers, and when they came to the moor they discovered silver deposits. They would have found tin, as well – they might have been hoping for gold. They brought gold with them, you see. Children's games and gold! Can you imagine what people must have thought? People would have assumed they were fairies or magicians. Maybe they were. Look at this . . . am I going too fast?'

'No, miss,' said Miles. 'You're doing great.'

'They were a wealthy people. They were a very spiritual people. Eleudin's the most amazing exhibit, though – we're very lucky to have him. In fact, we're fighting to keep him . . . but that's another story. Stand back, or you won't see – can you little ones come to the front? We have to keep him in the dark.'

'This is scary,' said Sam.

'Oh no – it's just that he's falling to pieces. The name Eleudin means "One who is lost", by the way. Can you pull that string, please? What's your name?'

'Tomaz.'

'The string works the curtain, Tomaz. Ellie, would you turn all the other lights off?'

Vicky turned a switch and, as she did so, the curtain moved. They were plunged into darkness and a curious silence descended. The curtain shifted and the glass case was revealed, glowing in soft blue light. There was an earthenware pot in the centre, but it was broken into three pieces.

Another bulb came on and some of the children gasped and pressed closer. The pot contained something small, made of what looked like twigs – but now they could see better, they realised that it was, in fact, a tiny child. The sections of the pot had been separated, so they could make out the little body, laying on the largest. There were tiny legs, which were folded so the knees were tucked under the bottom jaw of a delicate grey skull. Arms clutched the knees, and you could make out the curve of the spine and the shoulders. The skull was tilted slightly, as if the child was resting. The eye sockets stared as if they were concentrating hard. He was surrounded by feathers.

He only looked a few months old.

Chapter Twenty-Two

'Eleudin,' whispered Tomaz.

'What's the matter, Tom?' said Vijay, softly. 'What are you thinking?'

'I've seen him before.'

'You've seen him before? What do you mean?'

'Miles?'

Tomaz looked round and found that Miles was right next to him. He grabbed his wrist. 'I've seen him,' he hissed. 'Or maybe his brother . . . He's older than you think. I've seen him in the trees.'

Seconds passed as the children breathed and gazed. Vicky let them take it all in and Doctor Ellie stood at the back, waiting.

'Can you see what he's wearing?' said Vicky, at last.

'Bracelets,' said Sanchez. He had his nose pressed against the glass. 'Are they bracelets?'

'Ankle bracelets too,' said Sam.

'Gold thread,' said Vicky. 'There's a necklace as well, but it's hard to see. There were little earrings on his ears and there was a ring on each finger. They were sent off for carbon dating and never made it back – but it's the same principle as the Egyptians. Can you see the inside of the urn? How good are your eyes?'

'No, miss,' said Israel. 'It just looks like a pot. What's inside it?'

'The lighting's terrible. We applied for a grant, but it never came to anything. Look, if you hang on . . . I'm not supposed to do this.'

She produced a torch and switched it on.

'It's bad for the surfaces,' she said, 'but I want you to see. On the inside of the pot – how they did it nobody knows – but they drew the planets and the stars. Can you see now?'

Her torchlight picked out indentations and little swirls of dark colour.

'When the pot was intact,' she said, 'he would have been surrounded by comets. Comet tails. Moons – they loved the moon. We had someone examine it and he said there were seven planets, which is pretty amazing, isn't it, considering they had no telescopes. At least, we assume they didn't. There's the moon in all its phases and fourteen constellations, all of them accurate. He's got a map of the heavens to look at. Feathers to fly with.'

'Why though?' said Imagio, quietly. 'If the pot hadn't bust, nobody would see them.'

'Oh, but the baby would,' said Doctor Ellie. 'They weren't drawn for you and me – they were drawn for him.'

'Why?'

'I presume it was to help him,' said Vicky. 'I think, when he died, they made sure he had wealth – that's all the gold thread. They made sure he looked beautiful – he used to have long hair, but it came off when we moved him. Such long hair! You see, his parents carried him with them. They must have been taking him somewhere. And he had a map for whenever he needed it, so he could find God.'

A strange thing happened then.

Millie had been standing with everyone else, looking at the objects. And like most of the others, her mood had been shifting between curiosity and the mild boredom that cases of old remnants usually produce. But the skeleton-child was having an effect she hadn't expected and she found that she was trembling. She turned away from him, but was ringed in by Sam, Imagio and several orphans. Then she caught sight of Israel's black eyes and, when she looked back at the dead child, which she had to do, Vicky's torch made the gold around the wrists glimmer and a purple star blazed out of the pottery background. For a moment, in the glass, she saw not the Ribblestrop children, but the children of the tribe. She found her eyes were full of tears. She was about to cry and – worse – the crying was rising up from some deep place within that she couldn't control and, before she knew it, a terrible sob burst from her and her eyes were swimming. Eric thought she was laughing and grinned at her, but Millie was lost to a grief she didn't understand. She choked and put her hands over her mouth. She turned away again and broke out of the crowd. She thought she would fall, for the sobs were now coming one after another, and she could hardly breathe.

Strong arms held her.

Doctor Ellie had her arm right round her and was leading her to a chair.

'Don't worry,' she was saying. 'You're all right. Sit down, my dear.'

Millie found herself sitting and then her head was in her hands. The sobbing would not stop – the tears were pouring through her fingers. The rest of the children stared, bewildered. Tomaz was kneeling in front of her and Doctor Ellie was beside him.

'Take them upstairs,' she was saying to Vicky. 'Take them up to the conservatory.' Then she was pressing Millie's hands. 'It's all right, love. It's all right – he has this effect on people. You're not the first . . .'

'I'm fine,' sobbed Millie. 'It's nothing!'

'Anjoli, leave her alone. Go upstairs, please.'

'No, miss.'

'Go upstairs and leave us. Tomaz, too.'

'No, miss.'

There was a clattering of feet and the room emptied. Tomaz remained and Anjoli pressed himself against Millie's shoulder. She had her eyes closed now, because she was feeling sick. She felt Anjoli's warmth and had never been so glad of human contact, for she was as cold as a corpse. He moved so that he was sitting across her knees, hugging her. Tomaz was still there, kneeling, and she could still hear Doctor Ellie, but she was some distance off. There was a strange music in her head and she felt desperately tired.

'She'll be fine,' said Doctor Ellie. 'It's the heat, that's all it is.'

Anjoli had his arms right round Millie's neck and she hugged him. She let the tears flow and pressed him to her, feeling his heartbeat. She kept her eyes tight shut, and all she could see were moons and comets and the empty sockets of the child, drinking in the heavens.

'Don't leave me,' she said.

'Who is he?' said Tomaz.

'I don't know.'

'You've seen him before. Haven't you?'

'No. Of course not.'

'Why is he here, Millie? He shouldn't be here!'

But there was one last surprise.

The other children had followed Vicky back up to the ground floor, and she led them out the back to a glass extension. There was a single, solitary exhibit there and everyone recognised it at once: it was the white stone they'd used in the lay-by to prop up the car jack. It had been cleaned and polished, and it was laid against an almost identical piece, edge to edge. The crack between them was jagged and uneven and, though the stones looked similar, it was clear that they were two pieces of a puzzle that didn't quite match.

'You've been told about the flare paths?' said Vicky, quietly.

'We know a bit,' said Ruskin.

'If we could decode this stone, we'd know where they ran and what they led to. There's a flare path close to here.'

Sam said, 'Doctor Ellie thought she had the code. She thought this stone would help her crack it.'

'Oh, we've been trying. There's still a piece missing, though. I'm afraid it's the main piece.'

Caspar had come to the front. 'Where did you find it?' he said. 'You should have told me.'

He reached out then and put his hand on the surface. He let his fingers trace over the runes and the children waited for Vicky to tell him not to touch. She didn't.

'Are you looking for another one?' he said.

'It must exist,' said Vicky. 'Somewhere.'

Caspar turned and looked up at her. He went to speak, then thought better of it and looked back at the stones. He touched them both and shook his head.

'What's wrong?' said Asilah.

'I know where the missing bit is,' he said, simply. 'It's in the South Tower – where my gran lives. I climbed up there, about two weeks ago, when I was escaping. You know where the roof's pointed? You have to crawl right up . . . there's all sorts of things up there. But right at the top, where the weathercock sticks, that's where the rest of this stone is.'

He looked around the group.

'I'm not lying!' he cried. 'I've seen it. I've touched it.'

Doctor Ellie was at the door. She spoke very quietly. 'Are you sure, Caspar?'

'Yes.'

161

'You actually touched it?' said Sanchez.

'Why would it be in the roof of a tower?' said Eric. 'That makes no sense at all.'

'I'm telling you,' said Caspar. His face was red. 'Why do you always think I'm lying?'

'Then the last piece is the keystone of the house,' said Doctor Ellie. 'The keystone for Ribblestrop Towers. The south tower is the highest of the four, yes?'

The children nodded.

'It makes perfect sense. The builders, when they finished the south tower . . . they capped it with . . .' She licked her lips. '. . . with a stone they knew to be magical. Of course they did. They would always try to do that.'

Vicky had her hands clasped in front of her face, as if she was at prayer. 'How do we get it?' she said, softly. 'We have to get it!'

'Oh, you can't!' said Caspar. 'My gran would kill me. None of us are allowed anywhere near it.'

Everyone was looking at him.

'Forget it,' he said. 'It's not even worth thinking about! Apart from anything, it's holding up the roof . . .'

Chapter Twenty-Three

Things started to move fast.

The headmaster spoke to both Professor Worthington and Doctor Ellie, and agreed that Mr Ian's proposal regarding the Pioneers' Award was just too good to miss. Could it be combined into an ancient history project, involving the exploration of flare paths? Of course it could. He cycled into town the same afternoon and found a payphone. He got straight through to Mr Ian and the details were confirmed. They would all meet together in two weeks' time for the expedition of a lifetime.

On his way back to Ribblestrop, he was almost forced off the road by a convoy of speeding police cars. They swept past him and swerved through the school gates. He pedalled as fast as he could and was in time to see them disappear up the main drive, lights flashing. There were unpleasant interviews ahead, he knew, so it was a relief to dismount and push the bicycle quickly into the trees. Surely everything could wait until the camping trip was over? Perhaps even until the end of term? Professor Worthington had reminded him that they would all be facing court summonses in the not too distant future, but the incidents on the motorway and river now seemed in the distant past

– especially when the sky was as blue as it was that morning. The children had forgotten the chaos and were getting on with life! Surely the police would have the same, practical common sense.

'We've been caught out, sir,' said Captain Routon, as the headmaster approached the camp.

'Oh,' said the headmaster. 'Are they here?'

'They're waiting for you.'

'Oh dear.'

'I thought you'd forgotten, sir. I said I'd call them and I never did!'

Professor Worthington trotted towards them. 'It's so embarrassing,' she cried. 'The school diary's in your office, Giles, so nobody remembered! We haven't even got a pitch!'

The headmaster looked bewildered. 'Are we talking about the . . . police?'

'What police?' said Professor Worthington.

'We're talking about football, sir,' said Captain Routon. 'End of last term, we agreed to that fixture with the High School, and they've arrived. The new coach is quite disappointed.'

'Oh Lord. You mean it's today?'

'That's what we're saying.'

'We must gather the children! We can drum up a side, Routon!'

Professor Worthington was shaking her head. 'We can't,' she said. 'The children say they're too busy!'

'Oh Lord,' said the headmaster. 'We're going to look like terrible sports. And I really did want to cultivate better relations with the locals. Where are they?'

'Talking to Doonan,' said Professor Worthington. 'He's trying to sort out a cricket match instead, but nobody's interested. They're all geared up for football.'

The headmaster started walking. 'Let's go and talk,' he said. 'They used the goal nets for those wretched man-traps, didn't they? Dear, oh dear. Are they in the arena?'

'Yes, sir. It's chariot-racing till eleven.'

'This is going to be tricky . . .'

The teachers took a footpath where the trees thinned and were soon clambering down to what the children called 'The Coliseum'. The ground had been cleared with a bit of careful slash-and-burn, and there were hard tracks where the chariots had flattened the earth. It had become a popular spot for archery practice too and Miles had organised some simple gladiatorial contests.

The High School children were standing in green track-suits as one group. The Ribblestrop children were some distance away, looking sulky and irritated. The two chariots were parked where the ground was highest and the donkeys cropped the nettles.

'Now come on,' said Doonan. 'This isn't good sportsman-ship. Can we at least put the stumps in?'

It wasn't clear who he was talking to and it didn't actually seem to matter since nobody was listening. He had a bat and ball in his hands and was doing his best to work up some enthusiasm.

'I need two captains,' he shouted. 'Do we have two captains?'

One of the High School squad called an obscenity and clod of earth was flung high into the air. It burst at Doonan's feet.

'Doonan!' said the headmaster. 'This isn't going to work.'

A young teacher with large ears emerged from the High School side and trotted towards them.

'I'm very sorry about this,' he said, brightly. 'You're the headmaster, yes? I should have called you.'

165

'No, no, no – the fault is mine –'

'Easy to forget fixtures. It's no problem as far as I'm concerned.' He shook hands and smiled. 'We've had three suspensions this week, so our team's not what it should be. Johnny Jay, by the way. I'm old Cuthbertson's replacement. Trying to get things going again. Hasn't been easy, to tell you the truth.'

He grinned. 'I'm just out of college, so this is a real chance for me – bit of a learning curve too. It's so hard to get them to practise! They love playing, of course – they've been nagging me to organise matches. But can I get a decent practice? Never. Your lot look a bit . . . distracted.'

'They've been training the donkeys. They had a bit of breakthrough, yesterday, apparently.'

'Sports are taking a back seat this term,' said Professor Worthington. 'I fear you've had a wasted trip.'

'Pity,' said Johnny. 'It's the first time I've seen them enthusiastic.' He laughed. 'I've heard a lot of things about your lads. Good things, too – which one's Imagio? He's the genius, isn't he? The boys still talk about him – I was hoping to see him play.'

'The one to the right,' said Doonan. 'Sitting in the tree.'

'Some of our younger ones try to copy his moves. You wouldn't lend him to us, would you, so he could give us a demo?'

'He has renounced football,' said Captain Routon, sadly. 'I keep trying to persuade him otherwise, but –'

'Oh, look – a delegation . . .' said Johnny Jay.

The Ribblestrop teachers looked round and saw that Asilah and Sanchez had broken away from the group and were approaching. They both held spears and were bare-chested.

'We've got a suggestion, sir,' said Sanchez.

The headmaster smiled. 'That will be very welcome, Sanchez. This is Mr Jay, by the way. This is our Head Boy.'

166

'Mr Jay,' said Sanchez. 'We're really sorry about this. We're not trying to be rude. It's not that we don't want to . . . you know, play, it's just that we're doing other things at the moment. Next term, we'd be well up for it. What we were wondering . . .'

'It might seem a bit unfair,' said Asilah, 'as you're not prepared, but there's nothing to it, really. And the donkeys are much easier.'

'Easier . . . ?' said the headmaster.

'We know how to make them pull the chariots. So, what we were thinking – you know, just as a friendly – was what about a chariot race? Two teams, two chariots.'

'Wow,' said Johnny Jay.

'You can choose which one you want,' said Sanchez. 'You can choose donkeys, too. So, you know, we wouldn't have that much of an advantage.'

'A real chariot race?' said Johnny. 'Here and now? In the woods?'

Doonan said, 'It's a marvellous idea! There was a lot of bad-blood last term, Mr Jay. It might help to do something a little more lighthearted.'

'We don't have much of a course, though, do we?' said the headmaster. 'I mean, would you just go round in circles?'

'We could make a course, sir,' said Captain Routon. 'Couldn't we? Maybe incorporate a bit of javelin work – do you have javelin throwers, Johnny?'

'We do athletics every Wednesday. It's not popular, but they might give it a go. Let me consult.' He grinned. 'It's an imaginative idea – it might be just the solution. Give me five minutes.'

Five minutes later, he was back, with two tracksuited High School boys.

'This is Robbie, who's taken over as captain. Robbie, tell these boys what you just told me.'

'We're up for it,' said the boy. 'We've not done it before, but if you, kind of . . . you know, show us where things are. We don't say no, do we, Alex?'

'We'll give it a go,' said Alex. 'Could be a laugh.'

Chapter Twenty-Four

The two schools came together and there were awkward introductions.

The Ribblestrop children remembered the High School footballers all too well, for though they'd won the last football match, it had been on blood-soaked turf. Hands were shaken and names exchanged, and it was Doonan who realised that the important thing was to get everyone working. A course was decided on through the trees and out to the lawns. Miles unveiled the swords and daggers. After they'd been admired, the bramble-clearing began. An hour later, they had a good, wide track and the High School chose Robbie as their driver. Sanjay showed him how to steer and it was agreed that he and his team could have the rest of the morning to practise. The Ribblestrop children, meanwhile, would devise the various challenges, hazards and tests that would add a little spice to the competition.

The headmaster rushed off to organise light refreshments and by noon everything was ready. Both teams walked the trail together and agreed it was fair. When they returned to the starting gate the very air crackled with tension. Even the donkeys seemed aware that an important event was about to take place and were twitching nervously.

How had they been persuaded to work? It had been Eric's idea. He'd realised that the spears were ineffective, as well as cruel, and he'd mixed rum into their mash. Hours later, one sniff of alcohol and the beasts would do anything. There was now a bottle sitting in the back of each chariot.

The teams piled into the chariots and the drivers took the reins.

'We'll be timing you,' said Johnny Jay, 'but let's be clear. It's first past the post – simple as that. You take any route on the lawns, as long as you take the three challenges. Is that right, Captain Routon?'

'Absolutely, sir. Wall of fire is the first. Severed heads is the second. Finish up with Catch the Slave Boy. Where are the slaves?'

Nikko stepped forward and so did the smallest of the High School. They grinned shyly at each other and limbered up.

'High School has to catch Nikko, here. Ribblestrop, you've got to catch . . . what's your name, son?'

'Barney.'

'You've got to catch Barney. And there's no hiding up trees, boys, you stay on the open plain between the woods and the house. That's clear, isn't it?'

Nikko and Barney nodded and shook hands. At a nod from Captain Routon, they sprinted off together and were soon out of sight.

'Charioteers?' cried Routon. 'Are you ready? You need to get back here, fast as you can, with your prisoner and six heads. Are there any questions?'

There weren't.

'On your marks, then. Get set.' He nodded at Johnny Jay, who blew a long blast on his whistle. The teachers shouted,

'Go!' and the donkeys leapt like racehorses. Muscles straining, they hauled the two chariots forward and, as the ground sloped down, they picked up speed at once. The howls were deafening and the wooden carts creaked and plunged over ruts and roots. When it came to an uphill stretch, the teams jumped down and pushed. Here, Henry seemed to have the advantage because of his strength and size, but the High School boys were, on average, bigger than their opposition and they worked together well. The two chariots crashed through the woods side by side and it was obvious that it was going to be neck and neck.

Nikko and Barney had reached the lawn. They stuck together and made for the straw archway that Professor Worthington had thrown together with the older orphans. She was still putting the finishing touches to it and it stank of petrol.

'I'd stand back a bit, Nikko,' said Professor Worthington. 'It's going to go up like a bomb. You'll need to split up, as well.'

'Are they going to hurt us, miss?' said Barney, the High School boy.

'I doubt it.'

'They won't tie us up or anything? Or use the spears?'

'Well, you're a runaway slave, so you've got to expect to be restrained. My advice is once they've got you, don't resist.'

'I'm going to keep moving,' said Nikko. 'I'm not making it easy for them.'

'Yes. You'd better run fast, though. Here they come . . .'

There was a burst of cheering from the edge of the wood and the two chariots lumbered out of the trees. The donkeys were loving it – they had their heads down and their ears were swept back. The chariots were packed and the children were waving their weapons. The High School driver – Robbie – was clearly a natural and as they made for the archway he barged his chariot against the Ribblestrop vehicle, so it veered off course. As if the High School donkey sensed the advantage, its trot turned to a gallop and it forged ahead. The Ribblestrop team were lost in confusion.

Professor Worthington lit the fuse to the straw and ran for cover. There was a flash of light and in an instant the whole archway was ablaze, pouring thick black smoke into the sky. The High School donkey didn't even flinch. Its driver kept it straight as an arrow and seconds later the chariot plunged through the opening.

Twelve cabbages had been positioned on the other side of it – these were the 'severed heads' Captain Routon had referred to. The High School boys started to spear them, or try to – for it was a very difficult task on the move. Ribblestrop was gaining and there were now three orphans on their donkey's back, urging her on. Henry was pushing from behind and they were picking up speed. Their circus training was beginning to tell, for leaping on and off was second nature. As they came through the blazing arch, Eric hauled the reins back so hard that the chariot turned in a breathtaking skid. It fish-tailed just as he'd hoped and caught the High School chariot broadside, knocking it clean over. The High School boys tumbled onto the grass, in a knot of limbs. Some were winded and they wasted a precious half-minute righting the chariot. Again, Ribblestrop had the advantage, for Anjoli, Podma, Miles and Vijay had spent hours practising with spears. They soon had six cabbages on the floor of the chariot and could now attend to the final challenge: the capture of the fleeing slave.

Young Barney was jogging towards the main house and was wondering if he should just give up and let them take him. His mind was made up when he looked behind and saw the chariot steaming up to the driveway in a cloud of dust. There was a small boy standing on the back of the donkey drawing a bow and, as Barney swerved to the right, he felt the swish of an arrow over his shoulder. It drew a line of rope, clearly designed to entangle him. He jumped over it and sprinted away in sheer, undiluted terror.

The screams of his pursuers turned to a ferocious baying. This produced a surge of adrenalin and the boy made for the lake. Nikko passed the other way, for the High School chariot was now after him, and the two chariots crossed, the children trading blows as the vehicles grazed each other.

Again, Ribblestrop had the advantage.

Israel and Sam were the masters of the sling-shot and they were standing on the side of their chariot, legs held by a dozen hands. Little Barney was tiring and panicking. He was up to his knees in water, hoping the chariot wouldn't venture into the lake. Now he could hear it churning up the water and he was gasping with exhaustion. His one hope was to get to the bridge that looped over to the first island. It was a forlorn hope, however, for the chariot was at his heels. He decided to dive, but Sam loosed his weapon and the length of rope wrapped itself round his knees. He fell, splashing and gulping water. Then strong arms lifted him and he was suddenly safe amongst the hot bodies of the Ribblestrop boys.

'You all right?' said someone in his ear.

'Yes!'

'Nothing broken?'

They were shaking him and checking him for wounds. He felt an arm round his shoulders and he realised that he'd had the most exciting experience of his life. As the team screamed in triumph, he screamed too, and the donkey veered back towards the woods.

*   *   *

Nikko had been caught, too.

He had made the mistake of keeping to the drive, thinking he could move faster. The High School chariot had simply borne down on him and, when he'd dodged right, two sprinters had come for him and lifted him into the air. Then he'd been flung like a rugby ball into the back of the chariot and he too was howling with delight as they made for the finishing post. The Ribblestrop vehicle was drawing near and again it was close. They plunged amongst the trees together and it was a question of who was lucky enough to get the clearest passage through. The High School team was stronger, for Henry was tiring. They lifted their chariot over all obstacles, whilst Ribblestrop got tangled in brush. Asilah, Sanchez, Tomaz and Imagio were all on the ground pushing and heaving, but as they came within sight of the finishing line, the main axle simply snapped in half and the chariot was immovable. Ribblestrop watched in disbelief as they were beaten at their own game.

The High School pushed on, skidding down the slope towards the waiting teachers. Their captain leant out and touched the tree they'd started from, and applause, then cheering and finally laughter, rang through the forest. For the first time, High School boys and Ribblestrop children embraced, before they collapsed together on the ground.

'I enjoyed that,' said Johnny Jay at sundown. 'That was an education for me and we must do it again.'

The headmaster nodded. 'Your boys are very resourceful.'

'You ought to join us on the moor,' said Captain Routon. 'Do you do the Pioneers' Award?'

'Never heard of it.'

'It might be too short notice, now, but we'd love to have you with us,' said Captain Routon.

'Let me give you a map,' said the headmaster. 'It shows you where we're going.'

Johnny Jay was nodding. 'I'm always keen to try new things,' he said. 'I think the kids will be too, after this. They've made new friends – listen to them!'

The children were high above in the tree houses, eating and drinking. The teachers could hear excited chatter floating down through the leaves.

Johnny Jay studied the map. 'I know this area,' he said. 'I used to go mountain biking round there – it's fantastic. Would your lot be interested in a bit of cycling?'

'I expect so,' said Captain Routon.

'It's a passion of mine. Let me get back to you, I'm sure I could arrange it.'

'We've got the bikes,' said Doonan. 'Let's keep in touch.'

'Definitely. You're heading towards Lightning Tor, by the look of it. It's closed off, unfortunately – I'd love to take my lot up there. I've always wanted to see it.'

Chapter Twenty-Five

Lady Vyner watched the chariot race from her window.

She watched the wheels carve ruts in the lawn. She watched the archway burn out and collapse, and she watched everyone disappear back into the woods. Once again she noticed smoke rising from what had to be cooking fires. She trembled with rage.

'Cuthbertson,' she said, when he picked up his phone, 'how much do I have to pay you to rid me of these . . . hooligans? Close the door!'

'What? Who is this?'

'Who do you think it is? I'm talking to Crippen for a moment – wait. I can't hear myself think . . .'

Lady Vyner slammed the door herself and the television set in her lounge was instantly muffled.

'I've got old women here – three of them, now – and all they do is talk. It's driving me out of my mind!'

'They're staying with you?'

'Staying here, yes! It's a nursing home now, you know that. You're part of this SSS nonsense, aren't you? Why can't you finish the job?'

'You haven't paid your bill, Lady Vyner.'

'You haven't got rid of my squatters! They've just squatted elsewhere.'

'I'm not the boss, Lady Vyner. All I know is we haven't received a penny from you and it was never part of the deal to patrol . . . how many acres are there? We'd need hundreds of men.'

'Can't you just burn them out? There must be something you can do.'

Cuthbertson lowered his voice. 'I'm working on it. Believe me.'

'What?'

'I said I'm working on it.' He paused again. 'What sum are we talking about, anyway?'

'What do you mean, "What sum?"?' I'm asking you —'

'If we did a private deal, you and me. If I made sure they packed up and left, once and for all?'

Lady Vyner was silent this time.

'Why don't you come and see me?' she said. 'Disguise yourself again and we can talk face to face.'

'I need a down payment. Nothing happens till I've seen your money.'

'I can show you cash, Cuthbertson. Cash is not the problem.'

'I'll be with you today, then.'

'No. Another inmate's on the way, delivered this evening. Come in the morning and we'll draw up a nice little contract together.' Lady Vyner laughed. 'I'm putting my faith in you. You tried to drown that little girl, didn't you? That's what we need! A bit of aggression. Can't you organise a forest fire? You know where they are, I take it?'

'I've got an eye in the sky.'

'What are you talking about?'

'An ex-pilot – air-reconnaissance.'

'Give him some napalm.'

'It might be easier just to give the police the right tip-off – get those teachers arrested.'

'Excellent! Sort out the details.'

That same evening, Lady Vyner's doorbell rang long and loud.

She was waiting, of course. The letter of introduction had dropped onto the mat the previous day. A new inmate was arriving, requiring 'special care'. Rose was the woman's name and the letter suggested she was wealthy. *Expense, not a problem* had been scrawled under an undecipherable signature and a credit card had been clipped to the paper.

She looked around for Crippen. He was asleep and not even a crack across the knees stirred him. Her coat was missing and the bell rang again. Caspar had left a spare blazer on the hook, so she yanked it over her nightdress and started down the winding staircase. The hallway was dimly lit, for every window had been covered in steel mesh. When she hauled open the main door, she was confronted by an alarming sight and it stopped her in her tracks. Two tiny adults stood either side of a giant nurse. They were pushing a battered-looking wheelchair, which contained a slumped form, dozing or unconscious. It wore a wide-brimmed hat and heavy make-up.

'Are you Lady Vyner?' piped one of the minders.

'Yes.' She looked at the letter again. 'This is Auntie Rose, is it? We don't take corpses here. She's still alive, I hope?'

Sam smiled through his disguise. He was wearing the headmaster's jacket and Doonan's pith helmet. Beside him, Vijay was wrapped in one of Professor Worthington's summer dresses.

'Oh yes,' they said together.

'It's been quite a job wheeling her here,' continued Sam. 'She's a bit sleepy, but happy to be home.' He put his lips to the old lady's ear and spoke loudly. 'We're here, Auntie Rose. You're in good hands now!'

'How are you paying?' said Lady Vyner. 'That card you sent?'

'All taken care of,' barked Vijay. 'Can we get her upstairs? It's way past her bedtime.'

Before Lady Vyner could frame a reply, the giant nurse had lifted the wheelchair past her and it was rolling down the corridor. The little adults scuttled after it and they were soon climbing the stairs.

'She'll be no trouble!' warbled Sam.

'She doesn't eat or drink,' cried Vijay. 'Where's her room?'

It took five minutes to get to Lady Vyner's apartment.

Sam felt his heart go cold, for he remembered an encounter in his first term, when he'd had to get the old woman drunk. Vijay recalled the incident halfway through the second term, when Caspar had shot her clean through the shoulder and she had slapped Captain Routon as he stemmed the blood-flow. They could see stains on the carpet and new parts of the ceiling had collapsed. Something scuttled over the rafters above and the hot water tank in the bathroom chose that moment to gulp and groan. The noise from the television was deafening.

'What a lovely lounge,' said Sam, as they nosed into it.

'It won't be for her,' said Lady Vyner. 'She's next door, in my grandson's bedroom.'

They moved on, receiving friendly nods from the elderly guests on the sofa, who were sipping tea. They passed a kitchen full of stinks and stains, and there was a smell of burning from something that had boiled dry on the stove. Whether it was food or old underwear was impossible to say. The boys had never seen Caspar's quarters before and Sam couldn't silence a sharp intake of breath as the door swung open to reveal the saddest little cell he'd ever visited. Badly-made model aircraft hung listlessly from the ceiling and there was a grainy photograph of a baby in the arms of two mournful-looking parents. They all recognised the eyes as Caspar's and remembered with a prickling of guilt that nobody had really asked about the poor boy's Easter holidays and his period of incarceration. Nor had they ever asked about what had happened to his parents and why he'd had the bad luck to be living with such a monster of a grandmother.

A grey shirt hung on a coathanger, like the ghost of the child himself. The wardrobe yawned, emptily. A jigsaw was half-done on the carpet and there was a dirty cup with one dead cockroach stuck to the bottom. A Post-it note clung to the bed-head, for the child had been counting off his days of confinement. There were two clusters of five and an extra line in wobbly biro.

'Was he here long?' said Sam.

'Who?'

'Your grandson?'

Lady Vyner smiled. 'Eleven days. I was trying to teach him gratitude, but what was the point? Children don't know the meaning of the word any more.' She poked Auntie Rose's shoulder. 'She's waking up. What do you think of the room, you?'

'L-lovely,' whispered Auntie Rose. The word stuck in her throat.

'It's got the best views in the house,' said Lady Vyner. 'So I'll be charging a supplement. We share the bathroom and Crippen serves a hot meal every Friday. I suppose you'll want to say goodbye now and get to bed?'

'Lady Vyner,' said Sam, boldly, 'may we clean up a bit, before we go? So as to help our auntie settle?'

'Clean up where?'

180

'In here. So it's all . . . nice and fresh.'

'I cleaned it yesterday. Where's the mess?'

'It is a lovely room,' piped Vijay, 'but shouldn't we . . . open the windows, perhaps? Or do a bit of dusting?'

Lady Vyner chuckled. 'You do what you want. If your standards are higher than mine, you sort it out. Put her to bed and call me when you're done. I'll give you ten minutes, then it's lights out.'

The children watched her stomp off down the landing.

'Crippen!' she called. 'Keep an eye on these people! Don't let them pilfer . . .'

As soon as the door closed, Doctor Ellie leapt up from the wheelchair and tore off her disguise.

'She's an ogre!' she cried. 'She's a disgrace!'

'Shhh!' hissed Vijay. 'We've got no time to lose. Let's get Caspar out.'

They tilted the wheelchair backwards and removed the plywood seat. Caspar Vyner was scrunched inside the recess, his knees around his ears and his fists under his chin. He emerged with his mouth wide open, gasping with pain. He was lifted onto the bed and surrounded by a ring of determined faces.

'Where exactly did you see it, dear?' said Doctor Ellie. 'Up in the roof?'

Caspar managed to nod.

'How did you get up there?' said Sam. 'Is there a hatch or a door?'

'You'd better be sure about this, Cas,' said Vijay. 'If we get caught she's likely to murder us.'

Caspar nodded again, but was too stiff to point. 'I'm sure!' he squeaked. 'I . . . got . . . through the ceiling. In the – ow! – bathroom. I was slopping out and—'

'Too risky to go that way,' said Vijay. 'We'll try through here and cut across. Give me a leg up, Hen.'

181

In fact, he hardly needed one. He was on top of the wardrobe in seconds, leaping from Henry's forearm, and Sam was right there behind him. The plaster above their heads was so old and brittle that it broke under their fingers. An army of rats ran for their lives as light broke in on the mess of the Vyner attic. It was stuffed with rotting clutter and the boys pushed through with difficulty. In less than a minute, though, they were standing upright on the rafters, hauling Caspar behind them. They all had torches and the beams cut through thick clouds of dust.

'Don't make a sound!' hissed Caspar. 'She'll hear us on her side!'

There was a whistle from below. 'Pull me up, boys!' hissed Doctor Ellie.

Sam knelt down and put his head back into the bedroom. 'I think you'd better stay down there, miss. You can make a break for the stairs, later.'

'Not on your life,' cried Doctor Ellie. She was pulling on a dark balaclava, which matched her boiler-suit. The Auntie Rose disguise was on the bed. 'You're a thoughtful boy, Samuel and I love you dearly. But I am not missing this moment – not for anything in the world.'

She got a foot onto Henry's knee and then his shoulder. He took her feet in his giant hands and pushed her up past Sam into the recess of the attic. Sam watched in awe as she ascended. Henry turned and quickly rearranged the old lady's wig on the pillow. He drew the sheet neatly up to its edge and clambered up to join his friends.

The dust was settling around them and the timbers of the roof-space were emerging from the gloom. They were in a witch's hat of beams and struts, all furred over with birds' nests and cobwebs. Torches in their teeth, they climbed higher, clinging with their legs. The rats still squeaked in protest and fluttering things squawked in terror, but the intruders took no notice. There was something large under the apex and they inched towards it. Minutes later, they were squashed together, hunched in the dust like bats. They trained their torches on the thing they'd come for and Doctor Ellie reached up to touch it. It was pale grey and mottled with indentations. Under the grey – for she was rubbing a patch with a trembling forefinger – it was as white as sawn ivory.

'Oh Caspar,' she said.

'What, miss?'

She couldn't go on. She gulped and tried again. 'You have made an old lady very happy. You're a beautiful boy.'

'Well done, kid,' said Vijay, quietly.

'You actually came right up here, by yourself?' asked Sam.

'I was starving! I was desperate . . .'

'You're a hero,' said Doctor Ellie. 'Pure and simple. And when I write the history of the lost tribe of Ribblemoor, there will be a special acknowledgement of your courage. This discovery will be talked about for hundreds of years. It's the missing piece, no doubt about it.'

Caspar's face turned pink under the grime. 'It was just lucky I saw it,' he said.

'History, eh?' said Doctor Ellie. She had her breath back and managed to stand. In a moment, she was running her hands right round the stone, tracing those familiar patterns of moons and suns, dots and dashes. She had her nose against them and she could feel that, of all the three pieces, this was the most perfectly preserved. 'History is often made safe by recycling,' she whispered. 'The original piece – when it was one stone, I mean – must have been broken up on purpose. The tribe may have broken it themselves, you know. Perhaps they wanted their code to remain secret forever? Perhaps they deliberately sent the pieces to the three corners of the moor, so they'd never be found and joined ... And then your ancestors discovered this one, Caspar. They dug it up and felt its magic ...' She stroked the surface again. 'They must have sensed the charge – that crackle of energy, deep as magnetism. "Where shall we put it?" said the one who found it. "How can we utilise this force?" And someone must have said ...'

'"The tower,"' hissed Caspar. '"We'll put it in the tower."'

'Like a lodestone. Like a lucky-charm. Like the lamp of a lighthouse.'

There was a respectful silence.

'And it's been shining ever since, boys.'

'Miss,' said Sam. 'I think we'd better get it down. Do you think Miles is ready?'

'He'd better be,' said Vijay. 'We can't do anything without him.' He turned to Henry. 'Do the roof, Hen. Quiet as you can.'

Chapter Twenty-Six

Timmy Fox saw the hatch in the roof open.

He was making another recce at that very moment, taking photographs from a new angle. By extraordinary coincidence, he was glancing at the south tower just as Henry's powerful arm emerged, and he soon had it in his viewfinder. Henry's head appeared next and, in a moment, the boy had twisted around and was pulling off roof-slates. He passed them back inside and, in less than five minutes, the top of the tower was stripped. The pilot could just make out the five figures gathered under the rafters.

He tapped a number into his phone.

'Foxter here,' he said, when Cuthbertson answered. 'Strange goings-on at Ribblestrop. Thought you ought to know.'

'What can you see? Where are you?'

'I can see . . . Hang on. Development: there are children crossing the lawn. I need to get lower.'

'No you don't. You're paid for reconnaissance only. What can you see?' Cuthbertson's voice was tense.

'They're all carrying equipment . . .'

'What are they doing, Foxy? You said something strange . . .'

'There's a little gang of them clambering out of the tower roof. There's another band down on the ground with . . . it looks like ropes and pulleys.'

'Take photos. We're not going in.'

'There's a fair-haired boy. It's him, Cuthbertson!'

'Who?'

'The one who gave me the gobstopper!'

'I don't care about that! What's he doing?'

'He's got a bow and arrow, the blighter. He's aiming upwards.'

'Stay out of range!'

'There's a string attached. He's signalling to the ones on the roof. What on earth are they up to?'

Henry was now perched on the tip of the roof and was pulling at the Ribblestrop weathercock. Sam, Caspar and Vijay were close by, a little lower. It was a big golden bird and it was cemented onto the topmost point of the tower. Lumps of masonry were soon falling and in another moment the thing was teetering madly. Henry dropped it to Caspar and Vijay, who stowed it safely. The great white stone was now exposed, like a worn tooth awaiting extraction.

Sam gave Miles a confident wave and his first arrow soared upwards, carrying thirty metres of fine thread. The tip was blunted of course, so when it bounced off Henry's back it did no damage. Sam caught it and started to pull. The thread drew a line of string and the string drew a line of rope. The rope was tied to a cable, and Doctor Ellie helped pull so that in a short time they had a block and tackle in their hands. Henry wrenched the rafters back and put his arms round the stone. It was huge and it was heavy, but they'd lifted more awkward loads in their time. Vijay slung a rope round it and used a train-coupling knot he'd discovered in a library book. It was a knot that, once tight, could draw railway carriages, and he linked it to the cable with a steel clasp Eric had forged for the purpose. Henry took the strain over his back and Doctor Ellie watched her prize topple from its nest. It sank slowly towards the ground.

Miles, Asilah and Eric let it down carefully. Then, as soon as it touched the courtyard, Sam slid after it. Doctor Ellie followed his lead and Asilah was there to receive her as she stepped onto the courtyard. She was drunk on adrenalin.

'Hurry,' said Miles. 'If the old crow looks out the window—'

'She'll be pissed by now,' said Caspar, who had jumped the last five metres, and rolled paratrooper-style in the gravel. 'She'll be off her face.'

'Even so,' said Asilah. 'Let's get back to the camp. You did well, guys.'

'We'll have to leave the pulley,' said Eric, and he hauled the ropes through. Then he smiled. 'What's going to happen when it rains?'

'What do you mean?'

'You've taken half the roof off. Her flat's going to get flooded.'

'Good,' said Caspar. 'Let's hope she drowns.'

'What about Auntie Rose?' said Doctor Ellie, starting to laugh. 'What will your gran say when she sees that Rose isn't there any more?'

'She'll think she's dead,' said Sam, grinning. 'She won't realise for days!'

'Look,' said Miles. 'There's that balloon again. Shall we give them a wave?'

Everyone looked up and waved joyfully. Doctor Ellie was laughing hard and knew she was slightly hysterical. She looked at the precious stone and closed her eyes. She said a quick, silent prayer, thanking God for the ingenuity of children, and gave the thing a quick hug. Henry plucked it up and balanced it on his shoulder.

They crossed the lawns together, as fast as they could. Caspar was twirling and dancing, and Vijay was singing. The balloon rose higher – they could just see a burst of flame as the pilot lit the gas. It became a dot, high above the earth, and they forgot all about it. They reached the camp in time for supper and the headmaster brought his car as close as he could, so the stone could be taken, at once, to the safety of the Ribblestrop Museum.

Chapter Twenty-Seven

Ex-Inspector Cuthbertson called a high-level strategy meeting the very next day. The venue was his ice-cream van, which he'd driven onto to the edge of Ribblemoor. Its freezers had been stripped out and there was now a bank of storage lockers and radio equipment. Photographs of the Ribblestrop children were taped around the walls; the face of Andreas Sanchez was circled in red. Timmy Fox and Mr Ian squashed themselves onto stools as the wind howled across the wilderness and rattled the windows.

'Update me,' said Cuthbertson.

'We've agreed base camp,' said Mr Ian. 'It's a car park beside Flashing Tor, and we've agreed the date, as well. We'll be camping there next Tuesday and pushing forward the next day.'

'Outward bound?' said Timmy. 'What's the plan, exactly?'

Cuthbertson met his gaze. 'As far as you're concerned, it's flying a balloon in difficult weather conditions. We've got a job to do and you're going to be our eyes.'

'Right-o. I'll warn you now, though, there's always storms over Ribblemoor, and—'

'Can you fly, or can't you?'

'The Fox can fly anything,' said Timmy. 'All I'm saying is it won't be easy.'

Cuthbertson turned to Mr Ian. 'What if they postpone because of bad weather? Is that possible?'

Mr Ian snorted. 'They won't even check. They've left all the organisation to me and I've told them next week is clear and sunny. I've put them into groups – and the Sanchez boy's one of five. When it gets stormy, I'll get my lot back to base-camp. The Ribblestrop teams will probably lose themselves and they'll be well away from their teachers.'

'Hang on,' said Cuthbertson. 'If you take The Priory kids off, they'll do the same – they'd be fools not to.'

'They won't know what I'm doing. Communication's going to break down.'

'When do the two schools come together?'

'I don't know, exactly – sometime in the evening. We'll arrive by minibus. The Ribblestrop lot are arriving by . . . chariot. They said they'd be taking an "unorthodox route".'

'They are pretty unorthodox,' said Timmy.

'It's this history project,' said Mr Ian. 'Something about "flare paths" – they've got it into their heads that they can follow some of the old pathways, so they want to navigate independently. I didn't understand much of it.'

'This is the doctor, is it? Doctor Ellie?' asked Cuthbertson.

Mr Ian nodded.

'Will she be with them?'

'I don't know.'

'Have you spoken to her, Ian? Have you picked her brains?'

'Not yet.' He paused. 'Look, Cuthbertson, she can't stand the sight of me.'

'Few people can, lad, but that's not going to stop us. I want you to get on friendly terms with that woman. Set up a meeting, do you understand me? Take your lot to the crackpot museum and get her to do a lecture. Foxy, I want you out over Flashing Tor tomorrow, getting used to the wind. I want up-to-the-minute coverage by radio. Soon as they're clear of their teachers, we do the deed.'

'What deed?' said Timmy Fox.

Cuthbertson stared at him.

'I do need information,' said Timmy. 'The Foxter's part of the team now – he needs to know the plan.'

The ex-policeman reached up to the side of the van and plucked some of the photographs. He set them on the table and turned them so the Fox could see faces. 'These are our targets,' he said. 'That's Anjoli, all right? Small but wiry and violent. I've seen him in action and he's a menace. Miles, you know – Ian's going to deal with him. Vijay's another little beast, dangerous as the rest of them. Millie . . .' His finger lingered on her nose. 'She's the one I'll be looking after. We have scores to settle. You understand me?'

Timmy Fox swallowed. 'Look here,' he said. 'I'm not fond of the little beggars, obviously, but—'

'That's the one we're really after,' cut in Cuthbertson. 'Andreas Sanchez. That's the one we lift, because he's the golden ticket. Son of a Columbian and rich as Croesus. Believe me . . . if we ask a sensible price, it will be wired to us at once. He was kidnapped before and his father will be desperate. We wait for the money, then fly off into the sunset.'

The men were silent.

'So where do I send them?' said Mr Ian. 'We're meeting at Flashing Tor. Have you chosen the finishing post?'

'Oh yes.'

'Where? I'm going to need to set the co-ordinates.'

'I've chosen the perfect spot. I think the best thing is if I show it to you.'

Cuthbertson struggled into the driving seat and started the engine.

The road he took wound upwards into a range of sharp, grey peaks, and the wind got stronger. He turned right over a cattle grid and was soon lurching down an unmade road. He passed a notice saying *Strictly Private*, and squeezed between two enormous *Stop!* signs. Minutes later, the road was good again and they were rolling over a wide plain of scrubland and broken rock.

Mr Ian looked anxious. 'Cuthbertson,' he said, 'this is pure wilderness. They'll be lost for days.'

'This is Boundary One.'

They came to a wire fence. It stretched long and high and there were rubber claws fixing high-voltage cables all along it. *Keep Out!* said a blood-red notice. *Ministry of Defence Property. You Have Been Warned.*

'This is the way to Lightning Tor,' whispered Mr Ian.

'Correct.'

'This is totally off-limits. The public can't come here!'

'It's been decommissioned. Nobody knows but, as of yesterday, Lightning Tor is undefended and accessible. The army's packed up and gone – almost. So guess who's looking after it.'

'Looking after it? I don't –'

'While the ministry boys are sorting things out. You've got to have some kind of presence.'

'You,' said Timmy Fox. 'Stillwater Security Systems!'

'These are my men,' said Cuthbertson. 'Lazy and thick, every one of them. Hand-picked!'

A young guard was hauling open a gate and Cuthbertson saluted.

'You can't see Lightning Tor yet,' he said. 'It's up in that cloud. The road's a bit steep here, so hold tight . . .'

They drove on for another kilometre and were soon surrounded by angry shards of granite. There was no colour anywhere and the wind nagged at the vehicle, rocking it from side to side. Cuthbertson stopped.

'Listen,' he said. 'In a few weeks' time, the bulldozers arrive. There's silver deposits round here going down for miles and there's going to be quarrying.' He grinned. 'We're expecting protesters, of course. Always a few loonies trying to stop progress. So the deal is we're going to blow up the whole site.'

'Who?' said Timmy Fox. 'Who's going to blow it up?'

'The army's laying the explosives. Should be ready by Friday.'

'And you're going to detonate . . .?' said Mr Ian.

'When it's safe to do so. Yes. Do you want to see Lightning Tor?'

'You're going to bring the children here?'

'Everyone wants to see Lightning Tor, don't they? It's a special place.'

He let in the clutch and inched the van forward again. They curled left under a black shoulder of rock and passed a series of long, low sheds. The windows were boarded up and there were padlocks on the doors. Beyond that was a radio mast, bristling with antennae. They came to another gate, wrapped in razor wire, and a squall of rain splattered over the windscreen. The road dwindled into grass and gravel and it rose up sharply towards a misty cliff. Cuthbertson shifted into first gear and rolled forward. Almost at once, they were enveloped in cloud.

'Cuthbertson,' cried Timmy Fox. 'You can't see the road!'

'Don't worry.'

'Let's stop here!'

'I've been here before. Stop panicking.'

The tyres were slipping now and the engine was scream-ing. The ex-policeman revved harder and they were suddenly rising, swaying wildly from side to side. Timmy Fox let out a groan of terror and there was another flurry of drenching rain, hammering at the roof. Then, the cloud lifted and the whole of Ribblemoor seemed to spin around them. They were halfway up a crag, clinging to bare rock, and an enormous skull and crossbones was hanging close to their bonnet.

Danger of Death! said the sign. *Lightning Tor. Do Not Proceed.*

'Cuthbertson,' said Mr Ian. 'This is madness.'

'Now we have to walk.'

'You can't expect the children to come here!'

'Yes I can.'

'But the fences! The gates!'

'Everything will be unlocked. I'm organising it.' He turned and smiled. 'They'll think it's the most exciting place they've ever been. You know children. And we'll be waiting for them, Timmy, won't we? We'll be up there at the top, all ready for action. Now, come and see the best bit . . .'

It was hard to get the doors of the van open, for the wind seemed to be piling straight down on top of them. Cuthbertson dragged himself out and bent low. He pulled the hood of his coat up and staggered along a narrow path. Mr Ian followed him and Timmy Fox came last. Minutes later, they were forcing themselves through a narrow gulley. That's when they saw, rising above them, the snout of the volcano. It appeared and disappeared, for the clouds were caught in a vortex around it. Overhead, giant birds were wheeling, shrieking with rage.

'Up!' shouted Cuthbertson.

He led the way to a set of stairs carved into the rock. A metal rail enabled them to haul themselves upwards. They came, at last, to a narrow wooden bridge.

'My God,' shouted Timmy. 'This is impossible!'

They could look down, now, over the edge of the crater. The birds were everywhere and they could see where they'd come from: the crater was full of ancient, twisted trees – it was a forest, protected by walls of granite. The little bridge crossed just above the tops of foliage and ran to a central column on which sat a concrete bunker, under another enormous radio mast.

'What's down there?' cried Mr Ian. He was clinging to the side of the bridge, white-faced.

Cuthbertson put his mouth to the man's ear. 'The centre of the earth!' he roared. 'Now come and meet my brother.'

'What brother?'

Cuthbertson pointed to the top of the mast. 'He hates those kids as much as I do. He's in the control room, sorting out our equipment. And Timmy!' he shouted, gripping the man's shoulder. 'That's where we need the balloon. That's our launch pad – top of the aerial!'

Chapter Twenty-Eight

Meanwhile, the children were smelting.

They had been hard at work all morning, so they stank of charcoal and burnt metal. The furnaces had risen to a thousand degrees and they'd watched iron liquefy. They had guided it down earth channels into moulds; then they'd struck those moulds open so the axe-heads inside dropped hissing and glowing, like meteors. Their eyes were dreamy at the wonder of it, for this was real magic – the magic of the elements.

They showered in a nearby waterfall and lunched on nut roast – then they were ready for Captain Routon's briefing. Everyone knew that some kind of trek was being planned, and the word 'pioneers' had been whispered in many corners. But the details were still secret. Today all would be revealed. They met in the roundhouse, where Doctor Ellie had pinned an enormous map.

It was surrounded by flaming torches.

'This, my dears, is us,' said Routon, pointing to a cross. 'Just by the stream.'

'Sir,' said Miles. 'I'm not being funny, but isn't that chart a bit old?'

'It's very old. 1938.'

'If we're going into the wilds,' said Millie, 'we ought to have a modern one.'

'I don't know about that. Rocks and rivers don't really change, do they? I got this from the auction house, yesterday. All kinds of things coming in at the moment – a lot of it army surplus. They've just closed one of those old bases.'

'Is that where these came from?' said Vijay. He was holding the receiver of an antique-looking field radio. In a crate nearby there were rucksacks, helmets and battery packs.

'They were almost giving it away,' said Routon. 'I thought it might come in handy.'

Oli's eyes lit up and he crept forward.

'Look at it later,' said Ruskin. 'Let's find out where we're going.'

'Are we going up mountains?' said Eric. 'Is this for the flare path project?'

'Yes,' said Doctor Ellie. 'It's a combination of survival and archeological exploration, so it's going to test you to the limit. The mountains are actually known as tors, by the way. They're all over the moor and our tribe would have known every inch. They're volcanoes. Three hundred million years old.'

Captain Routon explained the proposed route in hushed silence. They would start soon, for Mr Ian was keen to get moving. They'd leave at dawn and follow what Doctor Ellie believed to be the first flare path. If they could trace it, it would lead them through farms, into the wilderness of the open moor. They would travel for a full day and meet up with the children of The Priory. That's when the competition would start.

Doctor Ellie pinned up the team lists.

They would be in small groups, fanning out across the valley. Each team would be making for a different destination, as it was a test of orienteering. They would have maps and a compass and, when they'd reached their first stop, they'd have to solve a simple riddle. This would allow them to locate Mr Ian's concealed boxes, in which they'd find the co-ordinates for the finishing post.

The winning team would receive the Pioneers' Award.

The children burst into spontaneous applause and instantly set about organising kit-lists.

'How many nights, sir?' said Israel. 'How long are we actually out on our own?'

'Just two,' said Routon. 'I was hoping for longer, but as it's your first outing, we're taking it easy.'

'So we live as the tribe did!' said Ruskin. 'We'll actually be the tribe, crossing the moor!'

'That's the idea,' said Doctor Ellie.

'Where do we end up?' said Millie. 'We meet up at the end, right?'

'Mr Ian's choosing the final destination,' said Captain Routon. 'It's a very closely guarded secret – not even I know where it's going to be at the moment. But I'm sure he'll choose somewhere interesting.'

Sanchez found Millie later that evening. She was feeding the camel and he stood watching, uncertain and nervous.

'How are you?' he said, awkwardly.

'Fine.'

'Do you need a hand?'

'She's off her mash. She knows we're leaving.'

'Isn't she coming?'

'Only two chariots, Sanchez. What's she going to do? You're feeling useless and rejected, aren't you, baby?'

'How can she know?'

'Sixth sense, I guess. Some creatures are very sensitive.'

Sanchez looked at her and she raised her eyebrows.

'Have I done something wrong, by the way? Are you here to lecture me about something?'

'Of course not.'

'Well, I'm going to take her down to the lake, so you can come with me if you want. Can you limp that far?'

Sanchez swallowed the insult and helped her open the paddock gate. He had learnt not to let Millie's belligerence provoke him. They had ridden horses together through Colombian coffee plantations. They had slept in the same tent up in the snowline and watched shooting stars. He could never understand how a friendship as close as theirs slipped so easily back into confrontation.

Millie led the animal through the woods. By the time they got to the water, the sun was low and the school building was golden again. Neptune reclined, gazing up at the sky. His face was as inscrutable as ever, though Anjoli had said it was just the bug-eyed look of constipation.

'Come on, then,' said Millie, as the camel lapped. 'What do you want to talk about?'

Sanchez decided to be frank. 'Okay,' he said. 'I'm worried.'

'What's worrying you?'

'I'm worried that we hardly ever talk now and things are happening too fast. Do you think we're ready for the expedition?'

'Yes. I think we're ready for anything.'

'What if something goes wrong? The last thing we want is for us to get lost. If we get lost, the police will get involved – they were here the other day. I heard the headmaster and he was saying they're still going to make a prosecution – they're just getting it ready. There's going to be a summons and—'

'When did he tell you this?'

'He didn't.' Sanchez looked embarrassed. 'He was talking to Professor Worthington and I kind of . . . overheard.'

'Spying, Sanchez. That's bad.'

'If they all get prosecuted, it will mean the end of the school. They could be arrested again and that means we all get split up. What would the orphans do?'

'I don't know.'

'Things are getting dangerous.'

Millie looked at him. His eyes were full of tears.

'What's on your mind, Sanchez? What are you thinking?'

'I've just got a bad feeling about the future. I think there are . . . omens. And I'm frightened.'

'Omens?'

'Yes.'

Millie smiled. 'It's usually the other way round, isn't? I'm usually the one warning you.'

'Have you spoken to Tomaz?'

'Yes,' said Millie. 'Have you? He thinks you've been avoiding him.'

Sanchez blushed. 'I have been – I admit it. But I spoke to him this morning.'

'Have you spoken to Miles? Sanjay? Asilah?'

'Yes, I've spoken to them all. But . . . you're going to think this is silly. I thought I was the only one. That's why I said nothing.'

'The only one?'

'Getting visits. Hearing things.'

Millie was silent for a moment. Then she spoke, firmly. 'Maybe you sleep deeper than most people, Sanchez. But everyone sees them – just in the corner of their eye . . . they're just shapes at the moment. Tomaz lived with a ghost, don't forget. He's sensitive that way and he says they're all around the tree houses – he's been saying it from the start. Miles is sure as well. They hear stuff and they get given stuff. And I believe them.'

'I was woken up last night. I received a gift.'

'Are you talking about feathers?'

'No. I know people keep finding feathers, but I was thinking so what? There are birds in the trees. There's nothing special about feathers. What I found was . . . can I show it to you?'

He slipped his hand into his pocket.

'I was given it last night. By a child.'

Sanchez opened his hand and revealed a flat stone. It was a cream colour and had been chipped sharp around the edges. There was a web of strange, rusty orange over the surface, fine as thread. Millie took it and stared. She saw that along one side there was a ridge, like the backbone of some creature. From the backbone, on either side, little ribs formed the pattern of a feather, or a fish.

'It's a fossil,' said Millie. 'You're saying someone put it in your pocket?'

Sanchez said, 'It's got a hole in it – can you see? It's like the one in the museum, I don't know if you saw it. I was hearing wind in the branches, like we all do. There's leaves moving all the time, but I was lying awake and there was Miles on one side of me, Eric on the other. The tree house was moving, of course – we're used to that. But I felt someone sitting right by me, close to my shoulder. I heard him laugh and I . . .'

'What?'

'He touched my hair.' Sanchez paused. He was flushed. 'I had my eyes open. I was not asleep, but everyone else was. I swear it. I was wide awake and when I looked . . . there was nothing, obviously. Just the laughter again. Not mean laughter – not spooky, even, just . . . playing laughter and a hand pressed me. Just here.' Sanchez touched his chest. 'I sat right up and the next morning I find this under my pillow. A gift.'

'You think it was a ghost?' said Millie.

'I know it was a ghost. I know it. And what I want to know, Millie, was what you saw in the museum that made you so upset. You know, when we were standing round the urn with the little baby inside – Eleudin. What did you see that made you crack up like that?'

'I don't know.'

'Was it just the fact it was a skeleton? Did it scare you?'

Millie looked hard into his eyes. 'No,' she said. 'It didn't scare me at all. What's scary about it?' She paused. 'Look . . . this is really hard to put into words, but I was . . . staring, like everyone else. And the glass . . . you know how you see reflections, so you see yourself? We were all standing around him and it was just that, for a moment, for a second, the glass wasn't there and I saw us. It was our child and he was one of us. We were gathered round him and it was us putting the thread round his wrists and feet and . . . do you remember? She told us they even had earrings for him and he had long hair. We were there with him, like they must have been. He was one of ours. All we wanted was for him to get to heaven and I thought, *Poor baby. Poor us, grieving for him.* It's not them, it's us – we're no different. History's about studying ourselves.'

Sanchez nodded. A tear rolled down his cheek.

'I showed the fossil to Asilah,' he said. His voice was shaking. 'He said he has one. He said Nikko has one too and Nikko found it in his pocket. Just a little one, but sharp as a razor.'

'What does it mean?'

'I don't know, but they're all around us! I showed mine to Doctor Ellie and she said it's a protective thing to ward off . . . whatever's out there. So I don't think we should go out on the moor. I think something really bad's coming.'

Millie touched him gently on the shoulder. 'I know it,'

she said. 'I'm sure you're right and everyone feels it. But whatever's coming is going to find us, wherever we are, isn't it? It's going to push us to the limit, because it always does.'

Sanchez sighed. 'We don't have to go! We can just stay here!'

'No we can't.'

'Tell me we're friends, please. We are friends, aren't we? You and me?'

'Yes.'

'And you think we should just wait? And see what happens?'

'Sanchez, yes. What else can we do? We stick together and we look after each other.'

Chapter Twenty-Nine

The next sensation was at the museum.

Doctor Ellie had sent a message that everyone was to meet at two o'clock on Wednesday. The children had been upgrading camp defences, for they didn't want the place spoiled in their absence. A new man-trap was dug, close to the main access trail, and camouflage had been renewed to disguise the tree houses. They would leave for the moor properly armed, so axe-heads were fitted onto hard wooden poles, which were left in water to swell and tighten. Swords and daggers were sharpened twice a day.

They decided to rest the donkeys by cycling into town, and were through the doors right on time. They piled their cloaks in a heap and those that had dared to wear their weapons – for the teachers still threatened to confiscate any they saw – remembered in time and hid them. Sanjay led everyone through to the conservatory and was stopped in his tracks. A dozen children in smart blue blazers had got there first and were sitting crosslegged in rows. They swung round at the intrusion and gazed at the Ribblestrop pupils, open-mouthed.

'Wow!' yelled Anjoli. 'There's kids here! Little 'uns!'

The children in blue could only gawp as the savages piled

in. Asilah fought his way to the front to restore order, but it was a chaotic scene.

'Hey, look who it is!' yelled Sam. 'Look at that, guys, it's Scottie!'

'There's Jacqueline!' shouted Kenji. 'What are you doing here?'

Sure enough, the two children they'd met with Mr Ian were in the group, looking as pale and bewildered as the rest.

'Hey,' said Imagio, kneeling down beside a frizzy-haired eight-year-old. 'What's with the clipboards, man?'

'Look at this!' said Israel. 'They got questions!'

'You guys doing a test?' said Eric.

'They're making notes,' shouted Vijay. 'Look at this guy's handwriting! Look!'

'That is neat,' said Imagio, squatting next to him.

Miles had pushed through, straight to Vicky. 'Miss!' he said, hugging her. 'You've started without us! Where's the stone gone?'

Vicky struggled to make herself heard above the din and fought her way out of Miles' embrace.

'Listen, please!' she cried. 'Listen! We're double-booked, I'm afraid. There's been a bit of confusion, so . . . please! It's going to be quite a squeeze. I'm sure we can do it if we're organised. Can everyone just sit down for a second?'

It was just at that moment that a voice bellowed from the hall and the glass shook in the windowframes. Even the Ribblestrop pupils were silenced and Vicky jumped as if she'd been struck. All eyes turned to the teacher, pressing through the tangle of bodies; it was, of course, Mr Ian.

'Silence, the lot of you!' he yelled. He waited for two seconds and then said in a serpent-like hiss, 'What the hell is going on? Who are these ruffians?'

'Hey, Mr Ian,' said Miles, from under his nose. 'You're looking good.'

'Better than ever,' said Anjoli.

Mr Ian changed colour. His face went pale, as if the blood was draining into his beard, and his lips twitched.

'Excuse me,' said Tomaz, from behind. 'We've got to get Henry in still. Can you move up a bit?'

'I don't understand,' said Mr Ian. 'I thought . . .'

'Oh, this is my fault!' said another voice, from even further back. 'Is that the Ribblestrop children? I'm afraid we got muddled – we get so few school groups and now we have two at the same time.' Doctor Ellie was easing herself into the room, pressed to the wall. She slid round to the front, eyes shining. 'What an absolute treat!' she cried. 'You're going to have to forgive me, Mr Ian – it's a genuine mistake. Your children can squeeze to the front, can't they? Can you move forward, dears?'

'This is intolerable . . .' said Mr Ian. 'I reconfirmed this only yesterday!'

The look of horror on his face was intensifying. He was taking in the details, now, as his eyes sprang from child to child. Sanjay was wearing multiple necklaces of stones and birds' feathers and his blazer had no sleeves. Kenji had tied his hair up in dreadlocks and was wearing nothing but shorts. Every inch of skin was painted deep red, though the red was slashed with black tiger stripes. Henry was actually breathing down Mr Ian's neck as he was led past. He wore the yellow and black of Ribblestrop and even had a tie on. He was carrying a dozen dead rabbits, though, that Sam had killed with his slingshot on the journey. They hung from a stick, tied by the feet, and The Priory children couldn't take their eyes off them.

'This is impossible,' whispered Mr Ian.

'Oh, we'll manage if we work together,' said Doctor Ellie. 'I suggest everyone sits down and Vicky finishes her introduction. The Ribblestrop children have heard it before, so they'll just have to be patient. There's the big surprise coming, don't forget. So let's get on. Anyone for juice, by the way?'

The two schools settled.

Vicky resumed her lecture, but Mr Ian was more entertaining. His expression switched from horror to hatred and then to nausea. Millie and Miles sat next to him, one on each side, and because of the limited space they were obliged to press quite close. His blue-blazered pupils scratched away at their clipboards, heads down. Each child had a cap folded neatly into their right pocket, and Anjoli removed one secretly and put it on. The boy they'd already met – Scott – noticed this and stared, blinking at the blasphemy. Then, suddenly, he grinned, and the joy in the room passed from child to child like a dangerous, silent electricity.

Mr Ian was powerless.

When Vicky invited questions, there was a forest of hands.

'Where did they get the gold?' said one boy.

Vicky explained that they had brought it with them, from far-off places.

'Why didn't they just bury their dead?' said someone else. 'I mean, why didn't they have graves, like most people?'

Israel answered this one, reminding the girl who'd asked that they were always ready to move. Ruskin said that in any case, putting someone in the earth must have seemed so rude, and it made much more sense to keep someone you were fond of close by.

A high-pitched voice then broke through the debate and the frizzy-haired boy stood up. 'What I want to know, miss,' he said, 'if you can tell me, please, because I find this ever so interesting, is where these "flare paths" actually lead to, and do you think there's any treasure at the end?'

'Harry,' hissed Mr Ian. 'Grow up and shut up.'

'It's a good question,' said Millie. 'What's wrong with that?'

'He's always asking about treasure,' said Jacqueline. 'It's a bit of an obsession.'

'Well,' said Doctor Ellie, 'it's a question that actually gets to the heart of the matter. Your name's Harry, is it? I can tell you, Harry, that there is undoubtedly treasure out on the moor. The idea that everything's been found is ludicrous. As to where the flare paths lead, well, that's harder to answer – and Vicky and I have been hoping to find out for many, many years.'

'And we're closer than we were,' said Vicky, smiling broadly.

'Much closer. Thanks to a discovery made by our resident explorer, Caspar Vyner – who's sitting at the back and deserves a round of applause. As I think you know, Caspar, the stone is now complete, thanks to your eagle-eyes.'

There was a burst of applause and Caspar turned pink.

'The flare paths lead off in different directions,' resumed Doctor Ellie. 'Tracing them has been a very difficult job, because so many stones have been uprooted and moved. The only way to really see them is to get out into the moonlight and look. But even that's not easy because they don't always shine the way you expect.'

'Why not?' said Eric. 'I thought you said they just kind of . . . glowed.'

'Not exactly. It's hard to say how they work, but my theory is that they were cut at very precise angles. The moonlight falls on the reflective side at very particular times – the moon has to be aligned in just the right way, you see.

So in other words, you can stand in the darkness looking for them and see nothing. And then, when the moon climbs into right place, they light up like someone's pulled a switch. Of course, at some point, they all go off again.'

'Have you seen that, miss?' said Imagio.

'Yes, I have. It's very moving. It's rather frustrating, too.'

'So where do they lead?' said Sam. 'Where do you go if you walk down one?'

'Well, this is the point, Samuel. We've never been able to walk down one for any distance. And when we do, it's guesswork and we tend to veer off in a wrong direction. So . . . I can't really answer the question, because I just don't know.'

'We think,' said Vicky, 'that they probably lead to a very special place. Tomaz, what's the matter?'

'Nothing, miss.'

'Are you feeling unwell?'

Tomaz put his head down and Vicky continued. 'If it is a special place . . . sorry, I've lost my thread. If the flare paths lead to a special place, then it would have to stay a secret. You wouldn't want people going there, unless they had good reason. I wonder if it's actually a sacred spot . . . some kind of graveyard, perhaps.'

'Like for that kid in the vase,' said Vijay.

'You think they would have buried them,' said Jacqueline, 'in the end?'

'In most cultures, even wandering tribes create a necropolis. That's a place for the dead – a final resting place.'

'And you think it's on Ribblemoor?' said Miles.

'It's a theory.'

Vicky took over. 'Would it be easier if we just went outside, Ellie? I'm worried about Tomaz. I think we need fresh air.'

209

'Outside where?' said Mr Ian. 'I don't want muddy shoes.'

'Can you open that door, Sanchez?' called Doctor Ellie. Everybody was on their feet. 'I think it's time we showed you the stone.'

Chapter Thirty

The conservatory doors opened onto an overgrown garden and Sanchez threw them wide.

Thirty-five children were soon pushing through long grass towards a set of crumbling steps. There had been a rain shower that morning and everyone was soon wet-footed, slipping and sliding. They climbed down past shaggy trees and sprays of bramble – the temptation to shove was over-whelming and there were shrieks of laughter. When they got to the bottom, however, a silence descended, for the last section of the garden was a curious oval shape, almost completely surrounded by an ancient wall, and it held in its centre – like a jewel – a circular fish pond.

Out of the water rose the stone, white and shining.

It was cracked in two places, but the cracks were thin, and it was obvious that the structure was now complete. The whiteness gleamed far brighter than the Ribblestrop children remembered, but what was so beautiful and extraordinary was the perfection of the stone's reflection. The water was still and black, and held the reversed image as clear and exact as a mirror. It was as if the stone had doubled itself and, when the children peered down, they saw themselves and the sky and some immediately felt dizzy, for it was like looking down into a perfectly inverted world into which you could all too easily fall.

'It was Vicky's idea,' said Doctor Ellie quietly.

'Well, not really . . .' whispered Vicky. 'It was just a suggestion, because—'

'Because we were getting nowhere,' said Doctor Ellie. 'Let's be honest, we'd been up all night with it. We'd been copying the symbols and cross-referencing every piece of text we thought might help us. Could we work it out? No, we couldn't.'

'I started to look at it upside down,' said Vicky. 'I was very tired and I think I had a line of symbols the wrong way up and they seemed to make more sense that way. So I got a mirror and we looked at it then through the mirror.'

'We saw things differently. We saw that what we'd thought were simply runes, or lines, were actually trees. We began to see fish and feathers. And the fish repeat in certain ways that we think might replicate the flare paths themselves. How good is your Ancient Celtic, Mr Ian?'

'Non-existent.'

'Are you familiar with Bede?'

'No. We don't study that period.'

'Do you study the lives of the saints? Paganism and Christianity?'

'We do twentieth century.'

'Nazis,' said a boy.

'We've been doing Nazis for three years,' said another.

'That's because they come up in the exam,' said Mr Ian. 'If you can write an essay on the Holocaust, you sail through. Even the stupid can understand Hitler.'

'Yes,' said Doctor Ellie. 'That's a comforting thought. Well, Bede was an eighth century monk who translated many texts, including some very early ones that were based on old, oral traditions. There's a fragment of an epic poem

– nobody knows where it comes from and very little exists. It's called ''Hymn to St Caspar'', and the more we looked in the mirror, the more we thought of it.'

She concentrated hard, and spoke carefully:

'When the river runs full and the valley fills,
When the fire leans to the wind in the hills:
Look not for the children, if they choose to be lost,
For the earth stays warm under summer frost.
In through the pool of the solemn-eyed,
Look not for the dead, for they have peace –
You'll find the soul of those who died,
Changed yet again, when the birds fly east.'

'But that's so similar,' said Miles, quietly. 'That's almost the same. Isn't it?'

'As what?' said Vicky.

'As the poem we know. About the sword, last term! That's got such similar words.'

'Bede said it was about one of the earliest saints, but we all know he had a habit of mucking things about to suit his purposes. St Caspar was a holy man who passed through here. According to legend, he prayed here – in this very garden.'

'Miss,' said Tomaz quietly, 'you've got to stop this now.'

Doctor Ellie laughed. 'What do you mean, Tom?'

'How do you read it, then?' said Ruskin. 'It it left to right, or –'

'Look down into the water, children. If you look hard and if you wait a moment – don't disturb the surface. Kneel down, some of you, then everyone can see. Can you see the feathers? They're carved in deeper and under them – in the reflection, I mean – can you see the flames? I think a feather might represent death, I don't know. Or possibly the soul. What's happening?'

'It's the sun, miss.'

'Wait a moment . . .'

A cloud had moved by as they were staring and the sun was suddenly brighter than it had been all morning. It was as if it leant in close and burned, hard as a searchlight. The stone flashed whiter than ever and the light caught the edges of the carvings and silvered them. Down in the water, the reflection was charged with life and the symbols of trees, or feathers, or streams, or flowers – whatever they were – stood out in columns rather than lines. For a moment they pulsed, shining in the blackness like white letters on a black page.

'Oh my God, you read downward,' said Vicky.

'They all end in feathers,' cried Doctor Ellie. 'Every column, look! Every column is a flare path and they all end in feathers. They end in the same place, perhaps . . . The necropolis, do you think? . . . Tomaz!'

Tomaz was in the water, wading to the stone.

He had jumped and the resulting splash made some of the younger children squeal. It wasn't a deep pond, so the water only came to his knees and he kicked the surface hard, from side to side, soaking Israel and two of The Priory children.

Mr Ian jumped back and roared. 'How dare you!' he yelled. 'Get out at once!'

Tomaz kicked and splashed, and it was as if he was erasing the reflection. He spun round in the water so waves destroyed the surface. Then he was the one shouting.

'What if they don't?' he cried. 'What if they don't? What if they don't?'

Sanchez jumped in after him and so did Miles. They tried to grab him, but he twisted out of their grip and fell back against the stone.

'What if they don't *want* to be found?' he panted.

214

'Look,' said Mr Ian. 'I've had just about enough!'

'Who?' said Doctor Ellie. She was moving towards Tomaz. 'Who are you talking about?'

'Tom!' said Miles. 'Calm down! This is —'

'No! No!'

Miles tried to hold him, but it was impossible.

'What right have you got?' cried Tomaz.

He was sobbing. He was soaking wet and his thin body was still pressed against the stone as if he was trying to conceal or protect it.

'Please tell me what's wrong,' said Doctor Ellie. 'I can see you're upset and I promise I —'

'You've got no right to go looking for them,' sobbed Tomaz. 'You think you can poke around and . . . what are you going to do? What if you're right? What then? Don't you understand – look at them! Look! Look up there, on the walls!'

He was gazing up at the top of the surrounding walls and everyone swung round to see what he could see. There was nothing, but Tomaz remained wild-eyed. 'They don't want to be found!' he said. 'Why is that so hard to understand? Leave them alone!'

With that, he turned and pushed with all his might, against the stone. Vicky cried out and Caspar leapt into the water to stop him. It was too late, though: the stone fell in three pieces and the water was lifted into a geyser as it fell. Tomaz walked over it, climbing out of the pond on the far side. He went across the grass, to where the wall was broken and started to climb. He was crying, openly. Miles followed and so did Imagio and Vijay. Asilah called something in his own language and everyone watched as the four of them disappeared and the disturbed water slowly settled.

Millie felt something against her cheek and grabbed at it. She saw Anjoli do the same and she saw that one of The Priory children had one too.

There were feathers in the air, blowing randomly over the pool, catching at some of the children, then rising up and soaring over the walls of the garden, out of sight.

Someone was laughing.

Chapter Thirty-One

Back at the village, the mood was sombre.

Tomaz had not returned and nor had the boys who had followed him. In the absence of the main chef, Captain Routon cooked the rabbits and, though it was a rich, wholesome stew, it was hard to swallow. The teachers usually stayed in the camp until after bedtime, but on this occasion they withdrew just as the sun went down and walked to their own camp. They had two tents pitched close to Doctor Ellie's van and would often enjoy a nightcap together under the stars.

'I wonder what's brewing,' said Professor Worthington, gazing up at Orion.

'It's been going on all week,' said Doonan. 'There's been something not quite right, but I've not been able to put my finger on it.'

'Tomaz is a deep, fragile boy,' said the headmaster. 'We've always known that, ever since he fled after that business with Miles. He's seen the rough side of life, has Tomaz. Like Imagio and Asilah. And all the orphans, of course . . .'

'And Millie and Sanchez,' said Routon.

'Yes.'

'And Henry,' said Doonan.

'Yes. All of them, really.'

'I suggest we stay well out of it and let them deal with the situation.'

'You don't think we should have a meeting?' said Doonan. 'Try and talk it out?'

'No. I don't.'

There was a silence.

'Tomaz is loved,' said the headmaster. 'If his friends can't help him, I'm quite sure his teachers can't. What was he seeing, on the walls? He saw *something*. Who's he protecting?'

The children, meanwhile, gathered in the roundhouse.

Nobody had any intention of going to bed, so they lit torches and played cards. Some decorated their weapons and one or two made jewellery out of the countless items that had been gathered during the day – the grasses and the pebbles and the drops of waste metal. It was nearly midnight before Miles came back. He stood looking at his friends, hands on hips.

'Well?' said Asilah.

'He won't talk. I think we all need to go to him.'

'Where? Where is he?'

'Up a tree. We lost him for a bit, after he ran for it. So we wasted time going down Neptune. We thought he might have gone back to his house.'

'So what did he do?' said Sam. 'Are the others with him?'

'Yes, but he won't say anything. We should have come to get you earlier, we would have found him sooner. You know the elms, up by the edge? We should have guessed.'

'I went there with him,' said Israel. 'He loves that place.'

218

'Come on,' said Miles. 'There's a pretty good moon, we won't need torches. Vijay found him and it's my hunch we need everyone.'

The children put their cloaks on and walked out of the village in single file. Now that the defences had been strengthened, they were obliged to go carefully, for there were a variety of concealed traps on the pathways and it would be unpleasant to spring them. Miles led the way and they were soon on a well-worn track that led up to the rocky outcrop known as Ribblestrop Edge. The trees thinned and the moon poured through them. Soon they were climbing up through scrub and gorse, and they saw the six great elms that dominated the skyline. Trees had meant very little to the children before the history project had begun. They were simply things that could be climbed occasionally. In the last few weeks they had learnt that every patch of forest had its own character and that a tree could be friendly, hostile, indifferent or awkward. The six elms were giants: strong, patient and benign.

'Is that where he is?' said Sanchez, gazing upwards.

'That's where he is,' said Miles. 'He's just being stubborn.'

'Has he talked to you at all?'

'You know what's wrong, Sanchez. I was talking to Millie. I know you know.'

'What can we do about it, though? I *don't* know, Miles – I'm lost.'

'What I think he wants is solidarity. If he gets solidarity, he'll come down and be normal again. Come on.'

'I'm going to need a rope ladder to get up there.'

'No you're not.'

The children gathered round the trunk of the central tree. There were lumps in the higher branches, that could have been birds' nests or clumps of leaves. Asilah called

219

something in his own language and Vijay answered with a whistle.

'You go first, Nikko,' said Asilah. 'Show us the best way.'

'I can't do this,' said Ruskin. 'I'm going to stay down here.'

'I've done it,' said Miles. 'It's not difficult.'

'Yes, but you're not frightened of anything,' said Ruskin.

'Just do it, fat boy,' said Millie. 'It's the getting down that will be harder.'

Nikko had reached the first branch even as she spoke. Sanjay was behind him, and they could see now how there were ridges, and if you fitted your hands and feet carefully, it was like a vertical staircase. Some of the bigger orphans stayed behind Ruskin and Sanchez, just in case they needed support – and Sanchez did get stuck once when he over-reached and found himself teetering backwards. A hand on his back righted him and another hand supported his heel. He was able to move on and soon he had both arms round a manageable branch. In five minutes, the tree splayed out into a multitude of easier pathways and there was little difficulty in ascending. They moved up into the leaves, clambering on and on, and soon the tree was thick with children and the breeze was whispering among them.

Tomaz had found himself a comfortable 'v' at the very top of the tree. He sat there, curled in on himself, and was soon surrounded. Nikko, who was the lightest, actually moved up above him, into a little cluster of twigs. He swayed close to Tomaz's head, and Tomaz said nothing.

'How are you feeling, Tom?' said Sanchez, at last.

Still he said nothing.

'This guy's in a sulk,' said Anjoli. 'I've met moody people, but this guy takes the prize.'

'I think he's in love,' said Miles, and a number of boys chuckled.

'You get a housepoint for soaking Mr Ian,' said Vijay. 'That was cool.'

'What upset you, Tom?' said Sam.

'We're off on the trek tomorrow,' said Sanjay. 'We should be sleeping – it's an early start.'

'I'm not going,' said Tomaz quietly.

Sanchez said, 'Not going where?'

There was a silence. 'I'm not going on the trek,' said Tomaz. 'I don't even want to talk about it.'

'What's making you angry?' said Millie. 'You might as well tell us. We're all here, listening.'

'You know as well as I do. You know what they're like, and . . .'

'This is the tribe you're talking about?'

'You heard them. Well, I've seen them, all right? And I'm telling you, it's just like what the poem says. You don't go looking for people who don't want to be found. What right do you have? I know what they're going to do – I can see it. Doctor Ellie, Vicky . . . they're going to go busting up something they don't even understand.'

'Doctor Ellie's nice,' said Oli. 'What's she breaking up?'

'Okay,' said Tomaz. He adjusted his position on the tree branch so he could look around more easily. 'You think she's nice. I'm sure she is. You think Vicky's nice, and I'm sure she is too. But they're so much into this history thing and finding stuff out and cracking open secrets that they're going to . . . They're going to do a lot of damage. What do you think they're looking for? You know what they're after – they think the flare paths are going to lead to some special, sacred place where there's going to be treasure. Bones. People. What are they going to do? You think they're going to arrive and say, "Oh, this is nice – we'd better not disturb all this!" Oh no. They're going to call in the archaeologists, the TV crews, the newspapers. They're

221

going to dig it all up and bung it in some filthy museum. Millie, didn't the little boy in the case make you feel bad? Didn't it?'

'Yes.'

'It makes me feel sick. They're going to find a whole lot more of that kind of thing and . . .' He was lost for words again. 'I'm not going to be part of that,' he said. 'If you want to go, you go. All of you. But I tell you one thing: if you go with them and do this terrible thing, then I will . . .' His voice started to crack. 'I left here once before. I can do it again, you know. I'm not staying with a bunch of people who do that to the dead by digging them up and putting them in glass cases. I thought you were all good and responsible, but I'm not living here . . . not staying here . . .' He was openly crying now and the sobs were choking him. 'I can't do it,' he spluttered. 'I just can't.'

Ruskin had a handkerchief and he passed it up to Sanjay. Sanjay got it to Anjoli who got it to Nikko and in a moment – via a stick – it was in Tomaz's hand. He dabbed his eyes and blew his nose.

Nobody said anything.

'I think you've misunderstood, Tom,' said a voice. 'I'm so sorry.'

Several boys nearly fell and the tree shook as hands clutched branches. There were gasps of disbelief.

'Vicky!' said Millie. 'What the hell are you doing here?'

'You followed us!' said Caspar.

'Well,' said Vicky, in a small voice, 'that isn't quite true. We didn't follow you, exactly. We were here anyway . . .'

'You're up a tree,' said Miles. 'You're halfway up the same tree we're up, but you didn't follow us?'

'I followed you up the tree, but we were already on the Edge. We heard you, you see, so . . . we wanted to check you were all right.'

'Who's the "we"?' said Asilah. 'Are you telling us Doctor Ellie's here, as well?'

'She's down on the ground.'

'You'd better come a bit higher, miss,' said Sanchez. 'If we're going to talk it would be easier.'

'I'll try. I haven't done this for years.'

The tree shook again and the figure of Vicky Stockinger, museum curator, emerged from the darkness and came to the upper branches. Tomaz stared at her.

'I don't know what you heard,' he said, 'but I'm not going to take anything back. I don't want to . . . offend anyone, but what you're doing is bad.'

'Tomaz,' said Vicky, 'are you the one who's been writing notes?'

There was another silence.

'What notes?' said Imagio.

'We've received three,' said Vicky gently. 'They've been delivered to the museum and they're never signed. But they're . . . they're very angry and upset notes, aren't they, Tom? They're saying that Doctor Ellie and I should leave things alone and that we have no right to do what we're doing.'

'That's what I think,' said Tomaz, in a small voice. 'That's what I said. Okay, I should have put my name on, but . . . I was so angry. You don't understand, miss! What you're doing is . . . It's just wrong.'

'But, Tom. You've never asked us what we're doing.'

'You're always going on about it! Walking the flare paths. Finding the grave sites. Digging things up.'

Vicky was shaking her head. 'No. You're wrong. That's not what we do.'

'I think Tomaz has a good point,' said Ruskin. 'I can understand curiosity. But—'

'Shhh,' said Millie. 'Sorry, Ruskin, but let Miss Vicky talk, will you?'

'How is Tomaz wrong?' said Imagio. 'I've been listening hard and I think he has a good, solid point that nobody here's even thought of. And if he's not going on this trek thing, then I know for sure I'm not.'

'I'm not,' said Podma. 'Eric's not, either.'

'I don't know how the misunderstanding happened,' said Vicky softly, 'but there has been one. It's my fault, for never taking the trouble to explain. And you're quite right; when Ellie and I get together, we just get excited about things and we don't stop and communicate. What happened today, by the pond, was a terrible lack of communication. You see, that child in the room downstairs – the skeleton . . .'

'He shouldn't be there, miss,' said Tomaz.

'I know that. The British Museum have been wanting him for a number of years —'

'Then you have to say no.'

'Shut up!' said Caspar. 'Let her finish.'

'We've always said no,' said Vicky, 'but the museum's very small, and it's already moved once. It's going to close soon, we all know that, and the collection will be broken up. That's just fact. A few weeks ago, someone from the British Museum came down and made another attempt to persuade us. But you see, Doctor Ellie and I . . . for a number of years – ever since we met, actually – we've had this dream that one day we could find the flare path that led to the . . . I don't know what to call it. The sacred spot, or the sacred grove – whatever it is. And we want to put the little boy back where he actually belongs. We want . . .' She broke off. 'You know I said to you, Millie, that he affects quite a lot of people the way he affected you? He affects me very badly. I can't sleep sometimes, because I can hear him.'

'You *hear* him?' said Anjoli.

224

'Yes. Do you understand me, Tomaz? I'm still not sure I'm being clear. That little boy is lost. When he was found, when he was dug up, he became more lost. We want to put him back with those that are looking for him. And I think . . . I think you probably want to help us do that, don't you?'

Tomaz was looking down at her. Vicky's eyes were full of tears now and he was reminded of pools.

'I think you want to help us,' she said, 'because we're actually on the same side.'

Chapter Thirty-Two

Down on the ground, they found Doctor Ellie.

She was sitting on a rock, patiently, and the children stood in clusters, unsure what to say.

'Vicky will look after him,' said Doctor Ellie. 'She'll get him ready tomorrow, Tomaz. We've been ready for a while, but we think we ought to take the plunge now. We'll wrap him and we won't disturb him again. Vicky will make him comfortable. I think he's ready for the journey.'

'Why did you come here, miss?' said Anjoli. 'Why tonight?'

Doctor Ellie smiled. 'It's a rising moon,' she said. 'This is the best place to look from.'

'Let's go,' said Asilah.

Miles had his arm round Tomaz. They walked the short distance to the Ribblestrop Edge and it was as if the ground they walked on was luminous. The very air seemed to be shining and when they got to the lip, and gazed out over the landscape, the light was silver. There were distant railway tracks shining and they could see the woods and farms that gave out onto moorland. A stack of rock, rising like a distant volcano, was the angry outline of Flashing Tor, and there were columns of cloud that looked like smoke. The children sat down and gazed at the moon.

Everyone heard the laughter at just the same time – a single peal, then a hush.

'Don't move,' said Imagio.

'Don't even speak,' said Miles.

There was a silence and it was as if everyone was holding their breath. Tomaz stood up, very slowly, but he didn't look round. The moon shone a little more brightly and silvered him. 'Why feathers?' he whispered at last. 'Tell us why feathers.'

The children gazed out over the moor, determined not to look behind them. The laughter came again, and this time it was the laughter of two, or maybe three – it was breathless, as if a game were in progress. Sanchez wanted so badly to turn round, but something told him not to, and he was aware that everyone was still – that if a single head turned, the laughter would vanish. And there were footfalls now, soft on the rock. There was a squeal and a gasp, and something metal fell upon stone. There was a peal of laughter that blazed louder than any other and then there was the sound of a flute – one note, long, sustained, with the laughter swirling around it. Then the moon must have tilted and the earth must have leant towards it, for the light altered yet again. As the children laughed and laughed, and as the feet jumped and ran, a trail of white stones became visible all across the moor. It was as if stars had fallen – they were that bright and clear. There was a trail and it led in a great curve over a hill, into darkness, then appeared again, narrowing to nothing. It was a path, unmissable, heading north.

'Don't go,' said Tomaz. 'Please don't leave us.'

Imagio took his hand. Sanjay took his other hand and Miles found Millie's wrist. In a moment everyone was connected and everyone felt it at the same time – there was a pulse and, when they looked down, they saw that the ground was covered in feathers.

The flare path had disappeared.

'Why feathers?' whispered Sam. 'What's special about feathers?'

'Oh God, look!' said Vicky.

Everyone turned now and saw that she was pointing. There was something on the ground, where the ghosts had played. They remembered the metal sound – the clink on the rock – and whatever had fallen was still there. Vicky knelt beside it and the children pressed around her.

'Look . . .'

'What is it, miss?' asked Caspar.

'I've seen it before,' said Israel. 'There's some in the glass case, downstairs in the museum. You said they were playing cards.'

'But it's new,' said Vicky. Her hands trembled and for a moment she didn't dare touch it.

Doctor Ellie had a torch out and the metal disc shimmered in the beam, silver, bronze and copper. There was a bird etched skillfully, with a bright eye and cruel beak.

Vicky picked it up and instantly it corroded almost to nothing – it was a leaf, suddenly, of oxidised, corrupted matter that might have come from a bonfire.

She fell to her knees. 'Oh no . . .'

'That wasn't a playing card,' said Podma.

'Is that what they were playing with?' said Oli. 'They were throwing it. Is it a weapon?'

'It's just a throwing game,' said Kenji. 'Frisbee. But they were catching it on sticks.'

'How do you know that?' said Miles.

'I could hear. That's what the knocking sound was. They were just playing a game, throw and catch. Throw and catch. We do the same, Miles. They're us.'

'I think we have to go, don't we?' said Doctor Ellie. 'If the flare paths are that clear, then this is the right time of the year. When's the longest day? Next week? Next Monday?'

Vicky said, 'Did you see how beautiful it was?' Millie put an arm round her shoulders, for she was distraught. 'Before I touched it. Did you see how gorgeous it was? They made that.'

'What's their name again? The name of the tribe?' asked Millie.

'Caillitri,' said Vicky, softly. 'It means, "Those who pass". "Those who are leaving".'

'We can follow them now,' said Asilah. 'We can leave tomorrow – that's ahead of schedule, but that won't matter. We're going to be slow, so the sooner the better. This Pioneers' Award thing, is it important?'

'It is to Captain Routon,' said Podma.

'The flare paths are more important,' said Sam, 'but we can do both. We can do the challenge *and* look after Eleudin.'

'We've got to be clear, though,' said Miles. 'If it comes to making a decision, the priority is finding his home. Are we agreed on that?'

The children nodded.

'Did anyone see them?' said Tomaz. 'The ghosts, I mean. Did anyone turn and look?'

'I tried,' said Anjoli, after a silence. 'I couldn't move, though.'

'Nor could I,' said Millie.

Miles stood up. 'Let's get back to the camp,' he said. 'If we're leaving at dawn, we ought to get some sleep.'

Chapter Thirty-Three

What had the police actually been doing all this time and why had they been waiting?

The answer was simple: they'd been sorting out the paperwork.

Officers and clerks had been organising file after file into binders and ledgers. Every document had to be indexed and copied, checked and re-filed. There were eye-witness statements, reports, photographs and recommendations. There were inventories and estimates, plus a range of odd little jottings collected by ex-Inspector Cuthbertson over the months when he'd been in charge. There were accident reports, expert analyses and boxfuls of drawings. There were physical samples, such as the gobstopper that had been retrieved from the windpipe of Timmy Fox, and the ruined trousers of a police officer who'd fallen into the lake. Of course, the evidence and documentation also went way back to the autumn and spring terms, when the children had accidently brought the whole of the south west's train service to a halt and set fire to a Travellers' Sleepeasy. There was a smashed-up burger van to be considered and one whole filing cabinet was dedicated to traffic violations. There were copies of licences that had never been applied for and warning letters that had never been acknowledged. An insurance consultant in Exeter had drawn up a three-hundred page document on the policies the headmaster should have had, but hadn't got, and there was a section at the end that estimated the amount of money he could be sued for by the people who weren't properly protected from the accidents they might have had. A policewoman in Taunton had interviewed Lady Vyner over the phone and spent the following week listing the hazards to which the Ribblestrop children had been exposed. They ranged from unprotected eye-level coat pegs to wild cats, lethal reptiles and loaded guns. The Ribblestrop children had been exposed to so many risks it was a wonder any of them were still breathing.

The prosecution team was at last ready for a first hearing, and it was judged essential that the teachers being investigated should appear in person. Unfortunately, there had been no word from the headmaster, as even the hand-delivered letters had gone unanswered. When the final deadline passed, the Chief Constable took out his special pen and signed four arrest warrants. Norcross-Webb, Worthington, Routon and Doonan; the four names were inked onto dotted lines and the papers were stamped and sealed. They were scanned into a whole network of computer systems and the arrest appraisal team met to confirm date, time and strategy. A police van was sent to Ribblestrop the following morning, along with two cars from Exeter HQ. Dog handlers were brought up from Bristol, and child-protection officers were flown in from London. Lady Vyner was consulted and it was agreed that the Ribblestrop children would be taken into temporary care. This would involve the immigration service too, so they scrambled a specialist lawyer 'to observe', while places were found in secure units round the country. It was known that some of the children were under ten years old, so there was a slight delay while the appropriate soft toys were located.

By mid-morning, however, things were ready. The police station car park had overflowed along Ribblestrop High Street. Apart from the prison truck, cars and dog vans, there was a fleet of minibuses, a firearms unit and the satellite control vehicle.

'Gently does it,' said the officer in charge. 'The last thing we want is to alarm anybody.'

'We've had the weapons report, sir,' said a supporting officer. 'Sixty-two per cent risk, so that's alert level amber.'

'There were gunshots last term,' said a firearms officer. 'So we'll be covering your backs. I don't expect resistance —'

'What if the kids just run for it? Any air cover?'

'We've a chopper standing by,' said a reconnaissance expert. 'The armed officers will be flanking you; the wooded area's the hot spot.'

'Right,' said the chief constable. 'Deidre? Do you want to say anything?'

'I do, Brian. Thank you.'

'Do you all know Inspector Moorhouse? She's our child-liaison officer.'

Deidre smiled briefly and put on a pair of large glasses.

'Good morning,' she said. 'I just want to remind everyone that in an operation like this, the children come first. What we want is to avoid anything traumatic for them – it's their interests we have to keep uppermost in our minds. Now Lady Vyner's agreed to come with us, as her own grandson's involved. There's quite a lot of little ones, of course, and I think most of them will be pretty desperate by now. We've got hot drinks, we've got sweets and toys. We're going to be nice and reasonable, and I really don't foresee any problems if we all stay calm. I think the grown-ups will see sense.'

Somebody laughed.

'I know that sounds strange,' said Deidre, 'after what we've been reading, but when they see we mean business, I agree with Brian. I think they'll come quietly.'

Brian turned to a flip chart. 'Two squads,' he said. 'There's a back way, off a kind of cart-track here. I'll take four in that direction. Deidre will lead the advance party in through the front door, as it were – she'll make first contact. That's a narrow path through the woods, and I think three's enough for that. We don't want to overwhelm them.'

'No, we don't want to panic them,' said Deidre. 'We arrive nice and slow – a walk in the woods. We show the ID, take the teachers aside, and it'll be over in a minute.'

'I'll lead them out to the lock-up,' said Brian. 'No cuffs. No physical contact, not where the kids can see. We cuff them in the truck, not outside.'

'I'll stay with the kiddies,' said Deidre. 'We'll get them nice and settled, try and get a sing-song going . . . and then bring the buses in.'

'Any questions?'

There were none. Fifty doors slammed and the vehicles moved off in a long, slow convoy. The car at the front put its blue flashing lights on, and Lady Vyner sat in the front seat, trembling with excitement. The lights flashed and flickered all the way to the school. Minutes later, the doors were opening again, and a first aid tent was pitched. The various units took up their stations and the two arrest squads moved into the trees.

The dogs whined and barked, and the back-up officers settled down to wait.

What Deidre reported afterwards was the 'uncanny silence'.

She knew she was close, because she could smell a bonfire. She was also aware that the track she was on had been used by many feet. She stopped and radioed to the second squad.

'Are you close, Brian? Over.'

'Close enough. There are a lot of cart-tracks, pretty fresh. Hooves, as well. The ground's quite churned up around here – looks like horses. Can't hear anything. Over.'

'I can't either. They might be having a nap, I suppose.'

'I'll ask Lady Vyner – hang on a minute. What do you think, ma'am? Have they flown the nest?'

Deidre heard Lady Vyner say something obscene.

'We should check the museum, Brian – they were there yesterday.'

'Right.'

'Very, very quiet.'

'Too quiet, Deidre. I'll press on. Over and out.'

Deidre clicked her radio off and moved forward.

The officer behind her whispered, 'Wait! What's that there, guv'nor?' He pointed into the bushes.

It was a black-and-gold tie, looped round an eye-level twig a few metres ahead, and it did its job just as the children had intended. Eric had fixed it in place, under Oli's direction, and it was a very simple distraction tactic. It was designed to ensure that anyone moving forward on this particular section of the path would keep their eyes up, rather than down. The tripwire – which was spread at ankle height – would not be noticed.

Deidre didn't notice it and, as she went to retrieve the tie, she kicked straight through it. The wire released a powerful sapling that had been bent almost flat. As it sprang to its full height, it yanked the pins on several machines and the officers were suddenly assaulted from the right, from the left, and from the rear. From the rear came a volley of lethally sharp arrows. Six bows had been positioned and two sent their missiles way too high – but the swish as they passed overhead was terrifying. One arrow went straight past the nose of a policeman and

234

embedded itself in a tree. Two more swerved wide, but the last one caught Deidre full in the buttock. She slammed her hand to the wound and went down on one knee. The movement probably saved her life, because the second trap was a rock tied to an enormous branch, which swung across the path at head height and would have knocked her senseless. The branch crashed into the undergrowth and released a second sapling. This one was more ingenious than the first and had been Anjoli's idea based upon an African tale he'd read in Doctor Ellie's library van. The little tree swished upright and smacked a spike, hard, into a carefully chosen oak. The spike drove deep into a hollow part, and in that hollow was a large, thriving wasps' nest. The wasps were jerked from their midday snooze and, assuming they were under attack, rose as one. They didn't notice the sapling or the vine that had held it. They noticed only the five panicking police officers – and they dive-bombed together. The officers covered their faces and howled as their hands were stung. The cleverer wasps went for ankles and bald patches. Several found the unprotected flesh above shirt collars. In a moment, the officers were running, and they ran straight into the final trap – which was simply a pit, covered by brush. They found the ground gave way beneath them, and they ended up winded and helpless in wet mud. A part of the nearby spring had been diverted to keep the mud thick, and it was impossible to struggle out of it for the walls were sheer. Miles had wanted to put sharpened sticks at the bottom, but had been overruled. The officers clambered to their feet and were helpless. The wasps re-grouped for another attack and those waiting on the drive heard the screams on their radios. Back-up moved in and the chopper was soon overhead. The dogs were unleashed and raced through the woods. Armed officers soon surrounded the camp – but within a few minutes it was clear that the children and their teachers had long gone.

Deidre's face was so swollen she could hardly talk. 'Are they human?' she blubbered. 'Are they human beings? I mean . . .'

'It's war,' said Brian. 'They've declared war – simple as that.'

His group had fared no better.

He had also kicked through a tripwire and two of his men had been knocked into the camp latrine. Lady Vyner had been whisked off her feet in a goal net and was now dangling from the top of a conifer. A fire engine with hydraulic crane – the one vehicle nobody had thought to invite – was being called up from Exeter. It would take two hours to get there.

'Secure units,' sobbed Deidre. 'All of them. These children should be in cages!'

Ex-Inspector Cuthbertson heard about the raid that evening.

It frightened him, because he realised that he had forgotten just how dangerous – and resourceful – the Ribblestrop children could be. He made a resolution not to forget again. He checked the equipment in his ice-cream van. He had various restraints – plastic cable ties were the easiest for thin wrists and ankles, but he had nylon cord and chain for when they got to Lightning Tor. The Sanchez boy could be doped quickly with chloroform and belted into a bodybag.

Cuthbertson checked his personals too. He had a false passport and a brand new credit card. He had money in both sterling and dollars, and it was all in a small backpack that could be grabbed at the first sign of trouble. Timmy Fox had the hot-air balloon ready, safe and neat on its trailer. That was hitched to the van, which had been serviced the day before and was full of petrol. He had food, stove, tent, sleeping bag, night-vision goggles and waterproofs. His brother had been in touch – the fourth member of the team – and they'd devised a neat little plot to deal with Captain Routon. The ice-cream man disguise was fresh and ready on its coathanger, so he relaxed again. He telephoned The Priory.

'How's it going?' he said.

Mr Ian paused. 'We've had a set-back,' he said.

'What?'

'One of the boys has got chicken-pox.'

'So what? Put a pillow over his face.'

'You don't understand. It might be an epidemic, so we've got to check the rest and possibly postpone the camp—'

'Get your brats onto the moor, Ian.'

'I'm doing my best, Cuthbertson!'

'I don't care if they've got pox or leprosy, I want them on the moor with Ribblestrop. That was the plan! If you're not there, they won't proceed.' He lowered his voice. 'If you don't make the rendezvous, friend, I will personally rip the beard off your face and feed it to you bristle by bristle. Then I'll put you in jail.'

There was a silence.

'I'll see what I can do,' said Mr Ian.

Chapter Thirty-Four

The chicken-pox turned out to be an isolated case and Mr Ian nearly wept with relief.

The boys and girls of The Priory finished morning prep in the usual frigid silence and at half-past twelve put away their books. Some went to the library for periodical reading, for there was a current affairs test twice a week. A select group went to practise their university application letters, while those doing the Pioneers' Award put their blazers into polythene wraps and filed to the gym for the dreaded final kit inspection.

Mr Ian had organised a line of tables and each child set out the items it intended to take.

'What's that, Perkins?'

'My reading book, sir.'

'Rejected. You will not have time for reading.'

'Sir.'

'Hubble. Re-fold those socks.'

'Sir.'

He moved down the line and the children sensed his tension. Jacqueline stood with her hands behind her back, eyes down. Scott was beside her.

'You let me down, you two,' said Mr Ian quietly. 'You were not loyal.'

The children blinked. Jacqueline licked her lips.

'I'm not going to punish you now. I'm going to observe you, in the hope you'll win favour over the next three days. If you fraternise with those ... lowlifes again, I'll assume you want to undermine me. And when we're home, you will experience the full hell of my retribution. Do you understand me?'

'Yes, sir,' said the children together.

'Why are there feathers in your kit, Scott? Matron told me about this.'

'They were given to me, sir.'

Mr Ian picked one up. 'A feather collection,' he said. 'You're an effeminate boy, aren't you? Who gave them to you? Speak up.'

'They were given to me at the camp, sir. I just like them.'

'Rejected. I don't want clutter on this trip. I'll say this to all of you ...' Mr Ian raised his voice. 'If you're taking toys, get rid of them now. Do not think you can conceal a toy, I will find it. Last term it was Charlie Johnson, wasn't it?'

A fair-haired boy at the end of the row jerked to attention. 'Yes, sir,' he piped.

'What did you conceal?'

'A toy car, sir.'

'What did we do with it? When we got home?'

'We smashed it up, sir.'

'We took a hammer to it, didn't we, Johnson? We agreed that toy cars were inappropriate, even if they had been given to us by a much-loved, much-missed grandparent. We smashed it to pieces and we put the pieces in the bin. When we're out on the moor, we're a unit working together. One weakling and the whole group is weakened. If you spot weakness, tell me about it. Toys, knick-knacks, reading books. They have no place on Ribblemoor. So ...'

239

He moved out to the front where everyone could see him.

'I will call an item of kit. You will pick it up and hold it above your head. Start with your compass. Come on, hold it up!'

The children did so.

'Good. Survival muesli bars, six-pack.'

They put their compasses down and held up their muesli bars.

'Okay, let's speed this up. Toilet tissue, pack of ten. Grey shirt. Get it folded, Tutton! Good, Fisher – very neat. Outward-bound neck-tie – let me see it! Good!'

The list went on, and Mr Ian marched up and down the line, checking his squad. At one o'clock he was done and they all went to lunch. Then they moved their packs to the waiting minibus. At two-fifteen, exactly on-schedule, Mr Ian nosed the bus out of the school gates and set off for the moors.

As he did so, two elderly donkeys made their way up the long flank of Corriemor Hill, drawing chariots that bulged with weapons and equipment.

The Ribblestrop children and their teachers were walking beside them, drenched in sunshine. The sky overhead was a dome of cloudless blue and skylarks poured down song, as fresh and clear as water from a spring. They had all set off at sunrise and had already walked several kilometres. Doctor Ellie checked one of the old maps, which flapped in her hands.

'Off the path, I think!' she cried. 'If we swing northwest, we'll go past a little wood. That's where the flare path was leading, I'm sure of it.'

A gust of wind almost tore the map from her hands.

'Where exactly are we going?' shouted the headmaster.

Doctor Ellie put her mouth to his ear and shouted back. 'We saw the path last night! But the stones aren't easy to spot, you see. It's a far cleverer system than I'd thought!'

'Look behind!' shouted Sam.

Doctor Ellie turned and saw that most of the children had paused and were gazing in the direction they'd come. Their cloaks flapped and their hair streamed. The higher they climbed, the more the wind tugged at them. The land folded away below them, a great duvet of greens, yellows and browns. They could see the track they'd ascended and they watched the shadows of clouds steaming across the landscape. The camel brayed with joy – it had been impossible to leave her, after all – she'd cried all night. Now she carried Professor Worthington, who sat back in a classroom chair that Sanjay had lashed over the hump. She was reading under a parasol.

'Why haven't we been out here before, sir?' said Imagio to Doonan.

Doonan shook his head. 'I don't know,' he said. 'It makes me want to be out here every day.'

'I don't ever want to go back,' said Eric, holding his hand.

'Oh, but you can't leave Ribblestrop. You can't be serious!'

'It's so beautiful, though!'

'Come on,' said Asilah. 'We've got six hours of walking ahead. Let's move it!'

'But who's actually navigating?' cried the headmaster. 'We do have a destination in mind, don't we?'

'Follow me!' yelled Captain Routon.

He trotted down the hill towards them, waving his arms. He was in a bright red army coat, courtesy of the Ribblestrop auction house, and was impossible to miss. It flapped behind him like a scarlet cloak and he was grinning from ear to ear.

'The first tor's in sight, sir,' he panted. 'Just over that ridge. Then we push on through the valley, all the way to Flaming Tor. And that's where we meet The Priory children.'

'Right.'

'Mr Ian's got the final co-ordinates. He knows where we end up.'

Miles jumped onto a rock. He drew his sword from his belt, and raised it, so that it flashed in the sunlight. The donkeys brayed again, and the chariots rolled forward.

'Heave!' cried the children, turning the wheels. 'Heave!'

The tribe moved steadily on.

Millie hung back for Doctor Ellie.

'Where's Vicky?' she said.

'Looking after Eleudin,' said Doctor Ellie, quietly. 'She's going to meet up with us later, when we find the main flare path – when we know where we're going. We've all got those field telephones Captain Routon bought, yes?'

'You think they're going to work? They're ancient.'

'I have more faith in ancient things than you do, my dear. And Oli seemed hopeful.'

'I'm just not sure how we're going to keep together,' said Millie. 'We're going to be splitting up and we're not even sure what we're looking for . . .'

'But you can feel it, can't you?' said Doctor Ellie. 'Something's guiding us.'

'I just don't want to be lost out here,' said Millie.

'You can't be lost at home. And this was their home, remember.'

They ploughed on, up ground that got rockier and rockier. When they came to the next ridge, they stopped again, for the world had changed and the new landscape stunned them. The softness they'd come through came to a sudden and dramatic end, and they were peering down into a gorge that was wild and forbidding. The grass had been nibbled to almost nothing and a bridleway wound down towards a stream that hissed and gurgled across a plateau of rock. In the distance, they could see an upthrust of savage, grey stone. It reared up like the volcano it was, cut off flat at the top. Beyond it was an even larger one and this was topped by a spike of granite that pointed like a dead finger right up into the sky. It was a prehistoric land and, had a brontosaurus sauntered into view, nobody would have been surprised.

'That is crazy, isn't it?' whispered Miles.

Tomaz was next to him. 'What is?' he said.

'I just didn't know there were places like this on our doorstep.'

'It's mad,' said Imagio. 'We're just a few hours from school – and this has been waiting for us.'

'We're going back in time. How can this be here when we're . . . doing lessons?'

'It's awesome.'

Everyone climbed onto the chariots now, for they were rolling downhill. Sanjay and Israel had the reins and the donkeys took the strain easily. Nobody spoke, for as they descended, the rock rose up on either side and enclosed them in a silence they didn't want to break. Even the skylarks hung back, and the only sound was the wind sawing at the occasional bush and the water grinding the rock.

They forded the stream easily, up to their chests in icy water. They hauled the chariots back onto dry land and set off into the Stone Age. The grass had given way to lichens and there were gleams of silver and quartz under foot. The first volcano now towered over them and they could see its black fissures and the piles of debris that had collapsed down its sides, strewn around it like rubble.

'Why don't we climb it?' said Sam.

'Not that one, lad,' said Captain Routon, cheerfully. 'That's a baby compared to where we're going.' He held one of the maps in his hand and studied it, turning it this way and that. He jogged on ahead and waited.

'That's Killer Tor, that one,' he said when they were together again. 'That's the first, isn't it?' He scratched his head, aware that an old war-wound had come to life. 'That means we're coming in here, just where we wanted to. The next one is Silver Tor, then you've got Hammer Tor and Broken Tor. We've got to get past all of them.'

'Sam's right, though,' said Kenji. 'We ought to climb them.'

'You'll get plenty of climbing tomorrow,' said Captain Routon, zipping up his coat. 'Don't you worry about climbing. Okay, forward march, everybody! Follow me!'

The chariots rolled on. They had refilled their water bottles and snacked on dried fruit. Everyone had plenty of energy and the only worrying thing was how small they suddenly felt. It was as if they were shrinking. That morning they had been part of a lush, green landscape. Now they felt like insects on the moon.

When they saw the hot-air balloon, high above, it seemed comforting. They had felt cut off from civilisation, all alone in a valley that had existed quite happily without them for millions of years. It was nice to know another human being was aware of their presence and they waved their arms.

Timmy Fox got straight on his radio.

'The eagle has landed, old boy,' he said. 'Are you there, Cuthbertson?'

'Clear as a bell, I'm here all right.'

'You're on Lightning Tor, are you?'

'Right by the main mast – that's why reception's so good. What have you got?'

'The Foxter's got them in his sights; they're dressed rather strangely and riding in chariots. Unorthodox route. They've come past . . . I think it's Silver Tor.'

'You think? Or you know?'

'Silver Tor. ID positive.'

'Ian's on the move too. They'll rendezvous tonight.'

'Good. Bang on schedule, then.'

'Have you heard the weather forecast? That low pressure's doing just what we hoped.'

'I can feel it. It's pretty tempestuous up here, so foul weather is on its way.'

'You can stay up for a while? Keep track of them?'

'I'll be all right. I'll be with you after dark, after touch-down.'

'You can see Routon, can you? Big chap, bald on top?'

'I can see him. Red coat – stands out a mile.'

'We're going to need to identify him tomorrow, once my brother gets here. Keep high and don't screw up. I'm entering the codes.'

'What codes?'

'The explosives, Timmy. I'm entering the explosive codes – have you forgotten the plan?'

'No. I'm . . . on the ball, Cuthbertson. I'm up to speed.'

Chapter Thirty-Five

The Ribblestrop children reached Flashing Tor after six hours, and sang when they saw it.

It was a spontaneous song, led by Israel – a chant he'd learnt from an old monk in Tibet, used for paying homage to creation. Their voices rose and they flung the chorus at the landscape, for the sun had turned into a great ball of red gold and its heat was gone. As they came to the foot of the crag, it rolled lower, and rested on a shoulder of cloud. Flashing Tor seemed like a vast and mighty mountain, rearing up and begging to be climbed. When they had sung the song five times, they set off at a run – they had to make the top, for the sunset would be the miraculous climax to a miraculous day. They scrabbled up, using hands and feet, for the slopes were steep. After half an hour they came to a great granite plug, that was more like a chimney. They swarmed up it as one and they found there was just room for everyone to sit on its sloping summit.

They watched a melting world. The cloud had been stirred into a furnace of black, pink and red, and the sun was at last being swallowed. The dark of the evening came down like a soft ink-wash, bleeding through a papery sky, and when Sanchez found a hand holding his own, he realised with a little lurch of joy, that it was Millie's. She pressed against him.

'It's even better than Columbia,' she said. 'Isn't it?'

'No.'

'All right, then. It's as good.'

'How can anything be the same after this?'

'What do you mean?'

Sanchez found that the words he wanted to say were thick in his mouth and useless. He felt an arm round his shoulders and saw that Miles had squeezed in from the side. He was grinning and his eyes were full of sunset. Sanchez gave up on words and pulled his two friends closer, with all his strength, as far off in the valley there was the first, distant flash of lightning.

'You think they sat here?' said Sam.

'Who?' said Ruskin.

'The tribe – the Caillitri. You think they would have come up here?'

Ruskin took his glasses off and cleaned them, thoughtfully. 'I think they would have,' he said. 'They'd have been stupid not to. What would they have talked about, though?'

Sanjay leaned in. 'Maybe they imagined us.' He grinned. 'Maybe they sat here and said, "You think they'll ever be kids up here, wondering if we existed?"'

The teachers had stayed at the bottom, looking after the donkeys and camel. If their maps were right, then the rendezvous point with Mr Ian and The Priory children was just three kilometres further, on the far side of the tor. They drank water and moved on along the track.

'You know,' said Professor Worthington, from her perch, 'this feels like a holiday to me. I haven't actually relaxed like this for quite some time.'

The headmaster looked up at her and smiled. 'I agree,' he said. 'Once term starts, it's absolutely non-stop. When they disappear off in their groups, I'm going to do some serious reading. Some of the books in your library, Ellie, are quite extraordinary. I'm getting all sorts of ideas for the end of term. A nice series of tests, perhaps, to consolidate what we've been teaching. How are you, Routon?'

Routon was driving the second chariot. He had zipped up his hood, so only his eyes were visible.

'Caught the sun, I'm afraid, sir. I should have known better.'

'I think the weather might be changing,' said Doonan. 'I can smell rain.'

'Well, Ian's the expert on that one,' said the headmaster. 'He's our reconnaissance man and he says it'll be fine. Are you going to be out there with them?'

'We're not supposed to be,' said Doonan.

Captain Routon nodded. 'According to the rules, the children have got to go it alone. We won't be far away, though – me and Ian.'

'What's the finishing post?'

'I'm afraid that's classified, sir. Only Ian knows that.'

Doctor Ellie laughed. 'I must say this has whet my appetite,' she said. 'You ought to have a staff team, next time. I'm tired of the children having all the fun.'

'How are supplies?' said Doonan. 'Do you think they've got what they need?'

'If they haven't they'll be sorry,' said Captain Routon. 'It's the only way to learn, you know. I was in Siberia once, crossing the steppes with a husky team – everything in tins. Food, water, fuel – all in tins. We'd gone through that list so many times and do you know what? We got to base camp and we'd forgotten the most important thing.'

'What was that?'

'A tin opener.'

'What on earth did you do?' said Doonan.

'As it turned out, we were very lucky. There was a youngster on the team who'd lost part of his jaw in a sniper attack. Smashed up his bottom teeth, so his dentist had replaced them with metal. He had to open his mouth, and we had to press his head against a box, and I had to kind of rotate the edge of the tin between two molars. You find a way when you have to.'

'They've got what they need,' said Professor Worthington. 'And whatever they lack in equipment, they make up for in spirit. Ah, look down there! Can you see what I see?'

'Is that a minibus?' said the headmaster. 'That will be The Priory.'

'By the way, sir,' said Captain Routon, 'did the High School ever make contact about that bicycle outing? I thought that young teacher was just what they needed.'

'Johnny Jay? He was good, wasn't he?' said the headmaster. 'He left a message on my phone – said it was a bit short notice this time, but he's still hopeful.'

'It was nice to see that co-operation,' said Professor Worthington. 'We should build on that, Giles. Our lot can be very shy with strangers. Are we late, by the way?'

'We said just after sundown,' said Doonan. 'We're right on time.'

The Priory had arrived.

They had taken the road, of course, and it ended in a gravel car park, with a toilet block at the far end. Beyond that was a lawn area with a sign reminding the public that camping beside Flashing Tor was allowed if all fees had been paid in advance and licences obtained. There was another, larger sign screwed to the gate, listing various things campers shouldn't do. Park rangers, it said, had the authority to remove people if the necessary paperwork was not produced. One such officer was going through Mr Ian's file, ticking boxes on a checklist.

'How many have you got, sir?'

'Fifteen,' said Mr Ian, coldly.

'And the other school? Ribblestrop Towers?'

'Twenty-two. They'll be here later.'

'Good. We've had a severe weather warning, you know. Thought you might cancel the trip.'

'We won't be going far.'

'No? So you're just here for one night? You've booked in for three, but—'

'We'll see how it goes. We didn't expect bad weather.'

'Happens all the time round here. Spoils a lot of plans. Do you need any extra bin bags, by the way? Oh . . . sir.' He was peering through one of the side windows. 'Is that a gas stove under the seat? Behind the little lad's feet? With a T36 gas cylinder?'

'Yes. It's to heat our evening meal.'

The ranger shook his head. 'I'm sorry, sir, you're not up with the latest regulations.' He pulled out another form and began to fill it in. He smiled at Mr Ian. 'Bit of an incident with a T36 last summer, so they're on our "not permitted" list. Seems the valves can be a bit unpredictable in hot weather, specially if they're kicked over. You can phone for a pizza delivery, perhaps?'

Mr Ian closed his eyes. 'We've been using these stoves for fifteen years. It's how we cook supper.'

'Can't allow it, sir. If it was up to me, I'd turn a blind eye. You should have said it was a TD50 – they're allowed if the user has a certificate. If you could just sign here and here, to say you've agreed to comply. Have you got any dogs with

250

you? No? In that case, I'll show you where you can put your tents.'

He pulled out two small, orange flags.

'Can you stay in first gear, sir? I'll guide you into your bay.'

Chapter Thirty-Six

The ranger beckoned and waved, and Mr Ian was soon on his allotted patch of grass. The children clambered out and once they had their tents unrolled the man departed. Everyone worked hard and fast and three blue tents were soon neatly parallel to one another, the guy ropes just touching. They'd brought a small storage tent, which housed other equipment, and they sited their windbreaker. Two boys went to fill the water container and pots and pans were set out ready to go. Mr Ian put up his own tent and then checked the children's. Their sleeping bags, torches and pyjamas were arranged properly, according to the diagrams he'd issued.

He gave the order for the relaxation of the dress code and the children removed their ties and pullovers. These were stowed in specially designed travel bags and the official Priory jeans were pulled on. If the children felt cold, they had blue Priory fleeces. If it rained, they had blue Priory waterproofs, which were ready in plastic tubes. Mr Ian himself had an all-weather Gore-Tex jacket in the same shade. He'd had the school crest embroidered onto it and he lay it carefully by his boots. Then, checking to see that the park ranger really had left them to it, he assembled the illegal stove.

'I hope we won't get into trouble, sir,' said Hubble.

'Why should we?' said Mr Ian. 'The man was talking nonsense. Get the potatoes peeled – that's your job, isn't it? Jacqueline – sausages!'

'Yes, sir.'

'Johnson. Do you think you're strong enough to open a tin?'

'I've got it here, sir –'

'Decant it, then, and use your initiative. A meal cooked out of doors always tastes better – you did an essay on that last term.'

The Priory children were soon hard at work and as Mr Ian's watch turned to eight o'clock he lit the burner.

At that precise moment, the Ribblestrop children attacked.

It wasn't a real attack, of course, because the schools had established such friendly relations – it was a charge for the sheer joy of charging. Sanjay had seen the minibus from high above and it had been Miles and Anjoli who suggested creeping down to surround them before the Ribblestrop teachers got there. They'd slid down the side of the tor in silence and then fanned out, rabbit-crawling through the scrub. They used the sounds of skylarks, ravens and owls to communicate, though The Priory children were far too intent on preparations to notice them. Miles raised his arm when everyone was in position – it was just visible as a black silhouette – and pointed to the blue tents. With blood-curdling whoops and howls they raced in together, vaulting the hedges. It took only seconds to let the tents down, and then Eric led the assault on the children themselves.

The Priory pupils recognised their friends and fought back vigorously. Ignoring the cries of Mr Ian, there were soon several scrums as hand-to-hand combat turned into fierce wrestling. Eric was shouting, 'Take them prisoner!

253

Take them prisoner!' when a hand was slammed over his mouth and he found himself on his back. He was pinned by the sharp knees of a boy he dimly remembered – a spiky-looking child with frizzy hair. Kenji and Nikko were rolled up in one of the collapsed tents and then The Priory children regrouped to repel Miles, Sam and Anjoli.

Anjoli, unfortunately, was so excited that he ran straight through the windbreaker and tripped over the stove. Mr Ian could only watch in horror as the sausages tipped onto the grass, and the hot fat caught fire. Worse than that, the gas canister was booted sideways and the nozzle sheered clean off its tube.

It became a flame-thrower.

There was only one object in immediate proximity, and that was Mr Ian's personal tent, sited a discrete distance from the others. He raced across to save it, but couldn't get near: his sleeping bag, his boots and his beloved water-proof were caught in a furnace, melting together into a sticky mess of zips and rubber. It was Asilah who managed to block the gas and soon everyone was stamping out the flames.

'Oh man,' said Podma. 'That was a close one! That could have caught the bus!'

'Look at your food!' shouted Miles. 'You got ash in the beans.'

'Look at his stuff!' said Sam.

'Who trod on the sausages? Look at that – they're ruined.'

Israel was holding his eye. 'I got punched!' he said, in disbelief. 'By a girl!'

Mr Ian looked from face to face. It was too dark to see who was who, though some of his own children had torches. He was so angry he couldn't speak – his mouth would not work. His rage was throbbing, but he realised that he had spent so much of his life getting worked up about trivial things – about tie-knots and untucked shirts – that he had no reactions huge enough for a real atrocity. That a group of children could do so much damage in such a short time and stand there smiling at him, eager and happy . . . His heart was unable to pump enough blood to his brain. He was about to have a blackout.

'Something wrong?' said a voice. 'What on earth's that smell?'

He turned and the nightmare got worse. He was tipped from one ring of hell to the next. A donkey was staring at him and in the chariot it pulled was the Ribblestrop head-master, carrying a flaming torch. Behind him there was a camel and the stinking savages of Ribblestrop were forming a ring around him. There was a hand on his shoulder.

'We'll do the fire, sir,' said Captain Routon. 'You'll have an accident if you're not careful.' He called out to the chil-dren. 'We need a bit of light, first of all. Vijay on the shelters, please – squad of eight. Everyone else, wood gathering – except Tomaz. Tomaz, can you pick your team for kitchen duty?'

Doonan called out over the noise, 'Mr Ian's lot? Do you mind helping us all for a bit? Miles and Millie, can you explain what needs doing?'

Mr Ian climbed into the minibus and locked the doors.

For the next hour, the work was fast and efficient, and he tried not to look. Wooden poles were going up, right by The Priory children's tents. They opened up into what looked like a tripod and then a large canvas skin was being unfurled to complete a genuine teepee. There was laughter floating in the night and the sounds of metal hammering on wood. There was the occasional squeal and a steady stream of chil-dren emerging from the nearby trees, their arms full of branches. Soon, the whole camp was bright and hot, for a huge campfire was blazing inside a perimeter wall of torches.

When the headmaster rapped on the glass, Mr Ian ignored him. There was no point trying to get control – wherever he looked, some new outrage was being committed. A boy with long hair had a piglet on a spit. There was a pan of what looked like stew and he saw with a shock that Jacqueline and Harry were helping prepare it. They were chattering happily and laughing. The tents had been re-pitched, even closer to the Ribblestrop teepee, and the flames cast long, demonic shadows. He could see a Ribblestrop boy in a Priory fleece. Two of his own children were shirtless and seemed to be trying on some kind of garland or necklace. Logs had been dragged from the forest and were being sited around the fire, which was sending columns of sparks up into the night.

When the singing started, he covered his face. The Priory children were learning the Ribblestrop school song and he knew there was nothing he could do. Only hunger drove him out of the minibus and he took his place at the far end of a log.

'Does your school have a song?' said Millie. She was crouching right next to him, speaking almost into his ear.

'Yes.'

'How's it go?'

'Oh, wow!' shouted Miles. 'I can almost remember it. Something about pain, yes? *In pain we learn stuff* – something like that.'

Two Priory children immediately began singing, their treble voices piping happily.

'*Persevere in labour, persevere in pain!*
Though the path is thorny, dawn is on her way.'

Hands started clapping in rhythm.

'*Triumph in disaster, labour not in vain!*

256

We will pull together, come what may!'

There was a burst of applause and whistles.

The children soon had spoons and plates to bang, and the songs were sung alternately. Several Priory children were in their school choir and taught soaring descants, which they flung up to the stars. When their voices were hoarse, Imagio sang a very dirty township song in Spanish, which was so full of swearwords that Sanchez had to stop translating them. Just before midnight, the pig was roasted through and Tomaz and Caspar carved it with their daggers. Baked potatoes were brought out of the ashes and the stew was ladled into bowls. Doonan distributed the bread and there was silence as they ate. Finally, a great tray of coconut ice was produced and it went round the circle three times before it was finished. It was soaked in rum and sugar, and the feast was at an end. The headmaster served hot chocolate in little earthenware cups the children had made and Doctor Ellie played her flute.

There was peace.

'So where are they now, miss?' said Tomaz.

'Who?' asked a Priory pupil.

'The Lost Tribe,' whispered Kenji. 'That's who we're following.'

Doctor Ellie finished a tune, and said, 'Gone from here, I'm afraid.'

'Where to, though?' said Israel.

She smiled. 'They disappeared two thousand years ago,' she said, into the silence. 'Nobody knows where, because it was never documented.'

'Maybe they stayed and just joined other tribes,' said Doonan.

'I'm sure some of them did. The Romans came west, of course. They may have fled the Romans. They may have turned themselves into sailors and sailed to the Americas.'

'Why feathers, miss?' said Sanjay. 'Did you find out why they had a thing about feathers?'

'Birds,' said Sam. 'Maybe they turned into birds and flew away?'

Millie laughed. 'Sam's drunk,' she said.

'I did identify the species,' said Doctor Ellie. 'I'll need to verify it, because it's ... well, there's something rather strange. According to my bird book – and I checked this with a friend from a local bird sanctuary – the feathers belong to a hawk that used to be common here. You get them in Asia, too, but they died out in England years ago. Silver and bronze in the feathers and –'

'The River Falcon,' said Asilah.

'Yes.' She paused, and looked at him. 'How did you know that?'

'It's where we grew up, miss,' said Vijay. 'You get them in the mountains. They fly higher than any other bird.'

'And further,' said Kenji. 'They can fly forever.'

'That's not true. That's a myth!'

'The last one was seen round here thirteen years ago,' said Doctor Ellie. 'It was never verified, actually, because the spotter wouldn't give her name. She worked at the listening station on Lightning Tor – I told you about that place, I think. She said there was a whole nesting ground. They live as a colony, apparently. But ... that may all be mythology as well. We may never know – that place is still off-limits, I'm afraid.'

Chapter Thirty-Seven

Captain Routon addressed everyone the next morning at dawn.

Tomaz had the coffee on before sunrise, so by the time the children were awake and dressed there were three large pots steaming and Imagio was stirring a huge saucepan of porridge. There was an early-morning mist hanging inches off the ground and the Ribblestrop children were wrapped in the blankets they'd woven in Doonan's loom classes. Some of The Priory children were wild-haired and wide-eyed. They always rose early at school, but they had never seen a sunrise like this one. The grass was wet, the dew gleaming and glimmering. Flashing Tor reared up into a sky that seemed higher, bluer and brighter. There were even stars, fading.

'Everyone sleep well?' asked Captain Routon. 'I hope so, because it's a tough day ahead. Your lot all ready, Mr Ian?'

Mr Ian nodded grimly. He had spent a cold night in the minibus wrapped in Captain Routon's coat. It had hurt his pride to accept it when offered, but as he had no tent, no bedding and no spare clothes, he was obliged to.

'Mr Ian has the co-ordinates and will hand them out in due course. You all have maps already. That's good, because as of today, everything changes. No more fun and games.'

'We're ready,' said Miles. 'We just need to know where we're going.'

'Carry only what you need,' said Professor Worthington. 'You'll be on your own and you don't want to be bogged down with useless equipment. You must, however, take a field telephone.'

There was a murmur of disappointment. The telephones were heavy and cumbersome.

'I will now hand over to the expert,' said Captain Routon. 'Mr Ian, sir?'

Mr Ian stood up and produced a metal box. 'I'm going to give each group a sealed envelope,' he said. 'In the envelope you'll find a map reference and a clue. You go to the map reference and when you get there – if you find the right place, that is – the clue will lead you to a box, just like this one. Inside it will be the co-ordinates of the finishing post, and you get to the finishing post as fast as you can. That's where your teachers and I will be waiting.'

'We're not allowed to help you,' said Captain Routon. 'If you get lost, then you're out of the game. You phone in for help, or come back to base.'

'How can we get back here if we're lost?' said Millie.

'Map-read,' said Mr Ian, with contempt. 'Failing that, you follow your eyeballs – you can see Flashing Tor for miles, however lost you are. That's why we chose it.'

'What if it's night?' said Oli.

'You wait until day,' said Eric. 'Dimwit.'

'What if it's misty?' said Sanjay. 'Doctor Ellie, you told us the weather can turn in half an hour –'

'Are you scared?' asked Podma. 'You come all this way, and suddenly you're scared?'

'I'm not scared, I'm just asking—'

'You want to stay with the donkeys?'

'Sanjay's right to ask,' said Doctor Ellie, mildly. 'The weather systems round here are very unpredictable and when the mist comes down you don't see anything. You don't even try to move. Mr Ian, you're our weather-man—'

'It's clear and bright.'

'You just said it was unpredictable,' said Miles. 'So how can you predict it?'

Jacqueline said, 'The man from the National Park said the weather was bad. He said—'

'Shut up!' snapped Mr Ian. 'This isn't a debate. This is a briefing, and my forecast is based on satellite photography and the advice of meteorological experts. Maybe you Ribblestrop children would find that hard to understand.'

'Yeah,' said Imagio. 'We just use seaweed, man.'

'We do a rain-dance,' said Anjoli.

'I pick my nose,' said Podma. 'That tells me everything, whether it's wet, or dry, or—'

'All right!' said Doctor Ellie. 'I think we can move on from the weather. What else is there to say?'

'I need a word with my lot,' said Mr Ian. 'In the van, please, quick as you can.'

'Special advice?' said Millie. 'I hope you're not cheating, Mr Ian.'

There was laughter.

Mr Ian rounded on her, red in the face. 'We actually take ourselves seriously, young lady, and try not to leave things to chance.'

The headmaster stood up. 'Very well,' he said. 'Ribblestrop: get into your groups, sort out your packs, and take your envelope.'

*   *   *

The Priory children sat silent in the minibus.

Mr Ian turned to look at them and, one by one, their eyes dropped.

'I hope you're proud of yourselves,' he said. 'I hope you're feeling good about your behaviour last night, because frankly . . . I'm disgusted.'

Nobody said anything.

'Not a word, eh? It doesn't surprise me. Take those feathers off, Scott. Give them to me – who gave them to you?'

'Sanjay, sir.'

'Sanjay. You even know their names. Well, I thank God that from now on we are divided, pursuing separate paths. I'll tell you now, you are not camping out on the moor.'

He turned to the glove compartment and removed a small box.

'I'm going to give you a mobile phone, Harry. Look after it. It's been charged and it's got my number. It's also got the number of mountain rescue and the school office. But if anything goes wrong, I want you to call me first. Have you got that?'

'Yes, sir.'

'You are staying together. One group.'

'Sir,' said Scott. 'You divided us up. We're in groups of five –'

'I am now un-dividing you. You stay as one large group.'

'Then how do we compete?' said Jacqueline. 'You said split up –'

'Fifteen's way too big,' said Charlie. 'We're supposed to go in different directions.'

The slap left a red mark on the boy's cheek and there was a terrible silence. Charlie's lip quivered. He held his face.

'Anybody else?' said Mr Ian. 'Because there's plenty more where that came from. I have had it up to here with the lot of you. This is not a seminar. This is me, giving you your orders – and if you want to challenge those orders you can expect a Darkroom thrashing as soon as we get home. You will split up, briefly, and you will then re-group. You will make your way to first base – you've all got the same co-ordinates. You will call me as soon as you get there. Is that clear, Johnson?'

Charlie Johnson nodded.

'I didn't hear you.'

'Yes, sir.'

'Good.'

Doctor Ellie was waiting for Mr Ian as he emerged.

She smiled at him, warmly. 'They've got a lot of spirit, your children,' she said. 'I like them. I'm afraid I was rather rude when we first met. Got off on the wrong foot with you, too. It takes a lot of effort to set something like this up and I respect you for that.'

'Would you excuse me? I have to get them packed.'

'Wait a moment.'

'What?'

'There's definitely rain in the air, you know. I've walked these moors for years and I can always tell, whatever the satellites say. We're in for quite a pounding.'

'I doubt it.'

'The Ribblestrop children can cope – I'm not worried about them. It's your lot I'm thinking of. Do they know what they're in for?'

'They've got the equipment they need, Doctor Ellie. Their kit comes up to military standards and I checked it myself. That . . . rabble over there. You say they can cope? I have to say I wonder. I haven't seen a single waterproof.'

'They know what they're doing.'

'I hope so.'

'What did people do, Mr Ian, before the age of plastic and polythene? Do you think they sat under the trees wishing they were equipped?'

'Tell me what they did. I'm sure you're going to.'

'The human skin is waterproof. The human foot can withstand just about anything if you know how to walk. Earth, air, water and fire – that's what these children are dealing with.'

'I saw the fire last night.'

'There you are then.'

'What took place last night was completely illegal. The lighting of a fire, I mean. On Ribblemoor. Maybe you haven't read the Country Code, or the National Park by-laws, but I –'

'Fires have been lit on Ribblemoor since the Palaeolithic Age. There are flint tools which suggest –'

'That wood over there is tinder dry!' cried Mr Ian. 'Every year there are forest fires. And people like you let children strike matches and –'

'We're arguing again, aren't we?'

'Yes!'

'What different views of the world we have. You see, I didn't notice anyone being irresponsible. They dug a pit. They gathered only fallen wood and the forest won't miss it. They live with the land, Mr Ian, that's what you don't understand – and they're not scared of it. They're not enslaved to it like you.'

'Nonsense.'

'They don't oppress each other. You don't protect; all you do is possess and control and intimidate. It's horrible and I will fight you to the death if I have to.'

'It will be your death,' said Mr Ian. 'Hopefully.'

'What can you mean?'

'Yours and theirs together. Now will you excuse me?'

Doctor Ellie looked into Mr Ian's eyes and for a moment there was silence between them.

'I made a mistake,' said Doctor Ellie. 'I thought I could communicate with you. And I was wrong.'

Chapter Thirty-Eight

Gary Cuthbertson had arrived.

He was sitting in a small, steamed up-car, about two hundred metres from the car park. He'd found a lay-by and was waiting for instructions from his brother, for both men were as corrupt and violent as each other. They'd been sacked at the same time, too, so revenge was an extra bond between them.

'Ready to go, Darren?' he said. 'Ready to get him, are we?'

'We're ready,' said Darren.

'What about you, Gordon?'

He was talking to two of his former football team – bitter young men who had also been excluded from the High School. Darren had been the promising striker, until young Imagio had humiliated him. Gordon, his friend, had spent most of his sixteen years stealing, cheating and causing pain.

'If you want him dead,' said Gordon, 'why don't you do him yourself? Why are *we* taking the risks?'

'And where's the money?' said Darren.

Gary Cuthbertson smiled at them both.

'That's really not the attitude, lads,' he said. 'You were keen enough last night and we discussed the financial rewards very carefully.'

'He's a big bloke,' said Darren. 'Captain Routon's ex-army – he's not going to go down easy.'

'He's a stupid bloke as well, lads. And he's not expecting an attack. You surprise him, hit him hard, and if it's in the right place—'

'What if he recognises us?'

'He won't. You'll have your hoods up, your faces covered. You're just a pair of hikers, walking the moor. It's a chance encounter.'

He pulled out an envelope of banknotes and waved it.

'Routon has no idea we're here, Darren. That's why it's easy. He's going to be out there on the rocks, keeping an eye on things. When the kids go off, Ian'll send him to a nice, high place to keep watch.'

'Where?'

'That's what the balloon's there for. Foxy's going to tell us. Routon's wearing a bright red coat – he's unmistakable. So all you do is get behind him and whack him.'

The boys nodded.

'Whack him with what?' said Gordon.

'You shove him off the cliff, lad,' said Gary Cuthbertson. 'You give him a great big High School farewell. Hit him, if you want. But get the idiot out of the game – get him down and chuck a rock on his head. What I'm giving you now is just the deposit.'

'When do we do it?'

Gary's phone was ringing. 'That might be the news we're waiting for.'

He clicked his phone open. 'Mr Ian?' he said. 'Do we have lift-off?'

'Yes,' said a tinny voice. 'Are you in position?'

'I am, lad. With two very capable and enthusiastic young murderers.'

'Everything's ready. The children are moving out now.

I've told Routon to get as high as he can. Foxy's checked in and he'll call you himself with an exact location.'

'We'll be ready.'

Meanwhile, at the camp, there was a final round of hugs and handshakes.

The co-ordinates had been received and checked, and the routes were being plotted. Some of the teams would be heading in the same direction at first, so the teachers organised time delays to avoid congestion. Captain Routon blew his whistle and Sam's team set off first – Sam, Henry, Caspar, Oli and Ruskin. They were so proud to be leading that they moved out of the camp at a swift jog and disappeared round the flank of Flashing Tor, their backpacks juddering up and down. The first Priory team went second and then Asilah moved out with most of the orphans. Fifteen minutes later Millie's group set off and then Mr Ian's second team, who turned off sharp right and plunged down into the valley depths. After a long fifteen minutes, the final groups were released and the camp suddenly seemed horribly empty.

'It's a question of waiting now,' said the headmaster. 'I have to say I feel rather tense.'

'They'll be all right, sir,' said Routon. 'Have they let us down yet? Ever?'

'They know what they're doing. I just hope the weather holds.'

'It doesn't seem to trouble that balloonist,' said Professor Worthington. 'What a view he must have.'

'I've always wanted to go up in one of them,' said the headmaster, dreamily. 'It was one of the things I wanted to do before I was sixty.'

'That's next week, isn't it, Giles? You're going to have to get your finger out.'

'I'm going to take a wander,' said Mr Ian.

The teachers looked at him.

'I want to get up high, where I can see the teams. Routon, you go up Flashing Tor. I'll take the path up to Hangman's Drop.'

'Right-o.'

'I'd go up to the top, if I were you.'

'You don't mind me keeping the binoculars?'

'Not at all. There's a plug of rock at the summit – you'll see everything if you stand on top of it.'

Doctor Ellie stood up. 'I'm going to go for a stroll in the woods. There's one of the oldest oak woods round here, you know. One of the flare paths cuts right through it.'

'Routon,' said Mr Ian. 'Can I keep this coat on? Mine's ruined.'

'Course you can, sir. That's a shooting-range coat, that is – visible for miles. If you got shot in one of them, you knew it was on purpose.'

Mr Ian managed a laugh. 'I'll see you all later,' he said. 'I'll come back here and get a weather update.'

The red figure seemed tiny from above.

Timmy Fox could see him easily, just with the naked eye – he was a little speck inching along a footpath. He'd let the balloon drift into the centre of the valley and could see most of the children in their different groups. The Sanchez group was the one he'd been told not to lose and they were already way out in front.

He got the red coat in his sights again and radioed ex-Inspector Cuthbertson.

'Foxter, here. The children are moving and our subject's all on his own.'

'Where's he heading?'

'North-north west and climbing. Hangman's Drop, I'd say – I've got it on the map.'

'I'll call Gary. He should be moving.'

'There's a nice shortcut through the woods – cut him off nicely. He's got twenty minutes, I'd say.'

'I want to know when he's up on a ridge, all right?'

'I'll keep you posted.'

Cuthbertson cut the radio link and took out his phone. His brother answered at once.

'Percy.'

'Gary. Just had word from on-high. Routon's moving.'

'We're ready.'

'Hangman's Drop – you got it?'

'We'll find it. What about the kids?'

'They're all on the moor, Ian's just checked in. He's going to round his up before lunch and pull back. The Ribblestrop lot are heading straight for the storm and the Sanchez group are on their way.'

'Lightning Tor?'

'Lightning Tor tomorrow.'

'Good. We'll sort Routon – get that job out the way.'

'Hit him hard, Gary. Don't take chances.'

Chapter Thirty-Nine

Back at the museum, Vicky Stockinger was putting on thin rubber gloves.

She would have preferred to work with Doctor Ellie, but everything was happening so quickly now – she could feel a terrible sense of urgency. Only that morning she'd received a letter from Ribblestrop District Council, confirming that their modest grant was to be withdrawn at the next round of budget cuts. That would mean a deficit and that would mean the collection would be divided and re-housed.

Eleudin had to be moved – at once.

She unlocked the side panel of his case and folded it down.

The child lay back on the pot that supported him, exposed to the world and its harsh, corrosive air. She allowed herself one photograph, then set the camera aside to get on with the important job. She had bandages, impregnated with Egyptian spices. She had moulded them together into pads and they were moist and thick as cream. She was tempted to dust the bones, but she was terrified he'd crumble into nothing. The restorers had wired him together, years ago, and he had been sprayed with a chemical that had, over time, turned brown-yellow. The little skull looked like paper – there was something so bird-like about him, so delicate.

She unfolded a mat. With trembling fingers, she took the ribcage. She supported the head and laid him on his side, folding the little arms. The pelvic bones were no longer attached, so she positioned them afterwards, and set the legs carefully against the chest, so he was hugging himself. The gold around wrists and ankles gleamed under the lamp. He did look peaceful. He wasn't sleeping, he was meditating, patiently, but it seemed so wrong that he could no longer see the stars and meteors he'd known through the centuries. She lay bandages over him, gently swaddling the body, wrapping so that the paste cooled and preserved him. When it came to the little face, she arranged the padding so he could just peep through a gap, and then she lay the largest part of the pottery on top.

She paused.

There were so many cases, and so many tiny treasures. She took her keys again and unlocked one after another. She took out coins and a hair-grip. She took out a ring and a necklace, and then she took the discs they'd once thought were playing cards. She lay all the treasures around him. Then she did her best to place the other sections of the pot so he was properly encased. More bandages followed, and soon she was looking down on a huge white cocoon. She had a box ready – one of the re-enforced plastic kind they always used for moving treasures. She packed foam and polystyrene into every gap and sealed the lid. That was when she heard the footstep, and stifled a gasp of fear.

There was somebody in the museum, on the floorboards above – and whoever it was, was moving quietly.

A board creaked and there was a footfall on the stair. She saw a black shoe and, above that, a dark trouserleg.

The shoe was shiny and she knew at once that it was a policeman.

'Miss Stockinger?' said a voice. 'Are you in the basement?'

Vicky didn't trust herself to speak.

The foot was joined by its twin and, with a creak of timbers, they climbed down the final steps. It was a man, with three stripes on his arm. He had a lean, boxer's face and a shaved head. His eyes swept round the open cases and came to rest on Vicky's hands.

'Having a clear up?' he said.

'Yes,' said Vicky.

'The door was open. You are open, are you?'

'Yes.'

'Wouldn't think so. No lights on upstairs.'

Vicky licked her lips. 'I just wanted to . . . get this little job done.'

'What little job?'

'We're closing. Some of these things . . . the more valuable . . . are moving to London.'

'Where's Ellie Mold today? Is she with you?'

'No.'

'Do you know where she is?'

'No.'

'Does she carry a phone?'

'No, I don't think the does.'

The officer was silent. His eyes were raking over the cases again. He turned and stared at some photographs.

'Is she all right?' said Vicky. 'You want to . . . speak with her, do you?'

'We need a little chat. You had the Ribblestrop children here, didn't you? Last . . . Tuesday.'

'Yes. We did.'

'Were their teachers with them?'

273

'No. I think . . . maybe one of them was. There's a teacher called Doonan. I think he was looking after them.'

'They've gone awol, Vicky. Absent without leave.'

'Who have? The children, or—'

'All of them. Every man, bird and beast.'

There were footsteps on the boards overhead again. Vicky's eyes flicked upwards.

'That'll be Deidre,' said the policeman. 'Child Protection. So where would those Ribblestrop children and teachers be, Vicky? Where would you go looking for them, if you were keen to track them down?'

'Well, . . . at school, I presume.'

'I just told you, my dear. We made a visit there yesterday morning and they've flown the nest.'

'Then . . . I don't know.'

The second police officer was coming down the steps. She appeared to be limping, slightly. When she emerged into the light Vicky could see that her face was a mass of boils and swellings. The right eye was heavily bruised.

'Where are they?' she said. The woman's voice rasped, as if her throat was damaged.

Vicky tried to reply, but couldn't find any words.

'How does a school disappear?' said the policeman. 'Where could they have gone, do you think?'

Vicky managed to speak. 'I don't know,' she said, 'but if you want to leave a number, I'll get back to you if I hear anything.'

A child laughed and both officers swung round. There was a footstep again, light but unmistakable. A puff of dust burst from the ceiling, as if the foot had stamped on the bare boards and dislodged it. The sound came again, but this time it was behind Vicky, in the corner of the room.

'Who's that?' said Deidre.

'Nobody,' said Vicky.

The officers looked at each other, frozen.

'I'll check upstairs,' said the policeman quietly. He was about to move when the lights went out. They were plunged into total darkness and there was a scurrying of feet. The police officers cursed. One of them took a step and tripped.

'Where are the light switches?' cried the woman. She was fumbling in her bag.

'It's the fuse box,' said Vicky. 'It's always—'

'Oh my word . . . Stay where you are . . .'

Deidre found her phone and seconds later she had the flashlight on. The thin light cast dramatic shadows, lining the room in black bars that swung and shifted as she turned. They made their way quickly up the stairs. The museum was still and empty, and the only footsteps were their own.

'What is this?' whispered the policeman. 'Where the hell did all this come from?'

'I don't know,' said Vicky, looking where he was looking. Her voice was shaking.

'How can you not know? Have you got the children here?'

'No! I don't know where they're from. They . . .'

Vicky dropped to her knees.

The floor, that she had brushed herself that morning – it was one of the first things she did – was completely covered in feathers. Some were long and large, and others were light as down. Some were still floating in the air, white, with a little brown and silver. The police officers strode through them to the main door and the feathers whirled.

'How many ways out are there?' said Deidre.

'Two.'

'I'll stay here, Brian. I'll hear if anyone moves. You go upstairs, see if they went that way.'

275

'There's nobody upstairs,' said Vicky. 'I'd have seen—'

'Shut it,' said the policeman. 'Don't say another word. We're not messing about here. We're not playing games with these kids – not any more.'

Chapter Forty

Miles, Sanchez, Millie, Anjoli and Vijay were making excellent progress.

The map was easy to follow, for there was a whole range of very simple landmarks. There was Flaming Tor itself, which was now some distance behind them. There was a bridleway, clearly taking them alongside the stream, which they crossed together, so they could make their way round Robbers' Tor. Robbers' Tor was a huge, lumpen thing, and their first destination – Hell Tor – was on the far side of it. Once they'd climbed that, they were confident that Mr Ian's clue would be easy to solve. It read, *Two black eyes, that's what you can see. Look between, that's where I'll be.*

'Black eyes,' said Miles. 'That's going to be two black pools, or shiny stones or something.'

'That or a dead sheep,' said Millie.

'Maybe a crow,' said Vijay.

'Thing is,' said Miles, 'we need to get to the top by evening. You think we camp up there?'

'Depends how exposed it is,' said Millie. 'Let's decide when we get there. Keep moving.'

They were all out of breath.

Their packs were not heavy, for they were carrying only bare essentials. Vijay had a sling-shot and would kill rabbits later that evening. They knew they'd be passing springs, so they hadn't bothered with water. They each had a long stick and Anjoli carried a roll of canvas that would do for the bivouac shelter. They each had a dagger for digging and Miles also had a sword and a hand-axe. Sanchez carried the field telephone, though everyone else had told him to ditch it.

Most of the children had found that it was more comfortable to wear shorts and shirts again, as the sun had blazed on their bare skins and made them sore. Miles had his hair tied back and had put a wild flower behind his ear. He peered up at the summit of Robbers' Tor, selecting the best path.

'Let's go up it,' said Vijay. 'If we head straight, we can do some proper climbing – get a view from the top.'

'Think you can make it, Sanchez?' said Millie.

Sanchez smiled and she put her arm round him.

The Captain Routon assassination squad was making progress too.

Darren led, having been set on the right path by Gary Cuthbertson. After the first cigarette break he came to a signpost. *Hangman's Drop* was carved into a piece of wood, and there was an arrow that pointed to a stile. Gordon went first and a track took them steeply upwards.

They raised their hoods and pulled the strings so just their eyes were visible. When they reached the viewpoint, they stared out over the moor, blinking.

'We shouldn't be standing here,' said Gordon.

'Why not?' said Darren.

'He might still recognise us.'

'Yeah, but he's going over. So what's it matter?'

'What are we going to hit him with?'

'Nothing. Just push him. Shove him.'

'No,' said Gordon. 'I want a weapon. I want to smack him one.'

There was a small information board beside them, screwed to a sturdy post. The two lads stared at it and learnt that Hangman's Drop was a one hundred metre precipice that had been mentioned in a poem by William Wordsworth. A number of the great man's friends had since visited and one had declared the spot 'truly sublime, raising one's spirits to heaven'. On a clear day, said the sign, the sharp-eyed hiker could see fifteen tors and three church steeples.

Gordon leant his full weight against the post and then jerked it backwards. It took a few tugs and a full-on kick from Darren – but at last they'd snapped it at the bottom and had a good, heavy-duty club. Almost at once, they heard an irritable voice.

'Is that Charles or Harry? I want you . . . What?'

A large man in a red coat came into view. He had his hand clamped to his ear inside a capacious hood. The hood concealed most of his face and he didn't notice the two High School boys duck out of sight.

'State your position, child. Have you reformed as a group?'

There was a silence.

'You know how to read a map! What do you mean, you're lost?'

Darren and Gordon peered out from their hiding place. Darren put his thumb up and then pointed sideways. 'Get round the back!' he whispered. 'Cut him off.'

The man in the red coat was speaking loudly. 'If you're by the stream, then I should be able to see you. Is that where you are?'

He stepped to the edge and gazed out across the valley. High above, he saw the hot-air balloon. Far below he could see a tiny cluster of blue dots.

'You're moving south!' he shouted. 'I can just see you. How many of you are there?'

Darren and Gordon jumped him together.

They were one either side and the distance was perfect for a good swing. Mr Ian turned, hearing the noise, but his hood got in the way so he never saw faces. He never saw the sign-board which caught him like a sledge-hammer and he never saw the expressions of glee at the perfect strike. The phone was crunched against his skull and he dropped like a stone. His legs didn't bend and he couldn't put his arms up because the blow had knocked him unconscious. He did a three-hundred and sixty degree loop and plummeted eighty metres into treetops below. Darren and Gordon watched and threw the sign after him.

They were breathless and excited and it was hard to make the phonecall.

'Done the deed?' said Gary Cuthbertson.

'What?'

'Have you . . . have you made contact with Routon?'

'We've smashed his head in. He's dead.'

'How do you know?'

'Coz I just watched him fall off a cliff after we battered him.'

There was a pause.

'Good lad. Get back to the car.'

'They knocked him over the edge,' said Timmy Fox. 'I saw everything.'

'He's definitely gone?' said Percy Cuthbertson.

'He didn't stand a chance. Is that . . . what you wanted?'

'It's part of the plan, Foxy. It means the Ribblestrop kids are in the valley, now. Unprotected. How's the weather?'

'Look, I can see the storm from here. It's heading straight for me, so I—'

'Are you losing your nerve, son?'

'No. I'll make for Lightning Tor now, shall I?'

'Yes.'

'I've got to find the right . . . air current, so it could take a while.'

'I'll call Ian. He can get The Priory kids out of the way, then it's D-day, Foxy. It's going to be real flying – that's what you wanted, isn't it?'

'I'm very nervous, Cuthbertson—'

'Think of the money. If you get nervous, think of the money. And the freedom.'

'Yes. We can do it – and then I'm off.'

'That's the deal, Foxter. Keep it in mind and don't screw up.'

Timmy Fox's basket shuddered and he felt a blast of wind drag him forward. He clutched at the safety cords. It reminded him of *Maisie* for a moment, the dear little plane that had once meant everything. Again, he felt the sickness of loss. The gust was an outrider for major currents, for there was no doubt about it: a real hurricane was approaching. He could see it, riding in from the ocean, and it was laden with foul weather. The sun was bright still, so he turned up the burners and rose. There were thunderclouds sitting on the horizon, moving towards him. He swallowed and licked his lips. That's where he was flying: straight into a storm.

Chapter Forty-One

Doctor Ellie was deep in the woods and had found another stone.

She was surrounded by some of the oldest trees on the moor and, though she'd come this way several times before, she'd never been so lucky. What made her stray from the footpath, she couldn't say – but she was amongst oaks more gnarled and knotted that anything she'd ever seen. They might be a thousand years old. Ever since she'd met the Ribblestrop children, she had known some force was guiding her – perhaps she was now more confident in simply obeying her instincts.

The stone lay half concealed by mossy roots.

She knelt over it with flashlight and paper. The carvings had all but disappeared, weathered away to so nearly nothing – but her eyes and fingers were trained and she could read the symbols like Braille. The feather, again – there was always the feather. There was a cluster of little trees all around it and a single flame. There was a spring, and another feather, and there was the bolt of lightning. She was used to reading them as columns now, rather than lines: the bolt of lightning, this time at the bottom.

What if she followed the oldest trees?

For the first time in a long time, Doctor Ellie did not note the location of the stone. She put her map away and looked up at the sun. Perhaps that had been the problem, she thought – this relentless plotting of routes? Instead of mark-ing the spot and cross-referencing, what if she just set off with her eyes open? She plunged into a thicker part of the wood and was soon in a gully. The branches swept the floor and she was climbing over them. There were flowers every-where. The light was green around her. She walked on and on, and when she came upon a stream she knew just what to do. She planted her feet either side of it, at the obvious cross-ing point and, as if at last she was reading the land correctly, she saw the next white stone.

It was in the water, flat on its back, and a fish was resting above it, gills wide. Feather, water, feather, fish. Fish, tree. Tree followed by larger tree – she felt the symbols with her fingers. Feather and, of course, the lightning. Somebody laughed to her left and she stopped. If it was a Ribblestrop or Priory child, he or she had come a long way off-course. She pulled her flute out of her rucksack and blew a loud trill – it was better than shouting.

The laugh came again, from close by, and she swung round nearly tripping on roots. She put her hand out to steady herself and, when she brought it close, she found she had a feather in it.

'Thank you,' she said, softly.

She listened to the water.

'I need a guide, my dear. More than ever.'

Almost at once huge raindrops started to fall, pattering through the leaves. She could not see the sky, but was aware that the light was dimming as clouds rolled in. She stepped into the stream and walked along its bed, the rain drum-ming all around her. She didn't look up. She knew she was going the right way.

Two hours later, in a part of the wood she knew she'd never explored, she found the third stone and there was a small fire burning beside it. She knelt down and touched the symbols gently, and then – as the rain fell harder and harder – she felt a gentle hand on her shoulder.

She looked round slowly, praying for contact. There were the prints of two small feet in the mud and there was laughter all around her, echoing through the trees.

Asilah, meanwhile, was leading two groups that had refused to separate.

The orphans liked to work together and felt anxious if they were too fragmented. Anjoli and Vijay had a streak of fragile independence, but the rest slept together, ate together, and fought together. They came upon some of The Priory children just before dusk, and it was lucky they did.

Two of Mr Ian's groups had met, but they didn't know where the third one was. They texted their teacher several times and tried to call him. When he didn't answer, they called their school number – and that's when the clouds rolled in and network coverage came to an end. They put on their waterproofs and reminded each other that they weren't lost. It was just that they couldn't work out how to get to the right side of Broken Tor, which was their destination. All they had to do was try again, but they'd come several kilometres out of their way.

'He's going to be mad at us,' said Charlie.

'It's not our fault,' said Jacqueline. 'He's still not answering, so do you think we just sit tight till he finds us?'

'No. We'd be better off pushing on.'

'If we try climbing in the rain, it's going to be slippy.'

'What do you want to do then?' said Harry. 'Stay here?'

'No.'

'Go back to camp? I'm not even sure . . .'

'I'm having a muesli bar.'

'It's not an emergency, Tutton! They're for emergencies.'

'To me, this is an emergency. You can eat yours during your emergency.'

'Shut up, both of you.'

When the orphans found them, they weren't desperate, but things were getting tense. They had decided to make a hot drink as they were cold and anxious. Harry found that the matches were damp, and their back-up lighter wouldn't work. The stove remained obstinately unlit, and when Eric whistled to them from the rock above, they almost cried with relief.

'Where are you heading?' said Podma.

The orphans carried lighters and flints, and the stove was soon blazing. Better still, they'd found plenty of dry brushwood in a nearby copse and they lit a proper fire in the mouth of a small cave. It was a bit smoky, but they had enough shelter to sit back and watch as the mist rolled up the valley. Mercifully, the smoke was visible for some distance and it attracted the final Priory team. Everyone came together, relieved and happy, and it was time to unfurl the blankets and get dry. The sun was nowhere to be seen.

'We've got to get to Broken Tor,' said Jacqueline. 'He said we should stay in one group and he'd meet us there.'

Asilah was studying the map. 'It's a long way back. You won't make it today.'

'He's going to be so cross.'

'Just tell him you had an accident,' said Kenji.

'He says only weak people have accidents,' said Scott. 'He says he's never had an accident in his life, and it's all mind over matter and keeping calm.'

'Why is he such a poisonous old devil?' said Israel. 'Is he ever nice to anyone?'

The Priory children shook their heads.

'You'd better all stay with us,' said Asilah. 'We're heading up Roman Tor, but I don't know if we should move in this.'

The rain was falling harder. He looked around and said something in his own language. There was a brisk discussion.

'No, we're going to camp here,' he said, finally. 'I don't think we should risk going any further.'

Tomaz opened his bag and took out three large fish. Nikko lent him his dagger and The Priory children watched, amazed, as he gutted them. The fire soon multiplied into several and a pot of rice was set next to a pan of black-eyed beans. Hot chocolate was bubbling and Tomaz began frying cumin seeds in butter. His pack had been noticeably larger than everyone else's and now they could see why.

Night fell.

'You guys cold?' said Imagio.

The Priory children were as close to the fires as they could get, without burning themselves.

'How come you're not?' said a little girl called Tilda. 'You're not wearing much. How come you stay warm?'

Israel said something in his own language and there was laughter. 'You know where I lived before I came to Ribblestrop?' he said.

'Where?' said Charlie.

'I lived in a place so cold your pee froze. You know what "bonded labour" is?'

'Course they don't!' said Kenji.

The Priory children shook their heads and Sanjay said something in his own language again, which made everyone laugh.

'Bonded labour,' said Eric, 'is when your parents sell you. Like, for a debt. We got families so much in debt they had to sell us, so we ended up working in strange and crazy places.'

'I worked on ships,' said Sanjay. 'I been round the world three times.'

'Liar.'

'Nearly three! You seen Australia, boy?'

'No.'

'Then shut your mouth – you've been nowhere.'

'I don't understand,' said Harry. 'How could your parents sell you?'

'Huh?'

Asilah said something quietly.

'Didn't they love you?' said Scott. 'Or did you do something bad?'

Asilah looked round the group. It was hard to tell who was who, for everyone was huddled in blankets. 'They probably liked us a lot,' he said. 'They just didn't get to know us too much . . . And they had to let us go.'

'Do you ever see them?' said Tilda.

Nikko smiled and looked down. 'Every night,' he said. 'Every damn night – they don't leave me alone.'

'He means in dreams,' said Israel, grinning. He punched Nikko lightly on the shoulder. 'You don't want to sleep near this one, man, he howls like a dog.'

'Not as loud as you,' said Sanjay. 'I remember you at Christmas!'

'Tell us about the cold,' said Charlie quickly.

'What about it?'

'Were you serious? About your pee freezing?'

A few children giggled. 'I was serious,' said Israel. 'You had to break it off in little pieces, there was no other way! This was way up in China, minus thirty, okay? I ran tea to the railway workers there, and hot tea froze solid before I could get it to them – serious. I saw a man once and he just leaned his head on a rail – next thing he couldn't get off again. Men had hammers they couldn't put down – the cold's worse than the heat.'

287

'Show your feet, Eric!' said Kenji. 'Do your feet thing.'

Eric grinned and unsquatted. He put his legs out straight, holding his ankles.

'You want to see a miracle? Look at this – I did this in the circus.'

He put his right foot into the fire and trod down on red-hot embers. He held it there and only when Nikko said something did he take it out. The whole sole was black and there was a smell of roasting.

Imagio said, 'You want a toe, anyone? This boy's better than pork.'

'You could hammer a nail in me,' said Israel. 'We don't feel stuff any more.'

There was a clink of glass.

'Guys,' said Asilah to The Priory children. 'We have rum about this time. It might not agree with you, but you can try it if you want. That's what really keeps the cold out.'

'Hey, let's sing your song again,' said Imagio, as the liquor was poured and the fish unwrapped.

The rain burst over them, then, and it was difficult to hear voices as they sang. The shadows on the cave walls flickered and everyone ate heartily. When the downpour eased, they told stories. They sang again and the Priory children learnt another filthy ballad – this one about a Bengali farmer who did bad things with a buffalo. They got drunk together and when they heard the laughter of strange children, they assumed it was their own. When they slept at last, listening to the buffeting wind, they didn't notice the feathers around them.

They did not feel soft hands drawing blankets up to their chins and touching their hair.

Chapter Forty-Two

Sam, Ruskin and Oli were arguing over the map.

Henry stood back and watched, waiting to be needed, and Caspar was too tired even to listen. The problem was that Sam thought the stream should be on the right, whilst Ruskin and Oli thought it was in the correct place. Sam explained that if they turned the map round, then the stream corrected itself, and that would mean that they were moving in the wrong direction.

'The thing is, Sam,' said Ruskin. 'We're lost. Even if you're right, we're lost.'

'We're not lost if we know where we are on the map,' said Oli.

'That may be true,' said Ruskin. 'If we were on the phone to someone we'd be able to say where we were. But if we can't work out where to go, you know, relative to the things around us, then that is a definition of lost. Isn't it? And that's what we are.'

'I can tell you the exact map reference,' said Oli, sulkily.

'I think we should just wait here,' said Caspar. 'This is a footpath. It stands to reason somebody's going to walk down it. Some time.'

'I think we're quite a long way from civilisation,' said Ruskin. 'I've forgotten which tor we were making for.'

'Red Tor,' said Sam. 'And I think it's that one.'

'It's not red,' said Caspar.

'It might be at the top.'

They gazed up at a great, looming headland, with another granite plug sticking up out of it. It seemed to have its mirror image opposite and something similar further off. As they watched, the valleys in between filled up with mist and the first raindrops fell.

'Typical English summer,' said Ruskin. 'All promise. No delivery.'

'What do you want to do?' said Caspar.

'I say press on. A footpath leads somewhere and . . . we'll find ourselves eventually. I say walk for another hour and then pitch camp.'

'Are you hungry?' said Oli.

'Not yet. I will be, though.'

Ruskin struggled into his backpack and took his glasses off. 'We should have pinched one of the orphans. Vijay or someone. They never get lost.'

'Where do you think The Priory —'

'Shhh!'

'What?'

The boys stood, listening.

'What did you hear?'

'I heard a groan,' said Sam. 'Or a kind of . . . howl.'

'Which direction?'

'In among those trees. Listen again.'

They waited, and sure enough there was a mournful moaning. It lasted a few seconds and died away. Then there was the unmistakable word: 'Help!' This was followed by another moan.

The boys moved towards it and soon found themselves clambering down a steep bank.

'Hello?' shouted Caspar. 'Who's shouting "help"?'

The voice came back immediately. It was weak, but it was fired by desperation. 'Hello!' it cried. 'I'm here.'

Ruskin laughed. 'If only people would stop and think about it. "Here" is meaningless, isn't it? You know, unless you can physically see them.'

'He must be where the trees are bit thicker,' said Oli. 'Come on.'

The boys hurried down a slope into thick woodland. When the voice came again, it seemed to be above them, and now that the light was going it was very hard to see. Eventually, however, they saw something red – high in the branches, spread-eagled. Sam and Caspar clambered up to it and the riddle was solved.

'It's Mr Ian!' cried Caspar. 'He's kind of . . . wedged.'

They managed to lift a part of him and a bough that had been half-broken suddenly gave way. The body slithered and cartwheeled, screaming in pain – and it was lucky that Henry was in just the right position. He caught the body in his arms and laid it gently on the earth.

'What on earth was he climbing trees for?' said Ruskin. 'He's fainted, by the look of it.'

The boys gathered around and shone a torch into Mr Ian's eyes. The face was deathly pale and yet again there was blood in the beard. The coat was ripped and his hands were badly grazed.

'He's in shock,' said Ruskin. 'What on earth's been going on?'

'Maybe he was picking fruit,' said Caspar.

'I'd say he's been attacked,' said Sam. 'A wild boar or something with tusks – and he climbed the tree to get away.'

The eyes blinked open and the pupils dilated with pain.

'Mr Ian?' said Sam. 'You've been injured.'

Everyone nodded.

'Can you walk?' said Caspar. 'In fact, do you know where we are? You've been here before, haven't you?'

'Oh God,' said Mr Ian softly. 'Help me.'

'Which way did you come?' said Oli. 'Do you think you can you remember the way back, if we show you the map?'

Ruskin held it, close to his nose. Mr Ian gasped and they saw there were tears in his eyes.

'Leg,' he said.

'What?'

'He's trying to say "left", said Oli.

'Left?' repeated Sam. 'Or leg? Which direction did you come in? If you can tell us that, we can retrace your steps.'

Ruskin looked down.

'Oh my word,' he said. 'Oli, look at that. He must have said "leg".'

Oli had stood up, and his hands were over his mouth. Caspar had changed colour too, for Mr Ian's right leg was resting at a horribly awkward angle. The knee was almost upside down and then there was a dramatic kink below it, at thirty degrees. The foot looked twisted too and the ankle was so swollen it might have been inflated.

'That's broken,' said Oli. 'That looks just like Uncle Abel after dad's ladder gave way.'

'We're going to have to carry him,' said Sam.

'This is bad,' said Ruskin. 'And I know one thing. We're going to have to give up any idea of winning this Pioneers thing; this is an emergency and the casualty takes priority. I suggest you get on the field phone, Oli, and we'll see if we can rouse Mountain Rescue. If we can't, we'll have to make a splint and a stretcher. Thank God we've got Henry with us.'

'I'll give him water,' said Sam. 'We ought to get some food down him too – and keep him warm.'

The boys busied themselves around the body, which seemed to be fading in and out of consciousness. Oli soon had the phone out and, though its red light flashed importantly, the earpiece relayed only a constant buzz of static. He wound the handle furiously, but there was no connection. Mr Ian coughed up the water they tried to pour down him, and they were forced to stop.

'Jake,' said Oli, quietly. 'It's the pain of the leg. That's the problem.'

'We ought to straighten it,' said Sam.

'Why?' said Caspar.

'Sam's right,' said Oli. 'You have to set a broken limb. We might not find a hospital for days and . . . when our uncle broke his, the doctor said the most important thing was to get the bones back in line, straight away, or you'd be crippled.'

Sam said, 'How do you do that, though? Did you see the doctor set it?'

'You kind of pull it,' said Oli. 'You have to be quite strong, because . . . well, you have to stretch the bones, and then everything knits together again. I didn't see it, but he explained it to me.'

Ruskin shook his head. 'I wish Imagio was here – he's the medic.'

'Yes,' said Sam, 'but you know what Professor Worthington says about the human body – she told us when we were stitching Miles. People just kind of . . . adjust their pain thresholds. Like in the old days, they didn't have anaesthetic, so they got on with the pain.'

Ruskin knelt by Mr Ian's shoulder. He spoke slowly and loudly. 'Mr Ian!' he said. 'You're in shock, but you're going to be fine. We're going to get you back to camp. But first of all, we're going to make your leg comfortable.'

'No,' said Mr Ian weakly. 'Don't touch it.'

'Henry's the strongest. He's going to stretch it for you, and that . . . that should make it better.'

'Don't,' said Mr Ian. He was blinking and managed to focus on Ruskin's face. The child gazed back at him, smiling kindly. He felt a hand on his brow.

'Think of nice things,' said Sam. 'That's what my mum said when I had a tooth out.'

'Please don't,' whispered Mr Ian. 'I beg you. I implore you . . .'

He felt two large, powerful hands around his ankle and smaller ones pressing his shoulders down. Ruskin was smiling, and he saw him nod and raise his thumb. Then there was the most terrible wrench and the world exploded into a million comets of pure, soul-wrenching agony.

The Sanchez party heard the scream and froze.

They had reached their first destination and found the metal box. They had the co-ordinates of the finishing post and had checked them on the map. They were feeling proud and fulfilled.

'Wow,' said Miles, listening. 'What animal was that?'

'Sounded like a bear,' said Vijay. 'A bear with a spear up its bum.'

'Listen. Shh.'

They strained their ears, but there was only silence.

'Must be dead,' said Millie.

'You think we're safe?' said Anjoli.

Millie laughed. 'We've never been safe, little boy,' she said. 'There's too much evil in the world.'

Vijay strained his eyes into the gloom. 'Lightning Tor,' he said. 'You think we'll find it in weather like this? That's definitely where we're heading?'

'Yes.'

'You checked it, Sanchez?'

'Twice. There's something I don't understand, though. It's the place Doctor Ellie was talking about, ages ago – the army place she tried to get to. Closed to the public.'

'So what?' said Vijay.

'So why would Mr Ian send us there?'

'Maybe it's now *open* to the public.'

'Doctor Ellie said it wasn't. She said she'd tried to get in and it had fences and guards. It's the one place she really wants to explore.'

Millie laughed. 'That answers your question, then. She must have chosen it with Mr Ian. Maybe that's where she's going to meet us with Eleudin.'

'Where's Eleudin now, d'you think?' said Anjoli.

'On his way, hopefully.'

'Hey,' said Millie. 'Put your head up.'

'Why?'

'Look at the sky – just do it for a second. Look.'

Everyone watched, as Anjoli rocked back where he was sitting and gazed upwards. Millie started to laugh. 'You look just like him,' she said. 'You're even wearing the bracelets.'

Anjoli smiled then and there was the first, distant peal of thunder. It was as if the rain was encouraged and decided to start beating the earth properly. The children heard the new note of intensity, for the rock they were on was being scoured. They put more sticks on their fire, huddled closer, and the cave filled up with warmth.

'We're staying here, then?' said Vijay. 'For the night?'

'Yes,' said Millie. 'Soon as it's dawn, we'll push on again. There's no point walking in darkness.'

Everyone nodded.

They were a silent for a while, gazing out at the weather. Then, after some time, Sanchez spoke. He talked about a mountain he'd climbed in Columbia. It was like the one they were on and he'd scaled it with his bodyguards.

'You getting homesick?' said Vijay.

'No.'

He started to tell them more and Millie suddenly realised how little she knew. He told them about his strange upbringing in a vast hacienda in Old Bogotá. He told them about the servants and tutors, and his parents' parties that had gone on night after night.

'I was always getting presents,' he said. 'Gifts, from people I didn't know. I never knew why.'

He talked about the clothes that were tailored for him and piano lessons on a huge veranda surrounded by jasmine. There'd been a cook that used to let him sit in the kitchen and make pastries. At last – after another, long silence – he told them about his mother and how wild she'd been. He was smiling as he spoke. He'd had to tell her off sometimes, he said, because she was never serious – she used to hide and read stories to the servant girls.

'Always laughing,' he said. 'She was like a sister. Well, that's not true. A friend. Then a mother at night, I guess. Especially at night. Whatever time she got home, she came in to see me. Woke me up to say goodnight. Ha!' He laughed.

'You got kidnapped, right?' said Vijay.

Sanchez nodded. 'My driver,' he said. 'He'd worked for the family thirty years, but he had no money, and they promised him a fortune. I guess my dad didn't pay high-enough wages.'

He talked more and again he was uninterrupted. He described where they'd taken him and the negotiations. He told them about the moment they'd come for him again and cut his foot. He talked about the phonecalls – the crying and screaming – and at last the shoot-out, bullets smashing through glass, and the eventual rescue. Finally, he spoke of his mother again and how he had come home to find her gone.

'They didn't tell me for a while,' he said. 'I was in shock. And when they did, I couldn't believe it – not for ages and ages.' He smiled. 'They said she had a weak heart. But I never understood that, because she had such a big heart. I never understood.'

The children sat close and Anjoli gently fed the fire.

Sanchez described the funeral and the grave, and how on the Day of the Dead the whole household had gathered, to talk to her.

He said: 'My father kept saying, "Shhh!" He got so drunk. We asked him, why are you shushing us? He said he was waiting to hear her laughter. We listened all night, but . . .'

'What?'

'Nothing. I pretended I heard it, but it was just to keep him happy.'

'Who?' said Millie

'My father. He was crying, you see. He was saying, "I can hear her! Listen!" So I pretended I could, but I didn't hear anything.'

As night fell, a small ice-cream van moved through the same storm.

It was rocking in the wind and the Cuthbertson brothers sat crammed inside it with Timmy Fox. They parked on a high shoulder of the moor, where satellite reception was better. The antennae stood bravely upright, searching the air for signals, but Mr Ian's phone remained unobtainable.

'Nothing,' said Percy, slamming his own down. 'Sounds like he's got the wretched thing turned off.'

'He should have been back ages ago,' said Gary. 'Or at least checked in.'

'I know.'

'If something's gone wrong, then it means his kids are still on the moor.'

'What do we do?' said Timmy. 'Should we abort?'

'Shut up. No.'

'All I'm thinking—'

'We're going through with it, Foxy! There's nothing to discuss, because this is the last chance. Ribblestrop won't be opening again – it's as good as closed.'

'How do you know that?' interrupted Gary.

'I heard this morning. The police are moving in again. First light tomorrow.'

'Police? On the moor?'

'I've still got my contacts,' said Percy, 'and that's what I've heard. They're going to raid the camp and grab everyone in it. So this is "final conflict", boys. I'll do it alone if necessary.'

Gary swore. 'We'll have to move fast,' he said. 'The police will come looking for the children—'

'Those explosives,' said Timmy Fox. 'Surely we can't detonate—'

'No changes.'

'But if the police are right behind us—'

'Everything is ready. We blast the lot of them – soon as we have the kid.'

The three men stared at each other.

'You sure they'll get to us?' said Gary. 'If the weather's this bad, they may turn back.'

'Give me the whisky. They'll make it, I know they will.'

He poured everyone two thick fingers of drink and they drank together. Then he pulled the photograph of Sanchez from the wall and stared into the soft eyes.

'Five million,' he said. 'His dad's worth . . . a hundred times that, but we're not going to be greedy. Keep it simple and quick.'

Gary touched Timmy Fox's arm and the man jumped. 'You ready, Foxy?' he said, softly. 'Those cables will hold?'

'Yes.'

'And you can fly in this? You sure you're up to it?'

Timmy Fox swallowed more liquor and his eyes welled with tears. He nodded.

'Trust the Foxter,' he whispered. 'It can be done and I'll do it. Up and out, yes? Up and out . . . and away, for the rest of our lives.'

Chapter Forty-Three

Dawn broke, but there was no sign of a sun.

The world was saturated, for the rain had come down all night until the ground was mud and sponge. The rocks ran with it and the streams were bulging. Clouds rolled into the valleys and rained yet harder, spurting water that the wind took upwards and sideways, creating cold, wet tornadoes that spun across the moor.

Sam's team had managed to sleep in shifts, for their canvas worked well under the trees as long as nobody moved about too much. Mr Ian was unconscious, with a waxy look to his skin. They found he had vomited in the night, which Ruskin said was a good sign.

'It's like when our cat got food poisoning. Do you remember, Oli?'

'Jake, he didn't have food poisoning.'

'He did. He ate that rat.'

'I meant Mr Ian. He didn't have food poisoning.'

'Yes, but what I'm saying is, the body always knows how to look after itself. Being sick usually means you're on the road to recovery.'

'He's a weird colour still,' said Caspar, poking his neck. 'He's cold, as well.'

'At least he's not shaking any more,' said Sam. 'He's stopped swearing at us, too. I say we get moving, quick as we can.'

'Move where?' said Oli, peering into the misty gloom of the woods.

'Back to the car park.'

'We'll need a stretcher,' said Caspar. He took an axe out of his bag. 'Can you give me a hand, Hen? It needs to be light, but strong.'

Half an hour later, they were ready to go.

They'd finished breakfast and rolled their casualty onto a kind of tree branch ladder. When they lifted it, they found Mr Ian's bottom sank through, so they had to roll him off again and put in more cross-pieces. When they tried a second time, his head lolled backwards, so they wedged in a large piece of tree bark. Ruskin and Sam led, with Henry taking the rear and Caspar carrying the packs. Unfortunately, this meant Mr Ian's feet were much higher, and it wasn't long before the whole body had slipped and slithered over the boys' shoulders, onto the soaking ground.

Mr Ian lay in the mud and started to cry.

They put the stretcher down beside him and tried a third time. This time they lashed him to the wood with his shoe-laces and tucked the canvas neatly around him. He was wet, of course, and the tree bark had spawned a hundred wood-lice, which were now busy in his beard. But there was a redness in his face again and when they lifted him they heard a familiar string of curses. They got him up on their shoulders and made better progress. Before long they were on the edge of the woodland and they stopped to catch their breath and gaze at the storm. The wind gusted noisily, nagging and scratching.

'This isn't going to be easy,' shouted Sam. 'I have absolutely no idea where camp is.'

Ruskin had to yell back. 'I think we go south!' he cried. 'I've got my compass still.'

They peered at the spinning needle. They were all cringing in the lashing rain and it was hard to keep the stretcher level.

'Where's the map?' shouted Sam. 'We ought to try and navigate.'

They set Mr Ian down and searched the navigation bag. The map, unfortunately, was watery pulp. They did their best to unfold it, but it came apart in their hands.

'You know what a lot of people would do now?' yelled Ruskin.

'What?' shouted Oli.

'They'd panic! They'd lose their heads!'

The boys nodded, wisely, and tried to wipe the rain from their eyes.

'We are not going to do that,' cried Ruskin. A jolt of wind knocked him backwards into the grass. His friends helped him back to his feet.

'We,' he roared. 'Are. Going—'

'What?'

'Where?'

'We. Are. Going. To. Get. This . . .'

'This what?' screamed Caspar. 'We can't hear you!'

'This. Man. To. A. Hospital.'

They looked down at Mr Ian and saw that he had opened his eyes. They were wide with terror and his mouth was open too, slowly filling with water. He was trying to move his arms, but he was too securely tied. He managed to roll his head and spit. As one, the boys gathered around him and lifted. As one, they set off along a path that was turning rapidly into a stream.

'This is south,' shouted Ruskin, studying his compass. 'And the one thing we know is that the car park is south.'

'Keep going!'

They bent their heads and marched, and it was Caspar who started to sing. *'Persevere in labour, persevere in pain!'*

'That's your song, Mr Ian!' said Sam, yelling into his ear. 'We're going to make it! Don't worry!'

They started again, singing together, and marching to the beat.

'Persevere in labour, persevere in pain!
Though the path is thorny, dawn is on her way.
Triumph in disaster! Labour not in vain!
We will pull together, come what may!'

'Oh God,' said Caspar, as they floundered in the mud. 'There are floods everywhere. We ought to turn back! This is terrible!'

As he spoke, the stream – which had become a river – burst its banks. The clouds spouted new volleys of water and the wind slashed the boys' bare knees until they staggered and swayed. Somehow they stayed upright and the song turned to a panting mantra as the weight of Mr Ian got heavier and heavier. Soon the water was up to their shins and the path completely disappeared. When they fell at last, it was into a raging torrent that was carrying all the mud from the Ribblemoor hills and rolling down the valley. They were suddenly up to their chests and Mr Ian was floating out of their reach. Henry lunged for him and managed to grab a foot. The shoe was loose, but he gripped the heel – a watery scream filled the valley once again as he was drawn around in a circle. Caspar dived and managed to get a fistful of beard; Oli, Sam and Ruskin trailed after Henry and they were all pulled out of their depth.

They bobbed together into the centre of the stream, one hand each on the stretcher. Almost immediately, they found themselves in white water. The rapids shot them north, into the wildest part of the moor.

Chapter Forty-Four

Asilah's team, meanwhile, was in good spirits.

The group had slept well, for the cave had proved warm. Everyone had been carrying food, so breakfast was hearty. There was also plenty of firewood and they'd had the sense to store it where it stayed dry – so the cave seemed like the cosiest place on earth. The Priory children told stories about their school and the orphans' eyes grew wide at the horrors they revealed. Nobody wanted to set out into the wild weather, so they sat, chatted, and watched the mist.

At last, though, Sanjay grew restless.

'Are we going to move out or not?' he said. 'I'm getting stiff just sitting.'

'Can I see the map?' said Tomaz.

They stretched it out and got their bearings.

'I don't think we should go any further,' said Jacqueline. 'I don't think Mr Ian would want us to try.'

'What would he want?'

'He'd probably want us to stay here and wait for rescue.'

'No one knows where we are,' said Eric. 'And this phone thing is useless.'

Israel laughed. 'We could be here a long time, man. The rain's getting worse.'

Imagio said, 'We can't sit here all day, guys, we'll go crazy.'

'We could split into groups,' said Nikko.

'No,' said Asilah.

'Stay together,' said a Priory boy. 'I want to say together.'

'What are you thinking, Tom?' said Podma.

Tomaz was staring at the map. 'I'm thinking we ought to explore the caves.'

Asilah frowned. 'I remember going underground last term,' he said. 'When they drained the lake, remember? That was the most dangerous thing we ever did.'

'Come on,' said Scott. 'We could give it a go – see where they take us.'

'Is anyone scared?' said Nikko.

The Priory children shook their heads.

'I bet we can get underground,' said Tomaz. 'We'll be able to tell which direction we're heading in, so if we're lucky . . . we'll find a way home.'

Imagio stood up. 'How many torches do you guys have?'

The Priory children produced powerful flashlights.

'Okay,' said Asilah. 'Let's do it.'

They packed the things they needed and kicked out the fire. Tomaz led, with Sanjay behind him, and they moved in single file. The cave they were in narrowed almost at once and ended in a thin crack. The roof lowered too, and they had to force themselves through, and then flop down onto their bellies. After some time, the passage opened and they gathered around for another conference.

Tomaz pointed at a corkscrew tunnel of rock that rose steeply upwards. 'You recognise that?' he said. 'You've seen one of them before?'

'No,' said Israel.

'Captain Routon showed me one. They're water holes. They were bored through in the Ice Age.'

'Is that good or bad?' said Charlie.

'It sounds bad,' said Sanjay. 'The way it's raining, I don't want this place to fill up.'

'It won't do that,' said Tomaz. 'If anything, the opposite. They'll keep the place dry. What I'm thinking is, they probably go a long way and they don't suddenly come to an end – you know, they have to lead somewhere. '

'You know it's in the wrong direction?' said Jacqueline. She was peering at her compass. 'It'll take us north and that's not getting us back to camp.'

'They go all over the place,' said Tomaz. 'That one probably bends round in a little while.'

'Let's do it,' said Sanjay. 'We can't just talk about it. We've got to do it.'

'After you,' said Tomaz. 'You can lead.'

Sanjay crawled into the corkscrew and started to climb. Behind him, the long line of children followed, torch-beams bouncing. They were led up for twenty metres, then back on themselves around an elbow. Then it was a steep climb down and they could feel the pulse of an invisible river, deep beneath their feet. When the roof came low, the wind got in from some unseen fissure or crack, and there was a sound like a flute, long and clear – almost beautiful. Then the tunnel plunged down steeper than ever, like a chimney, and they felt warmth rising. The rock was cracked with lines of silver and there were easy footholds. Sanjay led, down and down, and they weren't heading north, south, east or west. They were heading to the earth's core.

Millie's team had slept well too.

The children had breakfasted on nuts and fruit, and they decided to deal with the foul weather by walking straight through it. They were soaked, of course, and the wind had almost blown them off the ridge they were following, but it never occurred to them to give up or retrace their steps.

By midday they were looking down into a world of boiling cloud. They discarded any items that weren't necessary, preferring to travel with sticks in one hand and daggers in their belts. The canvas cloaks they wore were useless, so they dropped them. They could get no wetter, so the water ceased to bother them. They strode into the rain, exhilarated, letting the wind flow over them.

They didn't know if the path they trod took them in the right direction, for the maps had dissolved. Crags revolved right and left, and they had no idea which one Lightning Tor might be – or if it was even visible yet. They would climb over some rocky outcrop and see down into the depths of the valley for a moment – then the view would be filled with vapour. Sometimes they would have to stop, for they could see nothing – and they would hold one another and shout out their names. They waited, and their beating hearts would gradually calm, and the way would be clear again.

At last, they paused for a rest under a rocky overhang and ate more fruit. There was no chance of a fire, so they squatted close for warmth, smiling at each other. They were amazed at the distance they'd come and the wildness of the world.

'You think this is the way?' said Sanchez.

'It might be,' said Vijay. 'Who cares?'

'What does Lightning Tor look like?' said Miles.

'I guess it's big,' said Anjoli.

Millie started to laugh. They were surrounded by great granite plugs and peaks, and the realisation that they had no idea where they were going was suddenly funny. Their compass was gone and Sanchez had hurled the field telephone into the mist in a joyful display of carelessness. A roll of thunder drove up the valley, making the rock they leaned against tremble. Then it burst like a bomb over their heads and they looked up, expecting to see fireworks. The rain came down yet harder, pounding them.

'We are so lost!' laughed Miles.

Sanchez said, 'We'd better just pick a rock and climb it . . .'

'Climb them all!' said Anjoli. 'Why not?'

He was pointing into the rain, grinning. He crept out from the overhang and squatted in the full force of the downpour. His long hair was plastered down his shoulders and he held it back from his face. He pointed again. Millie joined him, putting her arm round his neck, and Miles did the same.

'What have you seen?' shouted Millie. 'What's out there?'

'Wait,' said Anjoli, into her ear. 'It'll come again. It was just above that ridge.'

Vijay joined them then and so did Sanchez. They waited together in a rain so hard and pure it felt like a waterfall. The sky was turning black as they watched, for a shelf of cloud had arrived, pushing in like a tide. The mist was sent scurrying out of the valley before it.

'Keep looking!' cried Anjoli. 'You'll see in a minute. You'll see the lightning.'

As he said it, a bolt flashed from the cloud and pierced the rock in front of them like a spear. It was like a crack in the sky and the air burned around it. The children screamed as it hit, and then – at once – there was a second bolt. Both had landed on the same peak, but what was truly remarkable was the image left behind. The sudden burst of brightness had turned the landscape black and white, and there was a phosphorescence in the air. The children blinked, for their retinas had been scalded.

The lightning had illuminated a trail of stones right up

the side of the mountain they were facing. The stones were bright white and laid out like markers. But the strangest thing was that they continued to shine, like runway lights. Millie stood and looked behind her and saw, with a gasp, that there were more. They trailed out behind, marking the very path they'd been walking. They had come exactly the right way, as if some guide had been leading them.

'It's the flare path!' she cried.

'What?'

'I said . . .'

The thunder rolled over them and her words were torn to pieces. She shouted again, but there was no need, because they could all see. It was the flare path to Lightning Tor – the mysterious path Doctor Ellie had so hoped to find. It ran straight, and it was lit not by the moon and not by the sun, but by cosmic fire.

The lightning struck again, three times in succession, and they saw the great fist of rock rising out of the crater that was Lightning Tor. They saw the mast above it and a ring of stones around the top. Their path was unmistakable. It was clear as a motorway – an airstrip – and it led to the top of the volcano.

Anjoli went first.

There was mist rolling on either side, but the stones were still aglow. Miles followed him, then Sanchez, then Vijay and Millie came last. They started to run, for the way had been beaten flat by many feet. When the lightning came again, directly ahead, it was reassuring. The white stones faded slowly and needed that burst of electricity to brighten them. They ran and ran, and came at last to where the ground dipped and levelled. They struggled over loose boulders to the foot of the tor they had to climb. Hand over hand they went, for it was protected by walls of rubble. They squeezed over and under, the rain still pelting them.

At last, they came to a fence. *No Admittance,* said a sign. *Strictly Private.* They climbed right over it and dropped happily to the other side.

The next fence they came to was much higher and topped with razor wire. They followed this to an enormous gate made of sheet metal. Amazingly, it swung open as they looked at it. The wind caught it and eased it back with a groan of old iron hinges. The padlocks were gone and the way was clear.

'This must be the place,' panted Sanchez. 'This is the finishing post – that radio mast.'

'I can see flags!' said Vijay.

The storm had died for a moment and the children stood still, catching their breath. The ground around them was covered in red-and-black flags.

'You think Captain Routon's up there?' said Miles. 'Up at the top? Do you think we've won?'

'We must have,' said Millie. 'You don't think anyone else will make it, do you? I bet they've all given up. The Priory kids will have gone straight back.'

'Let's go up. See if there's food . . .' said Miles. He stopped.

'I don't believe it,' said Vijay.

Millie started to laugh. 'That is impossible!' she gasped.

They had clambered up a shelf of rock and were in sight of a narrow track. Fifty metres further up, an ice-cream van had parked. Its roof was the shape of a vanilla cone, just like the one that had seen on the driveway to their school.

They were exhausted, but managed to run to the van, laughing and gasping. They huddled against it for shelter. There was one more stretch of path up to the crater, but the last sprint had worn them out. Millie could barely stand as another twist of lightning struck and they all screamed with joy. The world was drenched in whiteness so the children didn't see the three men until it was too late. They pounced with savage violence and it was over in seconds.

Vijay and Anjoli were slammed into the mud.

Sanchez found his arms twisted up his back and the breath driven from his body. Miles ducked a blow from Gary Cuthbertson and had the presence of mind to go for his sword. But the man was too quick and drove his fist hard into the boy's chest, knocking him flat on his back. They felt heavy knees on their shoulders and in a moment their wrists were bound. A length of chain pulled four of them together, while Sanchez was dragged aside and flung into the vehicle.

Timmy Fox bent over Miles.

'This is the one,' he said, breathing heavily. 'If it hadn't been for this one . . .'

Gary Cuthbertson drew him back and Miles coughed up lungfuls of mud, gasping for breath.

'Get the balloon ready!' he yelled.

'Let me look at him. I'm not a violent man, but—'

'Get the balloon up! I'll deal with them!'

Timmy Fox staggered off into the wind and Gary Cuthbertson turned to Millie. He rolled her over with his boot and knelt by her side. The rain poured upon them both and he grinned into her wide, frightened eyes. 'Think you can walk, girlie?'

'Where's Sanchez?'

'You recognise me? You weren't expecting this, were you?' The man started to laugh, for the child was speechless. He could see her mind racing, as the horror and helplessness dawned. All four were shivering now and he drew the chain that bound them tighter. 'I can drag you, if you want,' he said. 'I'll drag you like dogs and skin you on the rocks!' He took Millie's chin. 'You do remember me, don't you?'

Still Millie couldn't speak.

'Get them up to the top,' shouted Percy. He slammed the door of the ice-cream van and wiped blood from his nose. 'The boy's in the bag. I'll finish off up top and be back for him.'

They hauled the children to their feet together. Gary Cuthbertson yanked them forward, up the steps. When they tripped, he jerked them up again. The ex-policeman guarded from the rear, kicking them in front of him, and they made slow progress up towards the crater. They could hear Sanchez, yelling and kicking, but the wind soon obliterated his cries.

Chapter Forty-Five

What, meanwhile, had happened to the teachers?

The children were now spread across the moor – in mortal danger – and their teachers knew nothing. Dawn had broken and it was just as ex-Inspector Cuthbertson had said. The police were all around the campsite, waiting to spring. They had learnt from their mistakes and had arrived in darkness. Mercifully, however, Captain Routon had risen early . . .

He had been woken by the grumbling of the camel and noticed at once that its water dish was dry. Why that would make it anxious, he couldn't imagine; camels, he thought, could go for months without drinking. He took her down to the stream anyway and the donkeys followed. When he turned, the silhouette of armed officers was clear against the skyline and his training kicked in at once. In a second, he was on his belly. He squirmed along the bed of the stream and, finding cover, crossed to higher ground. He gasped in amazement. A long convoy of police vehicles stretched down the road. There were men everywhere – dogs, too. There was a bus and he read five dreadful words: *Child Protection Emergency Recovery Unit.*

Routon worked fast.

He scraped mud over his face and rabbit-crawled around the flank of Flashing Tor. Then he slid through the grass and got close to a policeman. There was little he could do, clearly – to take on a whole unit would be suicide. The main thing was surveillance. He toyed with the idea of infiltration, for the officer nearby was smoking, away from his mates, radio by his side. Routon sized him up, knowing that one blow to the neck would do the trick. He could pull on the uniform and be at the heart of the mission, working from within. It was a foolish fantasy, though, and the wise words of an old commanding officer came back to him. 'Watch and re-group, Routon! Don't ever be hasty.'

He lobbed a stone at a dog some fifty metres off and waited for the brute to bark in agitation. The distraction was all he needed. The young officer jerked round to see what had happened and Routon's arm moved in and snatched his radio from the rock. He rolled out of sight, somersaulting back down the side of the tor. It hurt to abandon his fellow teachers, but the children came first – they were the priority and he would get to them. He dived into the water and swam upstream, strong as a salmon. In half a minute he had lodged himself under the belly of the startled camel, his hands clutching its nipples. He kicked it hard and the beast broke into a hysterical run straight out towards the open moor. Behind him, he heard the first cry of warning, howled from a megaphone.

'This is the police!' It echoed over the moor. 'Do not move – you are surrounded!' The sirens started to wail.

The camel ran faster.

'Give yourselves up!' cried the voice. 'Resistance is futile!'

He closed his eyes at the thought of the poor headmaster. Professor Worthington, too – and the boy, Doonan – they would be in their pyjamas still and the police would take

315

full advantage of their terror. There was nothing he could do for them, nothing . . . The radio would tell him where they were going and a proper rescue could be attempted in due course.

He swung onto the back of the camel and urged it on. The main thing was to gather up the children.

When he came upon an abandoned field telephone some hours later, he nearly wept for joy. Communication was strength. Isolation was weakness. He wound the handle, but there was only the dull static of interference. He swung it over his shoulder and carried on.

Lightning Tor reared up before him at noon, the thunderstorm hammering it with rain and fire. Soon his beast was breasting the swollen river and cantering up the far bank. The gates they came to yawned open and they ran down the slope to the foot of the volcano. There were more peals of thunder, bursting like bombshells. The lightning was almost constant and he had to shield his eyes against the brightness.

Then he stopped and looked around him in horror.

How had he not seen them earlier?

He had run straight into a circle of Ministry of Defence warning flags. They were red with the black symbols he recognised from his days in the bomb squad. Red and black; if you were close enough to read the symbols, you were in mortal danger. They meant charges were right there, under your feet. They meant the fuses were in place and the switches primed – they were the last things the engineers laid before they cleared the area – concentric circles, warning you. He looked up at Lightning Tor and saw lines and lines of the same flapping colours.

For the first time in many years, Captain Routon simply didn't know what to do.

*   *   *

Vicky Stockinger was looking at police tape.

She had left Ribblestrop in the library van, reaching the Flashing Tor campsite just after lunch. It was wrapped in blue and white: *Police Line – Do Not Cross* ran the words, repeated again and again, criss-crossing into the trees and rocks. She could see a handful of officers sheltering under the remains of a teepee, so she climbed down and went towards them. A dog started to bark.

'No press,' called its handler. 'Nothing to see here.'

'I was meeting . . . a friend,' said Vicky.

'Were you, my dear? Why was that then?'

'Well, I was . . . going for a walk.'

'You picked the wrong day for a walk, darling. Pissing down.'

'Has there been an accident? Or . . .'

'Can't say at the moment – not till the Chief Constable's been.'

The dog was staring at her vehicle, growling, so Vicky ran back to it and climbed inside.

She checked Eleudin, wrapped and boxed as he was, and tried Doctor Ellie's phone again. Then she tried Captain Routon, and then Oli – every number went unanswered. She hadn't been sensible enough to bring a map, but she saw on the dashboard one of the old ones that Captain Routon had distributed.

There was a red ring around Lightning Tor.

It would be sealed off, she knew, for the public weren't allowed near it. But something told her she had to get there – and that a lot depended on her trying. A policeman was walking towards her, staring at her number plate. She started the engine and reversed fast. She could see him speaking into his radio and the dogs were barking again.

She did the fastest three-point turn she'd ever done and accelerated down the lane. She pressed her nose to the glass, gazing through the deluge. She put her lights on and floored the pedal.

Deep underground, Asilah's party was hurrying too.

They were in a cavern stretching high and wide, and they could feel hands on their backs, pushing. There was a whisper emerging from fissures in the rock and their torches revealed long threads of flashing silver.

'I don't know which direction to go,' said Sanjay.

'Look,' said Podma. 'Get over here and look at this.'

He was crouched over a low ridge in the floor that led into the next chamber. When the children gathered they saw a small footprint. There was another, just beyond it.

'What are they?' said Asilah. 'Are they fossils?'

'No,' said Tomaz. 'I don't think so.'

A Priory boy said, 'If they're fossils, that means millions of years. They can't be that old, can they?'

'Don't step on them,' said Jacqueline. 'Look! You can see the toes. Who . . . ?'

She saw him, for a moment, then – and didn't believe her own eyes. He was simply a movement at the edge of the torchlight, then gone again – too quick to be sure of. She heard his feet, but the quick slap on stone could have come from anywhere, so she couldn't trust her senses. She jumped forward in pursuit, but stopped. Israel heard the cry and spun around – and he knew this time. He grabbed Tomaz's wrist. Tomaz put his finger to his lips and one by one they all fell silent. They held their breaths.

'What did they say?' said Israel.

'I couldn't hear. It was a word, but – '

'It was our language,' said Asilah. 'Wasn't it? Did you hear what they said?'

'Ky-dián,' said Eric. 'Jaldi.'

'What does that mean?'

'It means, "hurry",' said Israel, 'But you use you it . . . you use it when something bad's going to happen. It means "move" – "get there!"'

'They're guiding us,' said Tomaz. 'They have been, for weeks.'

Something whistled over their heads and there was the clunk of metal on wood. Tomaz moved past Jacqueline and the tunnel narrowed into a crack. There was a circle of polished metal, like the one they'd found on the Edge. It was sharp, and etched with silver and bronze, and it lodged in the damp sand beside another footprint. The tunnel widened beyond it.

'Hurry,' said Eric. 'They're going to take us somewhere.'

'There's a tunnel. A proper tunnel!' said Tomaz.

'Have you been here before?' said Charles.

Tomaz was pressing through. 'There are tunnels everywhere,' he said. 'There's miles and miles of them, and . . . maybe they connect. I think we should run.'

They came to a staircase and the children flowed down it. At the bottom was a metal grille, twisted out of shape as if the rock had half crushed it. The gate had burst open and led them into a passage identical to the labyrinth that ran round Tomaz's home. There was sand on the floor and the walls were smooth.

'Look,' said Israel. 'Railway track!'

They shone their torches and saw metal rails gleaming back at them – long, thin, and curling into the distance. Ahead was north. Behind was south: every compass made it clear.

'South means Ribblestrop,' said Asilah. 'North means . . .'

'Shhh!' said Tomaz. 'Don't speak.'

'What is it?'

'They're waiting for us. Don't shine your torches! Put your torches down.'

319

They did so.

'Turn them off. There's three of them.'

'Who?'

'Turn the torches off. I think we have to go north.'

'Who did you see?'

One by one the torches were clicked off and the darkness took hold. It was a darkness so thick it seemed airless and the children stood motionless.

'They just want to look at us and . . .'

'Why?'

'They want to be sure. Stay still.'

They stood, like statues, though there were many who longed for the comfort of light. Some felt a hand on their arm and others felt fingers – delicate fingertips – in their hair and on their faces. Some felt what might have been breath on their feet. When Tomaz turned his torch back on, everyone winced at the shock of it. The trance was broken and at once they saw that things had changed, slightly – everyone was in some way different. In the seconds or minutes that had passed, wrists, ankles and necks had been festooned in a fine, golden thread – it was as fine as silk, woven, looped and knotted. Behind each ear was a flower and then, as they stood dazed by this, a small voice said the soft words again: 'Ky-dián . . . jaldi!'

It was written in the sand on the floor, and on the walls, scratched in dust. Sanjay raised his arms and saw the letters on his skin, in bright red clay.

'Let's go,' said Imagio.

They ran, fast.

The passage filled with the drumming of feet. They followed the rails and soon came to remains of a train, its carriages empty and windowless. They couldn't stop to inspect it. They came to rock falls and clambered over them, to resume their running. At one point a bird shrieked and flew bright white over their heads. A flurry of bats came from the rear and passed with the beating of a thousand wings. They ran through rain, for in places the roof sprayed fountains upon them, then the tracks led upwards over sand.

They came at last to an archway, where sand and dust poured from above as if the ground was moving. Beyond it were steps, hammered in pure silver.

'Oh God,' said Sanjay. 'Where are they taking us?'

'Go,' said a voice. 'Follow!'

The tunnel was alive with cries: 'Jaldi! Jaldi!'

The steps twisted up in tight circles and the children's torches made the walls glimmer, for there were ropes of silver marbling every surface. As they started to ascend, they felt a low rumble deep underground.

'What was that?' said Jacqueline.

The rumble continued and dust ran faster from the rocks above their heads.

'It's an earthquake!' said Charlie.

'No,' said Nikko. 'I worked in a quarry. I think someone's blasting.'

There was another long peal of thunder.

'That's explosives.'

Chapter Forty-Six

Cuthbertson had activated the switch codes he'd been given and he was ready for full detonation.

The main charges were linked to timers, for obvious reasons; what the children below had heard were what the setting engineers called 'testers'. The testers blew when everything was live and ready, for their job was to crack the heart of the rock. The cracks would allow oxygen to reach the high explosives deep inside the tor, for oxygen guaranteed cataclysmic reactions. The whole landscape would erupt and change forever.

The man's fingers were trembling, because everything was going so well.

Sanchez was safe in a bodybag, securely bound. He'd dragged the boy out of the van and given him a few more blows. That had subdued him. The Fox had hauled him up into the balloon basket, which was now anchored close to the radio mast. The other children were tied to the railings of the bridge, the volcano crater yawning below them. The storm raged on over their heads and Cuthbertson could feel the wind tugging at the control room's roof.

The computer screen was green. It now demanded final confirmation and Cuthbertson smiled. He had waited so long for this moment of destruction and he wanted to savour it. Fifteen minutes, they would have – that was the minimum countdown. Millie and her friends had fifteen minutes of life left, and he would be flying out with a boy worth five million pounds at his feet. He chuckled and tapped in the final code. *Are you sure?* he was asked, and he wanted to shout.

He typed one word. *Yes.* He re-entered the last four digits. One click and the job was all but done. He wiped his eyes and pressed the key. The screen turned red and the countdown started in clear white digits.

He pushed out into the wind and staggered as the rain hit him. The children were cowering on the bridge.

'You've got quarter of an hour,' he cried. 'Use it well!'

'Where are you taking Sanchez?' screamed Miles. 'We know what you're doing! We—'

The ex-policeman turned and slapped the boy hard. He couldn't resist it and Miles crumpled at once, bent double from the blow. Vijay, however, managed an extraordinary acrobatic manoeuvre, using Anjoli's back as a platform. The boys were bound together at the wrist, but he could still roll and bring his right leg high. He sent the ex-policeman staggering back with a kick to the throat and Cuthbertson fell against the handrail, teetering dangerously close to the edge.

He clutched his neck and stood gasping. He spotted a rock in the mud and toyed with the idea of smashing the four heads in, one by one. That was when he noticed a blue library van nosing up the track below, pushing through the mist. Then a giant shadow blotted out the light and he saw that the balloon was rising – the Fox and Gary were working the hydraulic winches together now, ready for the launch. A rope ladder dangled. It was time to get aboard.

He rubbed his throat and strained his eyes. The van had disappeared from view and there was now a roaring as the Fox opened the burners. He reached for the bottom rung, because his brother was yelling. Millie was screaming at him and it was suddenly raining feathers.

Cuthbertson turned again, mystified. He was completely surrounded by birds and the air was full of their cries.

The children underground had climbed until they were dizzy.

The explosions below rumbled on and they clambered faster and faster away from them. Then, suddenly, they broke out into daylight and rain. They found themselves among trees – but trees like they'd never seen. The roots emerged from solid rock and, in places, the trunks had fossilised. The children fanned out, gazing, speechless – it was a forest glade and there was foliage spreading over their heads. But they were enclosed in a crater, the walls rising almost sheer. Strangest of all, now that they could take in the details, they could see curious shapes hanging, suspended from some of the tree branches. Where branches were most entangled, the same objects sat together in clusters – they looked like earthenware jars, draped in ivy and lichen. Some had cracked wide open.

The children gathered again, under an ancient oak, and Sanjay pointed in astonishment.

The jar above him was tipped an angle and through a wide crack they saw a skull. It was peering down at them and behind it were ancient bones.

For a moment they were too frightened to move, for they realised they were entirely surrounded, and there was an unbreakable stillness. The trees were full of the dead and beside each jar stood a bird.

'Don't move,' said Asilah.

Tomaz said, 'It's the necropolis. We've found it.'

The birds watched the children, as if children were a rare species. The beaks were cruel and the eyes unblinking.

A voice came then, from high above. It was Millie's voice and it was a long, loud cry for help. Everyone looked up and, as if to complete the madness, a hot-air balloon rose into view. At once there was a whirlwind of screaming and a blizzard of feathers – for the birds rose as one and the leaves were sighing.

Ruskin's team saw the whole flock as it emerged from the crater.

He jumped out the library van just as the falcons rose and stood staring as they coiled around the balloon. He and his friends had been saved from drowning by Mr Ian's red coat. Their journey through rapids and waterfalls had been a long one, but luckily there had been air pockets stitched into the lining and they'd stayed afloat. When they'd come under a bridge at last, they'd managed to cling tight to it – and that had been just as Vicky roared into view. She'd come within inches of running Caspar down as he floundered into her path.

'Get in!' she screamed. 'Hurry!'

She got the passenger door open and everyone piled inside. Mr Ian was thrown into the back and they raced on, for Lightning Tor still seemed the only possible destination. Now the volcano towered above them and there was another peal of thunder.

The birds soared higher.

They could see Cuthbertson dangling on the rope ladder – he had been jerked off his feet. He was floating upwards and he had a foot on the bottom rung. The furious birds were all around him, and he had to use one arm to shield his face.

Millie was still shrieking, too, but her words were torn away by the wind. Sam pointed and raced towards the tor – more children were appearing on the rim of the crater, piling up from below. There were Podma and Eric, followed by a Priory boy – Scott was levering himself over a rock as the rain came down. Israel followed with Jacqueline. Kenji and Nikko helped each other, and in half a minute Asilah's whole party was swarming over the bridge towards the four captives.

Cuthbertson was looking down in horror and another bird snapped at his eyes. He felt talons on the back of his neck and he managed to punch at it. It sailed off, screeching in fury. The tor was seething with children and he saw that some had weapons – he could see someone poised to throw a spear. He could see the terrified face of Timmy Fox, shouting instructions of some kind. When he looked down again, he saw with horror that a giant of a boy was racing up the side of the volcano. He knew exactly who it was and his terror spurred him up another two rungs. A falcon tore at his hand and he almost fell – it had cut a tendon and the pain was unbearable. He touched the basket, reaching for his brother.

At that moment, he felt a searing pain in his arm and saw an arrow, just above his elbow. Two spears hit the basket and, fired by sheer astonishment, he made another rung. His wrist was grabbed and he had a surge of hope.

Henry was getting close, though, and the children were howling. The balloon plunged downwards into a vacuum and Cuthbertson was nearly jarred into the abyss – again he felt the bite of something sharp. The Fox was lowering some kind of harness and he managed to grab a strap. That's when Henry leapt and caught the bottom of the ladder in his powerful hands. At once, Asilah grabbed his leg and Israel grabbed Asilah. Miles was free, having had his bonds cut by Eric's dagger. He made a grab for Henry's ankle as the boy was lifted past him into the air. He felt Millie's arms round his waist and, when he glanced down, every child from Ribblestrop and The Priory was in the chain. Timmy Fox was trying desperately to cut loose: he turned the burners up to full and the balloon rose slowly upwards.

If it hadn't had been for Sanchez, all would have been lost.

He was still zipped inside the bodybag, with his hands and ankles lashed. He had been trampled, but he'd managed, somehow, to stay calm. His bodyguards had drummed it into him: if he was ever kidnapped again, he had to avoid panic. Control was everything and, as he lay there rolling in the darkness, he remembered the fossil round his neck – that gift in the night from unseen hands.

He'd used it twice as a tool, for the tribe had fashioned an edge as sharp as a razor. Now, he brought his legs up and wormed them over his wrists; his arms were painfully twisted, but they were in front of him and he could just bring his fingers inside his shirt to grab the little stone. It took seconds to cut the cable ties that restrained him, though he slashed his thumb badly in the process. Then his feet were free and he set about the bag itself. One cut from top to bottom and he was up like a dervish. Gary Cuthbertson's face was the first he saw and he leapt, headbutting hard with the full force of his skull.

The man's nose was squashed like a fruit, and Timmy Fox screamed in terror. He leapt back and a bird went straight for his throat. The balloon rose, but the children were hauling it down again. Ex-Inspector Cuthbertson had both arms through his harness and he watched in horror as Sanchez leant down and cut it loose with a single slash. Then he started work on the ropes of the ladder. The ex-policeman just had time to gasp, for he could see the future in an instant. The ladder dangled on a thread and the boy was hacking through it, rage in his eyes.

Cuthbertson jumped before he fell, lunging wildly. He caught the steel struts of the radio mast and, for a few bewildered seconds, he hung there, paralysed. Then he squeezed his battered arms and legs through the struts and watched the balloon sink slowly to the earth – for Sanchez had simply turned off the burners.

'Where's Oli?' yelled Ruskin, through the scrum of children. 'Where's my brother?'

A lot of the boys had rolled down the sides of the crater and were scrambling in the rubble and mud.

Vijay grabbed him. 'They've set explosives!' he yelled. 'Oli's in there, trying to shut them down!'

The word spread and, as one, the children clambered back over the bridge. It was a race against time now, for fifteen minutes had already turned into nine.

Timmy Fox and Gary Cuthbertson found themselves alone by the collapsing balloon. They were torn and traumatised, and their faces and hands were running with blood. Somehow, they blundered to the library van. Its doors were wide open. The key was in the ignition and they clambered inside. The Fox revved the engine and they made their escape.

They didn't hear the agonised cries of Mr Ian behind them. They bounced down the track and screamed onto the open road.

Chapter Forty-Seven

Where was Captain Routon?

He had been stranded among the warning flags, too frightened to move. Then he'd felt the ground shake beneath his feet and another series of instincts kicked in. In a moment, he found one of the detonation passages – it was marked by a yellow flag. He was halfway along it when the field telephone he'd strapped to his back rang weakly.

He snatched the receiver up and a polite voice said, 'Is that the headmaster?'

'Oli? No.'

'Oh. Can I speak to the headmaster?'

'Where are you, lad? It's Routon here and we've got an emergency —'

'We have too, sir. We're in quite a fix, actually. We're on Lightning Tor —

'What?'

Captain Routon heard a buzz of excited voices.

'Sir, we're actually in quite a mess. You know that policeman we never got on with, Inspector Cuthbertson? He's set explosives somewhere and we're pretty sure they're about to be triggered. I'm in the control room now. I've been trying to cancel the detonators, but I'm not getting anywhere.'

'You're at the controls? You're on Lightning Tor?'

'Yes.'

'Oh God. I'm following a wire at the moment – I'm under the ground.'

'Where, sir?'

Routon looked along the tunnel and saw the long, black cable looping neatly round a corner. He moved swiftly and came to some stairs.

'I'm right underneath you! I've found stairs . . .'

'There's a lot of passages, sir. Asilah said –'

'I'm going to look for the explosives, Oli. It's MOD work – it's a question of tracing the wires. How long have we got?'

'Seven minutes, just over.'

'I've come to a door of some kind, so it looks promising . . .'

The door swung open as he pushed it. There was a sign: *Ticket Holders Only*, so he continued into a hallway. Beyond this was a huge archway of brick, which opened into a vaulted chamber.

Captain Routon stopped in amazement. He was in a railway station and it was festooned with bright lightbulbs. There were two platforms and they were joined by an iron footbridge. The words, *Lightning Tor Listening Post* spread over a curving wall of dusty tiles and there was even a ticket office next to a wating room. He could see vending machines and old advertisements for hot drinks and cigarettes.

'Oli?' he said.

'Yes, sir?'

'You won't believe what I've found . . .'

'Six minutes, sir.'

He moved forward. 'This is unbelievable.'

Captain Routon walked to the edge of the platform and looked down at the tracks. He said a quick prayer of thanks, for he could see the beautiful logic of the installation. The MOD engineers had laid the explosives in a neat row, between the rails. They were wired in series and they stretched right to the buffers at the end wall. Fifteen metres of carefully wrapped nitramines and the letters HMX were stencilled on their covers – High Melting Explosive. The fuses gleamed, conspicuous in their tiny glass bubbles. The army boys who'd wired them had taped red warning signs to each one and the wires ran back to a control circuit in the centre, which lay under a perspex lid.

'I've found them,' he said, quietly. 'There's enough down here to end the world.'

'Oh,' said Oli.

Captain Routon jumped lightly onto the tracks. He lifted the perspex lid and saw the timer at once. It corresponded, no doubt, to the one that Oli was looking at. He had five minutes and twenty-two seconds left. He scratched his chin.

'Excuse me, Captain Routon,' said Oli. 'Are you able to do anything?'

'I don't know, son.'

'It's just that things are getting a bit tense up here. Millie says we're going to die.'

'Right.'

'There's quite a lot of disappointment, because we thought things were going our way.'

'Stay calm, lad. Keep your head.'

'I am, sir. But some of The Priory children are crying. So's Miles.'

'Bear with me. I just need to check a few things – I'm not up with the regulations any more, so it's going to be a little bit of guesswork. From memory, Oli, when you disconnect a battery that's been wired through an ARZ regulator, what's the disconnection procedure?'

'Oh Lord,' said Oli. 'That's tricky.'

'I know.'

'You have to work backwards, don't you? But it depends on how many terminals there are.'

'Seven.'

'That's a Horton-standard. Sam, be quiet!'

'Horton, yes. There's a procedure, isn't there? I did this at night-school, years ago.'

'Are you looking at it right now?'

'I'm looking at something similar. I'm afraid my hands are a bit shaky.'

'Look at terminals two and four, sir. Are they wired together? Do they have a shared live?'

'Yes. I think they do.'

'Then those are the last ones to cut, because live uses neutral. You go seven, six, five, three, one – then you come back to four, and finish with two. I'm pretty sure about that.'

Captain Routon produced his penknife and licked his lips. He started work, cutting back the insulation tape.

'We've got three minutes thirty-eight seconds,' said Oli. 'Miles wants you to get a message to his mum, but you won't survive if we don't, will you, sir? So—'

'Easy does it. Nice and steady.'

'We've lost Tomaz, by the way. He's the only one not here.'

'I'm disconnecting seven.'

'We're all holding hands, sir. We thought we might sing—'

'Shhh, lad. I'm concentrating.'

Captain Routon removed the screws one by one. He lay them to one side and eased out the wire.

Oli waited. He could hear the man breathing. At last, he said, as gently as he could, 'We've got fifty-two seconds left.'

'Don't need them,' said Captain Routon. 'We're safe.'

There was a burst of applause and cheering, and then a drenching wave of radio static as lightning struck the mast above them, again and again.

Captain Routon arrived at the volcano summit five minutes later.

There was a stink of sulphur in the air and the children had gathered outside the control room, gazing upwards.

There was something black at the top of the antenna.

A few birds were wheeling around it and now and then, one of them pecked and screamed. It was hard to see what the thing was, because it appeared to be half melted. It was a burnt mass, but as the children stared, they could make out a hand on the end of an outstretched arm and what looked like a boot. The lightning flashed again and the mass sizzled and glued itself harder to the metal frame. The children gasped then, for the flash had been just enough to illuminate a face, with boiled eyes that stared from a mask of absolute agony. Ex-Inspector Cuthbertson would never bother them again. He would need to be chiselled from the metal and brought down piece by piece.

Chapter Forty-Eight

Where was Doctor Ellie? Where had Vicky gone?

They were with Tomaz, still at the foot of the crater and the rain dripped down through the trees over the jars and onto their faces. They unwrapped Eleudin together, at the base of an ancient oak. Its trunk reared out of the rock, half-petrified, and they laid their bundle between its roots. The child's bones were crumbling.

'He's just dust,' said Tomaz, quietly.

'They're all just dust.'

'We can't leave him on his own,' said Vicky. 'Let's put him with friends.'

'You choose,' said Tomaz. 'Next to that one, maybe?'

There was an urn above their heads, wrapped in sacking. It dangled from a bough on old creepers and they could just reach up to it. They took Eleudin together, lifting him on his fragment of pot and placed him inside.

'Do the birds eat them?' said Tomaz. The falcons had returned and sat motionless, gazing at the new arrival. 'I mean, when they died and were brought here. Is that what the birds do? I don't really understand it.'

'Nor do I,' said Doctor Ellie.

'If they do, is it worse than burying someone?' said Vicky.

'It's different. I have a friend in India: he might know more. But the precise rites and rituals – how can we ever be sure? I still think they kept their dead with them, for some time. Maybe until they felt it was right, or maybe until the moon was in an auspicious place – maybe they had to wait for the lightning. Then they'd come here, perhaps. Hang them here, in the trees, and . . . would the birds break open the pots? I doubt it. But there are tribes in Africa that expose their dead to wild animals. The Parsis, as well, it's still done today. Vultures come, to take the remains and leave the soul free and clear.'

'I would like to be a falcon,' said Tomaz. 'I can understand why they wanted falcons around them.'

Vicky smiled and wiped her eyes. The raindrops ran down her face.

'This is goodbye,' she said. 'You think we can preserve this place? I don't.'

'No, of course not.'

'People will come and change it all.'

'The birds will need protection,' said Doctor Ellie. 'I can get some birdwatchers down in twenty-four hours. Set up a camp maybe, but . . . my protest days are over.'

'What do we do, then?' said Tomaz. 'We just leave him?'

Doctor Ellie looked at him. 'I'm going to suggest something to you both – something controversial. I'm going to suggest that we gather all the remains ourselves and hide them.'

'Where?' said Tomaz.

'In caves, down by the silver deposits. Out of view, where nobody will see. It's not perfect, but – they won't last long here and we don't want them . . . put under glass. Do we?'

'You mean bury them,' said Tomaz. 'Can we do that?'

'Their souls have gone, surely. They've got Eleudin back now – I don't see why they'll be waiting any longer.'

335

'They never wanted to be buried,' said Vicky. 'They like the light too much. And the rain and—'

'I know, dear, but I don't see how we can save them.'

'Who were the children?' said Tomaz. 'If their souls are gone, how come we were followed, wherever we went? Why were they playing with us?'

'Because they loved you,' said Vicky.

Tomaz covered his face.

Doctor Ellie smiled, but they could see how she too was struggling. 'I'm not an expert,' she said. 'I told you before, Tom, I'm just a dry old stick that's been pushing my nose in. Guessing. I don't even know how it started and I don't know what I'm going to do now we're at the end of it all. I don't know what they want.'

'Did they just want to look at us, maybe? Or did they know us somehow?'

'I don't know, Tomaz.'

'Because I never saw them,' said the boy. 'Not really – not to look at, full on. It's like when I see Lord Vyner. It's always a reflection in a mirror. I heard them, though, all the time.'

'They were always laughing,' said Vicky. 'So that must be good.'

'I was guided here through the wood,' said Doctor Ellie, 'but all I saw were footprints. And yes, I heard the laughter. Felt a hand—'

'I wish they'd take their dead for themselves,' said Tomaz.

'I know.'

'We can't bury them, Doctor Ellie.'

'I don't see what else we can do, love. There will be people here – soon.'

Tomaz felt a hand in his then and froze, because it was such a small hand.

Doctor Ellie turned, aware of a movement. Then she froze

as well and saw Vicky's mouth open and her eyes widen, for there were children everywhere. For a moment they thought it was Anjoli and Sanjay. They thought they saw Millie and long-haired Miles smiling – and then they thought it was bare-chested Nikko, staring with huge eyes, wreathed in flowers. Then they knew it wasn't.

The bodies were pale and the hands were white as if rubbed in chalk. The wrists were wrapped in gold thread and the skin was hennaed with complex tattoos.

Time stood still for a moment and the birds watched. The figures glowed. They were projections on the air, half seen – reflections in so many mirrors – but all around there was movement, for the leaves were trembling and there was sunlight. Tomaz would talk about what he saw, or thought he saw, but his version of events would differ from Doctor Ellie's. Tomaz said there was no laughter – just movement and rustling. Vicky said she heard them talking and she heard the sound of metal on stone. She said she saw one of the urns swing and lift, and she said she even saw hands passing it. She could not raise her head, though; it was all at the side of her vision.

Doctor Ellie said least of all, for she was too upset – she vowed she would write it down, one day, when she finished her history. She said that all she knew for sure was that the Caillitri children were leaving Ribblemoor, at last, and would never return. It dawned on her only at that moment that they really had been there in the valley and that the Lost Tribe was found again, in time only for farewell. They had returned to claim their dead.

When the three watchers came to and could move, the air around them was warm. They each found a flat stone in their hand and it was white, etched over with a fine pattern of silver and bronze. It had a word they'd never heard or seen before, carved over a feather.

337

'*Gaovida*' was the word, and there was a curious accent under the *o*.

When they went among the trees, every pot was gone – even the creepers that had tied them had been removed, as if the graves had never existed. There was another change, too, though it was hard to say what. A powerful presence was no more; a charge in the air, like the scent of electricity, has been dissipated. It was as if the sacred grove were sacred no longer.

The orphans translated the word for them when they all got back to Ribblestrop and were sitting in the dining hall. It was a word, said Sanjay, used by sister to brother, or parent to child – an intimate word, when one is setting out on a journey. 'Goodbye,' he said. 'But it's much more than that. It's . . .'

Anjoli said, 'It's when you're going a long way and you don't want to really say it.'

'Yeah,' said Eric. 'Kind of, "Goodbye, I love you – see you again".'

'But it kind of means you know you might not,' said Sanjay.

'It's a pretty sad word,' said Israel.

Asilah said, 'It's the one my mother used.'

Everyone looked at him. He had never spoken of his mother.

'She said it to me, the last time I saw her,' he said. '*Gaovida, chele*. It means . . .' He hesitated. 'It means, "Stay well, my love . . ."' He paused again, because his voice was shaking. '"Until I see you again. Some time, I don't know when. But I hope I do."'

Imagio was there first. He put his arms round his friend and hugged him, because for the first time in so long, strong, sensible Asilah had started to cry. Imagio kissed him and held him. 'Come on, man,' he said, quietly. 'Come on.'

Everyone gathered. 'It's a word full of love,' said Imagio. 'Isn't it? That's something, surely. That's what you hold on to.'

Epilogue

I

How did things end? Where were the teachers and how would everyone be reunited? Extraordinary events unfolded now, for the day was far from done. The children tore their eyes away from the remains of ex-Inspector Cuthbertson and it was just at that moment that there was a squawk of radio static.

It was the police radio, that Captain Routon had stolen. He put it to his ear.

'Oh my word,' he said. 'I'd completely forgotten!'

'About what?' said Millie.

It's not over, is it? – but what can we do?'

'What isn't over?' shouted Miles.

'The headmaster. Doonan. Professor Worthington. Shhh!'

Captain Routon listened to the faraway babble of electronic voices.

'It's bad, boys,' he said. He turned his back, cradling the radio to his ear. 'Very bad. They've been arrested. And taken—'

'Arrested?' said Sanchez. 'Arrested for what?'

'Wait!' said Captain Routon.

He clicked a button again and they heard the buzz of static.

'So where are they?' said Miles, unable to bear the suspense. 'Where are they at the moment?'

'Hang on, lad. I'm just getting an update.'

He turned a knob and listened harder.

'They're saying something about a train. They're being taken to London, by the sound of it, but . . .'

Millie grabbed the radio and shouted into it. 'Where are you taking our teachers?'

She held it close.

'Tiverton,' she said, after a moment. 'They're going to Tiverton Parkway.'

'Where's that?' said Podma.

Caspar said, 'It's the main railway station. It's the closest place to here, where the fast trains stop. The London trains . . .'

'Why would they go by train?'

'I know why,' said Captain Routon slowly. 'It's an outrage. It's what the police do sometimes, when they want to break you. They walk you in public, in your handcuffs. Leave you on the station for an hour. Let everyone see you.'

'But that's Doonan,' said Anjoli. His eyes were full of tears. 'That's Professor Worthington. The headmaster . . .'

'They haven't done anything wrong!' cried Kenji. 'You mean they're standing on a station in handcuffs?'

'How far is Tiverton?' said Eric. He grabbed at a map.

'How can we get there?' said Sam.

'I think it's miles away,' said Captain Routon softly. 'I don't think we can. We can stay together, we can write to them, or . . .'

Miles ran to the edge of the crater and looked down at the road. 'We've got the balloon,' he shouted. 'And we've got an ice-cream van.'

Sanjay said, 'What's that over there? I can see something – come round here!'

The crowd followed him back round to the rock and they gazed over the moors to where Sanjay was pointing. He strained his eyes and the children tried to focus.

'Coming down the slope,' said Sanjay. 'Just where the rocks are sharp – can you see them? They're on the next tor.'

'I can see . . . something,' said Eric. 'What is it?'

'They're coming towards us.'

'Bicycles,' said Imagio, in disbelief. 'Loads of them.'

'It's a . . . is it Mountain Rescue?' said Ruskin.

'They're mountain bikes,' said Millie. 'They're coming right for us!'

Captain Routon was staring too. 'It's that chap from the High School,' he whispered. 'Don't you remember? Johnny Jay! He said his boys loved an adventure! He said he'd try to join us! They've braved the elements!'

As he spoke, a young man with conspicuously large ears soared into view. He leapt from a rocky outcrop and hung in the air a moment. Then he plummeted ten metres to the ground below, where he bounced once and skidded through the mud. A dozen children followed him – girls and boys – standing high on their pedals, zooming into focus. From the skirts of the tor came those who preferred a more cautious descent. A cloud of dirt and debris rose behind them as they slithered down the hillside. It took a few minutes, but the flock were soon together again – led by Johnny. They crossed the dip and started the final ascent up the path to Lightning Tor, a great flotilla of brightly coloured waterproofs.

The Ribblestrop and Priory children hurtled down to meet them. It took seconds to explain the mission and turn the bikes round. The children paired up briskly. Some sat on handlebars and some shared the saddle. Every child found a place and they were soon pushing off again, fired by sheer desperation.

Millie held onto Miles and Sanchez. They watched the departure and the same idea was forming in their minds.

'It can't be that hard, can it?' said Miles.

'We've got to try it,' said Millie. 'Something tells me it'll be faster.'

'I don't know,' said Miles. 'I don't know if you can steer them, or what you do – you just hunt for different air currents.'

'Let's trust to luck,' said Sanchez. 'It's worked so far, hasn't it?' He jumped into the balloon basket and pressed the ignition. In a moment the crumpled skin was inflating and in less than a minute they were off the ground, rising into clouds that were breaking open around them.

'I think you just go high as you can,' said Millie. 'Oh my God, look!'

The birds were back for the last time, soaring as they rose. They swooped and dived and, as they did, a watery sun found strength and poured warmth and light over the moorland. The birds came together, caught in some updraft that spiralled them higher and higher. Then, in perfect formation, they were gone, like arrows.

'This is the end, isn't it?' said Millie. 'We can't hope to do anything. We're just going to . . . what? Say goodbye?'

Miles opened the burner as wide as it would go and they rose like a rocket.

'We can do anything we want,' he said, grimly. 'Look at them all down there! There's no goodbye, never.'

The moor below them was a vast patchwork of rock and rubble, and the river poured through it. They could see the High School bicycles, hurtling along its banks, and then fording it in waves of spray. They could see a camel, lolloping riderless behind, and an ice-cream van on the road, pursued by two loyal donkeys.

When the wind came, it caught them like a mighty hand and they were dragged across the sky. They clung to the sides of the basket and then they clung to each other. Higher and higher they soared, until the currents combined and pushed them south.

They saw the glint of railway tracks and then soon, in the distance, they saw the sleepy town of Tiverton. They came over a winking canal and green playing fields. At last, they spotted a car park and beneath them lay the main station.

'Can you see any police?' shouted Miles.

Sanchez was scouring the area with Timmy Fox's binoculars. 'No. We must have missed them. They're gone.'

'Can you see a train?' cried Millie. 'We could try and catch up, or go further up the line, or —'

'There is a police car!' said Sanchez. 'By the doors. Wait . . .'

They floated nearer and Miles adjusted the valve so they dropped.

'Oh no,' said Sanchez. 'I've got them.'

'Let me see!' said Millie.

She pressed her head next to her friend and they used an eye-piece each. They played the instrument along the track and came onto the platform. Sure enough, huddled in forlorn isolation, they saw the three teachers they loved.

'They're in their pyjamas,' whispered Millie.

'Slippers, too,' said Sanchez. 'They're not even dressed properly. I can see handcuffs – it's horrible – they look so sad! Miles, I think the train's coming – we're not going to make it . . .'

'Sanchez,' said Miles. 'Give me the binoculars, please. I can see something else.'

'What?'

'Give me the binoculars!'

Miles was leaning over the basket, gazing down in a different direction. He put the binoculars to his eyes and swore quietly.

'What?' said Millie.

'Look. You don't need these any more. It's incredible . . .'

'Where?'

'Everywhere. Look around you! Look!'

Miles started to laugh. He grabbed Millie's hand and put his arm round Sanchez. 'It's a revolution! It's a complete, total revolution! Look, Sanchez . . . they're everywhere! We're saved! They'll stop the trains, won't they? That's what they're here for!'

There were just two roads to Tiverton Parkway station and both were thronged with school children. They overflowed the pavements, so they marched in the centre of the road, and the traffic had come to a hooting standstill. A bus disgorged fifty more and there were minibuses arriving. Children as young as five were hand in hand with older brothers and sisters. Most were holding cellphones and a simple text message was flicking back and forth, back and forth. It had been passing through classrooms for the last hour.

Tiv Park. Get there. Close it.

II

Blocking the line was easy.

Henry was a quarter of a mile south of the platform, and found a level crossing. He was with two High School boys, and they simply lay down on the tracks and refused to budge. The traffic stopped and the signalman had to telephone ahead, to say there was an obstacle on the line.

Angry motorists argued with the children and one even tried to drag them off. They simply linked arms and clung to the rail. The hooting queues lengthened on either side. Jacqueline, Charlie and Podma did the same thing at a crossing half a mile north. They clambered over the barrier and walked up the line as if they were off on a picnic. They ignored the cries and threats, and sat down on the sleepers, smiling happily.

Tiverton Parkway was cut off and the south-west trains network had to be halted. Speeding expresses were held at other stations and the one bound for the Ribblestrop teachers came to a gentle stop – close, but not close enough.

Meanwhile, the texts continued to fly.

It had all been started by the High School children, of course. They made full use of their social networks and the airwaves were full – the world wide web buzzed with the outrage and then the solution. The word spread, mushroomed and magnified; the curiosity turned to determination, and anger turned to rage. Something wrong was happening – good teachers were under attack and the wrong had to be righted. Soon the pupils from a dozen schools were simply walking out of classrooms and it was a groundswell that could not be contained. Children hauled open their school gates and caught buses. They persuaded friends to drive them. They came on mopeds and bicycles, and many simply jogged. The access to the station was soon choked with children in green, black, blue, magenta, maroon – every colour of the rainbow. It was a fire of pure indignation.

Teachers ran among them, shouting and waving. They were ignored. A police car tried to push through and was blocked, helpless, by the throng of young bodies that refused to give way. When a child in a red striped blazer jumped on the roof and started to dance, he was cheered. It was a peaceful protest and few understood its object – but there was change in the air. *Get there*, flickered the message. *Get there now. Drop everything.*

The children of The Priory School got direct calls from their friends on the moor. They rose and left their desks. Soon, the place was empty, for every child was running. A pair of off-duty bus drivers were persuaded and both vehicles were crammed. They got as close as they could, but of course the traffic was gridlocked, so the children stepped out onto the railway embankment and walked. In Bristol and Exeter, camera crews were scrambled. Daytime television was interrupted. The Education Minister received a desperate phonecall and was helicoptered straight to the scene. She looked down, helpless.

From the balloon as well, it was an extraordinary sight and the three friends held each other, unable to speak.

Sanchez turned the burner off completely and they sailed low. Thousands of faces gazed up at them and hands were waving. The station car park was full and the railings had collapsed. In the distance blue lights were flashing, but

every emergency vehicle was covered in children and everyone was dancing.

Doonan, Professor Worthington and the headmaster were
standing together, gazing in disbelief.

They were guarded by just three policemen – the escort
hadn't expected trouble, so now they had no idea what to
do. Lady Vyner was there – she was in a wheelchair after
her man-trap experience, and had come specially to see her
enemies' final humiliation. Instead, she saw her own grandson walk confidently up the line towards her. Sam, Ruskin
and Oli were beside him, and a group of boys and girls
she'd never seen before arrived on bicycles, pedalling
between the rails. The station staff could do nothing. The
crowds were simply laughing at them. The police moved in
to safeguard their prisoners, but there were now five
hundred children swarming over the platform, and they
found themselves lifted off the ground by gentle hands.
When they struggled and resisted, the hands got firmer –
they were shoved into an office and the door slammed shut.

When they checked their belts, their keys were gone.

The three teachers were uncuffed and they raised their
arms. The children around them started to cheer. They were
embraced, then lifted high. They found themselves standing
on a bench, and the sea of children stretched almost as far as
the eye could see, and the cheering wouldn't stop.

It was easy to drop a rope to them.

Miles went down to help the headmaster and he was
soon clambering up to the basket. Professor Worthington
followed and Doonan came last. As he dangled, he saw an
ice-cream van limp up the railway track, its tyres cut to
pieces and its engine howling. Captain Routon got out onto
the van bonnet and waved both hands, but he didn't try to
reach the basket even though it came close to his nose.

Sanchez raised his thumb and the burner blazed once more. The balloon rose and rose, until it was dot in the sky.

'You know we're real fugitives now,' said the headmaster, as he looked down.

'We always have been,' said Doonan.

'What have you done wrong?' said Miles. 'Explain it to me.'

'I don't know. I just started a school.'

Millie said, 'How long shall we stay up here? Will they try and shoot us?'

Professor Worthington was laughing. 'You fought them,' she cried. 'You fought them and you won. We're free!'

'I can see Ribblestrop,' said Sanchez. 'Just look at it . . .'

The evening sun had saved itself, and was ready. It caught the old building in a spotlight of gold and the building glowed like a lantern. They floated close and the four towers caught fire. They saw the Neptune statue, white as pearl in a lake that was turning silver. All at once the sky turned lilac and the moon burst up from the horizon. It rose and rose and the flare paths blazed again. There was laughter, everywhere – for Millie was holding Sanchez, and he was holding Miles. They floated over the courtyard and hung there in silence.

It was dark when their friends came up the drive.

The Priory children were with them and the High School cyclists too – determined to camp on the lawns all night and tell tales forever.

They lit a fire, of course – and soon they were singing:

> 'Ribblestrop, Ribblestrop, precious unto me!
> This is what I dream about and where I want to be.
> Early in the morning, finally at night –
> Ribblestrop, I'll die for thee, carrying the light . . .

Ribblestrop, Ribblestrop, jewel within my breast.
I will hap'ly die for thee; I will stand the test.
Even when I'm dreaming and especially when I wake . . .
I will try to give to thee; I will never take.'

III

And Doctor Ellie's library van?

It was spotted as it approached Bristol airport.

One of its tail-lights wasn't working and a police officer pulled it over for a routine check. The computer revealed that it was a stolen vehicle and, when the young man opened the back doors, he found Mr Ian, sobbing quietly under a mountain of books. He called for back-up at once.

Gary Cuthbertson made a run for it, but security was so tight in the area that he was captured within minutes. He was arrested with Timmy Fox and taken into custody. Mr Ian would have joined them, but for his injuries. He was hospitalised and woke the next day surrounded by policemen.

Lady Vyner arrived home to find the locks and grilles had been torn from the windows. The whole building was full of children and she gave up all resistance. When she went up to her flat, she discovered that the recent rain had soaked through the ceilings and floors, and she had nowhere to live. The elderly ladies she'd admitted were nowhere to be seen, but she found them eventually, chatting with the orphans in their dormitory. They had agreed to share the job of matron and were already getting the laundry organised.

She sat down, trembling, and they brought her tea.

As for the prosecution of the teachers, it was halted at once.

The great truckload of police paperwork was mysteriously lost – after all, the Ribblestrop teachers were heroes now. When the chief constable visited the next morning, he spoke of 'misunderstandings' and 'breakdowns in communication'. His handshake was firm and reassuring.

The headmaster's telephone now rang constantly. Every educational expert wanted a consultation and the government asked him to chair a special committee on the future of schooling. He refused, of course, because he had a school of his own to run.

Doctor Ellie took a full-time job at Ribblestrop, and Vicky was taken on as art teacher. The real problem was how the school could accommodate the hundreds of children who now wanted to enroll. Queues formed every day, all down the drive. The Priory and the High School were to be partners, of course; three beacons of excellence, whose light would shine forever.

Life Is Dangerous! ran the motto. All three institutions adopted it. The words were stamped on all letterheads, and they fluttered on flags. They were there on every blazer badge, in gold and black, under the lion and the lamb. Most importantly, however, they came to form the mantra that would beat in the pupils' hearts: *Life Is Dangerous.*

For every child knows, deep down, that a life lived in safety – protected and controlled and deprived of all excitement – is a life not worth living.

RIBBLESTROP TOWERS

Due to massive expansion, RIBBLESTROP TOWERS
is recruiting teachers of English, Maths, Geography,
Martial Arts, Hindi and Sanskrit, Dance, First Aid,
Music (*with modern opera*) and Landscape Gardening.
A commitment to the life of a busy
boarding school is expected.

Accommodation will be available
once the substantial building programme is complete.

Hand-written letters, with CV and a photograph, should be
addressed to the headmaster. Applicants should state what
particular skills they can offer, making sure they address
the following questions in particular:
Do you like children?
Do you scare easily?
What will you bring?
How do you inspire?
What do you believe in?

Dr Giles Norcross-Webb
Headmaster, Ribblestrop Towers

ACKNOWLEDGEMENTS

I am grateful to my agent Jane Turnbull, who gave constant support, as usual, advising, approving, rejecting and enjoying. Michael Gee helped me with the history, but the mistakes are mine, not his. Advice and information also came from Martin Gosling, Mike Smith, Michael Hemsley, Canon Bill Anderson, Charu Misra, Mansi Prakash, Toyah Singh and Nancy Zuang. The series received an enormous boost from *The Guardian*: thanks to Philip Ardagh, Julia Eccleshare, Michelle Paver, Marcus Sedgwick and Julia Golding. Thanks also to my editor, Venetia Gosling, who worked on book one with me and stayed with the whole trilogy, so the children are hers as much as mine – and thank you to Ingrid, for her faith. I'm grateful to Serge Seidlitz for his unique visual inventiveness, and Melissa Hyder for such careful, creative copy-editing.

But it was Joe T who started it, and to him I will forever be in debt.

ABOUT THE AUTHOR

Andy Mulligan was brought up in South London and educated at Oxford University. He worked as a theatre director for ten years, before travels in Asia prompted him to re-train as a teacher. He has taught English and drama in India, Brazil, the Philippines and the UK. He now divides his time between London and Manila.

A dilapidated school with the most unpromising
of pupils and eccentric of teachers, led by an
educational maverick, must unravel the mystery
of what lurks in the cellars. Anything could
happen... and anything does!

It's a new term at Ribblestrop and the headmaster
is hoping for a bit more organisation. But secrets
remain under the ground, the new Chaplain is not
all he seems, and a truck load of circus animals
has taken refuge in the grounds . . .